Berkley Sensation titles by Darcie Wilde

LORD OF THE RAKES
THE ACCIDENTAL ABDUCTION

The Accidental Abduction

DARCIE WILDE

BERKLEY SENSATION, NEW YORK

THE BERKLEY PUBLISHING GROUP
Published by the Penguin Group
Penguin Group (USA) LLC
375 Hudson Street, New York, New York 10014

USA • Canada • UK • Ireland • Australia • New Zealand • India • South Africa • China

penguin.com

A Penguin Random House Company

THE ACCIDENTAL ABDUCTION

A Berkley Sensation Book / published by arrangement with the author

For information, address: The Berkley Publishing Group,
a division of Penguin Group (USA) LLC,
375 Hudson Street, New York, New York 10014.

ISBN: 978-0-425- 26556-7

PUBLISHING HISTORY
Berkley Sensation mass-market edition / September 2014

PRINTED IN THE UNITED STATES OF AMERICA

10 9 8 7 6 5 4 3 2 1

Cover photograph by Claudio Marinesco.
Cover design by George Long.
Interior text design by Kelly Lipovich.

To Tim, who is my happily ever after.

One

"Good evening, Mr. Rayburn." Sir Ignatius Featherington held out his thin, dry hand. "And a warm welcome for this chill evening."

"Thank you, sir." Harry Rayburn took the hand Sir Ignatius extended carefully. He was always afraid he might break the small, smiling man. Sir Ignatius, like the rest of his family, lived up to his name—being from a clan of small, slight, soft-spoken people. In Agnes, their oldest daughter, and the reason for Harry's visit this evening, that slight frame translated into a perfect, pale delicacy of the sort generally compared to all manner of flowers.

"Nancy, go and tell Miss Featherington that Mr. Rayburn is here to see her." The stooped, gray-haired baronet was still beaming as he gave his instructions to the parlor maid, and still attempting to give Harry's hand a hearty shake. "Now, Mrs. Featherington and I will be taking a bit of a drive. I'm sure our absence won't discommode either of you young people." He let one eyelid droop in an attempt at a wink.

"I sincerely hope not, sir." The jewel box made a reassuring weight in Harry's right pocket. He himself felt as light as a Featherington. His heart alternately brimmed with happiness and beat out of control from an emotion uncomfortably close to terror. Which in and of itself was as it should be, he decided. It made the moment real. Tonight, he would propose. After tonight Agnes—lovely, perfect Agnes—would be his flower, his jewel, forever.

The maid returned and curtsied. "Miss Featherington says she will be glad to meet Mr. Rayburn in the front parlor."

"Oh, no need, Nancy, Mr. Rayburn can go to her in the sitting room." Mr. Featherington patted Harry's back. "And let me say again, we are happy, very happy, to have you here, Mr. Rayburn."

"Thank you, sir," said Harry seriously. He tried to fish out some words about doing his utmost to make her happy, but none came. It didn't seem to matter. Sir Ignatius gave his hand another squeeze, blinked his watery eyes, and smiled with encouragement. Harry turned, squared his shoulders, and started up the hall.

When he reached the door, Harry put his hand in his pocket and touched the box as if for luck. Not that he needed luck. Everything was exactly as it should be. He had been courting Agnes Featherington for the best part of the season, ever since he'd come back from that last, disastrous trip to Calais, in fact. He'd spent the entire winter navigating balls and dinners and concerts, and doing absolutely everything required to make himself into a desirable beau. Sir and Lady Ignatius made no secret of the fact that they considered him highly eligible as a suitor for their beautiful daughter, which was a relief. Harry was a merchant's son. This meant there were plenty of matrons who considered him second-class goods, despite the fortune he brought with him. The senior Featheringtons, however, possessed no such scruples, and from the beginning had welcomed his presence. Harry's parents had seemed quietly content to let the matter take its own course. Indeed, the only hitch in the entire affair had been his sister Fiona's habit of calling the object of his intentions "Agnes Featherhead."

But now was not the time to worry about Fiona. Harry ran his hand over his hair (ruthlessly slicked back), and down his side whiskers (freshly trimmed). He straightened the cravat he'd spent hours tying in the new "Grecian waterfall" style, and brushed down the sleeves of his coffee brown coat. He checked the location of the ring box once more—right pocket, just where it had been all the other times he'd checked. Only then did Harry take a deep breath, and knock on the door.

"Come in," answered the sweet, entirely feminine voice from the other side.

Harry pushed open the door, and there she was, just as he had pictured her. Agnes Featherington sat on the chintz sofa. The rich evening sunlight streamed through the bow windows and glimmered on the golden ringlets that trailed across her swanlike neck. She wore a white evening frock with delicate primrose trim. Dainty primrose slippers peeped out from under her hems, and her fair head was bent over a piece of embroidery, also primroses.

Harry's heart swelled with a flood of fresh affection. Agnes was slender, pale, and lovely; the perfect girl, in every way.

From his basket by the fire, Percival, Agnes's unfortunately overfed Maltese dog, lifted his head and growled.

For once, Harry was able to ignore the beast. All his attention was fastened on Agnes. She was like a fairy-tale princess seated in her bower. Agnes was everything that was pure and true and lovely. She would do credit to the home of any man, and she would bring him everything he needed to make a good, settled life.

She was no fool, either, no matter what Fi thought. There was a great stack of books on the table at her elbow—poetry and novels and histories. They'd have plenty to talk about in the evenings when he came home from his work, on those occasions when they felt like talking. Harry rather expected there was a whole host of far more energetic activities that would be filling their evenings after the wedding.

Agnes lifted her heart-shaped face, and her blue eyes widened. There was the tiniest hint of maidenly hesitation before her tiny pink mouth bent into a smile. "Oh, Mr. Rayburn! I wasn't expecting *you* this evening."

Which was perhaps a little odd, considering he'd just been announced. Harry decided she was joking, and smiled as he made his bow. "I hope I'm not inconveniencing you by calling?"

"Not in the least." Agnes laid her embroidery aside. "Won't you sit down? Shall I ring for tea?"

"No, no thank you. I don't want anything." *Except you.* But of course he couldn't say that. Agnes was dainty and innocent. He could not shock her with such a blunt statement. That was also exactly as it should be.

Harry sat on the edge of the slick velveteen chair, which creaked ominously under his weight. The furniture had been chosen to suit a family of Featheringtons, meaning it was delicate and spindly, and perhaps a bit overgenerous in the matter of curlicues and gilt trim.

He did not let himself touch his pocket again. "Miss Featherington . . ." he began.

Agnes clasped her pale hands in her lap and blinked her china blue eyes. "Yes, Mr. Rayburn?"

His mouth had gone dry. He shifted his weight. The chair creaked. Percival barked once in sharp warning. "Miss Featherington, Agnes, I'm here for a very particular purpose."

"Yes, Mr. Rayburn?" She blinked again. For a moment he thought she looked perplexed. Could it be he was her first suitor? Her first love? That was perfect, too. He would have to be very gentle with her. Indulgent. She'd have little whims and small worries. That was all right. He'd make a home that was just as perfect as she was; a beautiful, peaceful setting for this priceless gem.

He felt too big for this delicate room, for this perfect, tiny golden girl. He realized he was trembling a little as he moved from the chair, down onto one knee. He took her doll-like hand between both of his.

"Agnes, it is my wish, my very great hope, that you will do me the honor of becoming my wife."

He brought out the box and opened it to reveal the ring. He'd spent days agonizing over the purchase. It had to be rich, but not ostentatious. He'd settled on a blue diamond, to match the shade of her eyes, and double-cut for the shine. He held it out now and watched those blue eyes widen. His heart swelled. This was so right, so perfect. The rough life he had known was behind him. He could settle down for good now, and forget everything but being a husband worthy of Agnes. She, in return, would make his home an oasis of calm and beauty.

Agnes lifted her eyes from the ring. Those eyes were bright with wonder, and she pressed her free hand to her lips in utter surprise.

"And then she says, 'You must be joking, Mr. Rayburn!' "

"Oh, Harry, I'm sorry."

Harry didn't even bother to look at Fiona. Instead, he stared at the small, red box in his hands. He knew coming back home was a bad idea, but he'd been unable to think of where else to go. After all, he'd fully expected to be spending the evening happily ensconced in the Featherington's home with his new fiancée, receiving congratulations and discussing wedding plans.

Instead, here he was on the sofa with his sister—his married sister—staring at the little velvet box with its half-carat, double-cut blue diamond on a band of eighteen-karat gold. It would be perfect for "the young gentleman's purpose," or so the jeweler had assured him as he wrote out the bill. Harry turned it over in his fingers again.

"I did everything," said Harry to the ring and the memory. "I waltzed. I quadrilled. I had to beat off at least six other fellows at every ball to get onto her dance card. I fetched more cups of punch than I can count. And those endless poseys." Harry closed his eyes against the fresh pain of remembering how many hours he'd wasted in the flower shops, thumbing through that ridiculous little pamphlet on the "language of flowers" and debating the exact right combination of white, pink, yellow roses, forget-me-nots, pansies, and Lord knew what else to send Agnes. She'd even worn some of them. "Her parents were all for it. Anxious for it, in fact."

That, he supposed glumly, should have been some sort of clue; not that he had been looking for clues. He hadn't been looking for anything, except Agnes's little hand on his arm.

"I walked her blasted dog, for God's sake. I've got the scars to prove it!"

"Don't swear at me, Harry," said Fi tartly. "I just told you it wasn't your fault."

"I know, I know. I'm sorry."

Fiona, now the Honorable Mrs. James Westbrook, was not long back from her own wedding trip. Married life, a trek across the Continent, and a new, grand home in the Lake District, all seemed to agree with her. Fi might look the part of the quintessential English rose, but she'd always been too clever by half. Her seasons in London had been marked by all sorts of interesting adventures, until James Westbrook arrived to take her in hand. Since she'd been back, though, it seemed to

Harry his sister's cleverness had mellowed. She seemed both more contented and more, well, grown-up than he'd ever known her to be. She was staying with their parents because James was off in Cornwall on business and she hadn't wanted to be in London alone. From the way Mother was humming as she moved around the house, Harry suspected there might be something in the wind involving a new branch on the Westbrook family tree.

"It's really not your fault." Fi reached out and squeezed his hand. "You're a nice man, Harry. Steady. Solid. That's not what a girl like Agnes Featherhead wants."

"Featherington."

Fi did not bother to acknowledge the correction. "She wants a poet or, better still, a highwayman who will come riding in off the moors with a bunch of lace at his throat and a pistol at his side."

"In short, she doesn't want me because I'm boring." He shouldn't have come home. The last person a man disappointed in love wanted to pour his heart out to was his happily married sister. He could only thank his lucky stars that his parents weren't home. They'd of course been aware of his errand. Probably Father had taken Mother out somewhere to distract her until Harry returned with the presumably happy news.

"You are not boring, Harry," Fi was saying. "You're . . ."

"A perfectly nice man. Solid. Steady." *So solid I live with my parents in their town house rather than in rooms like a proper bachelor about the town. So steady I hold down a job in a warehouse rather than spend my days swanning about the moors with lace and a pistol.*

He was actually quite a good shot. Perhaps if he'd demonstrated that to Agnes, he'd have taken on some of the romantic bronze she seemed to want. No. Harry pushed his hair back from his forehead. If he'd had a pistol to hand, he would have been far too tempted to shoot that vicious little dog.

No. He wouldn't have, either. Because he was nice, solid, steady, Harold Syverson Rayburn. But even as he thought this, an image flashed through his mind, unbidden and entirely unwelcome—of the cobbled alley, the shouts, the last shove, and the man sprawled at his feet . . .

No. He snapped the ring box shut. That wasn't him. That

was someone else. He'd left that other man behind in Calais when he came home. He really was steady Harry Rayburn, and he didn't want any other sort of life. The problem, it appeared, was that Agnes did.

"There are far worse things to be than steady," Fiona was saying. "One day . . ."

"Yes, yes, yes, all right." Harry got to his feet and started for the door before he had to listen to Fiona parroting their mother's words about how he would one day find a girl who could appreciate all his good qualities.

"Harry?" said Fi behind him. "Agnes Featherhead is an idiot, and she could never be the sort of woman you need."

She did not say, "As I told you," and she did not say, "What were you thinking?" Harry, for his part, did not demand to know how his sister could possibly understand what sort of woman he needed.

"You'll let Mother and Father know?" he asked instead. "I need to be . . . somewhere else."

He heard Fiona agreeing, but didn't bother to look back. Instead, he retrieved his hat where he'd left it on the hall table and headed out into the street. What he needed was a drink or a dozen, and to be away from women.

Harry settled his hat lower on his head and across the square toward St. James Street, and the one place he could be sure of an entirely masculine welcome.

When Harry arrived at the Silk Road Club, it wasn't even ten o'clock, and the club room was less than half full. Most of the members would still either be home at dinner, or out on the town. But Nathaniel Penrose was there, and he raised his glass as Harry walked in. Harry grunted in answer and headed directly for the sideboard and its collection of bottles. Most of the club members were merchants of one sort or the other, and club rules required they help keep the cellars stocked. This meant that the Silk Road had some of the best, and hardest to find, spirits in London, which was exactly what Harry wanted.

He'd hoped the walk here would help clear his head, but the more he played the farce of his proposal over in his thoughts, the harder bitterness dug into him. Wine, port, and brandy were all far too weak for what he needed. He unstoppered the scotch whiskey.

"I take it things did not go well," said Nathaniel. Nathaniel was not in trade, at least not directly. He worked with the naval office, but he never said exactly what he did there. It was widely suspected it involved ferreting out smugglers and insurance frauds, but if anyone knew for sure, they held their peace on the subject.

Harry poured a good two fingers into a glass and swallowed it down in one burning gulp. He set the glass down with a sharp clack, and poured another.

"That bad?"

Harry saluted Nathaniel with his glass, and knocked back the second whiskey. "You can't be serious, Mr. Rayburn," he drawled.

"Ouch. Better bring that over here."

Harry collected glass and bottle and dropped into the chair beside Nathaniel. "What the hell was I thinking?" he demanded.

"You weren't." Nathaniel took up the bottle before Harry could, and poured out two measures of whiskey, both, Harry noted grumpily, rather smaller than the ones he'd just downed. "It's what girls like that count on."

"You are speaking of the love of my life Miss Agnes Featherhead." No. That wasn't right. He shouldn't call her that. Christ and damn, he didn't even have the excuse of being drunk yet. It must be the heartbreak. Heartbreak made a man mean.

"Harry, everybody makes an ass of himself once in a while. This was just your turn."

"The consolations of philosophy." Harry raised the glass in a toast and gulped down the drink.

Nathaniel shrugged. "It's true. Eventually, every man meets a woman who makes him go out of his mind."

"I thought that was this 'true love' I keep hearing about." He reached for the whiskey, but somehow, Nathaniel had gotten there first, again, and was pouring his own glass, and taking his own damn time about it.

"No. True love doesn't make you loose your wits. It lets you find them." He refilled Harry's glass—in that same confounded leisurely fashion, and nowhere near far enough—but Harry couldn't exactly snatch the decanter out of the man's hand. Not here in London, where he was nice, steady, boring Harry.

"I don't know what came over me." Harry stared into his

glass. "It's not like I'm some schoolboy. I was only even at that ball because of Fi. But when I saw Agnes she seemed . . . perfect."

Nathaniel shrugged. "There's marriage in the air. When a man like Philip Montcalm finally takes to it, the rest of us bachelors start looking about and saying 'Perhaps it's time.'" Nathaniel spoke the name of their mutual friend, and the man who had, until recently, been known about town as "the Lord of the Rakes." "The next thing you know, you see some young lovely who's everything you've been told to want, and that's that."

Was Nathaniel right? Had Harry wanted Agnes just because she'd *seemed* perfect? The idea left him with a very bad taste in his mouth and Harry took another swallow of whiskey to wash it away. What if the real problem was that he hadn't remembered, or hadn't bothered, to look beyond appearances?

No. That couldn't possibly be what had happened.

Could it?

Harry felt his eyes narrow. "Don't tell me *you* ever fell for some little English rose . . ."

"All right, I won't tell you. Point is, Harry, you're no more a fool than thousands of others." Nathaniel paused and eyed Harry over the rim of his glass. "Unless there's something else behind all this?"

"No, nothing."

"Because to some of your friends, it looked like the whole thing proceeded in a tremendous hurry, especially for someone who always talked about how love should be the lifeline of the heart . . ."

"I said there's nothing behind it." *Nothing at all*, he repeated to himself. Then he had to tell himself it was just the whiskey making that feel like a lie. "I thought I fell in love and I thought she did, too. Apparently I was wrong, but as you say, I was no more wrong than thousands of others."

"If that's really it then, finish your drink, be thankful for a narrow escape, and next time find someone who wants Harry Rayburn, not Lord Byron or Dick Turpin."

"They should advertise," said Harry. "Or wear signboards. 'Maiden seeks dashing highwaymen, no plodders need apply.'"

Nathaniel chuckled. "I think the chaperones might prefer it. Maybe the matchmaking mamas could post the notices over those little chairs where the candidates sit."

"*Women!*" sneered Harry, lifting his glass high.

"Women!" echoed the entire room.

Two

Dear Mrs. Wakefield:

I am writing to request the favor of a private interview, tomorrow. There is a matter that has long been on my mind to discuss with you. As it intimately concerns the future security and well-being of yourself and those to whom you are most nearly connected, I am certain you will find the proposal acceptable.

 I intend to call at four o'clock. I trust I will find you at home.

Your servant,
Terrance Valloy

Leannah Morehouse Wakefield laid the letter down on the desk. Had there ever, she wondered, been a declaration of intent less calculated to rouse tender sentiment in a maiden's bosom?

Not that Leannah could be considered a maiden by any stretch of the imagination—especially once her five years of marriage and another year of widowhood had been taken into account. Neither did she harbor any idea of romance ever playing a part of her life. Still, it would have been nice if Terrance had made some small effort to sound more like a suitor and less like a solicitor.

This unfortunate thought brought with it the equally unfortunate image of Mr. Valloy seated behind his vast desk and handing across a marriage license tied in red ribbon. *Everything's quite in order. You just say, "I will," and the matter's settled. You will? Excellent.*

Leannah's late husband had been far older than she, but he had done his level best to be good to her. Still, there had been a point when she hoped any second marriage might be more compatible, perhaps even more passionate. In her private heart, she longed for a union where she was not seen as a girl to be indulged, cosseted, and, not to put too fine a point on it, bred. She had thought, perhaps, that if there was to be a next time, it might be with someone who knew the ways in which she longed to be touched and who understood how to ease the deep ache that came when she was alone.

Now I'm just being ridiculous. Leannah made herself look again at the ledger where she'd been entering the household accounts. *Romance is for those who can afford it. Terrance will make a civil, amiable, and steady husband. That is what I need.*

What we *need.* Leannah closed the ledger so she would not have to see all the red ink she'd entered just this evening. She'd let the fire burn down to its last coals and was working by lamplight with two shawls over her shoulders and her thickest stockings and slippers on her feet. Although it was finally April, the weather had yet to turn warm. She yearned to go up to bed and burrow under her quilts, but Genevieve hadn't returned yet. Leannah wouldn't be able to sleep a wink until she was sure her sister was safely home.

But she had finished the accounts, and she felt too tired to read. That meant the only thing left was to answer Mr. Valloy's note, and assure him she would be at home when he arrived at four tomorrow.

Today, she reminded herself. She glanced at the clock. It was almost two.

"Leannah?" A man's anxious voice reverberated through the study door. "Leannah?"

Oh, no. Leannah rose at once and hurried out into the cold, dark hallway.

"Leannah?"

Octavian Morehouse Leannah's father, stood on the stairway landing. His dressing gown hung open over his nightshirt, and his thick gray hair stood wildly on end. He swayed on his bare feet, looking about him like a child who had lost his way.

"I'm here, Father." Leannah hurried up the stairs to grasp his hands. "I'm right here."

It took his pale green eyes a moment to focus on her. "I couldn't sleep," he said. "I thought they were looking for me again and . . ."

"Shhh." Leannah patted his hands, appalled to feel how cold they were. "It's all right now. There's no one here but us."

"Leannah?" A new voice drifted down from overhead. "Is something wrong?"

This time it was Jeremy, the youngest of the Morehouse siblings, leaning over the upstairs railing and rubbing hard at his eyes with the heel of one hand.

"No, nothing's wrong." Young boys were supposed to sleep deeply, but her brother never had. This, combined with a youth's unerring instinct to head straight for wherever the most trouble might be, made it impossible to protect him from scenes such as this. "You can go back to bed, Jeremy. Father, come into the study. You'll catch cold out here."

"I'm sorry," Father murmured as he let her lead him down the stairs. He hadn't brought so much as a candle with him. Given the way his hands shook, however, that was probably for the best.

Leannah sat him on the end of the sofa closest the hearth and set about building up the fire.

"There now, that's better." She tried to sound cheerful as the fresh flames sprang up, but the collier's bill was on the desk along with all the others. "You take a moment to warm yourself."

Father stretched his trembling hands out to the fire, rubbing them over and over as if trying to clean off some stain. Leannah looked away. She didn't want him to see her expression just then.

When she'd been a girl, Leannah's father had seemed a giant of a man. He could carry her and Genevieve together—one on either shoulder. She'd loved his booming laugh, and the way everything around him was always the best, the finest, the grandest. The Morehouses were the flower of England, his daughters the fairest and the finest girls. When Jeremy arrived, Father held the infant up high, declaring before the entire neighborhood that his son was the brightest of boys and his future was limitless.

But that was all long ago. Father's collapse had left him a bent and haggard old man whose spotted skin hung loosely off his bones. He looked lost in his own dressing gown. Leannah suddenly hated the worn, forest green garment. She should buy him a new one. And a new nightshirt. He shouldn't have to wear those old, flapping things.

She looked down at her own frayed sleeves and tugged them over her wrists.

"Are the curtains closed?" asked Father.

"Yes, Father. Closed tight. Try not to make yourself anxious."

"I don't want to be seen. I don't want to hurt anyone. You won't let me hurt you anymore?"

"No, Father. You cannot hurt us."

"But I can. You don't know. I keep reading the papers. I see the numbers and the reports of the markets. I keep thinking if only I had a little money, I could do so much for us. I start thinking how to get it, and it all begins again, all the schemes and the plans."

"I won't let anything happen, Father." At the same time, she thought irritably: *Who let you have the newspapers? I'll have to speak to Bishop about it.*

The problem was, Bishop had so much else to do. He was the man of all work, and their only servant now besides Mrs. Falwell. Father needed a real nurse who could watch over him properly and be there when he got anxious like this.

Leannah tugged on her frayed sleeves again. *And this is exactly why I have to make up my mind to say yes to Terrance Valloy.*

"Close the drapes, Leannah. Please," whispered Father.

She moved behind him and gripped the puce curtains—a horrid color but they'd come with the furnished house—and rattled the rings. "There, Father," she said. "It's done. Please try to rest."

"You're a good girl," he said. "I wanted to be a good father, but I failed in that as well."

Leannah's head was aching. She had to distract him. If he fell into one of his brown studies, there'd be no sleep for anyone tonight. She tried to be gentle, to be forbearing, but sometimes it all felt impossibly hard, especially when there was so much else to do just to keep the house running and looking after Jeremy and Genevieve.

"I thought we might go driving tomorrow," Leannah said. Never mind that she'd just spent the last half hour trying to decide whether it would be best to finally sell the team and the barouche, or if they could cut expenses far enough by just selling the saddle horse, Bonaparte. "I think we all deserve an outing, don't you?"

"I'd like to see you drive," he said. "Do you remember the Lady Day races back home? I was always so proud of you."

No one's going to beat a Morehouse at a race. You get right back up there. Leannah bowed her head. As a child, she hadn't minded how much time Father had made her spend learning to handle a team. She'd basked in his pride, and driving fast always felt like flying, like freedom. Even now, when she knew all about the cost of the lessons, the horses, and the carriages, and when she understood all of that money had been thrown away on the exercise of pure pride, she still missed it.

"Well, that's settled," she said. "If the weather holds, we'll all go out. The snowdrops are blooming in the park, and Gossip and Rumor certainly need the exercise." *I can put the stables off for another week. When Father's calmer, I'll be able to talk to him sensibly. If we sell the team, we can sell the carriage, too, and keep Bonaparte for Jeremy, and maybe me . . .*

"Where's Genevieve?" asked Father suddenly. "She shouldn't be out so late."

"Genevieve's at the Fosters' charity concert, Father. I told you about it." Genevieve had been glad to go, too, even though she hated charity evenings, and even though Leannah had insisted she take Mrs. Falwell with her as an extra chaperone.

"Oh, yes, that's right, you did." Father patted the chair arm restlessly. "Well. She'll be home soon then."

"Yes." Leannah glanced at the clock. In fact, Genevieve should already be home. Worry stirred in her. She pushed it aside. Probably her sister was lingering with friends over punch and ices. After a solid two weeks at home, Genny deserved an evening out. Especially now that she'd given up pestering everybody about Mr. Dickenson. Genevieve was a good girl, but she had all the Morehouse stubbornness. Well, Leannah's position regarding Mr. Dickenson had been made quite plain, and that whim was finished. Now Genevieve would be able to meet a man who would want her for the right reasons. Perhaps a political man. That would suit Genny very well. But in any case, he must be a man with whom she could be herself.

Not that I've provided her the best example on that score. Leannah very deliberately did not glance back at the desk, and the letter from Mr. Valloy.

"Would you like me to read to you, Father?" she asked. "Or would you rather just sit quietly?"

Father looked up at her, and after what seemed like great effort, he managed a smile. "I think I'll just be quiet a bit now, Leannah. I'm feeling much better already. You get on with your work."

Leannah drew a deep breath. She needed to tell him how matters stood between her and Mr. Valloy. She'd put that off for far too long, and she really didn't want it to come as any kind of a shock when Terrance asked to speak to him tomorrow. She needed him to understand the matter was settled and entirely for the best.

But before she could find the words, Leannah heard the soft but distinct sound of floorboards creaking outside the door.

"There, that's Genevieve now," she told him instead. *If it's not Jeremy creeping down to eavesdrop.* But then, Jeremy knew precisely which of the rented house's boards creaked by now. Come to that, so did Genevieve. "I'll just go bring her in, and you can say good night."

Leannah took up the lamp and went back out into the hall. She was just in time to see an aging woman dressed all in black put her foot on the first stair.

"Mrs. Falwell!" cried Leannah, and Mrs. Falwell spun

around. She clapped her hand against her mouth and her watery eyes grew wide. "Where's Genevieve!"

But Leannah needed no answer. Mrs. Falwell's shock told her everything. Genny was gone, with Mr. Anthony Dickenson. She hadn't given up on her whim after all.

Genevieve was on her way to Gretna Green.

Three

The problem, Harry reflected with bleary irritability as he stumped down the stairs of the club, was that he'd never gotten *comfortable* with her. He'd never been able to look at her without feeling like a bumbling schoolboy, or too big for the room, or both. A man couldn't be expected to charm the slippers off a girl when he was afraid of tripping over her.

How on earth did she manage it? Was it her eyes? The way she tipped her head and hid her pretty pink mouth behind her fan? Perhaps it was the sheer delicacy of her. That must be it. Harry wasn't used to delicate girls. Life at sea and on the docks did not accustom a man to the company of girls reared in the hothouse environments of the parlor and the ballroom. His sister's delicacy was mere physiological accident. The women he'd known in Madrid, Ceylon, and Constantinople were exotic, beautiful, intoxicating, but they were not delicate.

Delicacy was Agnes's primary characteristic. She'd been so timid, so in need of protection from everything bigger than her Maltese. She always declared herself in need of his arm, or of having this errand run, or that item fetched. She'd smiled so prettily when she thanked him that he'd always been glad to do whatever little thing she asked, and her laugh had gone straight to his head. Yes, he'd felt every inch the raw merchantman when around her, but at the same time, he'd fought for a chance to show her he was far more of a man than the dandies and puppies who sighed after her.

Harry started down the street, keeping to the walks to avoid the traffic. He wasn't drunk, exactly. Certainly not as drunk as he would have been if Nathaniel hadn't cajoled him into eating a decent supper and washing it down with strong coffee. Or if the whiskey decanter hadn't at some point been replaced by a bottle of wine. But he wasn't completely sober, either. No sense in ending this disastrous evening by stumbling in front of a carriage. Agnes might find it terribly romantic if her rejection culminated in his early, ugly death, but Mother would never forgive him.

The clock had struck two sometime back, and the stream of passing carriages had thinned down considerably. That just meant the ones that were still out rattled by too damn fast. In fact, he could hear the distinct rumble of some fool somewhere nearby driving his team too damn hard.

He'd been so full of plans. He'd pictured Agnes as the jewel of his home, and mother to a brood of beautiful children, the perfect blend of Featherington and Rayburn. He hadn't let himself dwell too much on the prospect of how those children were going to come into the world. It felt . . . indecent to be having carnal thoughts about such a young and frail creature. At the same time, he dreamed of teaching her to sail, of seeing her on the deck of a ship with all that golden hair being whipped by the wind. She loved Byron? Well, he'd take her to Greece, and to the Turkish coast, and a thousand other places; dress her in silk from China, rubies from India, feast her on tea and spices from all the islands. He'd show her the world.

Even now he could see Agnes standing on the deck of a ship, the wind blowing back her yellow hair. Harry blinked at the image, and leaned in, as if trying to take a closer look. Before when he'd conjured this vision, she'd always clung to his arm and laughed. Now, she clung to his arm all right, but she was bending over the rail being terribly ill.

Come to think of it, he'd never seen Agnes do anything more vigorous than walk through the panorama exhibit in Vauxhall Gardens. Even then, she hadn't wanted to stay because it made Percival the Maltese nervous. Harry had felt very gallant escorting her away. He had, hadn't he? Or had he just felt clumsy and bumbling for not having realized the grand scene was likely to be too much for Agnes?

What is that idiot doing to those horses? Harry looked up and down the empty street. *The fool must be drunker than me.* Maybe he was trying to outrun his own broken heart. Well, if he wasn't careful he'd break the horses and the carriage and probably his neck, and serve him right.

Harry stepped into the street. He needed to get out of town himself. Go to Carlisle, maybe, or Barcelona, or Athens. It didn't matter much, as long as it was somewhere he wouldn't need quite so much whiskey to wash away the memory of Agnes Featherington.

Not Calais, though. Calais would be a very bad idea.

Harry scrubbed at his face and looked up at the soot-dimmed London moon. He cursed, slowly and thoroughly, in four different languages.

"Why?" he demanded. "What the hell is the matter with me?"

The moon didn't answer. Instead, a woman's voice erupted from the darkness.

"Out of the way!"

The thunder of hooves, the crack of a whip, and the bang, crash, and rattle of a carriage being driven at neck-or-nothing speed—it all toppled over Harry's miasma of heartbreak and whiskey. He whipped around just in time to see the horses bearing down on him. The team reared, and Harry stumbled back. Wind, and the edge of one flashing hoof, knocked his hat away. The woman screamed something and the horses whinnied high and sharp in outraged answer. They crashed down hard enough that their iron shoes struck sparks from the cobbles and lurched forward.

Runaway. Runaway team, with a woman on the box.

That was Harry's last clear thought. Because what he did next happened too fast for thought to keep up.

Harry jumped again, forward this time. His hands slapped against the carriage's stanchions and closed down, which was good, because he was instantly yanked off his feet.

I'm going to die.

But his scrabbling boot found the running board, and the absolute, overwhelming desire *not* to die gave Harry enough strength to heave himself over the edge of the open carriage's door and topple onto the seats. He bounced.

The team bolted around a corner. The carriage tipped up

onto two wheels, and the woman cried out. Harry flailed about, but this time he failed to catch hold of anything and tumbled onto hands and knees. The wheels crashed down. The jolt slammed Harry's teeth together and he barely missed biting his tongue.

Harry forced himself up onto his knees and grabbed the edge of the seat in front of him. The carriage—an open-topped barouche—pitched and rolled like a ship in a storm. The woman on the box had somehow kept her seat as the panicked horses tore blindly ahead. They took another sharp corner and again the carriage tipped, but this time Harry braced himself and kept his place. If he'd still had his hat, though, he would have lost it against the corner of the stone house. Again they righted, and again the horses took on a fresh burst of speed, straight down the middle of the high street. Carriages, curricles, vans rose up around them. The woman shouted and she screamed, and she still kept her seat as they threaded the needle between the slower traffic again.

Harry found his balance, and his wits. He crawled up onto the seat and clung to its back right behind the driver's box. The carriage banked, going up onto its two wheels again. Again he braced himself. They were going to die. The carriage couldn't stand this, and the horses certainly couldn't. One of them would stumble. The carriage would overturn. They'd lose a pin on the wheel or break an axle. He was going to watch this woman thrown to the stones, to break her head and neck. As it was, the strain of holding the reins had bent her nearly double. God, what nerve she must have to even keep a hand on them at all. Probably saved them both doing it. He'd remember to thank her, after he got the carriage stopped.

Wind whistled past his ears. The traffic had cleared out. Moonlight and lantern light flashed just bright enough for him to make out the empty, macadamized road before them. They'd reached the highway, probably the Great North Road. Harry breathed a prayer of thanks. Not only would it be near empty this time of night, it was also smoother, so there was less chance of a horse breaking a leg or the carriage breaking a wheel than on cobbles.

Unfortunately, the horses also felt the change in the road under their hooves, and put on a fresh burst of speed.

Harry gritted his teeth, and didn't let himself think about what he was doing. With the carriage rocking at breakneck speed, the horses straining against rein, bit, and bridle, he clambered over the carriage seat trying to get to the driver's box. His hand slipped and his elbow buckled and he was staring at the rushing pavement, but he caught the edge of the box again, and pulled and swung himself around just so, and he was up beside the woman.

He slapped his hands down over hers; had just enough time to realize she wasn't wearing gloves and that they were skin to skin, before he pulled back hard.

"What are you doing?" she cried.

"Let go!" he shouted. "I've got them! They're slowing!"

"I don't want them slowed, you idiot!"

The butt of her whip caught him in the guts. The blow—aided by sheer and complete shock—toppled Harry backward, onto the seat, and then onto the boards.

"Get up! Get up, there!" The woman cracked the whip over the team's head. The horses charged forward.

Harry pushed himself to his knees again. Outrage cleared the last of the fog from his eyes. It also let him see the situation. The woman—bent low, lashing the space between her horses' ears—was not panicked. She was not trying to hold on to runaways. She was driving at the absolute limit of the horses' speed and the carriage's endurance.

"Stop!" Harry shouted.

"No!" she shouted back. "Sorry!" she added.

"You'll crash us!"

"Watch me!"

Did he actually hear *pride* in her voice?

I'm being abducted, Harry thought as he pushed himself back into a sitting position. *By a madwoman.*

Except she wasn't a madwoman. She was handling the team like she'd been born on the box. She'd been in control that whole time they'd threaded the streets of London, and Westminster, and taken those daring, near deadly turns. Dear God, what kind of woman was she?

At this, absurdly, Harry laughed. Maybe it was the remainder of the whiskey burning through his blood, maybe it was just speed and danger addling his wits. But it occurred to him that he'd been wishing he could get out of town. Now he was doing exactly that, and at top speed. Admittedly, he hadn't considered abduction as a means of gaining distance from Agnes, but here he was, and there didn't seem to be anything he could do about it. Not unless he wanted to risk climbing back onto the box and trying to wrestle the ribbons away from his surprisingly strong and well-armed lady abductor. Abductress?

Harry laughed again. He clambered carefully onto the seat, gripped the rail, and settled back to see where this madwoman would take them both.

Four

❦

If Leannah had been able to spare a thought from driving, she might have used it to wonder how the night could possibly get worse. As it was, she needed every ounce of concentration, and all her strength, to keep Rumor and Gossip from overturning the carriage. The two mares were having the time of their high-strung lives. Their necks strained forward, and their ears pressed flat against their skulls. Gossip fought to get the bit between her teeth, and Rumor was picking up on the idea, making the reins twice as tricky to hold. They could feel her hands were tiring and her grip was weakening, and both were trying their best to try to outrun the annoying, rattling contraption they'd been harnessed to, again.

And now there was a man in the barouche. How'd he even gotten there? Had he actually managed to jump aboard? Leannah found herself impressed, although very much against her will. Such a feat made him either a hero or a lunatic, but she had no leisure to work out which it could be. They were coming up on the crossroads and the signposts, and the straight, white ribbon of the Great North Road. Leannah pulled on the reins, but the team resisted. She cracked the whip over Rumor's ear, catching the mare's attention and turning her head. She saw the open way now, and the chance to really run. The team swerved sharply to the right. Leannah had just enough strength left to rein them in and prevent the barouche from tipping up on two wheels yet again. She should slow them. She was risking the team, the carriage, her own neck, not to mention the neck of whoever it was riding behind her. But if she slowed too far, she'd never catch up with Genevieve and then . . . then . . .

The barouche jounced over a pothole, landing hard in a noise of straining axles and springs. Her last pin fell away and her hair tumbled in a great, heavy mass down her back. Wind stung Leannah's ears and cheeks and set her eyes watering. It caught in her hair, flinging it backward.

Leannah thought she heard a sound from her unwelcome passenger. It sounded almost like a laugh.

Is he a madman? Or simply drunk?

She'd just have to hope he wasn't drunk enough to do something even more stupid than try to take the reins—like jump out and break his neck in a ditch, because she didn't have time to go back for him. She had to catch up with Genevieve. She had to stop her sister from making the worst mistake of her life.

She should have known something was brewing. She should have smelled it in the way Genny hadn't made any trouble for the past two days. She hadn't complained at all about hearing Jeremy's lessons and had even taken him to the circulating library and the park. Leannah had let herself believe that, for once, someone in their family had come to her senses before a disaster rather than long afterward.

She should have known better. She should have listened when her friend Meredith Langley warned her that something might be in the wind. But with Father doing poorly and Jeremy at home, there had been so much to do that she hadn't been watching Genny as carefully as she should have. That, and she'd so wanted to believe everything would be all right.

They were well past the city walls now, in the land of scattered cottages and open fields where the city folk would retreat or retire when they'd earned enough. Clouds scudded thickly across the moon and the stinging wind that rushed through her hair brought the smell of rain. Smooth macadam shone in the carriage's lantern light. There were no other lanterns on the road ahead. They had the way to themselves, and at least two miles to the tollgate. Leannah eased up on the reins just a little. If the team wanted to run now, let them run.

She wished she could enjoy the ride. It had been years since she'd driven like this. She'd pull them back in a few minutes, when she could be sure she really had gained on Genevieve, and that lecherous scoundrel Anthony Dickenson. She'd allow them just one more minute of speed, of flying free. This would be the last time, after all, before she had to sell them both. Before she had to take up her life with Mr. Valloy so she didn't have to sell anything else.

But that wasn't yet. Now there was the rush of the wind and the tension of the ribbons in her hands, and the giddy speed of driving, and no one to see or know or care that she was a woman driving herself.

No one, of course, except her passenger. Well, she'd dealt with everything up to now. She'd deal with him when she had to. But for just another minute, she and her team would run. Just one minute more . . .

The black, animal shape flashed across the white road. Gossip reared up, pulling Rumor with her. This time Leannah's hands did slip. Both horses came down short and hard, and she heard the ring as the shoe skittered free across the macadam. Gossip whinnied and the team stumbled to a halt.

"No!"

Leannah jumped down from the box and ran around to Gossip's flank. Both horses were blowing hard and working their bits. The sweat on their necks gleamed in the lantern light. Gossip pawed the ground, but showed no sign of pain.

But the shoe was gone. She'd heard it go. Had she wondered how things could get worse? They just had.

"Are you all right?" asked a deep voice behind her.

Leannah turned to face the man she had inadvertently abducted, and her breath caught in her throat.

She'd abducted a positive Adonis—a disheveled and thoroughly wind-blown Adonis to be sure, with some rather overdone sideburns, but he carried it magnificently. He was tall enough to look down on her, something Leannah seldom encountered. The moon came out briefly to mix with the lantern light and show him to be fair-haired, with dark brows and a square chin that would send any lady novelist into raptures. His shoulders were broad and the arms beneath his coat were well shaped. She remembered the strength of his hands as they clamped down over hers and hauled back on the ribbons, hard but evenly, to try to slow the team.

She'd yelled at him, and kidnapped him. Did she remember hitting him? Leannah knuckled her eyes. If it wasn't for Genevieve, it all might have been funny.

But there was Genny, now well on her way to Gretna Green, and they'd never catch her. *Stupid,* irresponsible child.

"Are you all right?" the stranger asked again.

"No. Yes. Oh. I'm so sorry, Mr. . . . Mr. . . . Oh, *God,* what a mess!" Leannah whirled away from him to face the highway, straining eyes and ears for some hint of a carriage. All the exhilaration of the drive and the thrill of her borrowed freedom were gone. "I'm going to murder that girl!" *I'm going to kill myself if Gossip is lamed, and how are we ever going to be able to afford the farrier's bill and what if I don't catch Genevieve . . . ?*

Tears of anger and fear streamed down Leannah's cheeks. She wiped at them and the salt stung her raw palms. Two strong hands gripped her shoulders from behind. They didn't exactly shake her, but they did turn her irresistibly to face her disheveled Adonis. Leannah gulped air. She couldn't breathe. She could barely think. The man said nothing. He just held her still long enough for her to see that his eyes were set deep above sharp cheekbones, and that those eyes were kind, as well as sane and sober. His hands curled around her shoulders and she was highly conscious of their warmth seeping through her thin sleeves. He was not only strong, he understood how to control that strength. She was no one's fragile blossom, but if she struggled against him now, she wasn't sure she'd be able to break this grip.

Why am I even thinking of that?

She slowly became aware that the man was breathing in a deliberate fashion—one deep, slow breath in, and then one just as slow and just as deep out again. The rhythm of it was oddly steadying, and allowed Leannah to breathe more normally herself. A flush of warmth and embarrassment crept up her throat, because as her breathing steadied, Leannah also became aware she'd been behaving like an hysteric.

"Are you all right?" Adonis asked, his voice quite calm. "Can you tell me what's happening?"

"My sister." Leannah took a deep breath and another and reined in her thoughts as firmly as she would a mettlesome team. She felt she should lie, or at least evade the question. This man, with his strong hands and magnificent eyes, was completely unknown to her. He might be anybody at all. He might be trouble.

He is trouble, whispered a voice from deep inside her, because he hadn't let go of her yet, and she hadn't pulled away, which she should do. She should also lie.

But she didn't do that either. "My younger sister's run off to Gretna Green with a man named Anthony Dickenson." Condescending, priggish, Anthony Dickenson, who spent half their conversations subtly reminding her that he was the one with money and that she should be grateful he even consented to be seen with Genevieve. "I thought I might be able to catch up with them, but now that's gone and she's out there alone with him and . . . *Oh, the little IDIOT!*"

All her hard-won calm shattered and Leannah clapped her hands to her face. She was shaking and the tears had started all over again. This was a scene, she realized dimly. She was making a pitiful, pointless scene, but she couldn't stop herself. She had worked so hard and so long to keep the family together; to give Genny and Jeremy a chance at some kind of life, and now her sister did . . . this . . .

Leannah felt herself being pulled forward. Sweet warmth enveloped her as the man wrapped his arms around her. He held her gently. She could step back at any time. But she didn't want to. She pressed her face against his shoulder and let him— this perfect stranger—hold her. He was once more breathing slowly and evenly, and she had the very keen sense of him controlling himself. It was grossly indecent to be out here in the dark of the highway in a stranger's embrace. Leannah found she did not care. Her palm rested against the hard plain of his chest. The worsted cloth stung her ungloved hand badly, but she didn't care about that either. She wanted to stay here just as she was. She wanted to relax her body against his, to tilt her face up, to look into his eyes, and then . . . and then . . .

Slowly, painfully, her hand curled into a fist where it rested against the man's chest. *No. I must stop this at once. I cannot be the thoughtless one. I do not have time.*

At least she had stopped crying. She had also regained enough control over her limbs to step away. Her stranger let her go, as she had known he would. But he was breathing fast now, and his face was entirely flushed. He also was looking down the road rather than at her.

"What kind of start does your sister have?" he asked.

"An hour, maybe two." She'd have been on the road much sooner if she hadn't had to deal with all Mrs. Falwell's stammering evasions. Then there'd been all the delay of getting to the stables, and convincing the manager that this really was an emergency, not just an attempt to get the horses away without paying the bill, not to mention getting the horses brought out and harnessed.

Her—passenger? victim? Leannah had no idea what to call the man—unhooked the right-hand carriage lantern and held it up to peer into the darkness. He was still breathing far too quickly for a man who'd done nothing but stand still for the last few moments.

He's also putting distance between us, murmured that treacherous, trivial part of her, the same part that had let her be held by this stranger. *He doesn't trust himself.*

She had to think clearly. She could not, however much she wanted to, fall to pieces again, or waste time yearning after things she could not have, like another moment in this man's arms. Leannah made herself look past his back, a feat almost as difficult as stepping out of his arms had been. The highway was empty. The silent countryside spread out black and gray in the last shreds of moonlight still able to find a path through the gathering clouds.

"There's still every chance," he said. "It's a dark night, and we're on the edge of rain. It's some three hundred miles to the border. They'll have to stop somewhere. If nothing else, they'll need to change horses frequently if they're to go at any kind of speed. We can ask at the gatehouse if they've been seen. We might even find them at the inn there."

She couldn't help noticing the way he said "we." Leannah opened her mouth to tell him she could manage very well, thank you, but at the last moment decided against it. She might not want him here, but here he was and she could hardly abandon him by the roadside, even if Gossip hadn't thrown her shoe. If he could be useful, she shouldn't discard his help out of hand.

"You're right. I'm sorry, Mr. . . . ?"

"Harry Rayburn." He performed a credible bow. "At your service, I suppose, Miss . . . ? Or is it Lady?"

"Missus," she answered. "Mrs. Wakefield."

"*Mrs.* Wakefield." The surprise and disappointment in his voice were positively flattering. Leannah wished she had time to enjoy them. The trained reflexes of courtesy made her hold out her hand. That, however, proved to be a mistake. When he took her hand so that he might bow over it, she winced. Mr. Rayburn, who could apparently number quick observation among his fine qualities, turned her hand over. The lantern light showed harsh lines along her palms where the leather reins had bitten into her skin. A dark smear of blood spread across her skin. Leannah pulled her hand away and hid it in her skirt.

"Is she all right?" Leannah nodded toward Gossip. Of course she'd check for herself, but for reasons she could not quite understand, she did not want Mr. Rayburn to be looking at her just now. The rush of the drive and the distraction of Harry Rayburn's touch were fading, and the pain had begun to creep up past her wrists, into her arms. It would be bad later, but she couldn't worry about that either.

Mr. Rayburn quirked a brow at her, as if to let her know he understood this was meant as a distraction. Nonetheless, he did move carefully around Gossip, who stamped and whickered at him. He patted her shoulder, murmuring soothing nothings as he ran his hand slowly down her leg. Whatever his station in life, Mr. Rayburn was a patient man, and one who understood horses. Probably she'd gotten hold of some Newmarket dandy, or member of the sporting set who would be all too delighted to regale his comrades about his midnight ride, probably expanded and improved upon to tell how he'd stopped the runaway team and saved a damsel in distress.

Then she remembered his rough hands with their controlled and well-judged grip. Those were not a dandy's hands at all.

"I think she's all right," Mr. Rayburn said as he straightened up. "I can't find any swelling or tenderness. Just lost the shoe."

She nodded. Despair threatened again, but she pushed it

aside, hard. "We're about two miles from the tollgate, I think. It makes more sense to head there than try to turn back to town."

"I agree." He raised the lantern a little higher and met her gaze. "There's still every chance we can catch up with your sister. If this fellow she's with is in a great rush, he's just barreled up the high road, and we'll get word of them at the inn. If he decided to be evasive and take the side roads, we will be ahead of them."

Unless Gretna wasn't their destination after all. Unless there was no marriage planned. Leannah couldn't believe that of Genevieve, despite her radical, bluestocking views. But what of Anthony Dickenson?

Leannah drew in a deep breath and let it out slowly. It would do no one any good to say so much now. "We should be on our way at once."

He nodded briskly. "I think this one . . ."

"Gossip," she told him. "Gossip and Rumor."

He cocked his eye at her again. She shrugged. "They're the fastest things in the world."

That earned a startled chuckle, and despite everything, Leannah felt herself smile. "Gossip here will walk, if we take it easy. I'll lead," he added before Leannah had any chance to protest.

She shivered. "All things considered, you'd be within your rights to leave me here."

He didn't answer that, at least not directly. "Have you a shawl or any such?"

He'd seen her shiver. He was too observant by half, this Mr. Rayburn. She was going to have to be very careful around him, or she'd give something important away.

"I left home in rather a hurry." *Without gloves or a hat or . . . oh, no, without any money.* She'd been so intent on catching up with Genevieve before the worst happened that she hadn't even paused to consider such things. Leannah shuddered again.

"Here." Mr. Rayburn stripped off the caped overcoat he wore. "Take this."

"You'll be cold."

"Not as cold as you'll be up there. Come now. You've wounded my pride by abducting me, you can at least permit me my chance to play the gallant."

He settled the coat around her shoulders and she felt the barest brush of his fingertips against the bare skin of her throat. The coat smelled of whiskey, salt water, and, surprisingly, spices. A treacherous shiver trickled down her spine.

Oh, don't, she whispered in the dark of her mind. *I mustn't be curious, or intrigued.*

If Mr. Rayburn thought this latest, so very treasonous shiver might be anything more than cold, he was gentleman enough to remain silent. He held out his hand, and Leannah realized belatedly that he meant to help her back onto the box. She let him, noticing he took her arm, not her injured hand. His own arm was steady as a rock as she leaned on him. For a brief moment she imagined having those arms around her again, and she thought of how those hands would feel as they settled against her waist to pull her close, here in the dark, where no one could see, no one could know.

I should leave you here, Mr. Rayburn. Gossip could run a little way at least, if I gave her her head. I could leave you behind and let you walk back to town and away from me.

But Mr. Rayburn already had Gossip's bridle. "Come on, old girl. We'll take this nice and easy. Here we go."

Leannah took up the reins. The pain of the leather against her bare palms nearly made her gasp, but she swallowed the sound and gave them a single shake. Rumor snorted in complaint but took up a walking pace at Gossip's side.

"Thank you, Mr. Rayburn."

"For what?"

She thought she'd spoken too softly to be heard, but apparently she'd failed in even that much. "For not saying if I'd driven less like a maniac, my horse wouldn't have cast a shoe, and I still might catch up with my sister."

"All part of the service, Mrs. Wakefield. For what it's worth, I've a sister, too, and I've had to make a mad drive or two myself on her account."

"Why do they do it?"

"If I knew that, I'd write a book and make a fortune. Are you going to be all right?"

"I'm going to have to be." *Again.*

I must stop this. Leannah scolded herself at once. *Feeling sorry for myself is not going to help.* She drew in a deep breath.

Vanilla, cinnamon, sandalwood, and oranges hung in the air around her. Whoever Harry Rayburn was, he carried the world with him. A sailor? A merchant man? It would explain his steady nerves, and strong arms.

I'm a widow, she wanted to tell him. *I have been for over a year. There's no living husband, or anyone else to protect me, or protest what I do.* There was Terrance Valloy, but she did not feel she could count him.

But she must count him, and all the other people who in their turn counted on her. She had no business fantasizing about a stranger, no matter how warm his embrace or gallant his manner. This wasn't a ballroom where she could watch the men and dream about them later. Genevieve's future was at stake. Every second was precious and their walking progress was excruciatingly slow. And yet, she couldn't help looking at this man who turned from being abducted by a stranger—a woman no less—to playing the rescuer and barely batted an eye.

Who are you, Harry Rayburn? Leannah inhaled another deep breath of spices. *Where are we going together?*

Five

Harry had never once had cause to be grateful for a thrown horseshoe in his life, but he was now. That shoe let him lead Gossip the mare, instead of requiring him to ride up on the box next to Mrs. Wakefield.

If Harry'd had any breath left after that carriage ride, the sight of Mrs. Wakefield by lantern and moonlight would have knocked it clean out of him. From his vantage point during their wild ride, he'd had an idea his abductress might be good-looking, if a trifle mad and rather unconventionally accurate with the butt of her whip. Because she wore no coat or cape, he could plainly see she had the full curves of a well-grown woman. He'd watched with interest when her mane of hair tumbled down her back to be tossed and teased by the night wind. But those hints and glimpses were nothing compared to his first, full look at her.

For one thing, Mrs. Wakefield must have been married right out of the schoolroom. If she was more than twenty-five, he was a codfish. For another, she was almost as tall as he was. He'd spent so much time stooping down to talk with Agnes, and his sister, he'd more or less formed the idea of all girls being tiny things. To be able to stand with straight back and see something other than the top of the other person's head was comfortable, and surprisingly enjoyable. It made him feel more himself. It also allowed him to see the flush in Mrs. Wakefield's cheeks and the flecks of brightness that glimmered in her green eyes. Whatever had brought her out onto the road at this hour, her outrageous drive had left her not frightened, but invigorated. Her magnificent hair curled wildly about her shoulders and down her back—all the way down her back to the swell of her derriere, he could not help noticing. It was fair hair, with hints of red, he thought, although the light was not good enough to be sure. He did know for certain she smelled of lemon and jasmine.

But as arresting as the sight of her beauty had been, it was nothing compared to the sensation of embracing her. God! What had he been thinking! He hadn't been thinking. He'd seen her distress and he'd taken her in his arms. At the moment, it had seemed quite simple and natural. But what he'd felt as her full breasts pressed against him was anything but simple. His body had been instantly on fire, and hard as stone. The whole of her delectably curved form felt soft and luxurious, and yet he knew how strong she was. She'd scarcely seemed to notice how badly she'd cut herself by driving without gloves.

The sight of Mrs. Wakefield's wounded hands had bitten into Harry almost as hard as his sudden need. The moment he saw those cuts, he wanted to embrace her again. He wanted to swear to protect her forever, just as soon as he hunted down this Dickenson who'd caused her to be out on this road alone at night. He'd teach the fellow to never again cause a woman— this woman—pain. She'd tip her face up toward his, and those gorgeous eyes would be alive with gratitude. He'd see how much she wanted to be in his arms again and then . . . and then . . .

Harry's mouth went dry and his breath came shallow. If his breeches didn't loosen soon, he'd strangle himself.

Once, home from school for the holidays, he'd overheard Fiona and some of her friends reading some story from a lady's magazine. He remembered, quite clearly now, how he'd laughed up his sleeve. After imbibing such tales of overblown rescue and harebrained gallantries, the girls would be shocked to find that no real man would be so stupid. Why would a real man risk his neck over some silly girl? Especially one he'd just met?

It seemed he was finding out.

Stand down, he ordered his overeager member. *Stand* down. *She's alone, and in trouble and she's married.*

Which was just as well, because at the moment the thought of her husband was all that kept him walking down the highway, leading this stumbling, complaining, entirely too high-strung mare. Who in God's name let a woman drive such a creature? Harry's opinion of the as-of-yet-unknown Mr. Wakefield had not been terribly high to begin with, and it dropped a little further with each yard they progressed. Where was Mr. Wakefield anyway? What kind of man let his wife go tearing about through the streets of London alone to chase down her eloping sister? Was he overseas?

Perhaps he was in his grave. Perhaps this mysterious beauty was a widow.

The thought sent a shudder straight through him that was equal parts desire and disgust. How could he, of all men, wish someone in their grave? Especially over a woman he didn't know?

It's the dark, he told himself. *It's the isolation and the excitement of that ride, and all after being turned down by Agnes. That's what this is. That's all.*

Because under normal circumstances there was no possible way he could come to feel so much so quickly. He wasn't a man to fall in love at first sight. He didn't believe in that nonsense. Which did not change how intensely he wanted to kiss Mrs. Wakefield. He wanted to kiss her hands, right across the welts left by the reins. He wanted to kiss the worried lines on her wide, pale brow and to discover the taste of her lips and the sensation of her tongue sliding against his. He wanted to surround her with his embrace and discover what those luscious curves would feel like crushed tight against his body as he slowly, tenderly, took the chill from her skin and the pain from her hands, replacing both with warmth and with pleasure.

"Was she all right?" asked Mrs. Wakefield suddenly.

"Sorry?" Startled, Harry stumbled over a loose stone. Gossip made a sound very close to a snicker and Harry swallowed a curse.

"Your sister, the one you said caused you such worry. You seemed so well acquainted with, well, circumstances, I thought, perhaps . . ."

"Oh. You mean did she elope? No. Fi—my sister, Fiona— she wasn't doing anything so conventional as eloping. She was chasing after someone." He was babbling. He was thoroughly aware of the fact, and yet couldn't seem to stop. "And yes, she's fine. Married to a future baron just last June."

"I'm glad."

Mrs. Wakefield fell silent again, which dried up Harry's own stream of conversation. *Say something!* He ordered himself. *Put her at her ease. Be witty, charming, soothing . . .*

But he did not feel any of these things. He felt cold and bereft, not to mention randy as a prize bull, and absolutely helpless to do anything about any of it. The more he tried to steer his mind away from the lush beauty holding the carriage reins with injured hands and making no complaint at all, the more his mind's eye showed her to him as she'd been before—wild as a barbarian queen, lighting down easily from the carriage to stand in the circle of the lantern light.

She was also quite naked in this vision, and she seemed to be holding her arms open for him. She had skin of honey gold, he noticed, and her nipples were dark buds at the tips of her beautiful, full breasts. Harry bit down on another curse.

"Where'd you learn to drive?" he made himself ask.

"Where I grew up in Devon, there's a tradition of a girls' race on Lady Day."

"I imagine you won quite a bit."

"Every year." She sounded oddly hesitant as she spoke. Harry risked a glance over his shoulder. She wasn't looking at him. Her gaze was on the road, and yet he had the strongest sensation that she wasn't seeing it. She was lost in some memory. He wished he could see her face well enough to know if it was a good one.

"You've come to London for your sister's season, I imagine." Harry cursed himself as soon as the words were out. Bringing up her sister was exactly the wrong thing right now.

"That's one reason." For a moment, her shoulders drooped, and Harry cursed himself again. "What of you, Mr. Rayburn? What brings you to London?"

"Oh, I'm quite the town man," he said. "My father's an importer. I work in his warehouses. I'm afraid, Mrs. Wakefield, your gallant knight is nothing but a coarse member of that class the haut ton are pleased to call the 'counterocracy.'"

"I can't think of anyone else I'd rather have with me."

The swell of pride that came with this statement was entirely unwarranted, and, unfortunately, his pride wasn't the only swollen part of himself.

You need to stop talking now. But Harry couldn't be sure whether that thought was meant for her or for himself.

"I did think you might be a merchant," she was saying.

"What gave me away?"

"You smell of spices."

Something in those few words shot straight through him. She might have said "your coat," but she didn't. She said "you." She was remembering being in his arms. They'd been close enough to breathe each other's breath and feel each other's heartbeat. Did she like it? Did she like him? Did she want to be near him again?

"And you're far too st— calm to be the usual ballroom beau."

She'd meant to say strong. He was sure of it. Yet more absurd pride sang in Harry's blood and he found himself wishing something new would happen. Perhaps this Mr. Dickenson could turn up with a cutlass, or a pack of highwaymen.

God in heaven, what is happening to me? I'm turning back into that damned schoolboy, just like with Agnes.

Except what he was feeling for Mrs. Wakefield was nothing at all like what he'd felt for Agnes. When he'd gotten near the faint and dainty Agnes, he'd never dared to do more than kiss her hand. He'd always been worried he'd break her, or shock her. With Mrs. Wakefield, though, he felt the power of his own body. He felt quick and decisive and ready, not to mention rough, and he liked it.

That thought was a slap in the face, and the heat in his blood dimmed. He'd felt this surge in his blood before, the dangerous delight that robbed a man of thought and restraint. It could be like a drug, and the touch of it could turn excitement to darkness in a single heartbeat.

Harry cursed again, making sure to keep it all under his breath. It seemed that heaven heard him anyway, and decided to teach him a lesson for lust, and blasphemy. Because the clouds chose that moment to unleash their torrent of icy spring rain. Harry cursed in earnest now and the impatient off horse— Rumor?—pranced uneasily and shook the harness.

Rain pounded in cold, hard drops on his skull and shoulders. Harry welcomed it. The cold and discomfort did a great deal to dim his undisciplined body's more painful urging. But he'd no coat and his hat was long gone. His hair was soon plastered to his scalp and the drops hissed against the carriage lantern. The candles guttered. If they lost the light in this storm, they would be in genuine trouble. Harry turned, meaning to tell Mrs. Wakefield they should raise the barouche's cover, so she could have some shelter. He could handle the horses without her on the box.

"There's a light." She pointed up the road.

Now Harry saw it, too, the glimmer of torchlight on the right-hand side of the road.

"That'll be the inn at the tollgate. The Three Swans, I think it's called." he said. "We're there."

We're done, said another part of him. *Good.* Because this night had turned him into someone he didn't want to recognize, someone far different from the dependable Harry everyone believed him to be and who he wanted to be.

And he'd liked it far more than was good for anybody.

Six

Leannah nearly cried aloud in relief as she saw the inn's light.

The rain soaked her to the skin and trickled down under the collar of Mr. Rayburn's too large coat. The cold mixed with the pain in her hands, so that she could barely keep her fingers curled even loosely about the reins. Once, when Mr. Rayburn was watching the road, Leannah had looked down at her palms, and saw the cuts bleeding afresh.

This was bad. Even if she got her hands bandaged, she might not be able to drive. She couldn't control Gossip and Rumor with weakened hands. If she couldn't drive herself, she was never going to be able to catch Genny. She also wasn't going to be able to get away from Harry Rayburn. It was rapidly becoming clear that getting away from Mr. Rayburn was nearly as important as catching her sister.

But it might all be over now, she told herself. *Genevieve and Mr. Dickenson might be at the inn, waiting to change of horses or just taking shelter from this rain.* Guilt at sitting on the box in a good wool coat while Mr. Rayburn walked ahead without even a hat was as cold as the rain. She'd have to find a way to repay him for his kindness.

No. You mustn't think about that.

But it was too late. She knew what he wanted. She knew it from his ragged breathing and the flush in his cheeks. And yes, she knew it from that long, warm moment in his arms when she was close enough to feel the contours of his taut body against her. She knew that if there came a moment when no one could see, if she went to him, and she offered herself, Mr. Rayburn would say yes.

At an inn, for instance, where they would be forced to wait while her horse was reshod.

I'm a widow, murmured her needy self. *The rules are different for widows.* Widows' affairs were daily winked at, provided there was some little discretion. She could lay down with Harry Rayburn and there'd barely be a murmur from society.

Don't. Don't. Leannah closed her eyes against this new pain. *It's impossible. Even if Genevieve manages to get as far as Gretna and does in her reputation all on her own, I must keep some kind of respectability. There's still Father, there's still Jeremy, and heaven knows what will happen next. I have to keep us all together.*

Because that was what was important. That was what would always be important. She was responsible for her family, and she could never forget that, not even on a night like this. Especially not on a night like this. They'd reached the inn's cobbled yard and Mr. Rayburn brought the team to a halt in front of the door. The sign swaying on its chains proclaimed the public house as the Three Swans, but except for themselves, the yard was empty. Disappointment rushed over Leannah. She'd been hoping so hard that they'd see some sign that Genevieve and Mr. Dickenson were inside.

Now I'm just being ridiculous. No one could leave horses out in this weather.

Leannah climbed quickly down from the box, ignoring the fresh pain in her hands as she did. She didn't want to give Mr. Rayburn any excuse to touch her again. But it was no good. Now that they were face-to-face, she could see clearly how the rain had plastered all his fair hair to his head, and ran in rivulets down his wide brow. She resisted the urge to reach out and wipe the water away. She made herself drop her gaze from his fascinating eyes to his dripping and dispirited whiskers, which were really quite absurd. He wasn't a perfect Adonis, this man. He was a nice, but bedraggled stranger with a sense of decency. That was all.

He was also eyeing the inn door, and she understood at once

why. "This could be awkward," he bawled to be heard over the rain.

She leaned forward to make her answer into his ear, which was another mistake, because it brought her far too close for comfort. "We could say that I'm your sister."

He smiled ruefully. "I don't think anyone would believe it."

She reminded herself sternly that he was speaking of their looks, but it was too late. The thrill was already threading through her blood, because she knew what he really meant. The way they looked at each other, the way they stood like this, so close and familiar and yet so filled with tension, this was not the way of a brother to his sister.

"Wife then?" she said. *Oh, this is dangerous.* She shouldn't think about being his wife, not even for a moment.

Harry hesitated. "It might make it more awkward to explain to Mr. Wakefield later."

"I'm a widow."

She hadn't meant to tell him, Leannah was sure of that. A husband, however fictitious, was protection from this man, and from her own overwhelming feelings. But the words were out before she could even think about stopping them. Something about being so close to Harry Rayburn stripped away her well-honed skills of polite deception as quickly as the rain had washed away any trace of warmth on her skin.

Mr. Rayburn went very still for a moment. She watched him suppress some strong emotion. She reached down, to cover his hand with hers and say it was all right. For tonight she would gladly be his wife. Here in the dark, even in the rain, there was no one to see them . . .

Except of course there was. The door of the house flew open, unleashing a flood of firelight, as well as the solid silhouette of the landlord, with an umbrella in one hand and a lantern in the other.

"There you are, sir!" he cried. "We been expecting you hours since! Trouble with the horses is it? That explains it all."

"We're *expected*?" Leannah asked sharply as she ducked under the umbrella the landlord held out. Reality had returned, and it was both hard and unwelcome.

"Of course! Of course! Your message came to us in good time, and everything's in order."

Which could only mean Genevieve had planned this elopement further ahead than Leannah had given her credit for. She owed Meredith Langley an apology for dismissing her warnings so casually.

"Martin!" the landlord bellowed over his shoulder. "Get your lazy carcass out there and see to the gentleman's horses!"

The landlord kept up a solid stream of orders to the unfortunate Martin, who ran out into the deluge with a tin lantern gripped in one hand to take Gossip's bridle from Mr. Rayburn.

"Careful, there," Mr. Rayburn said. "She's got a temper. Has anyone else passed this way?" he asked as he followed Leannah and the landlord inside the blessedly warm public room.

"No, sir," the landlord replied. "Been a quiet night and likely to stay that way." He nodded toward the rain as he shut the door. "You needn't worry about anything along those lines."

No, there's nothing to worry about, except that Genny is out in that storm, and I'm stuck here.

The landlord evidently saw her distress, and quite mistook its cause. "Now, miss, don't you fret. All's just as it should be. We've your room ready, and my missus'll be right out to see to what's needful."

But his reassurance did no good at all. Leannah began to shake. She clutched Mr. Rayburn's sodden coat closer around her shoulders. The cold had gotten into her blood and bones. It filled her, as heavy and solid as the mass of guilt, anger, and fear that lodged itself under her ribs.

"Now then, now then, you just step through there, miss." The landlord set his lamp down on the oak bar. "The fire's good and warm in the parlor, and I'll send Mrs. Jessop to you right away, as I see your servant's yet to catch you up. An' I suspect you'll be wanting some tea?"

"As well as whatever's on the fire in the kitchen." Mr. Rayburn fished about in the pocket of his dripping coat and laid several coins on the bar. "With our thanks."

"Yes, sir. Very good, sir."

The parlor was plain, but neat and well kept, with several slat-backed chairs beside a round table for dining, as well as a pair of armchairs before the fire and a sofa beneath the window. Mr. Rayburn did not accompany her into the room, which was just as well. Leannah needed to collect her wits, and stop this ridiculous shaking, and Mr. Rayburn's presence would be a decided impediment to both processes.

A brisk woman—presumably the landlord's wife, Mrs. Jessop—bustled in and immediately began to poke up the fire. She chattered comfortably as she worked, about how she'd have tea and a bowl of good hot stew in just a minute, and wasn't this the worst of nights, but still, mustn't grumble, and if Miss would just give over that nasty wet coat, the girl would be bringing in towels and a dry shawl presently.

Leannah wasn't listening. She sat in the chair nearest the fire and held her hands out to the flames. The rain drummed relentlessly against the shutters, and Leannah trembled from the strength of her fear as much as from the cold.

This is my fault. Why didn't I just let them all know I'm happy to accept Mr. Valloy? We'd be settled again by now, and Genevieve could finish up the season without any of us having to worry. What am I going to do? Jeremy's going to wake up and find us both gone. No. Jeremy will be fine. He won't think to try to come after us.

Except he would. At twelve, her brother very much felt himself to be the man of the family. Leannah squeezed her eyes shut at the thought of clever, stubborn young Jeremy calmly distracting the servants and walking out the door. He had the family way with horses. He'd have Bonaparte saddled up before anyone knew he was missing.

My fault. All my fault.

But she hadn't wanted to marry Terrance Valloy. She'd entered into her first marriage because her father had arranged it for the good of the family. It hadn't been so bad. Elias Wakefield was a good man. It had taken her years to discover exactly how good, but she'd felt his innate kindness from the moment she first met him. She had no such feeling about Mr. Valloy. In fact, it was the reverse. There was something about the way he looked at her and about the way his hands felt against her when they waltzed that left her profoundly uneasy.

But what else was there to do? The money was gone and Father wasn't getting any better. She couldn't be weak, or sentimental. That was a luxury allotted to young girls, and more particularly girls with fortune, education, and suitors in some combination. Sentiment, romance, even simple desire had no part and could have no part in her life. There was no good lamenting about the unfairness of it all. It simply was. This extraordinary meeting with the undeniably attractive Mr. Rayburn changed nothing.

There was a soft knock at the door. Leannah looked up, expecting to see Mrs. Jessop again, but instead, it was Harry Rayburn who shouldered his way into the parlor. He had doffed his rain-drenched coat and now wore just his shirtsleeves and waistcoat. The wooden tray he carried was loaded with clean cloths, towels, a steaming kettle, and a tin basin. He'd draped a thick, white wool shawl over his arm as well. She noticed how his fair hair was badly tousled from having been rubbed dry, as were his whiskers. Really, they were a sight to behold. Despite her worries, Leannah felt herself smile.

"I've had a word with the stable lad, Martin," Mr. Rayburn told her as he set the tray on the table by the fire. "He confirms what the landlord said. The only trade this evening's been the mail coach and some farmers stopping by for a pint before the rain came on. But they were, in fact, expecting a Mr. Dickenson and a young lady, and they were to have separate rooms ready."

"Which means Genevieve at least planned to come this way."

"And that this Dickenson meant for them to stay the night, within bowshot of London." Mr. Rayburn frowned as he poured hot water into the basin. "Not something I would have expected for an elopement."

Genny, what are you doing? Leannah automatically pushed her hair back from her cheeks and winced again. Mr. Rayburn moved toward her, but stopped in his tracks. Their landlord might be mistaken as to their exact identities, but they weren't alone anymore. He couldn't casually touch her now. Someone might see the violation of propriety.

Leannah didn't want propriety. She wanted someone else to be strong, just for a minute. She wanted to collapse and cry. But that wasn't allowed either.

"However, that's neither here nor there," Mr. Rayburn went on. "It's safe to assume they've been delayed by the rain. All we have to do now is wait for them to turn up."

"Oh, is that all?" Leannah repeated wearily. "I'd rather be trying to run them down."

"Believe me, I understand the sentiment. Here, you'd better get this shawl around you." Mr. Rayburn was trying to sound brisk but the words kept catching in his throat. "Mrs. Jessop is seeing about some dry clothes. I told her the luggage was delayed with the servants. And we need to get those cuts washed." He indicated the basin. "It's been my experience that dirt can slow down the healing."

"Thank you." She stood to reach for the shawl he held out at arm's length. It was thick, undyed wool, made soft by time and much wear. She took it carefully, so as to not let her hand touch his. Her body had come too close to betraying her enough times tonight. She could not court fresh temptation. "I seem to be thanking you a great deal, but you've done so much." She drew the shawl close about her.

"All part of the service," he answered with what she was coming to think of as his habitual smile.

Leannah found she did not want to look at Mr. Rayburn anymore. She did not need to see him with his collar and cravat loose, exposing the intricate lines of his throat with its sprinkling of golden stubble, or the swell of his Adam's apple. She especially did not need to see the curve of his shoulders and arms beneath the plain white linen of his shirt. Instead, Leannah got to her feet and turned her attention to the basin of steaming water. She plunged her hands into it. The heat was scalding, and Leannah hissed and jerked her hands back.

Of course Mr. Rayburn was right there. "Here," he said and she knew she did not imagine the tremor in his deep, patient voice. "Let me."

Leannah knew exactly what she should say in this moment. *No. Thank you. I can do this myself. You needn't trouble. Truly.* But she didn't say it. She only held out her hands. Mr. Rayburn dipped a cloth into the water and wrung it out. He took her right hand in his. With infinite gentleness, he dabbed at the raw, straight gash on her palm, clearing away the caked grime. It hurt, but the pain was nowhere near as powerful as the sensation of his skin against hers. She could feel every nuance of his fingers. If she'd been a properly bred miss, his callouses would have made her cringe. Instead, they fascinated her. She wanted to know what those rough hands would feel like caressing her bare arms, and tracing a warm line across the sensitive skin of her throat, or her mouth, or her breasts.

Leannah couldn't even grit her teeth against the image, because she didn't want him to think he was hurting her. Mr. Rayburn took up a long strip of clean white linen. Quickly and efficiently, he wrapped it around her injured hand.

"You've had practice at this," she remarked, struggling to find some kind of intellectual distance that would keep her from slipping away with the rising tide of her need.

"Well, working in a warehouse, you see a few injuries."

"I would not have thought to find myself in such capable hands on this night." Now it was her words that made Leannah wince. The list of things she should not have said was growing unforgivably long. She told herself it didn't matter. There was no one to hear. No one, except of course Mr. Rayburn himself. What would she do if he decided she was flirting with him? What was she going to do if it turned out she was?

He made no reply, only looked at her for a long moment. He didn't let go of her hand, and that, for Leannah, that was answer enough. He knew what was happening inside her, what his touch was doing to her. He saw it in her eyes, he felt it in the way her hand warmed as he held it. He had blue eyes, and they were startlingly wide and clear; the sort of eyes that could look straight through a woman's polished politeness and see what she really wanted. Firelight caught in his gold hair, and those overgrown, coppery sideburns. The scent of spices was gone. Now he smelled of clean rainwater, and a bit of whiskey.

Move, away, move away! she ordered herself. *At least, say something.* But her throat had closed. She could scarcely breathe, let alone speak. She did not in the least want to move.

It was Mr. Rayburn who broke the moment. He dropped his clear, blue gaze and let go of her hand, so he could soak the towel again. He was breathing hard, and although the firelight made everything uncertain, she was sure she saw his cheeks coloring.

He feels it, too. Leannah's heart pounded in the base of her throat. She hadn't been in any way mistaken. He wanted her, and now he knew how she wanted him.

"I can do the other," she said.

"No you can't," he replied gruffly. "You'll get your bandages wet."

He took her hand and laved it softly with the towel. She didn't protest. *Let him do this,* said that treacherous part of herself. *Enjoy it. It will never happen again. I can make a memory of this moment and save it for later. I will want it later.*

Later when she was alone in her own cold bed, filled with the aching, heated restlessness that gave rise to private fantasies and forbidden acts. Oh, yes, she'd want to remember Harry Rayburn's hands on her then.

I am a shameless, wicked woman. Hot-blooded, reckless, indecent . . .

But before Leannah could finish this silent litany of her faults, they heard the crash of the door slamming open in the public room, followed by a man's voice.

"Hullo! Anybody about?"

Leannah's heart froze. She pulled herself away from Harry, ran to the door, and pressed her eye to the crack beside the threshold. She was fully aware of Harry right behind her.

It took a moment for her eye to adjust to the dimmer light of the public room. But as soon as it did, she saw there, standing at the bar with rainwater dripping from the brim of his curly brimmed beaver hat, was Anthony Dickenson.

Seven

❦

Leannah opened her mouth. Probably she intended to cry out and burst into the public room. Probably she would have done it, too, had not Harry Rayburn clapped his hand over her mouth and pulled her back.

"Don't." His breath was warm and his lips brushed her ear softly sending fresh tremors of sensation across her skin. "Think a minute. Is that him?"

Leannah nodded. He seemed to be taking a very long time about letting her go. But then, she wasn't struggling to get away as she should have been.

"All right." Mr. Rayburn lowered his hand from her mouth, but he did not loosen his grip on her arm. His body felt solid and warm and infinitely inviting against her back. "Your sister will have stayed with the carriage while he makes sure the rooms are ready. You go out and get her. I'll detain this fellow."

Leannah nodded again and now Harry did let her go. Her mouth tingled from the press of his hand. She needed to tell him to stop touching her, even in these extremes. His touching her was adding entirely too much trouble to this extraordinary night.

But whose fault is that, really? Leannah moved away from the door, so she would not be seen when it opened. Harry seemed to have forgotten her, at least briefly. His gaze was fixed entirely on some distant point. Then, as she watched, his expression shifted. No, his whole stance shifted. In the space of a few heartbeats, Mr. Rayburn transformed from her intoxicating stranger into some bluff and hearty fellow, a little too tall for the space and a little too hale for civilized company.

In this character, he breezed out of the parlor. "Hullo!" she heard him cry. "Thought I heard a voice. Beastly night out there, ain't it?"

Leannah was uncomfortably aware that her mouth was hanging open. "What sort of man are you, Harry Rayburn?" she said under her breath.

But there was no time to puzzle out that question. Leannah turned quickly around and slipped out the parlor's side door. She found herself in a little stairwell. A second door led out to the yard. Rain pounded steadily against windows and shingles. She was still wet from her earlier dousing, but she mustn't let that bother her. Leannah felt herself smile. *Let me see. What would Harry Rayburn do now?*

He wouldn't hesitate, she was certain of that much. Fortunately, the innkeeper was diligent, and the hinges were well oiled. The door opened with very little sound. Leannah pulled the thick shawl up over her head, caught up her hems, and ducked outside.

The rain tapped insistently against her head, but she ignored it. Hugging the wall of the public house, she hurried toward the spark she knew must be a carriage lantern.

Leannah's eyes had adjusted to the dark now, and up ahead she saw a high-wheeled landau. What a ridiculous choice for elopement. Such a carriage was meant for short drives in the city or on a racecourse, not long jaunts at speed through the country. At least Mr. Dickenson had put the top up. But despite the rain and despite the dim light of the carriage lanterns, there was no mistaking the profile of the girl sitting on the side nearest the house. That was most decidedly Genevieve, waiting for her would-be fiancé to come fetch her inside.

Leannah glanced at the inn, afraid to see the door open and let out Mr. Dickenson, but it remained fast shut. Harry Rayburn was doing as he said and detaining the man. Leannah crouched low and ran forward, making a wide circle around the back of the carriage. She skidded badly in some mud once, but righted herself. The rain covered the noise, and she was able to come right up to the carriage door on the far side.

In one quick motion, Leannah yanked the landau's door open, and jumped inside.

Genevieve whirled around, her hand raised. Leannah grabbed her sister's wrist before the slap could descend. "It's me, Genny," she announced and let the shawl slip off her head.

"Leannah!" Genny cried. "How!" Leannah wished for better light. She was certain the look that crossed her sister's face in that moment was quite priceless.

"Next time you want to keep a secret, you shouldn't involve Mrs. Falwell," said Leannah acidly. She was tired. Her hands hurt abominably under the bandages Harry Rayburn had so carefully and expertly applied, and she'd spent a large portion of the night feeling scared to death. It was not a combination that inclined one to immediate sympathy with a sister's interrogation.

"Well, you have to go away. You'll ruin everything."

"Too late for that." Leannah nodded over her sister's shoulder.

The carriage rocked as Genevieve jerked herself around yet again. There, framed by firelight from the inn's open door stood Mr. Dickenson, gawping. Harry and Mr. Jessop stood directly behind him.

"Mrs. Wakefield!" Dickenson cried. "How?"

"Ah, well now!" The landlord clapped his hands together with an air of immense satisfaction. "I guess this makes it a family party, don't it?"

"Now, see here . . ." began Mr. Dickenson hotly, but Mr. Rayburn cut him off.

"Let's all get inside. We can sort this out where it's dry."

It was quite clear from the stubborn set of her jaw that Genevieve wanted to protest. But the wind chose that moment to gust, and it blew a curtain of frigid rain straight through the carriage's open side and into her face.

"Oh, very well." Genevieve sniffed and ostentatiously reached for Mr. Dickenson to help her down. For her part,

Leannah watched Mr. Dickenson closely, and made sure he knew it. Martin, the stable lad, hustled up glum and resigned to take the equally glum and resigned horses around to the stables.

"Mrs. Jessop!" bellowed the landlord as he led them all back into the public room. "You were right! The lady and gentleman were here ahead of their family!"

"Come, Genevieve, we'll go into the parlor." Leannah took firm hold of her sister's arm.

"Good idea," said Harry, before Mr. Dickenson could protest. "I'm sure Dickenson and I will do fine out here."

Leannah shot him a quick glance of gratitude before directing her attention to steering Genevieve into the parlor and shutting the door tight.

"Who is that man, Leannah?" demanded Genevieve as soon as she turned back around. "What have you been doing?"

"What have *I* been doing?" Leannah gaped at her sister.

"Yes, you! I'm gone a handful of hours and I find you running through the dark with a handsome stranger in tow!" Leannah couldn't tell whether her sister was shocked, or impressed. "And what on earth happened to your hands?"

This abrupt questioning was really more than Leannah could bear. It was only years of training in discretion that prevented her from shouting. "Genevieve, I have been chasing you down for most of the night," she answered as evenly as she could. "What happened to my hands is I was driving through London like a lunatic without my gloves. And you, incidentally, have no right to demand an account of my doings."

"Well, you are still my sister." Genevieve untied her bedraggled straw bonnet. Her auburn hair had come loose from its pins and now trailed in loose ringlets around her neck. "I have every right to know what you're up to, especially when it involves strange men."

Once again, Genny had successfully turned her well-deserved scolding around on Leannah. How on earth did she manage it? "And *you* are still *my* sister," Leannah reminded her. "My *underage* sister, and I am here to once and for all stop you from marrying Anthony Dickenson."

"Don't be ridiculous." Genevieve took off her dun-colored

topcoat, and shook it out to hang on one of the pegs by the door. "I want to marry him. I am passionately in love."

"I'm not even going to dignify that with a reply."

A knock at the door interrupted them. Mrs. Jessop, grinning from ear to ear, trooped in with her stout arms full of towels and drying sheets. A young girl, still blinking the sleep from her eyes, followed. She carried a tray laden with a teapot, bread, and bowls that, from the savory scent of the steam, contained the long-promised stew. Hunger cramped Leannah's stomach.

"There now," said Mrs. Jessop as she set all the things down on the table. "Mary and I will have the beds turned down presently. And, ahem, we've found some dry things for you, Miss . . . ?"

"Mrs. Wakefield."

"Just so. Mrs. Wakefield, and this is the genuine Miss More-house, I'm guessing? Yes." Mrs. Jessop nodded with satisfaction. Leannah suspected the retelling of this story would involve all the local housewives, and many more pots of tea. "Miss Morehouse's bandbox has been sent up to the room," Mrs. Jessop went on. "You just get some hot food into you and then it's all to bed, and everything will be right as nine pence in the morning." She must have noticed the sisters' doubtful expressions. "You may trust me, miss," she said to Genevieve. "Twenty years I've kept this house, and I've seen plenty of elopements go by. It's better you put things right with your people sooner rather than later. Now then, Mrs. Wakefield, I'll take you upstairs and we can get you out of that wet dress. Mary will see to things down here."

Meaning Genevieve would not be left alone, in case she was thinking of making another dash for it.

Leannah followed the landlady gratefully. The room upstairs was chilly, despite the fresh fire in the grate, but like the parlor, it was clean and neat. The same could be said for the plain shift, dress, and stockings the landlady helped her into. She smoothed her wet hair back from her brow. It was going to dry into a mass of tangles. She'd have to ask Mrs. Jessop for a brush or a comb or she'd never get it put right. There were, however, far more urgent matters she needed to attend to first.

Back down in the parlor, Leannah found Genevieve at the table, tucking into a bowl of stew. The girl, Mary, moved slowly about the room, collecting damp things and folding them all with painstaking neatness. At a nod from Mrs. Jessop, the diligent maid followed her mistress out into the public room, a mountain of wet clothing and towels in her arms.

Before the door closed, Leannah glimpsed Harry Rayburn standing at the bar with Mr. Dickenson. Their eyes locked, and that instant sent a flutter of nerves through Leannah. Harry raised a glass to her.

Then the door closed, and he was gone, but knowing he was on the watch made her feel obscurely better. How had this stranger managed so quickly to become a reassuring presence?

It's this extraordinary mess that's done it, she told herself. *That's all. My nerves are worn raw. I will be able to see things sensibly in the morning.*

But, she realized with a jolt she did not want to see things sensibly, not when it came to Harry Rayburn.

Genevieve was quite another matter. Leannah drew a chair up to the table, and the fire. She dipped a spoon into her stew bowl, all the while trying to work out what she should say.

The stew proved to be mostly dried peas and potatoes, with a bit of mutton for flavoring. Still, it was filling, and the bread was fresh, and the butter sweet. Leannah quickly finished her entire bowl and felt much restored, despite the strained silence that persisted between her and Genny. By the time she'd buttered her third slice of bread, she even felt as if she might be able to carry on a rational conversation.

If only her sister could be persuaded to do the same. "Genevieve . . ." Leannah began.

Genevieve dropped her spoon into her empty bowl with a clatter, and pushed it away. If the truth were to be told, she looked very much like a sulky child refusing her warm milk.

"All right, all right, I am not passionately in love with Mr. Dickenson," Genevieve announced. "But I'm marrying him all the same."

Leannah swallowed the dismissive scold that hurried toward

the tip of her tongue. "Why, Genny? You're not . . . he hasn't . . ." she couldn't make herself say the words.

"No! What do you take me for?"

"We're sitting in a public house on the road to Gretna Green and you need to ask me that?"

Genevieve opened her mouth. She closed it again. She looked at the fire a long time. "I'm sorry," she said finally. "But you'd made it plain you would never consent."

"So why are you doing this, Genevieve? You don't love him and you don't have to marry him."

"Of course I do," she shot back.

"But *why*?"

Now Genevieve did look at her, and her mix of sadness and determination cut straight into Leannah's heart. "So you won't have to marry Mr. Valloy."

She would need to be very careful how she answered this. She couldn't let Genevieve see even the smallest hint of her discomfort. "Nothing's been decided yet. Besides, Mr. Valloy is a perfectly amiable and capable man."

"He's a pig," Genevieve snapped. "A pig who wants to get his clammy hands on Jeremy's land!"

"Genevieve!"

But her sister gave no sign of having heard. "You already married to save us once, Leannah. You shouldn't have to keep paying for . . ."

"Stop," said Leannah softly. "Please, don't say it."

Genevieve fell silent, but it didn't matter. The words still hung in the air between them. *You shouldn't have to keep paying for Father's mistakes.*

"Should or shouldn't doesn't matter," Leannah said. "We all have to deal with what is."

"You've already saved us all more times than any of us know," said Genevieve.

"I haven't done so much. It was Elias . . ."

The sound Genevieve made was loud, dismissive, and entirely unladylike. "Elias never would have made Jeremy his heir if you hadn't remained so good and true. *And* it was you who stopped Father from selling off the land while he had management of Elias's affairs, and kept us together after . . . well, afterward."

Leannah had no answer. She could only wrap her arms around herself and sit in stunned silence. She had always believed she'd kept the extent of the family's troubles entirely to herself. It seemed she'd been underestimating Genevieve for a very long time, and perhaps not only Genevieve.

"How much does Jeremy know?"

"More than you want him to."

"That wouldn't take much."

Genevieve reached across the table and grasped Leannah's bandaged hand. "Let me help, Lea. Mr. Dickenson isn't a bad man . . ."

"He wants to marry an underage girl without the consent of her family."

"Only because I talked him into it."

"Which hardly speaks to strength of character on his part."

"But it should prove I'll be able to manage him."

You don't need a man you can manage, Leannah thought wearily toward her sister. *You need a man strong enough and quick enough to understand you. One who will see all the good and beautiful things you are, and love you for them.*

Leannah pictured Mr. Dickenson as he had been in their little dining room when she'd invited him to dinner. He'd stared down at the pale soup Mrs. Falwell ladled out to him. He'd seen the crack in the china plate, and the lack of meat among the vegetables. He would have turned up his nose at it if etiquette had permitted. No, Genevieve would not be able to manage this man. She was beneath him, and Anthony Dickenson was not one to let her ever forget that. He'd get her to sign her name and body over to him. Then, he'd take her away to a grand house and a life of misery.

But she could not say that. Genevieve would never listen.

"You expect me to trust so much in your judgment and yet you also expected to be able to get all the way to Gretna with only one bandbox."

Genevieve turned her face stubbornly away, but the color was already rising in her cheeks. Leannah's tired, troubled mind cleared. She thought on her sister's cleverness, and her many other fine but misapplied qualities. All those qualities had surely been in play when Genevieve conceived of this elopement. Further, it was clear Meredith had been correct, and this had all been planned days, if not weeks, ago.

"You'd never elope without at least one decent dress, and a pair of dancing slippers," Leannah said slowly. "What's going on?" But she didn't need Genevieve to answer. Even as she spoke, the remaining pieces of the puzzle tumbled into place. "Genevieve, please tell me you didn't involve Uncle Clarence in this scheme!"

Their uncle, Clarence Morehouse, was the priest at St. Timothy's in Vauxhall parish. As such, he could go to the archbishop at any time to obtain a special license. Once that was in hand, he could marry Genevieve to her intended anywhere—in a church, a sitting room, or the private parlor of the Three Swans.

Genevieve shrugged as if it was of no consequence. "If we'd had to go all the way to Scotland, you could have caught us."

"I did catch you."

Genevieve made no answer. Leannah tried to run her fingers through her hair, only to be stopped by the myriad of tangles.

"When was he to meet you?" she asked.

Genevieve glanced at the carriage clock on the mantel. "He should have been here already," she said and for the first time worry crept into her voice. "He sent a message to Mrs. Falwell once he'd gotten the license."

"How did you even get Uncle Clarence to agree? He's not the smartest man, but he wouldn't participate to a runaway marriage." Understanding, unwelcome and cold, dawned. Leannah felt the blood drain from her cheeks. "Genevieve, you didn't!"

"I wonder that you ask me anything at all," Genevieve sniffed. "You seem to know all the answers."

"You lied and told him there was a baby!"

"He wouldn't have agreed any other way. As it was, he still wanted me to confess to you and Father."

Now it was Leannah who couldn't speak. She stood and walked to the hearth. She was shaking again, and wrapped her arms tightly around herself. She couldn't even think. Her mind had gone entirely blank. Almost idly, she wondered how Harry

Rayburn was doing out in the public room. How much had Mr. Dickenson told him?

And what must he think of me now? she hung her head.

"What was I to do, Leannah?" said Genevieve from behind her. "It's not as if my season's been a roaring success."

Neither of them mentioned that this was in part because she'd spent a certain amount of that season closeted in her room writing letters to the women's newspapers that spoke against the dissolution of a woman's individual legal status upon marriage. Not that she'd told anyone that was what she'd been doing. However—as Leannah had pointed out when she confronted Genny—if she really wanted to remain anonymous, she should have chosen a better nom de guerre than "G. M. House."

"I'm all there is, Leannah. I have to make a decent match so we can survive until Jeremy's of age." Her face flushed, and Leannah steeled herself for the outburst, which was not long in coming. "We shouldn't have to do this!" Genny cried. "We're adult human beings! You have twice as much sense as any man I've ever met! Elias should have left you the land, not a mess of lawyers, a sick man, and a twelve-year-old boy!"

"But he didn't and we must live with what is, not what we want to be," said Leannah as calmly as she could. "You do not have to marry, Genny, and you certainly do not have to marry Mr. Dickenson. I would never, ever ask you to do anything so against your principals."

But Genny just shook her head. "My principals won't keep the family safe and together. I can't afford to stand on them while you . . . give yourself away yet again."

"I've made my choices," said Leannah quietly. "You should be free to make yours, you and Jeremy both."

"But what about you? You have as much right to your freedom as either of us."

"It's too late for me." But her thoughts had already strayed back to Harry Rayburn. What was he doing out there? Was he thinking of her? Wishing perhaps that they were the ones to share the inn's simple meal, and then, and then . . .

Unless of course he'd heard the whole, sordid story from Mr. Dickenson's cynical mouth, and had already left in disgust.

"It's not too late for you," said Genevieve. "You're just play-ing the martyr because you haven't the heart or the nerve to do anything else."

This blunt statement tipped Leannah over into genuine anger. "That's enough. If you think you will change our situ-ation one bit by running off with a man who doesn't love you, then you are nothing but a silly schoolgirl and what you really need is to be sent to bed without supper."

Genevieve clamped her mouth shut and turned her face toward the fire. Leannah didn't watch her. She faced the window instead, struggling to get her breathing under control. She'd done so much, she'd tried so hard—to have her little sister accuse her of cowardice was more than she could stand. It wasn't cowardice to do one's duty. When would Genevieve understand that they all must live the lives they'd been given? For Leannah, that meant holding the family together until Jer-emy was twenty-one and Elias's land could be released from the trust. Anything else was not only foolish, but dangerous.

This wasn't any lack of nerve or heart. This was cold, hard reality. It didn't matter what Genevieve thought she was doing or why.

"I'm sorry, Leannah," Genevieve's meek words interrupted her thoughts. "I shouldn't have done it, and I certainly shouldn't have involved Uncle Clarence."

Genevieve was sitting with her hands clasped in her lap, her green eyes wide and anxious—the very picture of worried repentance.

Do you think I'm going to fall for this again? But Leannah didn't say anything. Her heart was too strained and sore to continue this conversation.

You're just playing the martyr because you haven't the heart or the nerve to do anything else. It was infuriating. It was ridiculous.

She might have been able to continue in this vein if she hadn't also been thinking of Harry Rayburn and the sensation of his arms wrapped around her, the brush of his lips against her ear, and the press of his hand against her mouth.

Leannah sighed. She sighed for trouble and secrets and younger sisters with good hearts who truly did want to help.

But most of all she sighed for the thousands of things that could never and would never be.

"Let's go upstairs, Genevieve," she said, putting her back to the public room and the lingering, tempting specter of Harry Rayburn. "We'll start for home tomorrow."

Eight

Anthony Dickenson, Harry decided, was not a man who improved upon closer acquaintance.

As soon as the parlor door closed, he rounded on Harry.

"Now, look here! Exactly who are you? And what business of yours is any of this?"

Actually, it was a bit of a surprise to Harry that this fastidious dandy would be involved in an elopement. Dickenson's buff coat had at least half a dozen capes to it, and his Hessian boots were polished mirror bright, that is, where they weren't splattered with mud from the yard. His dark, artfully arranged curls had suffered somewhat from the rain, and when he pushed his coat open, Harry saw a quizzing glass dangling from the gold chain around his neck.

Harry's mouth twitched, but he managed to meet Dickenson's drooping brown eyes. "I'm Harold Rayburn," he said. "I'm a friend of the family, and I'm here to help Mrs. Wakefield bring her sister home, unharmed."

Dickenson lifted his quizzing glass and regarded Harry through the lens. Dear God, he hadn't met with this much affectation since he'd come home from university. "Yes," Dickenson drawled. "You look like the sort of friend she'd have. What's your trade?"

"It's not making off with young girls in the dead of night." That drew Dickenson up to his full height, which was still a good three inches or so shorter than Harry's. Harry watched various shades of contempt and anger flicker across the man's sallow face. His hands itched and his heart started pounding, but it wasn't fear that set his blood racing. God help him, he wanted the man to take a swing. He not only wanted some reason to fight, he wanted it badly. If Dickenson swung first, that was all the excuse he needed.

No, no, I don't want it. Not now, not ever. Unease warred with the unwelcome anticipation in his blood.

Fortunately, Dickenson didn't swing. He just twitched his pale mouth into a commonplace sneer as he looked Harry slowly up and down.

"If you were a gentleman, I'd make you regret that." Then coolly, deliberately, Dickenson turned his back. Absurdly, Harry found he had to suppress a shaky laugh of surprise. He'd just been given the cut direct, as if this were a tonnish ballroom rather than a public house. Dickenson thought he'd just won some triumph over his underling. It was really too much, especially coming from a man who wasn't even an honorable, and who also apparently had no idea how close he'd come to being laid out flat on the floor.

"Landlord," Dickenson cried. "I need a drink! Brandy, if there's anything decent to be had in that hole of yours."

Whatever's in the cellar's going to be a sight more decent than what's at the bar. But this time, Harry kept his mouth shut. His hands were still shaking and the frustration of action delayed or denied still sizzled dangerously beneath his skin.

Think about Mrs. Wakefield, he ordered himself as, inch by painful inch, he reeled in temper and nerve. *You are her escort and protector here. Think how it would look if you planted your fist in that smug face without provocation.*

He put his foot on the bar's brass rail and waited for Dickenson's next move, and it had better not be toward the parlor, or heaven help them both. He hoped Mrs. Wakefield was having a better time of it in there. He wished he could send her some word of reassurance. Although, if there was any way he could speak openly, reassurance was not the first thing he'd be offering her.

She's a widow, whispered desire's warm voice from the back of his mind. *There is no Mr. Wakefield in this world. She's out of mourning.*

She could say yes, if he asked. If he took her in his arms and he kissed her, if he whispered how very much he wanted to touch her, to arouse her passions, and then satisfy them all. She could say yes. She wanted to say yes. He saw it in her eyes, and he heard it in the hitch of her breath.

At least he thought he did. Harry's face twisted into a scowl. He'd seen her cheeks burning with heightened color and her eyes widen as she looked at him. He had held her against his chest and felt how she was so lush and warm and eminently desirable. She had let him take that liberty, but what did that mean? It might mean everything. It might mean nothing at all. Maybe she was only confused and tired and hadn't quite been able to pull herself quickly away. But it might mean she felt this same fire that burned in him.

At the moment, however, the point was entirely moot. Mrs. Wakefield was on the other side of that door with her runaway sister, and he was stuck here playing watchdog to Anthony Dickenson. He couldn't ask her what she thought of the weather, much less begin the delightful task of seducing her.

"Here you are, sir." Mr. Jessop set a glass of dark liquid on the bar in front of Dickenson. "That's the genuine article, you'll find," he added as Dickenson gave it a doubtful sniff. "And what can I get you, sir?"

"Beer for me, Mr. Jessop, and one for yourself," Harry fished another half crown out of his pocket and handed it across. Since he was feeling so much like an undisciplined boy, maybe he should act like one, at least a little. Harry had spent three terms at Oxford. He'd enjoyed the time and made some good friends, although it quickly became obvious he didn't have any genuine inclination to scholarship. But he'd also been forced to hold his own among scions of the aristocracy who didn't think a mere merchant's son, however wealthy, had any business walking their hallowed halls. He'd learned when to fight them, and when to speak and when to hold his tongue. He'd also learned several effective methods for getting under the skin of exactly Dickenson's sort of snob. One of the best was to simply spend generously and have a splendid time while they were trying to turn up their well-bred noses.

Mr. Jessop's eyes lit up at Harry's invitation, and the sight of the half crown. "Well, I'll not say no to that, an' thank you, sir. We've got an excellent bitter. My wife's nephew brews it." They both ignored Dickenson's pained groan. Mr. Jessop brought out an earthenware jug and plied it expertly, raising just the right amount of foam on the golden beer. "Now, you see what you think of that."

"Your health." Harry raised his glass and received Mr. Jessop's toast in return. He drained it heartily, and without any difficulty. It really was very good.

Dickenson on the other hand, looked like he was drinking vinegar rather than brandy.

It was then Mrs. Jessop and her serving girl emerged from the kitchen. Mrs. Jessop carried a tureen, and the girl had a plate of bread and a crock of butter.

"Now then, sirs," said Mrs. Jessop as they drew a table up to the fire and laid the cloth. "I know it's not much, but we've some lovely stew, piping hot, and the bread's fresh this morning and . . ."

"You can keep your stews, woman," snapped Dickenson. "Christ and damn, if it wasn't for this rain . . ."

"That smells wonderful, Mrs. Jessop. Thank you." Harry pulled a chair up to the table and began at once to tuck in. The food was plain but hot and good enough. Harry had certainly eaten far worse on board ship and in any number of foreign ports where Dickenson probably wouldn't be caught dead if he could help it. It didn't hurt that Harry was starved, and had the distinct feeling the already long night was going to do nothing but get longer. For one thing, he wasn't going to be taking his eyes off Dickenson, no matter what happened. The man was staring at the parlor door, clearly trying to work out if there was any way he could snatch up Miss Morehouse and bolt.

Harry tore off another hunk of bread and mopped up the last of his stew. Dickenson cast him another disparaging glance, and set about pouring himself a third brandy. Harry's itch to pick a fight had faded, replaced by a wholly immature glee at Dickenson's discomfort. Despite this unadmirable, but persistent sentiment, food and drink had steadied Harry and he felt much better able to handle the man in front of him. He watched Dickenson knock back a fourth brandy. Unless Harry very much missed his guess, the man was about to begin justifying himself, and there would be some insult as a digestif. That fight he'd so narrowly avoided before might just follow after all.

Consider Mrs. Wakefield, Rayburn, and keep your head.

Not that considering Mrs. Wakefield was the sort of activity calculated to help him, or any man, keep his head. When he'd walked into the parlor and seen her sitting by the fire with her red-gold hair cascading in shining waves over her shoulders and arms, he'd barely been able to breathe. When she'd taken off his coat to reveal that damp muslin dress clinging to every inch of her magnificent body, he'd almost forgotten he was a civilized man. He'd wanted nothing more than to catch her around the waist and to kiss her until she couldn't think straight. But that would never be enough, and he knew it. It wouldn't be enough even if he were to lay her down in front of the fire, peel that wet dress off her, and wrap her up in his arms instead. It wouldn't be enough until he was able to bury his aching member inside her. Until he heard her call his name and beg for more.

Dammit, he really was going to have to stop considering Mrs. Wakefield or he wouldn't be able to sit down anymore, let alone sit still.

"I suppose," drawled Dickenson, "that woman's been pouring her heart out to you and telling you what a horrid individual I am."

If she'd been able to give full vent to her feelings, Harry suspected "horrid" was the tamest word Mrs. Wakefield would choose. Harry rubbed his side, remembering the blow she'd so unceremoniously dealt him. He tried not to think about how it would feel to grab her wrist and wrestle that whip away from her, or to see those emerald eyes alight with the joy of the challenge as he tried.

"It's not as if any of this was my idea," Dickenson was saying. "I would have done the whole thing by the book but the confounded woman wouldn't agree. Probably holding out for more money, the greedy chit."

Harry's fantasies dropped away. All his attention snapped back to the room around him, and to Anthony Dickenson at the very center of it.

"What did you say?" Harry inquired.

Mr. Dickenson set his glass down on the bar. He straightened, but not steadily. "I *said*, Mrs. Wakefield's got no business being picky about who comes courting her sister. She's lucky to get any offer at all, after the way she's carried on."

He's drunk. Don't do it, Harry told himself. *Let it go.* But he wasn't listening to himself. He got to his feet. He walked over to the bar. That unholy eagerness was back and it had brought his frustrated lust as reinforcement. "You will be cautious, and polite, about how you refer to Mrs. Wakefield."

"Ohhh-ho!" Dickenson's eyebrows shot up. "The boy thinks he's got teeth."

Harry realized his hand had already curled into a fist. *It's the brandy. It's the brandy. Let him babble. It doesn't mean anything.* But all he could see was Dickenson's smug face. That sight got down deep in him and it was foul and filthy, and goaded him hard. The man thought birth and family made him, thought he could tread across other lives with contempt and disregard because they didn't measure up.

"Now, then, sir, there's no call for anything unpleasant," said Mr. Jessop. "Is the brandy not to your taste? I've another bottle, very fine . . ."

But Dickenson wasn't going to be distracted. "Or maybe you just haven't heard about the methods the good widow used to get her fingers into that property she's holding on to so tightly. Maybe I should enlighten you as to your *lady's* morals." He fondled his quizzing glass. "But being in trade yourself, maybe you don't object to a woman with such capital business sense that she's ready to sell herself and her sister off to the highest bidder . . ."

Probably Dickenson was an habitué of Gentleman Jim's, or some other fine establishment where they taught boxing as a science. Harry had learned to brawl on the docks around his father's warehouse among the men and boys for whom fighting was a way to stay alive. His first punch went straight to Dickenson's guts, and when the man doubled over, the second blow landed right on the back of his head, dropping him like a sack of bricks. But it wasn't enough to appease the vicious anger roaring in Harry's veins. He had to teach the man a proper lesson. He drew his foot back, ready to plant a kick in the bastard's ribs. Roll him over with that, get the next one in his back.

"Harry!"

Mrs. Wakefield's shout cut through the vicious determination of his thoughts and Harry's head jerked up. She stood in the doorway, her face shocked and pale as she stared at him.

"I'm sorry," said Harry to her. "I'm sorry."

But it was Mr. Jessop who answered. "No need to apologize, sir." He stumped out from behind the bar. "Very neat job you made of it, if I may say. Martin! Come help me get this mess off the floor!"

As Martin slouched out of the kitchen to help his master carry the unconscious Mr. Dickenson to the bench by the door, footsteps thundered on the stairs. A moment later, Miss Morehouse pushed out of the parlor past her sister.

"What on earth!" Miss Morehouse cried, and then she saw exactly what on earth. "Anthony!"

Harry didn't move an inch as Miss Morehouse raced past him and dropped to her knees beside the bench, and Dickenson's prostrate form. Harry's gaze did not waver from Mrs. Wakefield's. His hand hurt and his blood burned. The terrible, heady desire for violence boiled through him, and she'd seen it. She saw him ready to beat the living hell out of a drunken man who was already down.

"You brute!" Miss Morehouse shouted up at him as she jumped to her feet. Genevieve Morehouse was nowhere near as tall as her sister, and her hair was many shades darker, but they shared the same green-gold eyes, the same regal bearing, and, clearly, the same nerve.

"Leave him be, Genevieve," Mrs. Wakefield spoke softly, but the command still rang through the room. Even her sister, it seemed, could not find it in her to disobey. Miss Morehouse huffed, but retreated to sit on a stool and very ostentatiously take up the unconscious Mr. Dickenson's hand.

Harry noted all this distantly. All that was real was the

shock on Mrs. Wakefield's face and the pallor in her cheeks. The violence that anger and insult had summoned was draining away and shame crawled into all the places it left open. He couldn't face Mrs. Wakefield anymore. He couldn't face anybody.

Without a word, Harry turned and bolted out the door.

Nine

❦

Leannah watched Mr. Rayburn's abrupt departure, momentarily dazed. Then, fully aware that Genevieve had begun talking again, she ran out into the darkness behind him.

The rain had cleared and the moon was out. Harry stood alone in the middle of the cobbled yard. She could see his shoulders shuddering as he drew in one gasping breath after another, struggling for control.

Confusion filled her. Clearly Mr. Rayburn was in the grip of powerful emotion, but she could not see any trace of its origins. He had knocked a man down. She might not be an habitué of public houses but she knew that fights happened with great regularity, and were even regarded as something of a rite of passage, if not actual friendship in the rarified realms of male behavior.

And yet, there had been that moment when she'd first opened the door to see Mr. Dickenson fallen to the floor. Harry drew his boot back to deliver a savage kick. His good-humored face was twisted into such a mask of fury Leannah could not help crying out to him, because something was wrong. This good man should not look so violent and yet so gleeful.

Leannah took a tentative step forward, uncertain as to what she meant to do or say. Harry must have heard because he turned his face toward her. All the commonplaces and light quips that might have occurred to Leannah scattered like dry leaves before the shame on Harry Rayburn's face.

"Are you all right?" she asked him.

He made no answer, just flexed his right hand experimentally and nodded. Impatience overtook her and Leannah strode to his side. Ignoring her cuts and her bandages, she grasped the sides of his face, exactly as she had done a hundred times to her brother, Jeremy. She tilted him firmly toward what little light escaped from the inn's shuttered windows so she could look for bruises, scrapes, or blood.

There was not a single mark, and Leannah's reflexive maternal instincts bled away, replaced by the awareness that this was not Jeremy whose face she held. This was the man she'd been fantasizing about. She had settled her palms right over his whiskers and she could feel them, crisp and curling and yet oddly soft. At least, she could feel them where she wasn't bandaged. Warmth and tension coiled low in her belly as Harry gazed at her. A smile formed on his expressive mouth that was both rueful and sweet. She stared at his smile. She could lean forward and kiss him, here and now. She wanted to kiss him. But as they stood like this, far too close for anyone's comfort, she did not see the sort of desire she'd glimpsed in him before. Now there was shame and sadness. His hand trembled as he raised it to pull her away from him.

"What is it?" she asked. "What's the matter? Please tell me."

"I can't," he whispered. He didn't meet her gaze. He looked down at their hands, held together. "I'm sorry . . . I just can't."

Bashfulness and confusion overtook Leannah as Mr. Rayburn drew away from her. She clearly had intruded on some secret, and she was torn between the desire to extricate herself from the situation, and the desire to know more.

We're still strangers, she reminded herself. *I have no right to press for a confidence. I mustn't forget that.*

"He'd had too much brandy," Mr. Rayburn said to the darkness and the empty yard. "I should have just let it go."

"I'm sure he gave you no choice."

"There's always a choice. Sometimes it's not a good one, but it's always there."

He let his head fall back and gazed up at the sky, looking for what, Leannah could not tell. *I wish I could go to him. I wish I could hold him, and tell him . . . something, anything.*

But she couldn't. She had transgressed enough boundaries. She shouldn't even still be standing here. Her place was inside with Genny, not out here with this man, who was obviously unhurt.

He drew a shaky breath. "I'm afraid I've made a rather poor impression on your sister."

"I think, when she has time to reflect on it, we'll find Mr. Dickenson has made a worse one."

"I suppose it is hard to play the dashing hero when one is unconscious on the floor."

Leannah gave one bitter laugh. "I only wish Genevieve really was pining to be swept away by some dashing hero. Then it would be easier to deflect her attention."

His brows drew together. "So, she actually does love that smug . . ." he stopped. "Dickenson," he amended.

"The situation is complicated, and not in any of the more usual ways." She couldn't stand to have this man thinking Genevieve loose in her morals. Whether it made sense or not, she cared about Mr. Rayburn's opinion, just as she cared whether or not he'd been hurt, and wondered what made him seem so sad and ashamed just now.

"Does she . . ." he began, but stopped. "No, no, I'm sorry. I've made enough of a mess of things tonight. I'm sure you wish I'd just start walking back to town."

"That is not at all what I wish."

Those words turned her toward her. The moonlight shone in his deep eyes and Leannah felt the intensity of his gaze prickle across her skin. It seemed as if he looked straight through her and into her confused and unruly heart. She liked that feeling. She wanted to be bared to him, and not just in her thoughts. She wanted to be free to go to him right now, to kiss his shadowed face and moonlit eyes. She wanted to touch him, to press herself against him and know for certain he was hard. She wanted to use her hands, her mouth, her whole body to ease the pain of the secrets Harry Rayburn carried.

"It is not what I wish either," he breathed. "I . . ." he stopped, and he was smiling, shyly, ruefully. The sight of that moonlit smile robbed Leannah of her breath. "I do wish I knew your Christian name."

"Leannah," she told him at once.

"Leannah," he repeated and it was sweet to hear. "Thank you, Leannah."

"What have I done?" she asked. "I mean, beyond land you in a world of troubles that aren't your own?"

"You have showed me yourself," he answered. "And you have allowed me to share this little time with you, and that . . ." He lifted his fingertips and she felt them graze her hair, just barely touching her, just barely travelling across the bounds of propriety. "That I will cherish."

She couldn't speak. Her mouth had gone dry and her heart fluttered at the base of her throat. The ability to move had fled, but at the same time it seemed every inch of her had come utterly alive. She was waiting for Mr. Rayburn's kiss, longing for it. His kiss would shatter this paralysis, as surely as the prince's kiss in a fairy tale would wake the sleeping princess. If he kissed her, she would be able to move, to touch him, to return his kiss. She wondered if it would taste of the spices that scented his skin, or of the rain that had so recently drenched him. It should be spices, she decided. There was nothing bland about this man. All was fire, all was heightened, even to the point of delirium. Surely it was delirium that seized hold of her now and kept her rooted to this spot.

"I imagine you wish we'd met properly," he was saying, trying to make some joke that would break the heated tension of this moment and banish the unspoken need filling in the air between them. "In somebody's ballroom, over cups of punch."

She didn't want this. She couldn't bear it. This moment was all she'd ever have with Harry Rayburn. She would not let anyone turn it into light satire, not even he himself.

"No," she said. "I am glad we met this way. In a ballroom, I never would have seen you."

"Because I'm a merchant's son?"

"Because you would have been just another beau in a fine coat," she said. "And I never might have looked beyond that."

The warmth in Harry's eyes faded and he stepped away. Cold rushed across Leannah as he turned away.

"You should probably go check on your sister," he croaked. "You've been out here too long."

I don't care! she wanted to shout. *I want to stay. I will stay!*

But he looked over his shoulder at her, and she saw the plea in his eyes. He wanted to be alone. The cold she'd felt before sank under her skin, but she nodded. Then, she turned away and walked back inside the house.

Mr. Dickenson was still sprawled on the bench. Genny was nowhere in evidence. The landlord was running a cloth across the bar, his face studiously neutral. Leannah winced. She had been out there with him far too long. There would be talk, if only between Mr. and Mrs. Jessop.

"Is he all right?" she asked gesturing to Mr. Dickenson.

"Right enough," answered the landlord. "He'll have a bit of an aching head and bruised pride, but he'll be none the worse for that."

"Good. Thank you. I'm sorry for your trouble, Mr. Jessop. I—"

"Think nothing of it, ma'am." He cut her off. "There is one thing maybe I should say." He glanced toward the door. "None o' my affair a'course, but I thought you ought to know. The other gentleman, Mr. Rayburn, he wouldn't have laid a finger on this one if he hadn't taken to insulting yourself and your sister."

"That is good to know. Thank you, Mr. Jessop."

"You get along upstairs, ma'am. I'll keep an eye on things."

"Oh, but you must be tired."

He laughed. "Not the first time I've kept watch through the night. Don't you worry." He gave her a wink, and Leannah felt a weary smile form. She nodded her acknowledgement and started up the stairs to the room Mrs. Jessop had prepared for them.

There she found Genevieve, stretched out on her bed, fully dressed, with her arms folded tightly over her chest.

"It's about time," Genevieve announced as she sat up. "I was beginning to think you were the one who eloped."

Leannah did not rise to the bait. "You should be in bed."

"I am in bed."

"You know what I mean." She gestured for Genevieve to

stand up and then moved behind her to undo the laces and tapes on her dress.

"All right, I do know," said Genevieve to the fireplace. "But I was worried about you, alone out there with that brute."

"Mr. Rayburn is not a brute, and you are not to say so again."

For a wonder, her tone was enough to silence Genevieve for ten full seconds. Leannah swiftly pulled her sister's dress off over her head and hung it on the peg by the door.

"I could just as well stay dressed," she grumbled. "It's nearly dawn."

"Which would make it all the easier for you to run off with Mr. Dickenson as soon as it's light enough." Leannah turned away from her sister and lifted her hair off her back. "Now me."

Genny obeyed, but Leannah could tell she had not in any way given up. She could plainly feel her sister's eyes boring into the back of her neck while Genevieve undid her tapes and loosened the laces on the corset underneath.

When they had both stripped down to their shifts and donned the nightdresses their well-prepared hostess had left out for them, Genevieve was still glowering. Leannah sat in the slat-backed chair by the fire and picked up the hairbrush that waited beside the basin of clean water. If nothing else, she could make a start on untangling her hair. Probably she'd need a week to do the job thoroughly.

"There is something going on between you and this Mr. Rayburn," said Genevieve finally. "I can tell."

Leannah took up a handful of hair and started brushing, hard. Why on earth hadn't she had it trimmed like a sensible woman? To let this mess grow so long was sheer vanity, and nothing more.

"There is, isn't there?"

The brush jerked in her hand as it hit a snarl. Leannah pulled again, harder.

"Leannah, I'm not going to sleep until you answer me. Tell me I'm not wrong."

Leannah sighed. "You are not wrong."

"I knew it!" cried Genevieve. "Are you in love? Where did

you meet him? Have you known him long? What sort of man is he?"

Leannah eyed her sister through the screen of her tangled hair. "I thought you'd decided he was a brute."

"First impressions should not be taken too seriously. Tell me!"

"Genevieve, I'm exhausted. Please. Just, go to sleep." To emphasize her point, Leannah reached across to the lamp and turned the wick down. The light sputtered and died, leaving only the low fire to illuminate the room.

She heard more than saw Genevieve flop down onto the pillows. "You'll tell me sooner or later," she prophesized. "You know you will."

No, I don't. But this time, Leannah had the sense to keep the comment to herself. She just picked the brush back up and set to work on her hair again. She listened to the sounds of wind around the eaves, and the sound of Genevieve's breathing, waiting for it to slow and deepen into a sound sleep.

But her last question would not leave Leannah's mind. *What sort of man is he?*

I don't know what sort of man he is, but I wish I did, because then I'd know what sort of man it is I want so badly.

Almost against her will, Leannah imagined Harry lying in the room on the other side of the wall. Was he naked? He might be. The night wasn't all that cold, and his clothes were damp. She remembered how confidently he'd moved about the parlor downstairs in his shirtsleeves. She hadn't been able to stop noticing how well his buckskin breeches fit his strong legs and taut buttocks. He'd be magnificent naked. She wondered about his chest. It was broad, and it would surely be a match for his strong arms. His hands and face were bronzed. Was his chest pale, or did it carry the warm coloring of a man who sometimes stripped to the waist when he worked? Did he have much hair on his body? He was quite fair, so probably not. There would be just enough to be enticing as her palms slid across his skin, up around his shoulders to his throat, his face. She knew just what his face felt like under her palms. She could feel it now, and she could clearly picture the intensity his gaze would hold as she pulled him to her so she could kiss him.

Leannah felt sure there would be nothing tentative about a kiss shared with Harry Rayburn. She already knew the feeling of his hand, of his arms around her body, the lightest brush of his fingers on her hair. He had given her so very much to conjure with. He'd spear those calloused fingers into her tangled hair and press his mouth close against hers. She'd open for him, so he could slip his tongue alongside hers. He'd kiss her cheek, trace the tip of his tongue down the sensitive skin just beside her ear, to her throat. He'd slide his hands up her sides until he came to her breasts. She'd bury her face in his fair hair and inhale his scent. He'd grip her roughly. He knew she was no delicate flower. He wouldn't be afraid to show her his strength. He'd be merciless as he plumped and squeezed her. He'd make her gasp and they'd both revel in it. He'd take the very tip of her nipple between his fingers and chafe it. He'd watch her face. Would he be stern? No. That didn't fit somehow. He'd be smiling, perhaps even mischievous as he backed her up against the wall. He'd press his hips against hers to hold her there. She'd be able to feel how hard he was. He'd rub their hips together while his hands worked at her breasts, filling her with that bright, hot, beautiful tension. She'd try to be quiet, and she'd fail.

Please, Harry. Please! She'd shout it so all the world could hear.

Yes, Leannah. Oh, yes.

She'd run her hands across the ridge of his erection and make him gasp. She'd let him know at once that she understood the workings of a man's body. She could make him hard, and she'd enjoy doing it. She'd find the buttons on his fly. They wouldn't bother with much more than that. Their need would be too great, too wild. She'd free him and he'd shove her skirts up, and lift her. He was strong enough for that, she was sure. She'd wrap her legs around his hips and press her heels against his thighs, shoving him deep into herself.

What would he be like? Would he fill her? She wanted to believe he would. The wall would be rough and cold against her naked backside. She imagined the inn empty—no one to hear, no one to suspect what they did. He'd thrust fast and hard into her, all restraint and good humor gone. He'd be maddened by his need and hers. She'd beat on his shoulders, shout his name, demand that he take her harder still, and faster. And he would obey. He'd give her what she craved, give her everything, all of him, all of Harry Rayburn and she'd take it, gladly, wantonly, greedily, and return everything that she had.

Oh, no, no, stop. This is a mistake.

Leannah was no stranger to the power of private fantasy, but this was beyond the pale. She was flushed almost to the point of fever, and so dizzy with borrowed desire that her strength had fled. It was only Genevieve's sleeping presence that stopped her from thrusting her hand between her thighs to rub herself until some kind of release came from the craving that her fantasy of Harry Rayburn raised.

She'd made sure she was the one who took the bed nearest the door and now she regretted it. She wanted to open the window and get a breath of air, but she didn't dare, for fear of waking Genevieve. She glanced at the door. Could she go down into the yard for just a minute? She needed the cold to calm this fever of Harry Rayburn.

Along with the nightclothes, Mrs. Jessop had left out some knitted slippers. She supposed a woman who had seen so many elopements might take care to keep her house stocked with what was needed for such occasions, and probably prospered by her foresight. Leannah thought about the coins Mr. Rayburn had already laid out on her behalf. She'd have to pay him back out of the housekeeping. She couldn't remain in his debt.

Leannah wrapped the shawl around herself. Carefully, and once again grateful for the well-oiled hinges on the door, she crept into the dark hall. She did not have lamp or candle with her, but she remembered where the side stairs were, and was able to follow them by touch down to the side door.

Outside, the cold spring wind cut straight through the woolen shawl. Leannah took a deep breath and shook her hair back. The wind across her skin was sharp and invigorating. It smelled of late frost and early greenery and its cold eased the ache she'd brought onto herself with her wicked imaginings of Harry Rayburn. Leannah spread her arms out as if to embrace it.

She heard the sharp hiss of an indrawn breath.

She knew who it was. She knew from the warm weight of the gaze she felt settling across her. She knew from the anticipation prickling across her skin and the way her heart beat heavily beneath her breast. There was only one person it could possibly be.

Slowly, Leannah turned.

There by the inn's corner, stood Harry Rayburn.

Ten

"Don't," whispered Harry. He held out one hand in a gesture that was both reassurance and plea. "Don't be afraid of me."

Leannah realized she had clutched her shawl to her throat. She didn't remember doing it. All her attention was taken up by Harry Rayburn. He was staring at her and there was something wild, almost fey, in his gaze. Despite this, it was not fear, or anything like it that stole through Leannah.

Of its own volition, her hand lowered. The corners of the shawl fell open. Her nightdress and chemise were thin stuff, and she had no corset on underneath. A gust of wind pressed the cloth tight against her breasts and hips. Cold tightened her nipples to hard points, and Harry could see that. He could see all of her.

"I'll go," Harry said without moving. "I'll go now. You don't have to worry."

He would leave if she didn't do something. The thought stabbed into her. He must not leave. "I'm not worried." Her voice sounded harsh in her ears. "Please don't go."

She saw the shadow of his Adam's apple bob as he swallowed hard. Harry took one step forward. "You want me to stay?"

"Yes." *Like I want my heart to keep beating.*

"I will stay." He took another step forward. "If I may stay close."

There was moonlight in his fair hair and moonlight in his wild eyes. He slipped into the shadows with her, becoming for one instant a mere shape, a dark ghost of himself. He had the grace of a dancer. Each slow movement was fascinating to her and the anticipation from this deliberate approach tightened every fiber of her body. He was giving her a chance to cry off, to get away if she wanted to. But she didn't want that.

"Yes," she breathed. "I want you to be close, Harry."

And he was. He was right in front of her. Although he did not yet touch her, she could still feel the warmth of him on her skin. He still had his boots on and she was in slippers, which made him that much taller. She tipped her face up to feast her eyes on his magnificent face and the intensity of his gaze. A stray breeze caught up the ends of her hair and dragged them across her face.

Harry reached out, and gently pushed the curls back against her shoulder.

"Leannah." The sound of her name in his mouth made her shiver. His hand slid around her shoulder, under the curtain of her hair, and her neck to cup the back of her head. She did not resist. She did not speak. She only allowed her lips to part, just a little.

Harry saw. He understood. He bent down and he kissed her.

Leannah had imagined a wild, almost brutal kiss from Harry. This was nothing of the kind. The kiss he gave her was an easy, almost polite introduction of his lips to hers. It warmed her, comforted her, as did the way his broad hand cradled her head. All was calculated to make her understand that she was safe here with him. She could relax.

And she did. Leannah felt her whole body soften. She leaned forward so that her breasts could brush against his chest and she could answer his kiss better, opening just that much farther to touch her tongue to his lips.

She felt him smile into their kiss. His free hand stole around her waist, urging her forward. She needed no urging. A sharp, hot ache had blossomed in the center of her body, and she knew the only relief was to have the whole of him tight against her. She pressed closer, shamelessly rubbing her heavy breasts against him. The rasp of the wool and linen and the warmth of his hard chest beneath caused her nipples to ruche tighter yet.

She liked it. His hand on her back moved lower, sprawling across the curve of her derriere so he could hold her still and rub his hips, and his wickedly erect member against her mound. The sensation filled her with fiery delight, and that delight was only brightened by the understanding of how very much Harry relished her body, her touch, and this coming together.

Harry's tongue slipped deeper into her mouth, turning their kiss urgent. Leannah moaned. A fresh flash of desire sparked through her. She wanted more. She reached around his shoulders to pull him down closer to her, but to her dismay, Harry broke the kiss and pulled back.

"You mustn't," he whispered, taking hold of her wrists where they rested on his shoulders. "We can't risk you opening those cuts again."

"But how am I to touch you?"

He smiled, and that smile was as sweet and wicked as anything she had imagined. It lit sparks in his blue eyes that had nothing to do with cool moonlight or distant fantasy. Keeping hold of her wrists, Harry spread her arms out wide. Slowly, as if they were on the dance floor, he walked her backward, his gaze feasting all the while on her body, barely concealed beneath her nightdress. She felt the rough brush of the inn wall against her buttocks and back. Harry raised her arms up, bringing her wrists together over her head, and crossing them so he could hold both in one hand.

"There," he whispered, and he was kissing her again. She opened her mouth for him at once, and it was so sweet. She sighed, deeply content to let strength and sense drain away beneath the attentions of Harry's clever tongue as he explored, enjoyed, tasted, and took. She wanted nothing except to let him hold her exactly where he wanted her, and continue this wanton kiss.

But Harry was not content with so little. His free hand stroked down her throat to her collarbone, and down farther, to the curve of her breast. His warm, rough palm caressed her, and Leannah moaned into their kiss. It was slow and firm, that touch. He took his time discovering her curves and lines. His fingertips danced lightly across her aching nipple. She gasped at the sensation and felt him smiling again.

He pulled back, but only a little, so she could still feel the brush of his lips as he whispered. "Now, you stay just like this." He squeezed her wrists where he held them over her head. "And let me please us both for a while."

He dragged his right hand down the underside of her arm, down to her shoulder, down to cup her other breast. Leannah drew in a ragged breath, and Harry was kissing her again. She closed her eyes and gave herself wholly over to the sensation. Now he caressed both of her breasts, cupping, massaging, delighting himself and her with his wicked play. Desire's warmth deepened, weakening her, softening her, opening every inch of her to his touch. He pressed her breasts together, chafing them against each other while his thumbs teased the exquisitely sensitive tips, and she thought she might die from the pleasure of it. If he hadn't held her pressed against the cold wall, she would have fallen. Her strength was entirely gone. She had no room for strength within her. She was too full of the pleasure Harry brought to her with the press of his body, his wicked mouth and his busy, knowing hands.

She was gasping. She couldn't breathe. He moved his mouth from hers and instead pressed his lips against her throat, her ear.

"Leannah," he whispered. "Beautiful Leannah."

"Kiss me again," she pleaded.

"Oh, yes." She felt the curve of his smile against her cheek. "I will do that."

Her mouth opened eagerly for him. But it wasn't her mouth he kissed. His hands gathered her breasts, pressing them up and close and tight, so he could drop a kiss on the top of each. That was good. She wanted more of that. She tipped her hips forward, to rub against him and urge him on, and that, too, was very good. His member was exquisitely hard beneath his breeches, and the ridge of it pressed against her hard enough to part her folds and brush the most sensitive nub of flesh at their tip, just as Harry's wicked tongue darted out from his open mouth so he could take his first taste of her breasts.

"Yes," she hissed. Pleasure buckled her knees. He felt it. He pressed his hips closer, to hold her against the wall. With hands and mouth, he ravaged her breasts, and she arched her back to press her mound still more tightly to him. His fingers rolled her nipples while his mouth dropped kisses on her skin. She barely remembered she must be quiet. They could not be heard. It was shocking, what they did. It was forbidden. She did not know this man. She knew nothing but the urgency inside her, the hot dampness of her thighs and how her hips moved to rub against him and find the pleasure his body could give. He lifted her right breast so he could suck on her through the thin fabric of her nightdress. His mouth and tongue were hot and hard as they surrounded her nipple, taking her deep. All the while his left hand worked her, stroked her, pinched and plumped and played.

Oh, she was lost. Lost to bliss, lost to need. Lost to this man, this wanton pleasure, the touch of the night wind and the rasp of the lime-washed wall against her back. Her whole body was roused to a fever pitch and the source of her madness was the source of her release. His hips ground against her, and she welcomed that rough gesture as she welcomed his mouth and his hands at her breasts.

"Yes, Harry," she gasped. "Yes, hard, like that."

He was kissing her mouth again, maybe to keep her quiet, maybe because he needed to. Leannah didn't care. She thrust her own tongue into his mouth, hungry for him. No, starving for him. His hands scrabbled at the skirts of her nightdress, bunching the hems up around her bare thighs so he could caress her there. His calloused hands rasped across her softer skin and she gloried in it. She knew what was coming, and her whole body thrummed with anticipation. She was a mass of contradiction—soft and hard, weak and yet filled with wild strength. That was what came of this plain, graceless, wicked desire—desire for this man, for his body, his hands, and his mouth. She must feel every inch of him against her, and inside her.

His hand brushed the damp, tangled curls between her legs and she rocked her hips forward, forcing his fingertips into her folds so he could feel how wet he'd made her.

Yes, her whole body cried. *Yes, now. Yes.*

And then he was gone.

Eleven

Leannah's eyes flew open, unable to understand this abrupt and terrible absence of Harry's touch. It took a wild moment of searching, but she saw Harry was beside her now. He was bent over with his arms out straight in front of him and both hands pressed flat against the wall. His breath rattled in his throat. A trickle of perspiration ran down his temple and dripped onto the cobbles.

"No." He spat the word through clenched teeth. "No!"

She couldn't understand what he was saying.

"We have to stop," he told her.

"I don't want to."

He turned toward her and in his face she saw something painfully close to anguish. "Oh, my beautiful Leannah, we must."

Slowly, she realized her wrists were still crossed above her head. She brought her arms down and her bandaged hands automatically searched for the ends of her shawl to wrap around herself. The shawl was gone. Her skin was damp with sweat and quickly growing cold. She felt exposed, but that exposure no longer felt like triumph. Shame, as cold as the night wind against her skin crept into her blood.

"Was it . . . something I did?"

Her question straightened him up at once. He had been trembling a moment ago, but now as he reached for her, his hands were steady and gentle.

"You did nothing." He cupped her chin and lifted her face toward his. Harry's smile was suffused with such tenderness it raised a fresh ache in her breast. "You did nothing at all, except drive me to the brink of madness."

"And you don't want that."

The oath Harry uttered was blunt, and startling. "That's not what I mean. Leannah, I want you. I want everything you will give me, but not like this." His thumb caressed the corner of her mouth. "Not up against a wall where anyone might see us, see you." He brushed her trailing locks back from her cheek. "I will dare anything for myself, but I will not risk disgrace for you."

It's not disgrace, she wanted to shout at him. *It's perfection.* She wanted to grab him by the collar—never mind her wounded hands, never mind Mr. Jessop awake right on the other side of the wall. She wanted to kiss him until he forgot everything but her and their desire.

But he was right. She might hate that fact as much as she had ever hated anything in her life, but she could not deny it. She had been driven beyond caution by his kiss and his touch. She would have done anything in that moment and not cared at all. But if anyone had heard, or seen . . . If *Genevieve* had heard or seen . . .

Leannah's chill deepened. Reality came back, carried on dawn's cold wind. Genevieve was sleeping upstairs. Mr. Dickenson was sprawled on the sofa in the public room. She was Leannah Morehouse Wakefield and her family waited in their rented house for her to bring her runaway sister home and then settle back to dealing with all the other problems that had come with her father's many failures.

She was not free to indulge any shameless yearnings in the moonlight with this man, or any man.

Leannah shivered again and looked about for where the shawl had fallen. Harry spotted it first, lying in a crumpled heap by the inn wall. He lifted it off the ground. She saw him move to place it around her shoulders, and then think the better of it. Instead, he laid it across her arm.

He did not look away even for an instant as she wrapped the shawl around her shoulders. He stared at her hands as she raised the plain woolen folds to cover her bare, cold skin.

Regret tightened her throat and its bitterness filled her mouth to overpower the last of the sweetness his kiss had brought. Leannah lifted her fingertips to Harry's mouth, and ran them across his lips. Harry closed his eyes and swallowed hard, but he did not move away.

"Thank you," she whispered. "For giving me this moment."

He caught her wrist before she could lower it, and planted a soft kiss against her fingertips. "I would give you so much more if I could."

Leannah shook her head. "No. You're right. It's too dangerous."

She meant to turn away, but he put his hand on her shoulder. "Only here, only like this. When we get back to London, we can find each other then." He smiled and to Leannah it was as if the ground shifted beneath her. "I can even come calling if you like. You might not believe it, but I look very fine seated in a front parlor, and make excellent conversation with ladies of all ages."

Leannah could not help but smile herself at this. "I believe you, but it wouldn't be advisable."

Consternation knit his brows. "Are you promised to someone?"

"No. Not yet, anyway."

"I don't like the sound of that, Leannah."

She couldn't look in his eyes. She looked at her bandaged hand where it rested against the lapel of his coat. She didn't even remember placing it there. It seemed her traitor body was not ready to leave off touching Mr. Rayburn.

"I'm sorry," she whispered. "I'm so sorry."

"Tell me what's wrong, Leannah. Perhaps I can help."

But she shook her head and she stepped away. She had to put at least some distance between them. The echo of the passions they'd raised still rang in her blood and bones. He'd called it madness and that was the right word. But it was more than that. When he held her, Harry made her feel she could trust him, and she wanted that trust as much as she wanted his touch. There had been so few people in her life on whom she was able to depend.

But trust and dependence were both dangerous. Trust could be betrayed, even when it was knotted up with bonds of blood and duty, never mind the flimsy ties of mutual need.

Leannah glanced over her shoulder. The moon had almost set. The last rays tangled in Harry's fair hair and his blue, worried eyes. She'd meant to say something, but the sight of him—her hero, her mad and dangerous lover—robbed her of speech. She took a trembling step forward and another. She waited for him to shy away from her. But he did not. He stood still, waiting for what she would do. She lifted her face to his, and brushed her lips against his mouth.

Then she grabbed up the hem of her nightdress and fled back to the safety of the house.

Harry watched the inn door close behind Leannah as she fled from him. He waited, to be sure she wasn't coming back. Maybe there was still hope. Maybe she wanted to come back. Maybe she wanted his determination to fail him so he would push her up against the wall again, and take her in his arms, plunder her mouth, suck on her breasts, finish what they had begun.

Only when he was positive that damned door wasn't going to open again, did Harry stride away. The inn's yard was not a big one, but there were several outbuildings, as well as a chicken house and the stable with its small forge and anvil. He was almost running by the time he ducked behind the farthest shed he could find. Utterly ashamed, but driven by pain and pure brute need, Harry undid his breeches fly as quickly as his trembling fingers could manage. He plunged his hand into his small clothes, grabbed his member and started to masturbate.

He pumped himself ruthlessly, angrily. In his mind, he saw Leannah. He felt her, with every fiber of his being. He smelled her scent on the wind, felt the silk of her hair and the satin of her skin. His palm held all the memory of the hot flesh of her thighs as he caressed them. In his mind, he pressed her up against the wall again. He fondled her breasts, sucked her tight, responsive nipples, squeezed her lovely, full derriere. But this time, he didn't stop, he didn't come to his senses and tear himself away. He grabbed her legs and raised her up so he could plunge his aching, swollen member inside her.

She cried out. She wrapped her thighs around him as her

sheath surrounded him, hot and tight and wet. *Yes, Harry!* she moaned. *Like that. I like that. Harder! Harder!* She'd tighten around him, dragging him deeper in, demanding he surrender his body entirely to her pleasure . . .

Harry's release came suddenly, in a series of crude, violent jolts. He stayed as he was for a long time, doubled over, braced by one arm against the wall of whatever shed he was hiding behind. As soon as he could make his shaking body move, he shoved his now flaccid member back into his smalls and buttoned up his breeches tight. Then, Harry put his own back to the wall. He let his knees buckle so he slid slowly down until he was crouched almost to the ground. He wiped his streaming face with his sleeve, and began to curse.

He cursed slowly and thoroughly. He cursed moonlight and rain and thrown horseshoes. He cursed the club's whiskey in four different languages, along with whatever insanity drove a man to try to be a hero. When he'd exhausted this subject, he cursed his member for not understanding that when a lady closed the door, it was past time to stand down. It was not right to be in the back of a stable yard easing his lusts with the memory of Leannah Wakefield. It seemed utterly crude and distasteful to him.

As if almost fucking a woman he didn't know against the wall of a public house was refined. Harry hung his head and rested his forearms on his knees. He could barely believe it, let alone understand it. In the space of a few short hours he'd jumped aboard a careening carriage, been knocked down, aided a woman in distress, gotten into a brawl. Well, "brawl" was a bit much, considering Dickenson hadn't even raised his hand. But he had knocked a man down over that woman and her sister, come within an inch of brutalizing him, and then come within an inch of fucking himself and that same woman into delirium in the open air.

Harry knotted his hands in his hair. He wanted to blame the drink, or the blow Agnes Featherington had dealt to his pride. But that wouldn't be the truth. The truth was there was something about being near Leannah that drove him clean out of his mind.

God, but she was magnificent! From the moment his lips touched hers, it had taken every ounce of his self-possession not to fall on her immediately and ravish her. Not, he smiled, that she would have protested. She had made it clear she wanted him and he knew for a fact she was as strong in her passions as she was willing and eager. She'd be as wild a lover as she was a driver. He'd put her on top of him, slap that magnificent derriere of hers to take them both into a gallop, and she'd like it. He was certain she would.

His member twitched. Harry started cursing all over again. His rude little session of self-pleasuring had cured the immediate pain and pressure in his body, but that was all. It had done nothing to ease the aching desire he felt for Leannah.

Slowly, Harry realized it was no longer quite so dark. He pushed himself to his feet and tried to smooth his hair down with his clean hand. The landlord and his wife would be about soon—that is assuming they'd ever gone to bed. He moved out from behind the shed to where he could see the inn, and the window beneath the eaves on the second story. Was Leannah asleep up there? Or was she awake like he was, thinking of what they had done together, wishing it hadn't ended.

Why didn't she want to see him in town? Was she ashamed of the heated moment they'd shared? He didn't think that could be it, but it was so hard to be sure. Society winked and joked at the desires of men, but it frowned hard when those same passions found a home in women.

Perhaps it was the fact that he was a merchant's son. It was plain from Leannah's speech and bearing that she was gently bred. Perhaps she had a position to maintain that did not easily admit a man of his birth. At the very least, she must be her sister's chief guardian. He wondered about their parents and if they were living or dead. He wondered what was behind the "not yet" she'd spoken when he asked if she was engaged. Who was the man who earned a "not yet" from Leannah? Where was he now, while she was out here in trouble and alone? Any such man deserved to have his woman stolen out from behind his back.

A chuckle rose in his throat and Harry shook his head. Then, he did the only sensible thing he could. He strolled around the front of the inn to the horse trough. There, he plunged head and hands straight into the icy water.

The shock of it hit him at once and Harry welcomed it. He

held himself under the water until he felt his lungs would burst. When he did allow himself to come up, he whooped and gasped. Great gouts of water sluiced off his scalp. Someone, Martin, probably, had hung a cloth on the pump and Harry used it now to dry himself, only to find it was soaking wet from the rain.

The sound of a bolt being drawn jerked him around. *Leannah?* Light glinted behind the shutters, and his mouth went instantly dry. *Leannah, you came back!*

But it wasn't Leannah. The flickering lantern was held by none other than the importunate Mr. Dickenson. Harry let himself fade back against the inn wall and held his breath. Dickenson didn't see him. He just stumbled across the yard, making for the stables.

Well, well. Once again, Anthony Dickenson was showing his true colors. Harry heard the hoarse sound of that man's voice issuing orders, which was followed by Martin's mumbling. There was a long pause, with much noise from the horses and, Harry suspected, a certain amount of cursing from Mr. Dickenson. Before too much longer, though, the landau, with its lanterns lit and its chestnut bay horses walking dutifully in step, came around the yard. Mr. Dickenson sat on the box with the ribbons in his gloved hands. He paused the horses by the inn door. Harry decided now was the time for action. He stepped out of the shadows, and tipped Dickenson a salute.

Dickenson started as if he'd seen a ghost. In answer, Harry folded his arms, and waited to see if he would dare to climb off his perch on that ridiculous high-flyer of a carriage. But Dickenson did not so much as waste breath on a curse. He just snapped the reins, whistled up the horses, and set their heads toward London without a backward glance.

Well, that was one problem taken care of. Now what in God's name was he going to do about the other?

Harry glanced up at the window, only to see that it was open, and that Leannah was staring down at him.

Twelve

What is the matter *with me?*

It was still full dark, and Leannah sat in the chair beside the last glowing coals of the fire, trying to brush her hair, and to find some way to calm down after having so unceremoniously fled from Harry Rayburn.

What is the matter with me? Each syllable was accompanied by an angry jerk of the stiff-bristled brush. It hurt her hands, but Leannah didn't care. The pain helped remind her who she really was and how many responsibilities she had.

The brush tangled in her curls again. It took several hard yanks to work the implement free. Her hair, as she had predicted, had knotted into a solid mass. She'd probably have to resort to shears to take care of the worst of the snarls.

Which would be appropriate, Leannah thought grimly. *Don't they shave the heads of the deranged?* If she was not truly deranged, she was certainly giving an excellent imitation.

But who could know that insanity came with such a brilliant smile, such fair hair and blue eyes? Or that one kiss could make her forget who she was?

Leannah gave the brush another vicious jerk. The tangle she'd been working on abruptly freed itself, and sent the brush skittering across the room. Genevieve rolled over in her bed but did not wake. *Of course not,* Leannah thought as she stumped across the floor to retrieve the brush. *The only two people awake in this world are myself and Harry Rayburn.*

She was certain he was awake. The thought of him being able to go calmly to sleep after driving her so far into pleasure and longing was insupportable. It made him into a calculating libertine. She did not like picturing Harry Rayburn in this fashion. She should not be picturing him in any fashion at all. That way lay not only madness, but genuine danger.

Leannah was intimately familiar with the power of fantasy. Mr. Wakefield had been sixty-five when they were married. It was Elias's hope to get an heir on his blooming, healthy, nineteen-year-old bride, but he was the first to admit he was no passionate lover. She'd never betrayed him, but she had spent a great deal of time with other young wives on the edges of ballrooms, watching other men. She'd discovered there was a form of pleasure in imagining that they were the ones touching her, coaxing her, rousing her. When she'd been widowed and lay alone in her bed, she continued to dream about such men, just as she'd continued to stay away from them. By then she knew how to manage enough of her own pleasure to ease the basic physical craving. It had not been perfect, but it had seemed like it would be enough.

It wasn't until she'd moved her family back to London last year that she'd begun to feel something genuine lacking in her life. She was no longer among familiar countrymen and their fathers, all of whom she knew so well that they aroused nothing in her beyond friendship. It was in the glittering ballrooms, among crowds of officers and the gentlemen, sports, dandies, lords, and wealthy tradesmen that longing woke in her. A part of her that she thought she'd packed away long ago wanted to be asked to dance. She wanted to look up into a pair of fine eyes and feel the press of a man's warm hands. She wanted to be talked with and called upon. Flirted with. Seduced.

If nothing else, this encounter with Mr. Harry Rayburn was a reminder that one should be very careful what one wished for. She could not get herself and Genevieve away from here quickly enough. She would take them straight home. The moment she had locked Genevieve in her room, she would write to Mr. Valloy and let him know she would be at home when he called and that she was ready to accept his offer. He did not engage her heart, but the heart was a willful creature. This last night was proof enough of that. From now on, she would have as little to do with its undisciplined tricks as possible.

The sound of hooves and wheels clattered through the window. Leannah nearly dropped the brush as she sprang to her feet. All her sensible resolve of the moment before fled, driven out by the idea this sound might signal Harry's departure.

I've offended him, repulsed him. She barely remembered she must not jostle Genevieve's bed as she threw open the window. *He's going before I can explain . . .*

But no. That wasn't Harry. Dawn's pearl gray light showed her Mr. Dickenson's landau, and Mr. Dickenson himself, turning the team toward the highway. Harry Rayburn simply stood by the inn, and watched him go.

Leannah moved to close the window, but she wasn't fast enough. Harry turned his head, and looked up. The sight of him there, waiting for her like Romeo waiting for his Juliet with the first rays of dawn lighting up his curling hair took her breath away.

For his part, Harry Rayburn smiled his brilliant smile, and bowed. Despite her agitation and confusion, Leannah could not help but smile herself, and wave her own hand in imperious salute.

Then she did close the window. Forgetting the brush and her hair, she let herself fall back onto her bed.

What is happening to me? she thought, blinking up at the ceiling. *And what on earth am I to do about it?*

Leannah was still groping for some sort of answer to either question when she drifted into sleep.

At least, she did until the door banged open.

Leannah lurched upright, blinking stupidly. Warm daylight streamed through the window. Genevieve stood beside her bed, fully dressed, her hands on her hips.

"What have you done!" she demanded.

"What are you talking about?" Leannah groaned and brushed her hair back from her face. The details of the previous night roused themselves to some sort of order, and it occurred to Leannah that Genny had somehow managed to dress herself without needing help, or being heard.

"Anthony! He's gone! Without a word. You must have done something."

"I did nothing," she answered honestly, but her thoughts leapt to Harry Rayburn, standing down in the yard. Had he run Mr. Dickenson off? If he had, it was yet one more thing she had to thank him for.

Apparently, Genevieve's thoughts were running along a similar, but far less grateful, course. "If you didn't do it, you must have put that Mr. Rayburn up to it."

"As far as I am aware, if Mr. Dickenson left, the decision was entirely his own."

For a moment, it looked as if Genevieve would argue the point, but in the end she just plopped herself onto the edge of her bed. "Well, it's all ruined anyway, even if Uncle Clarence does still turn up." She paused. "Do you think something could have happened to him?"

"Other than that he may have met someone on the road who either needed help or salvation? No." Leannah kicked her way out from her covers and crossed the room to sit beside her sister. "I know you were acting out of good motives, Genny," she said as she took both Genevieve's hands. "But this isn't the way, and Mr. Dickenson has just proved more than amply he's not the man for you."

"Then what am I to do?" whispered Genevieve. "We're in so much trouble, Lea. I have to do something to help."

"We're not in that much trouble," Leannah told her, and she strove to mean it. "It's nothing we can't work our way through, as long as we keep our heads."

"Like you're keeping your head with Mr. Rayburn."

"Mr. Rayburn is not the subject of this conversation." This declaration probably would have had more force if Leannah hadn't also at that moment gotten to her feet and gone to the small table to adjust the position of the brush and the hand mirror.

"He should be," said Genevieve to her back. "Considering you were making calf's eyes at him and then running after him into the dark—entirely unchaperoned, may one add."

"Genevieve!"

"Well, you were. And that was after he knocked poor Anthony down."

"We are finished with this," Leannah said firmly. "I am going to get dressed, and find out how soon Gossip can be reshod."

"What am I to do in the meantime?"

"Get Mrs. Jessop to lay out breakfast in the parlor, and stop making up fairy stories about me and Mr. Rayburn. We have to get home before anyone else unwelcome turns up." *Or before I lose my resolve with Harry. Again.*

Fortunately, Leannah was not given time to brood on this possibility, or any of its most likely consequences. Mrs. Jessop arrived a short moment later, bringing them clean water and fresh cloths. Leannah was a little embarrassed to find Harry's caution with her hands had been warranted. She had broken open her scabs and blood stained the bandages. Mrs. Jessop tut-tutted and helped rebandage her palms. Then, between the two of them, they wrestled Leannah's hair into some semblance of order, and dressed her again in her own simple, powder blue dress. The garment was a bit worse for the wear, but it had at least been shaken out and aired.

When she finally descended the stairs, Leannah found Genevieve enjoying, or at least eating, breakfast in the parlor. Like the night before, the food was simple but hearty—porridge with treacle, fresh brook trout, more of the good bread with fresh butter, as well as strawberry preserves.

Leannah had just settled herself at the table when Mrs. Jessop bustled in with a pot of piping-hot tea.

"The gentleman's outside," said Mrs. Jessop as she filled their cups full of tea so dark it was almost black. "He sends his compliments and asks if he might come in and say good morning."

"Oh, yes!" cried Genevieve before Leannah could answer. "I do so long to see how Mr. Rayburn does this morning."

Mrs. Jessop ignored this too bright and too quick exclamation, and looked to Leannah.

"Please show Mr. Rayburn in," said Leannah.

She thought she'd spoken quite coolly, but there was so much good-natured understanding on Mrs. Jessop's face as she exited the parlor, Leannah could not escape the realization she had made a bad job of it. This was not helped by the infuriatingly knowing look Genevieve leveled at her.

Leannah ignored her sister and concentrated on schooling her features into an appropriately bland and polite expression before the door opened to admit Mr. Rayburn.

Harry looked as rumpled as she felt. He'd had some sort of rough wash, and his hair was plastered back against his head. Golden stubble gleamed on his chin. It was everything Leannah could do not to reach out and straighten his cravat for him. But they were no longer alone together, draped in a veil of moonlight and shadows. The sun was up. Genevieve was sitting right here. She must return to being Leannah Morehouse Wakefield, and quickly.

"Good morning, Mrs. Wakefield, Miss Morehouse." Harry bowed. "How are your hands this morning, Mrs. Wakefield?"

He spoke politely, almost casually, but there was nothing casual about the look in his eyes. His eyes were filled to the brim with the memories neither of them could mention.

"Much better thank you," Leannah answered with equal politeness. But she turned her own eyes toward his. *Please,* she begged silently. *Please see that this polite conversation is not what I would choose.*

"Won't you join us, Mr. Rayburn?" inquired Genevieve, gesturing to the empty chair.

"Thank you." Harry bowed once more. "That is most kind, but I've already had my breakfast, and must make an early start of it. It has been a pleasure meeting you, Mrs. Wakefield," he said, and again there was that burning glance, and the clear wish to speak.

A sick pain rose in Leannah's chest. The contradictions of needing him to stay and wishing desperately he would go squeezed her heart and lungs. But he must go and she must let him. She couldn't be herself when he was near. He turned her into something, someone quite different.

You only play the martyr because you haven't the heart for anything else.

Leannah pushed Genevieve's accusation aside, again, and steeled herself for the final end of this—what to even call it?—this scene? It certainly wasn't an affair. She parted her lips. She had the polite farewell ready on her tongue, but the plodding sound of heavy horses' hooves coming through the open window interrupted her as surely as Genevieve's delighted squeak.

"Anthony!"

Genny jumped up and ran from the parlor. Harry ducked back reflexively to avoid being bowled over.

"Surely not," murmured Leannah. Mr. Dickenson was far too proud to come back after being knocked down, unless he had a plan of some sort. Leannah got to her feet and brushed past Mr. Rayburn. Even though her thoughts whirled with all manner of improbable scenarios involving Mr. Dickenson, she was very aware how Harry followed close behind her.

But it wasn't the return of Anthony Dickenson that created the racket. A massive, antique travelling coach creaked across the yard, pulled by a pair of shaggy cart horses. As soon as the slouching driver halted his team, the coach door opened and a spry old man dressed in clergyman's black popped out. He clapped one hand to his head to keep his broad-brimmed hat from flying off, grabbed up a black bag in the other, and scampered to the doorway where Genevieve had stopped, stunned.

"Oh, my dear Genevieve, I am so sorry I'm late." The Rev. Clarence Morehouse grasped his niece's hands and planted a kiss on her brow. His white hair stuck out in every direction from under his hat, an indication of the speed with which he'd taken to the road that morning. "There were so many delays with the horses, and then my man declared with the rain we risked overturning. We were forced to take shelter until day. But, I'm here now and I have the license and . . ."

Leannah glanced up at Harry to see him with his brows raised and a small, wry smile on his face. Then, she stepped into the doorway. "I'm here, too, Uncle Clarence."

Uncle Clarence froze, blinking his round eyes and looking for all the world like Jeremy when he'd been caught raiding the pantry, again. "Oh. My. Leannah."

"Just so." Leannah felt her own tight smile form. "May I have a word, in private?"

"Of course, of course." Uncle Clarence reclaimed his bag, but paused to squeeze Genevieve's hand once more. "Don't you worry, my dear. Everything will be right, I promise."

Leannah cast Harry another glance. In answer, she received

a slight nod. He would not leave Genevieve unsupervised. Her sister would have no chance to take to the road again.

Leannah led her uncle into the parlor. She liked Uncle Clarence, she always had. He might have gotten a very good living out of his London parish. But Clarence Morehouse was not one of that species of clergyman who preached bland and reassuring sermons about the importance of obeying one's superiors, made themselves agreeable in the fashionable drawing rooms, and kept the fees that should have gone to their curates. Rather, her uncle took the Gospel's instructions to love one's neighbor and succor the needy quite seriously. He also could not refrain from saying as much. This combination meant that what little extra money came into his church went out again just as quickly.

"Now, you're not to worry about anything at home, Leannah," said Uncle Clarence as he hung up his hat by the door. "I sent Mrs. Morehouse round this morning, to offer whatever help might be needed."

"Thank you," she said, thinking again of Jeremy and Father. Did Father realize she and Genny had been gone all night? He'd be distraught. Jeremy would be furious, if only because he was missing out on the excitement. Guilt washed over her. She had been so wrapped up in her encounter with Harry Rayburn, she'd all but forgotten about how Father would be worrying about them. What if it brought on another attack?

Uncle Clarence saw her distress and hurried to her side. "Now, don't worry, Lea. It's much better that you are here." Uncle Clarence took her hand and for the first time noticed her bandages. "Oh, my dear, what's happened?"

"It's nothing, truly." She drew away and she sat down by the fire. She also hid her hands in the folds of her skirts. Uncle Clarence drew his own chair up close to her.

"Lea, please believe me, had Genevieve not told me of her circumstances in strictest confidence, I would have laid the whole of the matter before you. I did try my best to convince her she should speak to you herself. I knew you would understand and support her completely."

"There's no baby," said Leannah. It was a much blunter revelation than her uncle deserved, but she could not think of any other way to say it.

"What?" Uncle Clarence drew back.

"There's no baby. Genevieve was never in love with Mr. Dickenson, nor he with her."

Uncle Clarence was silent at this. He blinked at the fire for a long time. Leannah watched, angry and weary beyond description. How could Genevieve do all this without her seeing? She should have known. She should have been able to put a stop to the matter before it went anything like this far. That was, after all, her reason for being. She was the one who saw the family disasters coming and stopped them.

She knew she was being unfair to Genny and to herself. She could not be expected to know everything in the minds of those around her. Except it seemed that sometimes that would be the only way to keep them all safe and together.

"I seem to have been imposed upon," said Uncle Clarence finally.

"I'm sorry, Uncle. If . . ."

"No, no." Uncle Clarence waved her words away. "I should have realized. She's been so worried, about, well you, and your situation." He looked up at her again. "She meant well, Leannah, I'm sure of it. You must try to forgive her."

Which was exactly the sort of charitable response she expected from him. At the same time, it strained her patience to the breaking point. There always seemed to be so much to forgive and always something new she must come to understand.

But all Leannah said was, "I'm sorry you were brought out all this way for nothing. We'll pay for the license, of course." *After we've paid Mr. Rayburn back for this night, and paid the farrier for Gossip's shoe and . . .*

Uncle Clarence waved her words away. "You mustn't mind that. Can you tell me how matters currently stand?"

Instantly, Harry Rayburn's face rose up in Leannah's mind. But she did not speak of that either. "Mr. Dickenson has taken to his heels. Genevieve is angry, and although I can't exactly blame her, I can't say I'm sorry, either."

"I do understand. How may I best be of assistance?"

"I will have to ask you to take us home. Gossip cast a shoe on the road, and with my hands, well . . ." She spread her bandaged palms. "I may have to stable the team here until someone who can handle them can come fetch them." *Another expense, more arrangements.*

"Naturally." Uncle Clarence nodded vigorously. "Would you like me to speak with Genevieve? Perhaps I can help her see that while her intentions may have been excellent, her methods were not of the best."

Leannah smiled. "You're welcome to try. I've had very little success. Still, you can sit with her while I go see about Gossip and Rumor."

With Uncle Clarence still making all manner of reassurances to her back, Leannah took herself out the side door and made her way around the inn to the stables. Gossip and Rumor snorted in greeting from their boxes, which were, she noted, roomy and comfortable. She petted their noses, held out her empty hands to be lipped and to prove that, unfortunately, she had neither apples nor sugar.

A shadow fell across the floor. She knew it was Harry. She didn't need to see him. After last night, her skin had become perfectly attuned to his presence. She wondered how long it would take for that sympathy to fade.

"Good morning, again, Mr. Rayburn." Leannah was pleased with how calmly she was able to speak his name. It gave her the courage to turn her head to look at him. He was smiling, gently, wistfully.

"Good morning again, Mrs. Wakefield."

"I imagine it's you we have to thank for Mr. Dickenson's absence?"

"I'd love to be able to take credit for running the gentleman off the premises, but no. He took himself away in the wee hours." Harry paused. "You seem well acquainted with the clergyman."

Leannah sighed. Gossip, bored and seeking attention, shoved at her arm. She petted the mare's ears. "He's my father's brother. I could absolutely murder Genevieve for involving him in this business."

"But she needed him to obtained the license for them, so he could perform the marriage on the spot, no matter where they met up."

Leannah nodded. "She thought I might catch her if she had to go all the way to Scotland."

"Given the way you drive, she was probably right." Harry moved closer. Anticipation prickled across Leannah's skin. But Harry did not touch her. He simply stood beside her, breathing deeply, steadily. She could feel the strength it took for him to control himself. Almost as much as it took to make her keep her eyes on his when a wicked portion of herself urged her to glance at his breeches, to search for the most definite evidence of his arousal.

"Well," Harry said. "Now that you've your family with you, I can relinquish my role of hero and protector."

"Which you performed admirably." She said this more to Gossip than to Harry. "I shall be sure to recommend you to all my acquaintances who find themselves in need of rescue."

"You can assure them my rates are entirely reasonable."

Leannah tried to find a witty response, but there was none. Her whole body ached for Harry's touch. She wanted to take him into her arms and discover all the pleasures they'd left unexplored last night.

"I wish I could think of a way to take that look from your face," he breathed.

She shook her head. "I'm just tired."

"It was a very long night," he breathed.

"And a maddening drive."

His hand moved. Slowly, hesitantly, he reached for her. Leannah's throat seized tight. *Move away, move away. Speak. Tell him he must not do this.* But she let Harry take her hand with that gentleness of which he was so capable. His breathing grew ragged as he raised her fingers to his lips.

He lifted his eyes, and she saw the mischief there, the bright understanding. He ran his thumb across the very tips of her fingers, and Leannah had to clamp her mouth shut against the sigh.

"Maddening," he drew the word out. "Yes. My thought exactly."

"We . . . we should probably be grateful we are at the end of it."

He had been so quick on the uptake at every other point she could not believe he misunderstood her now. He was ignoring her, quite deliberately. Exasperation flared up in her, but it swiftly died, because he still had not let her fingers go. In point of fact, he kept right on rhythmically brushing his thumb across her fingertips. The soft caress threatened to reach directly into her blood and brain, and drain away her ability to think.

"Are we truly at an end, Leannah?"

"Where else could we be? My sister is safe. My uncle is waiting to take us home. Where else is this to go?"

Harry made a great show of considering her words, without letting go of her hand, or ceasing the thoughtful brush of his thumb across her nails.

"You may be right," he said reluctantly, but she didn't believe for a minute he meant it. "Unless you'd like to go to Gretna?"

The suggestion was plainly meant to be absurd and Leannah made herself laugh. "But who would drive? My hands are a ruin."

Harry raised her hand a little higher. "You think I couldn't handle your team?"

His breath was warm against her hand. Leannah's heart stopped and started again at a frantic gallop. With that infinite attention and gentleness, he pressed his lips to her fingers, kissing each one in turn. She was melting inside. The whole of her was softening, warming, growing at once relaxed and eager.

She had been selfish long enough and taken much more than she should of what Harry offered. But she would take just a little more, just one more moment to store up against all the lonely nights that would follow this one.

"No, I actually rather think you could handle them." She stepped closer until her hems brushed the tips of his boots. Leannah let her free hand brush his curling hair and trail across his brow. She wanted to memorize the particular blue of his eyes, with that dark ring around the iris and those tiny flecks of steel gray. "You seem very comfortable with spirited creatures."

Harry lifted his other hand and let his fingers trace a line of warmth down her cheek. Now she did sigh and tilt her head toward him. Harry answered by opening his palm so he could cradle her cheek. "Comfortable is not how I'd describe myself feeling around you."

"No," she agreed. He touched the curve of her throat now,

right above her shoulder. She closed her eyes so she could better concentrate on the exact spot.

"So, shall we go?" There was a smile in his voice, but a hitch in his breath. If she took one more step forward, she'd press against his body. His warmth would wrap around her, and his arms would follow a moment later. "Your uncle can take your sister home."

She could picture it—the pair of them side by side on the barouche box, with Gossip and Rumor tearing down the highway at the limit of their speed. She and Harry would laugh and shout and passersby would stare. They'd clatter over the bridge that marked the Scots border and he'd leap down and catch her around the waist and . . .

"Please, Mr. Rayburn, don't joke. You have no idea . . ." She couldn't finish that sentence. *You have no idea what you're doing to me. What you're turning me into.*

But the truth was worse. This was not something Harry Rayburn did to her. Her heart, her passion, her most secret self reached out to the impossible idea of being with him.

"What if I'm not joking?"

He'd lifted his hand away from her throat, but he did not let go of her fingertips, neither did he step back. She could not miss or mistake one nuance of his expression, and his face was as serious as his voice. He meant it. Heaven help them both.

"I can't."

He was smiling again. While Leannah watched, the idea took hold in him, and he welcomed it. In answer, Leannah's fear rose up just as quickly. But it was not Harry's seriousness that frightened her. It was that she could feel the terrible, wonderful temptation of his words.

"You've been considering marrying again, haven't you?" he said. "Well, I'm not titled or any such, but I've got excellent prospects, and plenty of money in my own right if that's a concern . . ."

"No! Well, yes, but, no. Please, *stop!*" She tore herself away. It was the last thing she wanted to do, but it was the only way she could make him see she was serious in her refusal. They stood like that, both breathing hard and unable to speak, with the horses looking on, restless and bored.

Harry swallowed. "I'm sorry. I shouldn't have." His fingertips rubbed together, as if they already missed her touch. "Will you at least tell me where I might see you when we're both back in town?"

"I daren't."

"You dared a great deal last night." For the first time his voice turned ever so slightly suspicious. "Why can't I even call on you in daylight?"

She smiled although she felt it might break her in two. "Because you make me feel anything but comfortable."

He chuckled. She liked the sound of it. "Flatterer."

"If you like."

Whatever she did next, she would not take her leave of Harry Rayburn with a lie. Lying might have been kinder. It might even have been more intelligent, but it was not what she wanted. This once, she wanted to speak the truth to someone, anyone. More than that, though, she did not want Harry to think she regretted what they had done together.

"If it was just me, I'd go to Gretna with you, right now, as we are," she told him. "But there's Genevieve, and I've a younger brother at home, and my father's not well. So you see, I can't just run away."

He did not answer at once. He let her words sink into him.

"I do see." He glanced down at his restless fingertips, and spoke to them instead of to her. "And I'm sorry."

She'd meant to stop there, but it seemed her tongue was running ahead on its own. "I've always had to be responsible. I'm not the one who can act from her own desire."

His smile at this was small and sad. "And I'm the stout fellow—solid, dependable, dull Harry."

She was lifting her face, lifting her hand. She was straightening his rumpled cravat as she had wanted to do when he first appeared in the parlor. She was leaning forward and touching her lips to the corner of his mouth. He turned toward her just a little. His arms wrapped around her waist to support and hold her as they opened each to the other. The kiss was easy as breathing, as natural as sunrise and just as welcome.

"It's still madness," she whispered against his mouth.

"So it is." He pulled her closer. Her breasts crushed against his chest as he bent them both back. He kissed her mouth, her cheek, her throat.

"People like us shouldn't engage in madness."

"Dull, responsible people." He lowered his head to kiss the exquisitely sensitive skin of her throat.

"There's too much at stake," she sighed. She remembered just in time she mustn't press her injured palms against him. Instead, she looped her arms and wrists over his broad shoulders. He lifted his mouth to hers so they could kiss once more. She opened wide for him, delighting in the sensation of his tongue sliding across hers.

"Besides," he breathed as he moved his attentions to her cheek, her chin, and back down her throat. "We can't possibly elope with only one team of horses and no luggage. The thing's impossible." He paused. He lifted his head, just a little, but he kept his hands against her hips. "Unless you think your uncle would agree to marry us instead?"

Thirteen

Shock straightened Leannah up, straightened them up.

"Mr. Rayburn, I've asked you to stop joking about this."

"And I've told you, I'm not joking."

"But why would you want to marry me?"

She meant the question to push him away, but it seemed that Harry had his answer ready.

He kissed her again. Not gently this time, but hard, deeply, almost brutally. She opened to him, first in shock and then in delight at this wicked plundering of her mouth. He had hold of both her wrists and pinned them, not over her head this time, but behind her, as he leaned his whole broad, hard body against her.

"I'd marry you because I don't want to give this up," he whispered. "I want to understand every part of this feeling, and of you."

"Some things cannot be understood."

"Maybe not in the mind, but in the heart." He laid his palm over her breast. "In the heart, everything can be understood."

He kissed her again, plunging his tongue deep inside her mouth. He was so hard. The length of his erection pressed insistently against her mound. The sensation was driving her to distraction. Her eyes closed and she gave herself over to his kiss, his body and her own growing need. She hated her clothing and despised his. She wanted him naked in her arms, and between her thighs. There was nothing else in all the world now, except this man, this kiss, and their need.

Except there was. With a sound like a sob, Leannah wrenched herself away. She stumbled up against the stable wall. The horses snorted, whether disconcerted or laughing at her, she couldn't tell. She pressed her hand against her mouth, against her belly. She was cold. No, she was on fire. She ached, and yet the pleasure she felt removed all possibility of pain.

"Leannah, don't leave me," said Harry from behind her. "Don't forsake this before we have a chance to find out what it means."

"And if it means nothing?" She couldn't turn around. She couldn't look at him. If she did, she'd run to him. Her weakness was too terrible, too complete.

"Then at least we'll know it," he said. "We won't poison the rest of our lives with useless wondering and wishing."

His words came perilously close to making sense, especially with her lips still wet and swollen from his kiss. She could feel fever's perspiration prickling between her thighs. Her mound throbbed, damp and hot from his attentions, and filled her with a longing for more.

I'd marry you because I don't want to give this up. How easily she could have spoken those words to him.

But she hesitated too long, caught between real fears and impossible hopes. "I'm sorry," Harry whispered. "I've gone too far. I apologize."

Leannah closed her eyes once more. She did not turn.

"I'll go. Good luck, Mrs. Wakefield, and God be with you."

She heard his boots rustling the straw. *Let him go*, she told herself. *Let him go.* It would be easiest, it would be best. Lack of heart, yes, and lack of nerve, and too much duty all made it wisest and best to let this man go his way.

But in that moment, it felt cowardly, and Leannah had never been a coward. She made herself look, not back, but forward. She made herself see her future. In that future, she was standing in the parlor with Father as Genevieve accepted a man very much like Mr. Dickenson because there was no other way to make ends meet. Jeremy was there, home from the boarding school he hated, waiting to come into full possession of a property none of them really understood how to manage.

She saw herself standing in front of Uncle Clarence and holding Mr. Valloy's cold, thin hand.

"Harry!" Leannah whirled around. For one terrible instant, all she saw was the open door and the empty yard. A sob tore from her throat and she pressed her fist against her mouth to stifle it. She was too late. Too late.

"Leannah! It's all right. It's all right. I'm here."

He was. He must have been just around the corner, but now he was in her arms, raining kisses down on her brow, her cheek, her mouth. She answered every one frantically.

"I'm here," he kept saying. "I'm here, Leannah."

"Don't leave." She grasped his face in both her hands, forgetting her bandages, forgetting everything. "Please. I can't . . . I can't . . ."

He pressed his fingers across her mouth, silencing her. "I will stay," he told her, "as long as you let me stay."

"Did you mean what you said?"

He nodded. "Every word. Will you marry me?"

It was all up to her now. She could act from sense, or she could act from need. She could agree to an affair, or to absolute separation, or this other way.

"I will marry you. But it must be now. If I stop to think, I might lose my nerve again."

He stopped her words with another heady kiss. She was drunk on this man, on his eyes and his smile and his touch. Any more of him and she would faint dead away.

"You could never lose your nerve once you made up your mind. And if you did, I'd be right there for you."

She laughed, giddy as a schoolgirl as he seized her wrist. Harry was grinning wildly and dragged her across the yard, right past Martin who gaped to see them, and through a flock of chickens that clucked insults as they scattered.

Breathless, they reached the inn door to find the mail coach had arrived without either of them hearing it. The yard now was filled to bursting with passengers, baggage, and boxes. Even this inconvenience seemed unbearably funny. Leannah giggled and Harry laughed out loud.

"Do you want me to come in when you to speak to your uncle?"

Leannah struggled to marshal her wits. It was very difficult with Harry holding her wrist and smiling at her. "No, you'd better not. He mustn't think you've coerced me. And . . ."

"And what?"

"I'll have to say a great many things to convince him to do this." A thousand realities threatened to overwhelm her. She bit her lip and laid her wrist on his shoulder, as if she could draw fresh strength directly from his touch. "Listen to me, Harry. My family is in bad circumstances. Our money has all been lost. My father . . ."

"Is not well. You've said as much."

"It's a disorder of the nerves. He may never get better. Genevieve, well you've seen her, and my brother Jeremy's just twelve." *And then there are the whispers about me. I need to tell you about those.*

Harry crooked his finger under her chin and lifted her face to his. "I'm the son of a goods importer. I learned how to brawl on the docks before I'd mastered my letters. I've been around the world, and I can drink, swear, gamble, and whore as hard as any sailor when I'm at sea. When I'm at home, I'm devoted to my mother and sister, and look forward to little more than inheriting my father's business ledger. I've already been turned down as too boring to be endured. I hate to waltz. My whiskers are entirely overgrown and somewhat ridiculous looking, and I'm told I snore."

Leannah blinked. "You snore?"

"I'm told I do."

She smiled. "So do I."

"Well, you see? It's fate." He kissed her lightly, playfully. "Go speak with your uncle. I'll wait in the public room. With everybody else." He eyed the crowd of new arrivals with such exaggerated ruefulness Leannah had no choice but to laugh. She kissed him once more for luck and strength and hurried inside. All the way she felt Harry's gaze on her and heard his voice inside her mind.

I will stay, as long as you let me stay.

When Leannah ducked inside the parlor, she found Genevieve pacing, and Uncle Clarence admonishing.

". . . I understand your sentiments, Genevieve, but if you

could be persuaded to see that patience will serve you much better than any dramatic and hasty union. The Lord will provide, my dear."

"The Lord has not provided very much up to this point."

"Genevieve!" cried Leannah, closing the door tight behind her.

Genny threw up her hands. "All right, all right, I'm a wicked girl, and I'm upsetting everybody and I'm sorry. Are you come to tell me it's time to go home, Leannah?"

Leannah felt herself smile. "Actually, I need to speak with Uncle Clarence a moment. Will you excuse us?"

Genevieve's eyes narrowed. "About what?"

"You'll know shortly."

Genevieve was clearly reluctant, but in the end, she did leave, out through the door to the public room. Leannah found herself hoping briefly that she would not frighten Mr. Rayburn away. But she smiled at this. Among his many other amazing qualities, it was easy to see that Harry was more than a match for Genevieve. Which in and of itself might be enough to make this insanity right.

"What is it Leannah?" asked Uncle Clarence anxiously. "How can I help?"

Leannah hesitated, but only for a heartbeat. Truly, there was no way to do this, save to dive in head first. "Uncle, I wish to be married to Mr. Rayburn."

"What?" The force of his shout pulled the mild little man to his feet.

Leannah did not so much as flinch. "You have a license with you?"

"Yes, of course I do, but that was for Genevieve and her Mr. Dickenson."

"Well, as Mr. Dickenson has left, he and Genny cannot now marry. So, I propose we make use of that license and your presence to marry me to Harold Rayburn instead."

Uncle Clarence paced in a tight circle in front of the hearth, rubbing his hand repeatedly across his mottled scalp. Leannah folded her hands and waited.

"Leannah, you're not talking sense," he said finally.

"It is unexpected, I know. But it is also our best course of action. Once Genevieve's elopement is discovered, she will become a scandal. The only way to avoid that is to divert attention as far as is possible. I am already a scandal, and we all know it. At least I will be a married scandal, and those tend to be much less interesting to society at large."

Uncle Clarence passed his hand several more times across his scalp and then ran his fingers through his fringe of white hair, as if he might pluck out an answer.

"No." He wagged his head. "I cannot in conscience do this thing."

"Someone must return married from this escapade, otherwise Genevieve's chance at a new future is gone." She hesitated again. "Uncle, Genny only did this because she wanted to secure us the money her marriage to Mr. Dickenson would bring. If I marry Mr. Rayburn, we are taken care of, and she's free to make a different choice, a better choice."

"No," Uncle Clarence said again. He took her hands and gazed up earnestly into her eyes. "I do know the money is a concern, Leannah, but you need not stay in London. You can all return to the country. I've often felt a quiet life would better suit the entire family."

"A quiet life. Yes, for a family supporting not one but two spinsters, and Jeremy left with a rundown inheritance he has no way to manage, and no education or connections." They were cold words, hard words. Leannah felt guilty about having to level them against her charitable uncle, who had never done anything but try to help.

Think on Harry Rayburn, she told herself. *Think about that touch and that smile. Think about for once not having to end a dream at dawn.* Warmth suffused her body as she did think about this, and she felt the color beginning to rise to her cheeks. It was a wicked and impossible dream, except it was not so impossible after all, if only she held firm.

"Leannah," said Uncle Clarence gently. "I understand you've been driven to an extreme, but this . . . hasty and imprudent marriage . . . is not the answer."

"Then what is?"

"You're Jeremy's guardian. You can properly arrange for a mortgage of some of the land to meet the expenses of his education."

She shook her head. "*Father* is Jeremy's legal guardian. I

might be able to help arrange the mortgage, but any money would ultimately fall under Father's control, and we don't know what will happen then." *Except we do know. He will invest it, all of it, and the disasters will all begin again.*

"He's changed, Leannah."

"I want to believe it, Uncle. But the land Elias left Jeremy is all we have. If it is mortgaged and Father lapses, we'll lose our last hope." Her voice turned hard. "What happens then? What if I cannot care for us all? Will Genny and I go for governesses? Can you take us onto the parish roles? Or will Jeremy leave school and go to work or into the navy? Uncle, *think*. Jeremy's a boy, and neither Genny nor I are fit or educated for work. We were supposed to be accomplished and pretty, with our father to care for us until we are passed to husbands who would take up the chore. That has collapsed. This is what's left to us."

The words fell from her like a shower of stones. Hearing herself speak the truth so coldly frightened her. If she married Harry for desire, that made her giddy and impulsive and perhaps even ridiculous. But if she married him for money, what did that make her?

"But you don't even know this Mr. Rayburn!" cried Uncle Clarence.

Leannah met her uncle's distressed gaze. "But I do." These words came to her as easily as anything she'd told him yet, and they were just as true. "He is a good man, and I want to be with him." She did not say the word "love." That one word would not come to her. She tried to tell herself it did not matter. If it was to come at all, it would come when the time was right. But that was too close to what she'd believed of her first marriage, the one that truly had been for money.

That is not what I'm doing this time. I will not think it. I will think about Harry, think about his hands on my body, about his kisses and his promises. I will think about enjoying his company and his banter and his smiles, openly, freely, and without fear. I will think about not having to be so alone, for a little while at least.

"Please, Uncle," said Leannah. "I am not asking you to do this only for Genevieve or Father or even Jeremy. This once, I'm asking something for myself."

Uncle Clarence met her gaze for a long time. When he did turn toward the hearth, he bowed his head and Leannah heard the faint breath of whispered words. She guessed he must be praying, and she made herself be still and quiet.

At the same time she could not help wishing she could run to the door. What was happening out there? Was Harry pacing? Was he even still there? Had he repented his hasty, heated proposal? No. He would not do that. He was not Mr. Dickenson. He would not leave her without a word.

But how do I know that? I want to believe I know him, but I don't. I only know I want him and I am trying to convince myself I am right to want him.

The thought had a bitter sting to it, and she tried to push it away. She wished Harry were standing here beside her. She wished a thousand things, torn between desire, doubt, and this reckless, dizzy sensation that was like too much champagne in her blood.

At last, Uncle Clarence turned to face her. There was resolution on his face, and Leannah's heart plummeted.

"Leannah," he said. "Because it is you, because I know the trust and care all our family places in you, I will do what you ask."

With the arrival of the mail coach, the inn's public room had become very loud and very crowded. Mr. and Mrs. Jessop, not to mention young Martin, the girl Mary, and four or five other servants, who had apparently arrived with the dawn, were everywhere at once, answering dozens of calls, for food, for beer, and for all manner of fetching and carrying.

Despite this, Harry managed to catch the landlord's arm and shout his own request for paper, pen, and ink. There were letters to be written, even if he had to elbow three or four local goodmen and farmers out of the way to keep one corner of the bar clear.

He couldn't very well bring Leannah to his parents' house for their wedding night, so other arrangements must be made. Then, a note had to go to Father, explaining he was well, only delayed and would be back home (and at work) shortly, and that he could reassure mother and Fiona that all was well. These had to be pressed into the landlord's hand along with enough coinage to make sure that they were given into the hands of the nearest available reliable messenger, and that Martin was set immediately to work on reshoeing Gossip. It was a good thing he'd remembered both purse and wallet when he'd left the house.

Harry glanced at the parlor door, which remained fast shut. He didn't want to be writing letters. He wanted to burst in there, throw Leannah over his shoulder, and show her what a proper abduction looked like.

Could he really be doing this? Could he be about to marry a woman he'd met only a few hours before? Apparently, he could. But only such a woman as Leannah. The memory of her heated kiss, the eager press of her body, the warm fullness of her breasts in his hands seized him. Harry felt his groin tighten. But it wasn't just the desire she aroused in him that drove him to this impulsive action. Her spirit, her courage called to him. He did not want to let her go, and if, for her own reasons, she would not let him court her in the conventional manner, then this was the way to have and keep her.

But why? he asked himself again. *Why is it the way?* A slender thread of doubt crept into his thoughts, but he let it go. Whatever her reason might be, they would face it when the time came.

A hand grabbed his elbow and turned him abruptly around. Harry saw at once that it was Miss Genevieve Morehouse and stifled the curse he'd been about to level. She fixed him with a surprisingly steely gaze and then, keeping tight hold of his elbow, marched him out into the inn yard.

As soon as they reached a distance where they were not likely to be overheard, she spun him around once more to face her.

"What have you done to my sister?"

Years of dealing with Fiona had taught Harry that when presented with such a look, and such a question, nothing could be worse than evasion. "I helped bring her here ahead of you."

"What else?"

"If there's any other information you require on the subject, you can apply to your sister."

"Huh. As if she'd tell me anything. I suppose she's told you I'm quite the irresponsible child."

"Actually, she's told me you are a most determined young lady who cares a great deal for your family."

"She did not."

"Only because she hadn't gotten around to it yet. It was rather a busy night."

"Then you're a shameless flatterer."

"When I have to be. Right now, I'm simply remarking on what I've observed. You could have started this conversation by taking me to task for Mr. Dickenson's departure. You didn't. You asked about your sister. That proves it is your family you truly care about."

Harry watched with satisfaction as Miss Morehouse subsided. She was not quite willing to concede the bout, but she clearly felt he'd scored a point. He had to work at not smiling. Whatever tiny doubts he might have about the headlong course he currently pursued, there could be none whatsoever on one particular point. Miss Morehouse and Fiona were going to get along famously.

"Do you know what she's talking to my uncle about in there?" Miss Morehouse nodded toward the parlor window.

"I do."

"What is it then?"

Harry folded his arms and turned his own attention to the window. He wondered what progress Leannah was making. What would she do if her properly concerned uncle said no? What would he do?

"Well you're her match for stubbornness, I'll give you that." Genevieve's tone was more thoughtful than he'd heard it yet. "Where did you meet her?"

"On the road last night. She abducted me."

While Genevieve was still gaping at this pronouncement, the inn door opened to reveal Leannah, with her uncle at her side. Her eyes met Harry's, and she gave him a nod. A shock ran through him, from his boots to the crown of his head. She was smiling, and with that smile, the promise of her delightful companionship, as well as that luscious body in his arms, tumbled over him.

Miss Morehouse stomped over to her sister. "Leannah, this, this, *man* says you abducted him!"

Leannah was still smiling, and her gold and emerald gaze did not waver from his. She was beautiful. She was perfect.

"I did abduct him, Genny, and now I'm going to marry him."

Fourteen

❧

I cannot possibly be doing this.

But she was. In the yard, there had been an entirely predictable interval of explaining, and arguing, with Genevieve. This had given Uncle Clarence time to put on his surplice and stole and find the appropriate page in his prayer book. He now stood in the parlor with his back to the fire, striving mightily to keep from appearing worried as Harry took Leannah's hand in his.

Uncle Clarence coughed. "Dearly beloved, we are gathered together here in the sight of God, and in the face of this congregation, to join together Leannah Marie Morehouse Wakefield and Harold Syverson Rayburn in holy matrimony . . ."

Mr. Jessop, feeling the sense of occasion, had managed to find Harry a fresh cravat and brushed down his coat. Mrs. Jessop supplied Leannah with a little bouquet of snowdrops and one early daffodil, tied with a bit of white lace. The landlady now stood beside Genevieve, as mismatched a pair of bridesmaids as Leannah could have ever imagined. But she didn't care. Harry was looking down on her, his bright blue eyes alive with merriment, although he'd schooled his face into an admirably solemn expression. She did like his face—his clear brow, the wide expressive mouth, and of course his eyes. Those eyes told the truth about him and at the moment, that truth was he was glad to be here, with her, and glad for what they were doing.

As for his whiskers, well, they were part of him, and they made her smile. He made her smile.

". . . not by any to be enterprised, nor taken in hand, unadvisedly, lightly, or wantonly . . ."

If Genny makes that noise again, I will throttle her.

Harry's wide mouth twitched as he fought to hold back a laugh. His hand closed gently about hers. She was glad she had no gloves. She liked the feeling of his skin against hers, even in this strictly limited way. It warmed her and sent a thrum of anticipation through her veins, sensations entirely different from those that accompanied her first marriage.

Leannah's wedding to Elias Wakefield had been a grand affair. Elias had insisted on it. "Every girl dreams of this day," he'd said. "I mean for you to have that dream. Spend whatever you need to have everything just as you wish."

The command had been dizzying. It had felt like freedom come at last. Leannah and her friends had spent months in shops and warehouses assembling her trousseau. Elias kept sending presents—a fan, gloves, a coral bracelet, and at the last, a pearl and garnet necklace that had been in his family for generations.

All had been well as she walked up the aisle. Father had been so proud and sure of himself as he gave her hands into Elias's. She faced her bridegroom with the thought that her family's worries were over. She held her smile in place as he lifted back her veil, and gazed soberly down on her, candlelight glinting in his gray hair.

Elias had been dead for over a year and her trousseau had all been sold or packed away, except the garnets. The garnets she'd kept.

". . . I require and charge you both, as ye will answer at the dreadful day of judgment when the secrets of all hearts shall be disclosed, that if either of you know any impediment, why ye may not be lawfully joined together in matrimony, ye do now confess it."

The pause stretched out. It occurred to Leannah that Uncle Clarence was waiting for her to speak and call a halt to this. *I should. I should not tie this man to me, to us.*

But Harry's gaze remained steady, and his bare hands closed around her injured ones. She remembered his arms around her and his body pressed shamelessly against hers. Heat blossomed at the very center of her as she remembered the kisses he'd already given her, and how much more delight there was for them to discover. She had known duty and kindness and so many other things, but until Harry Rayburn had tumbled into her life, she had not known passion.

Uncle Clarence was speaking again.

"Wilt thou, Harold, have this woman, Leannah, to thy wedded wife, to live together after God's ordinance in the holy estate of matrimony? Wilt thou love her, comfort her, honor her, and keep her in sickness and in health; and, forsaking all others, keep thee only unto her, so long as ye both shall live?"

The merriment was gone from Harry's eyes. His gaze had turned inward. Leannah imagined him searching his own heart, but for what, she could not tell.

"I will." He spoke the words clearly, seriously. Leannah felt them as surely and deeply as she had felt the press of his hand.

Her own heart trembled beneath the weight of all the things she had not said. She'd told him the truth, but was it enough of the truth? How much could be enough for such a deed and such a moment?

What am I doing, Harry? To you and to myself?

"Wilt thou, Leannah, have this man to thy wedded husband, to live together after God's ordinance in the holy estate of matrimony? Wilt thou obey him, and serve him, love, honor, and keep him in sickness and in health; and, forsaking all others, keep thee only unto him, so long as ye both shall live?"

When she'd stood before the altar at St. George's with Elias, his gloved hand had felt light as air. Leannah remembered how firmly she'd told herself she would come to love this man. He was, after all, a good man. Things were exactly as they should be—a good marriage, a comfortable home for herself and, eventually, her children, security and prosperity for her family. It was everything she could hope for.

She had not been sold to an old man so she could be bred off him. Father had not urged her into this union because Mr.

Wakefield had agreed to give over his fortune for him to invest and manage. That was not at all what had happened.

And today? What do I tell myself today? Not that I love you, Harry. I won't say that again without being sure. But I want you, so very much. Is it enough? Please, dear Lord, if You are watching, let it be enough.

Harry's hand squeezed hers. There was no doubt in his eyes, and that small gesture gave her the strength she needed. "I will," she said.

"Who giveth this woman . . . oh, dear . . ."

"It's all right, Uncle Clarence. I give myself."

"Oh, well. Yes. Quite right. Ahem." He ran his finger down the order of service, confusion turning his face beet red. "The vows. Yes. You will repeat after me . . ." he said.

Leannah faced Harry. Her heart trembled. She waited for him to stumble over his words, to betray some sign of doubt. She waited for regret, for weakness and, yes, cold, hard common sense to come racing in and stop them.

But Harry did not stop or stumble. "I Harold take thee Leannah to my wedded wife, to have and to hold from this day forward, for better for worse, for richer for poorer, in sickness and in health, to love and to cherish, till death us do part, according to God's holy ordinance; and thereto I plight thee my troth."

Leannah was shaking. She could not even begin to name all the emotions that seized her. This at last was genuine madness, this moment that would seal them together.

I promise, I will do my best by you, Harry Rayburn, whoever you turn out to be, she said in the space of her mind. *I will be honest and I will hold faithful, however far we travel together. I will try. I want to try.*

Now it was her turn to speak. They were all waiting for her. Harry most of all.

Harry watched the stream of thought and feeling ripple through Leannah's gold and emerald eyes; memories he had yet to discover, hopes, wishes, fears, and doubts he could empathize with even though he had yet to learn their names.

"I Leannah take thee Harold to my wedded husband, to have and to hold from this day forward, for better for worse, for richer for poorer, in sickness and in health, to love and to cherish, till death us do part, according to God's holy ordinance; and thereto I give thee my troth."

He could not take his eyes off her. Her beauty held him, but so did the depth of her feeling, the life and the mystery of her being that he'd just begun to glimpse. All manner of desires filled him as he, they, solemnized this strangest possible marriage, but the desire to stop, or even slow down was not among them. In fact, he was having to work to hold her hands gently. He wanted to gather her close in his arms. He wanted to shout his need of her from the rooftops. If there was anything that frightened him, it was this desire and his willingness to dare the world to claim her.

I promise, Leannah, I will make a good husband—a steady, kind, thoroughly English husband. I'll keep you safe and make you comfortable. I will take care of you, no matter what happens and however long or short the time we manage together. I will try.

"Is there a ring?"

"Yes," said Harry. Leannah looked down at his bare hands, but Harry reached into his pocket and with a small flourish, pulled out the jeweler's box that had been waiting there the entire night. He opened the lid to display the gold and diamond ring. Leannah stared. Behind her, Genevieve gasped.

"Where on earth did that come from?"

"Genny! Be quiet!" hissed Leannah.

"I won't be! What kind of man wanders around with a diamond wedding band in his pocket?"

"One who has recently been disappointed," answered Harry with as much calm as he could manage. He'd thought it might look a bit odd, but like every other imagined impediment, it had seemed trivial enough. "I'm afraid this was purchased for someone quite different." He watched Leannah anxiously as he said this. He did not want her to feel slighted.

"It's beautiful," she answered. "I'll be proud to wear it."

Miss Morehouse fell silent, but suspicion still screwed her face tight. Leannah cocked her head, giving Harry a wry look, as Harry handed the ring over to the clergyman. To Uncle Clarence, he supposed he should say. They were family after all. He seemed a good sort, and Leannah was obviously fond of him. He'd have to set about making friends with the man. They could invite him to dinner. This was a comfortably domestic thought, and Harry found he liked it.

Uncle Clarence laid the ring upon his book for a moment, and then handed it back to Harry.

"You will please repeat after me: With this ring I thee wed, with my body I thee worship, and with all my worldly goods I thee endow: In the name of the Father, and of the Son, and of the Holy Ghost."

Harry spoke the words. They came as easily as the vows, but as he tried to slip the ring onto Leannah's finger, it wouldn't go past her first knuckle. Confusion descended and he stifled a curse. Of course it didn't fit. It had been bought for Agnes, and her hands were much smaller.

Leannah just smiled, and wiggled her littlest finger. Blushing, Harry took the hint. He also repositioned the ring. It fit perfectly. But it wasn't right for her. It was somehow too showy and too small at the same time. Why, of all the possible concerns that could have raised their collective heads, was this the one that nagged at him? He didn't know. He just knew it was wrong for Leannah to wear Agnes's ring. He would fix that, and whatever else might come along, just as soon as they got back to town. Well, not just as soon. There were several other more personal and private things to be attended to first.

It was these things Harry kept firmly in his mind as he took both of Leannah's hands and Uncle Clarence said, "Amen."

"Amen," they all answered, even Miss Morehouse. Genevieve.

And it was done, just like that. A breath of words, a moment of agreement, and she belonged wholly and solely to him.

"Mrs. Rayburn," he breathed.

"Mr. Rayburn," she answered.

"Ah, never mind the priest, kiss her, young man!" boomed the landlord.

And he did. He gathered her to him and he kissed her, openly, shamelessly, and for a very long time. Long enough to be sure she understood his promises of desire and constancy;

long enough that they both knew he meant to make this mad dream real. She was his wife and he was her husband, and no ill-fitting ring, no rash motives, no disapproving sisters, uncles, or parents would put that asunder.

All would be right. He would make sure of it.

Fifteen

"A health to the bride and groom!"

A raucous cheer rang through the public room. Mrs. Jessop hadn't been able to stand the thought of Harry and Leannah leaving without some sort of wedding breakfast. The feast she provided was little more than cold meats, bread, and cheese. To go with these, Harry ordered several bottles of wine to be brought up from the cellar so the whole public room could drink their health, which earned them a hearty cheer and a round of rather overly vigorous hand shaking from the farmers and travellers.

Leannah had to admit the impromptu meal was most welcome, partly because it passed the time while Gossip was being reshod, and partly because it cheered and revived Uncle Clarence.

"Remember, my dear," he said as she drew him aside to thank him for his help, "we are your family. Whatever may happen, you can always come home."

It was hardly a rousing endorsement of her conduct, but she could not blame him for it. Her uncle did kiss her kindly, and went to shake Harry's hand without any show of reluctance. They stood together now, with Uncle Clarence talking earnestly and her husband nodding his head at regular intervals.

Her husband. She wasn't Mrs. Wakefield anymore. She was Mrs. Rayburn. It was all so strange. When she'd married Elias, she'd been chiefly aware of an unnamed, nervous loneliness, this despite the fact that she was surrounded by her friends and relations.

Now she was surrounded by strangers, one of whom had just sworn to love, honor, and cherish her. Her only two relations present were trying to put the best possible face on it all. This time, though, she felt filled with warmth, excitement, daring, and relief, and, yes, gratitude, too. She was worried, but for the first time in a very great while, she felt poised at a fresh beginning. That sensation thrilled her almost as much as the heated glance Harry cast at her from across the room.

She was so intent on watching Harry she barely noticed when Genny came up to her to beckon her over into the chimney corner, one of the few quiet spots left in the inn.

"Now you're not to worry," Genny said. "I will look after everything at home until you get back." She meant it, too. This was Genny at her most determined.

"I won't be too very long."

"No, I don't expect so." Genny didn't say this to Leannah. She was looking at Harry, and her expression was distinctly uneasy.

"Genevieve." Leannah laid her hand over her sister's. Her throat felt unexpectedly tight and she had to strain to keep her words even. "You do understand why I'm doing this?"

"Not completely, but I do know you deserve any chance at happiness. I just hope Mr. Rayburn proves worthy, even for a little while."

"Surely the fact that he proposed marriage speaks well of his character?"

"Perhaps. But I can't help wondering . . ." Genny shook her head, and squeezed Leannah's fingers. Then, much to Leannah's relief, she smiled. The expression was faint, but it was genuine. "No. Considering how we came to be here, I won't start casting fresh glooms now. I trust you, Lea, and you have the best heart of anyone I know. This is a great deal for a sister to admit, so I hope you won't ask me to repeat it."

"I won't." Tears stung Leannah's eyes. "I promise."

"And I promise you'll have all the help I can give to make everything right."

They embraced then, and there was nothing faint about this gesture. Leannah felt her heart might burst from love and gratitude. She felt there were a thousand things she should say—explanations, promises, and apologies. But she didn't have the chance. At that moment, the door opened and Martin—smiling for the first time since their arrival—shouted that the carriage was ready.

The crowd cheered again and parted as far as it could to let Harry make his way across to her, and bow with a flourish.

"Mrs. Rayburn?" He held out his hand.

Leannah stepped away from Genny, and let Harry lay her arm over his. This occasioned another cheer and many more hoisted glasses. The whole crowd formed up behind them, a loud and merry escort to the barouche. Mr. Jessop himself opened the door, and bowed.

With exaggerated care and solicitude, Harry helped Leannah into the carriage. Gossip stamped uneasily and Rumor shook her head, making clear their opinions of crowds, late starts, and bridegrooms. Leannah wished she could climb up onto the box to take the reins, but her injured hands made that impossible. She bit her lip and reminded herself that Harry had already proved himself to be an able man around horses. She sat on all her cautions and suggestions as to how he should drive them, and instead asked, "Where are we going?"

"It's a surprise." Harry was making a great show of shaking out the driving rug and laying it across her lap. His hands brushed her legs and her hips as he wrapped the rough woolen covering about her and he certainly took his time smoothing out every wrinkle across her thighs and knees. The feeling of his hands caressing her, even through so many layers of cloth was enough to set her heart racing.

"Perhaps I don't like surprises," she replied, with a dignified lift of her chin as she arranged her shawl. Mrs. Jessop had given Leannah the thick woolen shawl she'd worn most of the night by way of a wedding present.

"Nonsense." This word was accompanied by a bold twinkle in Harry's steel blue eyes. In time, that twinkle was going to become either endearing or exasperating, possibly both.

"If you say something horridly conventional like 'all women like surprises,' I will slap your face," she informed him.

At this, Harry flashed her one of his magnificent, sunny smiles. A pang of need shot through Leannah. The twinkle might be neither here nor there, but the smile could bring her to her knees. She swallowed. On her knees with Harry suddenly seemed like an eminently desirable place to be.

"If you don't like surprises, it's only because you haven't had the right kind," he was saying. "It's on the list of things I mean to remedy in your life, Mrs. Rayburn."

"You've made a list?"

"Oh, yes." Harry climbed up on the box and let Martin hand him the reins. "I think you'll find me a very thorough and methodical man. Now, do sit back, my dear, relax, and let me take care of you a little."

Leannah did sit back, but the heat in Harry's eyes and in those words was going to make it impossible to relax.

"The bouquet!" shouted some stout woman from the crowd. "Come on, missus!"

She'd all but forgotten the little bundle of snowdrops. Leannah turned. The first face she saw among the small knot of women who had assembled among the men was Genny's. Her sister was trying to smile, but it was clearly still difficult for her. Worry touched Leannah. She aimed carefully, and tossed the flowers. For a heartbeat, she thought Genny might let them fall. But she did not. She caught them, and even raised them high. The women around her cheered and laughed. Genny met Leannah's gaze, and nodded.

Also not a rousing endorsement, but it would do for now.

The afternoon had turned fair and relatively warm. All around them the first haze of spring green lay on the fields, and if the wind was slightly chill as it rushed through her hair, it was filled with the sweet scent of warming earth.

Leannah was used to being a passenger, of course. London society frowned on women driving themselves. But she never let any hired driver take charge of Gossip and Rumor without distinct misgivings. The horses realized as soon as Harry took the reins they were in the hands of a stranger, and they were up to all manner of tricks—falling out of step, working their bits, bobbing about in the harness like half-broken colts. Several times, Leannah almost started to her feet, but she managed to hold herself in check. Since she could not drive, it was futile to shout suggestions from the seats like a nervous duenna in a hackney.

It helped that from the start Harry had demonstrated he was a patient man, and experienced with horses. He certainly proved this first impression to be correct now. He gave the team just enough play on the ribbons to let them think they were being allowed their own way. Seeing they were not to be constrained by inexpert or harsh hands, the matched grays fell back into what they loved best, which was to run. As the road was clear and the weather fine, Harry let them run.

But where were they running to? Leannah gripped the carriage rail and watched the passing countryside. The fields with their new greenery and pale rows of last year's stubble were giving way to clusters of cottages as the city walls came into view on the horizon. Her mind kept turning over possible destinations once they reached town. Did Harry have a house or rooms to take her to? Or did he mean to try to find them a hotel, or another inn, or even a coffeehouse? From this consideration, her idle thoughts turned to imagining Harry in each of the different settings.

In bachelor rooms she pictured him as sly, mischievous. He'd sit them together on a sofa. Then, he'd gather her close and whisper stories of all the exotic ways he'd learned to please women on his many travels. His knowing competent hands would work the tapes of her gown. He would peel the layers of muslin and cambric slowly from her body and set about demonstrating each pleasure, in his thorough and methodical fashion.

In a gentleman's house, he'd be courtly and correct, leaving her in her own room to get undressed. A silk wrapper would be laid out for her. After a suitable interval, he would come to her, and slowly undo the sash of that same wrapper. His eyes would light up when he saw she was entirely naked underneath.

Gossip and Rumor had run themselves long enough to tamp down their first reckless impulses, and permitted themselves be slowed to a brisk walk. A burst of impatience skittered through Leannah. She did not want them to slow. She could see nothing of Harry but his back, but that view showed her his broad shoulders, and did quite enough to remind her of how solid and strong he was, and how wicked and willing she'd felt in his arms. With such thoughts as companions, the ride already felt interminable. Whatever this mysterious destination was, she wanted them to be there now, this minute. She had fantasized long enough. She wanted this man—her husband—in her arms and under her hands.

Unfortunately, wanting and wishing did not shorten the road. By the time they made their way through the gates and into the streets of Westminster, twilight had already fallen. The winding streets were filled to the brim with carriages, coaches, vans, and chairs, all jostling for whatever space could be found. These were just the sort of conditions Gossip and Rumor hated, which did nothing to help their progress.

Leannah's heated imaginings had faded, but her restlessness had not. If anything, it grew worse, and far colder. While they had been on the highway, she'd felt separate from her life. Now they were back amid the walls and crowds of London. Anyone or anything might be approaching them, and they'd never see it coming.

She wondered where Uncle Clarence's ancient slow-coach was now, and how late it would be when he and Genny finally arrived back home. Had they remembered to send a letter ahead to Father or at least Mrs. Falwell, saying that all was right and that they were returning? Aunt Clarence was with Father, and she understood him, but what if he grew badly confused as he did sometimes, or fell into one of his black moods? Then there was Jeremy to be thought of. He could not be entirely trusted to sit patiently at home if word had reached him that an adventure was underway.

Leannah closed her eyes against the looming city. Shadows, smoke, and noise carried all her responsibilities back to her in one great bundle, to be delivered to Mrs. Wakefield. Those responsibilities had never heard of a Mrs. Rayburn. They had no notion such a person existed.

But I am Mrs. Rayburn, she told herself with as much firmness as she could manage. *It is signed and witnessed. It is done. It is real.*

She rested her head back against the seat and did not open her eyes. It was as if she thought to hide in her private darkness like a child hiding in the nursery, stubbornly believing that if she could not see, she could not be seen.

She stayed like that for a long time.

"Are you awake, Leannah? We've arrived."

Leannah's eyes flew open.

She must have fallen asleep. She hadn't felt the carriage halt, let alone noted that the neighborhood had changed from winding Westminster streets to a ruler-straight London avenue. Stone and brick houses that spoke of trade and wealth surrounded them, and a steady stream of richly appointed carriages flowed past.

Harry had drawn them to a halt in front of one of the stone buildings. Two wings of three stories each spread out to take up most of the block. Stone steps led up to an Italianate entranceway flanked by fluted columns. Rows of casement windows showed velvet curtains shimmering in the light of good fires and clean lamps.

"It's the Colonnade. A first-class establishment," Harry added, with a trace of anxiety in his voice. "We often lodge our business partners here, although I've never stayed myself."

Before she could answer, a small army of men and boys in scarlet livery emerged from the hotel, to take hold of bridles and reins, to hold aloft torches and set steps in place so Harry could alight without accidently muddying his boots in the gutter.

"It looks lovely," Leannah murmured, but not with the level of reassurance she hoped to muster. She felt suddenly and keenly aware of her appearance. During the day, her plain, disheveled dress and windblown hair might have been explained away, as could her lack of bonnet and gloves. But evening was filling up the streets. No woman of substance should be abroad unless she was cloaked, gowned, and jeweled.

"Don't worry," murmured Harry. He reached over the carriage door to take her hand and kiss the back, right on the edge of her bandages. "I told you, I'm known here. There will be no vulgar mistakes. You wait here for a minute, and I'll go see that my note made it through. It was brief, so there may be one or two details left to sort out."

But not even the lingering warmth of Harry's smile could loosen the knot in Leannah's chest. A gleaming carriage drew up behind hers. Two ladies emerged from the hotel and descended the broad stairs. The torchlight allowed her to clearly see their suspicious and disapproving glances. She tried to smooth her hair, but it was to no avail. Nothing was improved by the involuntary way she kept trying to calculate the cost of even a single room in this place, never mind the expense of a meal, and of stabling the horses, all of which had to be added up with the sum Harry had already paid out to rescue herself and Genevieve.

Genny only did this because she wanted to secure us the money her marriage to Mr. Dickenson would bring. Her speech to Uncle Clarence came ringing back. *If I marry Mr. Rayburn, we are taken care of and she's free to make a different choice, a better choice.*

At the time, she'd meant those words to convince him to conduct the ceremony and sign the license. Now, enlarged and echoing, they sounded like the calculations of a gazetted fortune hunter. Or something much worse.

I can't go through with this. Panic descended and Leannah clenched her cold hand around the gold and diamond band on her little finger. The bit of jewelry had taken on the weight of an iron fetter. *It was an awful, selfish idea. I won't do this to him, or to myself. I'll tell him it was a mistake. I'll thank him for going through with the ceremony in order to get Genevieve back home, and I'll leave him here. I'll tell Genevieve . . . something. Something will occur to me. There's surely been no time for scandal to erupt yet. We'll work out what to say. Almost anything will be more believable than the truth.*

"Why, Mrs. Wakefield!" cried a woman's voice. "I was certain that was you!"

Oh, no. With the slow, syrupy sensation of impending doom that took hold in the worst of nightmares, Leannah turned. A closed carriage had halted alongside her barouche and a mature woman leaned out the window. Torchlight gleamed on her plum velvet cloak and the half a shop's worth of jewels that glittered in her dark hair. *Not Dorothea Plaice.*

If there was a greater and more persistent gossip of her acquaintance than Miss Plaice, Leannah could not think of her name, or his. A permanent and unusually wealthy spinster, Dorothea had helped raise her flock of nieces and nephews.

This seemed to have given her a particular taste for knowing and managing everyone else's business.

"I'm so glad we've met!" cried Dorothea before Leannah even had a chance to say good evening. "I heard the most dreadful rumor at Mrs. Ibbotson's this morning. Now you can absolutely contradict it."

There was no hope at all this rumor could be something small, like the price of a gown, or Mrs. Spinnaker patronizing yet another young painter. *Nothing to do but face it out.* Leannah rallied nerve and sense. "I'd be glad to contradict it if I can, Miss Plaice. What is this rumor?"

"Why that little Genevieve eloped yesterday! Mrs. Ibbotson said she heard it from her maid, who heard it from her cousin . . . well, never mind the daisy chain." She waved it all away with a wild flutter of silk-gloved hands. "The point is, if Genevieve had eloped, you would not be sitting here so calmly." She paused, and seemed for the first time to take in the state of Leannah's dress and general appearance. "Would you?" she concluded rather more sharply.

But Leannah never spoke her answer, because just then Harry trotted down the hotel steps.

"Everything is ready for us and . . . I beg your pardon. I didn't mean to interrupt." He bowed to Miss Plaice.

"I'm sure you did not," Dorothea replied somewhat frostily, drawing herself back inside her carriage. "But I don't believe I've had the privilege of your acquaintance, sir."

Leannah took a deep breath. For a heartbeat, she met Harry's gaze. She saw there a moment of fear and she understood it. *He's waiting to see if I will deny him.*

"Miss Dorothea Plaice, may I introduce Mr. Harry Rayburn. My husband."

"Husband!"

Leannah allowed herself a small measure of satisfaction at having made Dorothea's jaw quite literally drop.

"Delighted to make your acquaintance, Miss Plaice." Harry maintained an air of perfect aplomb as he bowed.

"You see, Genevieve isn't married," Leannah told her. "I am."

"Well!" Miss Plaice pressed her hand to her generous bosom. "I am astonished beyond measure. I do beg your pardon, Mr. Rayburn." She bobbed her head. "And do please let me wish you very happy. But it is all so sudden! Everyone is so very fond of Mrs. Wake . . . Mrs. Rayburn I suppose I must say now. There is not one of her acquaintance who has not longed to see her comfortably settled."

"But you thought perhaps there would be rather more warning of that highly desirable event?" said Harry smoothly. "I do understand. But we wished the thing to be done quietly."

"Yes, yes of course. Very prudent, I'm sure." Miss Plaice's eyes narrowed as she began sorting through her copious memory for every little detail it held of Leannah's past.

"So, you will contradict that rumor for Mrs. Ibbotson?" said Leannah, striving to match Harry's matter-of-fact air.

"Oh, I will. I most certainly will!" From the way she said it, Leannah suspected that she would be on her way to meet that lady immediately, never mind that it was well past the hour for paying calls.

They said their farewells and received another hasty offer of congratulations before Miss Plaice signaled her driver to touch up the horses.

"And that's the end of that," sighed Leannah as the carriage pulled away.

"The end of what exactly?" Harry motioned to one of the linkboys to position the step so he could help Leannah down from the carriage.

"Any chance at keeping us a secret. The whole city will know before breakfast tomorrow."

This revelation failed to cause Harry to so much as blink. "Well, then there's no bar to us taking the rooms I've arranged. Mrs. Rayburn?" He held out his elbow, and Leannah, with mingled feelings of relief and wonder, laid her arm upon his to be conducted up the stairs and into the glittering hotel.

Sixteen

❧

"Welcome to the Colonnade, Mrs. Rayburn." A gentleman in dark coat and trousers stepped smartly up to Harry and Leannah, followed by a woman of middle years in a neat black gown and white apron.

"This is Marshall," Harry told her as the man bowed. "He'll be looking after us, and this is Lewis." The maid curtsied. "She'll attend you until your own maid can arrive."

That she had no maid and hadn't for over a year was not something Leannah felt needed to be mentioned in the public lobby, especially one with so much marble and gilt gleaming in its golden lamplight. *It's a dream. It must be.* She had thought such establishments belonged exclusively to her past.

"We'll see the rooms now," Harry went on.

As they crossed the mosaicked floor, Leannah felt her attitude alter; spine and shoulders straightened, chin lifted. Her stride smoothed and her face settled into an air of quiet pleasure and dignity. Leannah's education had been as erratic as the family fortunes, but when there had been money, Father had engaged the best available governesses so that both she and Genny could be schooled in the arts of dancing, deportment, and dress.

No one's going to be able to find a speck of fault with my daughters, Father declared repeatedly. *Morehouses are fit for any and all society, however grand.*

At the time, she hadn't known how helpful it was to his own plans to have his daughters proclaimed as perfectly well-bred and ladylike. Whatever the initial reasons for it, all that training came back to her now. By the time they reached the sweeping marble and mahogany staircase, her whole air proclaimed that she was familiar with such surroundings and comfortable in them. She felt Harry's approval of her. It showed in the way he held her arm as they followed Marshall up the staircase and the way he kept his stride so steady. He did not try to hurry or hide her. As far as he was concerned, there was nothing wrong. Both of them belonged right where they were. That air of confidence from him made keeping her own countenance that much easier.

As it transpired, Harry had not engaged a single room, but rather an entire suite on the first floor, where a hotel's best rooms were most generally kept. Marshall threw open the doors to a lovely sitting room. The walls had been papered in pale blue silk. Turkish carpets covered gleaming floorboards and plaster rosettes decorated the ceiling. A fire burned in the spotless marble hearth and the whole place was supplied with all manner of comfortable furniture, including a pair of deep armchairs drawn up before the hearth. The rich blue velvet curtains had been drawn across the windows to shut out the night and prying eyes.

"If you'll follow me, madam," said the maid, Lewis, "I'll show you your room."

"Her" room proved to be every bit as delightful as the other. Like the sitting room, it was decorated in shades of blue and cream. The four-poster bed was hung with white lace and covered with white comforters and thick bolsters. A dressing room and closet waited to one side, and all the furnishings spoke to comfort and convenience.

"Yes, this will do very well," she told the maid calmly. What she really wanted to do was turn in place and clap her hands in delight, like some young miss fresh from the country. "If you'll wait a moment, Lewis, I have a letter I need delivered."

The room was of course supplied with a writing desk, paper, quill, and ink. Leannah scribbled a hasty note telling Genevieve she had arrived, and where she was staying. She told herself there would not be any emergency. Despite her recent behavior, Genny was not really flighty. She would look after matters at the house, and their aunt and uncle would be on hand to help. All would be well for one more night. She was not being thoughtless or careless. She must not give into guilt for having caused her family trouble. She could have this one night.

Leannah sealed the letter with one of the wafers in the desk drawer, wrote the direction, and handed it to Lewis, who curtsied and left to see to its delivery. Out in the sitting room, she heard the sound of Harry dictating instructions to Marshall. Leannah stayed where she was. She could not have said exactly why, but neither could she make herself walk out to the sitting room. Instead, she sank into one of the armchairs by the fire. She needed this moment, just to breathe, and to assure herself that this lovely room would not vanish if she blinked.

Out in the main room, a door opened and then closed. She turned her head in time to see Harry walk up to the threshold of her chamber, and stop.

"Is everything all right?" he asked.

"Yes. I just needed to write to Genny, so she knows where we're staying in case anything unexpected arises. I hope you don't mind."

"Not at all. I wrote my family from the inn. Do you like the room?" Harry didn't seem to know what to do with his hands. He put them behind his back, and then in his pockets, and then folded his arms, and then stuffed his hands back in his pockets. Leannah felt herself smile. She sympathized with his uncertainty. There was no accepted form of courtesy to govern their situation. Also, she couldn't help noting the fidgets made him look endearingly youthful.

This caused a whole series of new thoughts to cascade through her mind. "Oh!"

"What is it?" Harry pulled his hands out of his pockets as if he thought he might have to catch something.

"I'm sorry." Leannah smothered her startled giggle. "It's just . . . I realized I don't know how old you are."

"Twenty-eight," he answered promptly. "I hope that will suit? If not, it will be changing on the thirtieth of January."

"It will suit admirably. And the room is perfect." She paused. "Are you going to ask my age?"

Harry drew himself up in a great show of being affronted. "You will find, madam, that your husband is the soul of discretion," he told her stiffly. "With him, you will always be ageless, and any bonnet that arrives from the milliner will suit you perfectly."

"How terribly discerning of me to have chosen such a man."

"Yes, it does speak very well of your sound judgment and inherent good taste."

It occurred to Leannah that Harry was waiting for her to invite him in. He wasn't going to enter a lady's room without her permission, even when he had just married her. It was at once absurdly correct and completely charming.

She held out her hand to him, and she knew she did not imagine the look of his relief as he crossed the threshold to take it, and to bend to kiss it. A soft sigh of warmth travelled through her. They were alone again. No one could wonder at them, or remark on anything they did, and there were so many things she wanted to do.

"I'm twenty-five," she told him, mostly to see how he responded.

Harry's response turned out to be a surprisingly self-satisfied little smile. "I thought you might be."

"Are you going to be one of those tiresome men who is always right?"

"Would that bother you?"

"I'm afraid it would, yes."

"Then I shall endeavor to be wrong at certain discreet intervals." His brow furrowed in mock consideration. "Mind you, it will take some time to form the habit. I may have to start with small matters."

"But not the bonnets."

"Never the bonnets."

Silence fell, and as she watched, the humor in Harry's eyes turned to tenderness. Slowly, with that curious grace he possessed, he went down onto one knee before her.

"Leannah." He laid his palm against her cheek. She closed her eyes and leaned into his touch. "Beautiful Leannah."

There were a thousand things she should say. Explanations still needed to be offered, reasons and rationalities exchanged. Plans must be made. But Harry was raising her to her feet so they stood face-to-face, almost toe-to-toe. He held her wrists, being careful of her bandaged hands. Leannah felt the delicious sense of dreamlike suspension beckon, just as it had in the moonlight. She might be back in London, but real life was shut firmly outside these rooms. Here, there were none to disapprove or make new demands on her. There was only Harry. This marriage, this man, could still prove themselves nothing but a dream, but it was her dream. For this little space of time, she could be Mrs. Rayburn, and Mrs. Rayburn could do as she pleased with her husband.

Leannah stepped forward. She lifted herself up onto her toes. Harry held himself still, letting her come to him. She brushed her lips against his. The soft sensation sent sparks dancing across her skin. She touched his curling hair, his stubbled chin. His scent of leather, sweat, and country air trickled into her blood and brain along with the warmth of his body. The combination worked on her like a drug, leaving her body lax and heavy with desire.

She moved a tiny step closer.

Harry wrapped his arms around her, drawing her the rest of the way to him. Every inch of his solid body pressed against her. He lowered his head. His mouth brushed her ear, then her throat, and her shoulder. The sensation was at once feather light and bone deep and sent a fresh murmur of desire loose in her blood.

"Now." Harry lifted her trailing curls aside and kissed her neck once more. "I expect you'll want to get out of these things." He ran his palm down her sleeve. "You can't be comfortable."

She made herself blink, and draw back the tiniest bit. "But I've nothing to change into."

"Oh, dear." Harry's fingers traced her neckline thoughtfully. "And I thought I'd taken care of everything."

"I believe that you did." He moved his fingers to caress her collarbone, and Leannah could not help but sigh. "Except perhaps one point."

"Oh?" He was kissing her throat again, and her shoulder.

"I've sent the maid away. You'll have to help me undress."

She expected him to smile, and return another quip, but instead, Harry grew grave. Still keeping one arm firmly about her waist, he smoothed back the strands of hair that had come loose from her pins and let them trail through his fingers. He watched the light elf locks drift down against her cheek. His face though, remained so serious that she could not tell if he was pleased by what he saw.

Doubt threatened. "Harry?" she breathed.

She got no further. His mouth covered hers, and Leannah leaned at once into his kiss. Kisses, for there were many more than one. He tasted the corners of her mouth and traced the shape of her lips with his tongue. He took her lower lip between his teeth and tugged ever so delicately. It was surprising, it was playful and delightful, and the best part was there was no hurry. They could take this time. They could do whatever they wanted. Nothing was forbidden here.

Leannah brushed her bandaged palms across his chest, reveling in the breadth and hardness of it. She ran them up his solid arms and around his shoulders, all the while matching each one of his kisses. The taste of him, the heat of him, it was rich and complex. Each sensation woke her senses to anticipation, acceptance, and to the sheer enjoyment of this man and his touch.

Her hand stole up the back of his head and she knotted her fingers into his curling hair, to hold him still and close so she could take his lip between her teeth. Harry permitted this, for a moment, but then he grasped her wrist.

"Ah-ah," he breathed. "You're still hurt, remember? We must be careful with you."

Her free hand rested against his chest, and now it curled into a fist. "I don't want to be careful."

"But I do." Harry's voice deepened and his blue eyes grew dark, almost dangerous. "I want to be very careful and very thorough." He kissed her jaw, her cheek. His mouth found the delicate flesh of her earlobe and kissed her there. "I want to show you how very much I desire you, and your pleasure." He whispered this directly into her ear so she could feel each movement of his lips as he shaped the words. "Say yes, Lean-nah." He turned his hand, and let his knuckles glide slowly down her throat to her shoulder. "Say yes to me."

What had begun as a sharp thrill broadened and deepened, becoming a dark heat that filled her. Leannah felt the last of her strength flee. She could not resist this man, and what was more, she did not want to.

"Yes, Harry."

Seventeen

❧

"Yes," she breathed again, and the word itself felt lush and rich in her mouth.

"Good."

He was backing her up, just like he had in the darkness outside the inn. Keeping hold of her wrists, he steered her where he wanted her to go, turning his body gently with each step so his chest and hips swayed sensuously against hers. This time, though, instead of moonlight, there was the warm flicker of the room's fire and instead of a hard wall behind her, there was the bed.

Harry didn't lay her down, at least not immediately. He wrapped her in his embrace again, and lavished her with warm, deep, inviting kisses. She did not struggle against his grip on her wrists. It felt too good to relax in his arms and let herself be kissed this way. His hands moved up her back, and busied themselves with tapes and hooks until she felt the fabric loosen and fall open.

"You've done this before," she said in mock accusation as Harry's mouth moved from hers to kiss the line of her jaw, her throat, her freshly exposed shoulder.

"Mmm," he agreed without any sign of shame or regret. "And the experience is proving most useful." He pressed her dress farther open, sliding the sleeves off her arms, and letting the bodice fall to her waist. He ran his hands firmly, deliberately down her sides, all the way to her hips, pushing the excess fabric of her plain blue dress down and away, until it dropped into a heap around her ankles.

Now she stood before him in corset, shift, and stockings. He gazed at her, boldly, openly coveting all he saw of her form and flesh. Leannah felt a blush that had nothing at all to do with shame rise up from her breasts to color her throat and cheeks.

Harry slid his hands back up her sides and over her shoulders. He speared them into her hair. Patiently, he sought out her pins. Leannah's breath grew harsh and ragged. The sensation of his fingers against her scalp, combing through her hair was maddening. Her center tightened and she felt her thighs growing damp. She made herself look into his eyes, to see the lust and need he held in such tight control as he plucked her pins free so her tresses could tumble loosely down her breasts and back. Leannah pressed one hand against his hip. With the other she reached up and pulled out the last pin, letting it drop onto the floor to join her discarded dress.

Harry sucked in a sharp breath as the last of her curls cascaded down.

"Yes," he breathed. "This is how I've wanted to see you from the first."

The warmth he kindled at her core intensified. Leannah welcomed it. She liked standing in front of him, bared in this way. She wanted more. She wanted to be rid of shift and corset. She wanted him to be free of coat and shirt and crumpled cravat, all of it. She could see the shape of his arousal beneath his breeches, and she wanted to see it in truth. She needed this. She needed him.

Harry settled both hands on her shoulders and pressed down, urging Leannah to sit on the bed.

"You'll have to give me a moment, my dear."

"What for?" The words came out as uncomfortably close to a pout, but the smile Harry turned on her was worth it.

"My dear Leannah, there is no clever or amusing way to do this, but I've got to get these blasted boots off."

"Let me . . ." she began, but stopped, remembering her own hands at the last minute.

"Don't worry," he said as he sat on the bed beside her. "We'll have years to undress each other."

Will we? She let her fingers graze his shoulder, and his arm. *Or will it just be this once?*

It doesn't matter, she answered herself. *If it is to be just this once, then let it last, let it burn as brightly as we can make it.*

Leannah knew men who were as vain about their boots as any woman about her ball gown. Harry did not appear to be one of them. After several moments of hard, undignified tugging, and several muffled curses, he tossed the boots aside, closed his eyes, and stretched his legs out with a relieved sigh.

"You're not used to Hessians, are you?"

"Never wear the things if I can at all avoid it." Harry opened one eye to peek at her. "Not disappointed, I hope?"

"No, and if you'd had your toes stepped on as much as I have, you'd understand why."

He laughed. "I trust you won't mind if I also discard coat and cravat?"

Leannah shook her head, and Harry suited actions to his words. She felt herself staring. An unfamiliar sensation rose in her as he doffed his burgundy coat, and unwound the strip of linen that secured his collar. It was a species of hot hunger, and it made the desire they'd shared at the Three Swans seem a fleeting, paltry thing. That need had made her weak, this hunger made her fierce.

He was removing his collar now, and undoing his shirt laces, providing her with a tantalizing glimpse of his chest. The skin there was bronzed, just as it was on his face and hands. She had been right. Harry did strip down and expose himself to the elements, and the gaze of the world. Leannah had a sudden vision of him in a summer meadow, wearing nothing but a pair of thin breeches. A wave of dizziness swept through her. She was starving for his touch and for his naked body. Her hands itched to hold him, to show him that he was not the only one with a knowledge of intimacy.

Harry met her gaze, and he had the nerve to smile at her as he unbuttoned his waistcoat, and laid it on the chair with his other discarded garments.

Considering how unceremoniously they had just dropped her clothing on the floor, this really was the limit.

"Does Mr. Rayburn intend to finish his toilette sometime today?" she inquired.

"Oh-ho, is this pique I'm hearing?" Harry arched his dark brows. "Does Mrs. Rayburn perhaps wish to register a complaint?"

"Certainly not." She folded her hands primly in her lap. "But if Mr. Rayburn is feeling in some way unready . . ."

"*Unready?*"

"Oh, dear." Leannah blinked up at him. "Was that indiscreet?"

He advanced on her. Leannah did not let herself shrink back, or allow the placid mask of her expression to shift. He grabbed hold of her wrists and leaned her back, bearing her down against the mattress, kissing her all the while. There was nothing slow or languorous about this kiss. He crushed his mouth against hers, taking charge without hesitation or permission. He pressed his knees against hers until her legs opened and he could step between them. He kept kissing her as he raised her arms over her head. When she was positioned as he wanted her, he pressed his forearms against the counterpane on either side of her head. He rubbed himself against her, hard. She gasped as the ridge of his erection ground against her damp folds. It was a rough, rude gesture, and it was exactly what she wanted.

"Do I feel unready to you?" he growled.

Leannah made herself roll her eyes. Where did this impish willingness to play come from? Under Harry's sensuous attentions, she was turning into someone quite new—an impulsive woman, unafraid of the most daring sort of games. "I don't know," she drawled slowly. "Perhaps if I could see some *evidence* . . ."

"You little minx." He spoke the words with a burst of surprised laughter. "Very well. Since you see fit to doubt your lawful husband, I shall have to teach you a lesson."

He seized her, and in one swift motion, flipped her over so she was facedown on the counterpane. The suddenness of it made Leannah squeak, and he snickered. She struggled, but he had her wrists again and was pressing them down firmly against the shifting feather mattress.

"Oh, no. You stay just as I have placed you, or I shall have to tie you down."

"You wouldn't." She'd meant to sound outraged, but it was difficult with the covers muffling her voice.

"With much less provocation than you are currently offering." He ran his hands down her back to her corset laces, and she sighed as she felt him work the knots. His legs pressed between hers again, and she sprawled open, indecent and inelegant. He leaned close over her, lifting and pulling until her corset opened and he could draw it out from around her belly. The absence of boning and lacing allowed her to breathe freely, to stretch and writhe, and while she might still be facedown, she knew Harry watched every motion.

"Wicked woman," he whispered and grabbed up handfuls of her shift, bunching it up, to expose her thighs and derriere to his view. His hands closed possessively around her, pressing and working her so that the covers slid provocatively underneath her bared skin, adding a fresh sensation to his exciting, indecent caress. "You should be spanked for your impudence." He ran his hand slowly around the curve of her buttock. "But that's for later." There was a rustle of cloth behind her. "Turn over. Let me see you."

She did turn over. Harry had discarded his shirt, and stood before her naked to the waist. He stripped magnificently. A light dusting of golden hair decorated the sculpted planes of his chest. But the sun bronze highlighted the starburst of white at his waist, and a long, thin line down his right arm. From this angle she could clearly see the shape of his erection. Impatience filled her. He was taking his time, enjoying his mischief, and making her wait. She didn't want to wait. She had waited for him long enough, for years, for her entire life. She lifted herself onto her elbows and opened her mouth to make her own demands. He must strip the remainder of his rumpled clothing away, and he must hurry.

But Harry was already busy with his breeches fly. She sucked in a hissing breath as he shoved the unneeded garments down and kicked them away to stand before her, entirely naked and entirely magnificent. His member stood tall and proud against his taut belly and Leannah felt her mouth watering at the sight of it. Heat and anticipation tightened her center unbearably, and her legs fell open of their own accord. She longed to touch him and stroke him and take him into her. She hated her shift. She wanted to be as bare and unashamed for him as he now was for her.

Harry advanced, slowly. Leannah laughed and scooted backward in mock alarm until she was pressed against the bolsters. Harry climbed onto the bed, on his hands and knees. There was nowhere to go, no escape, even if she'd wanted one. He lunged forward, caught her around the waist and rolled, bringing them together so he could grasp her breast through the soft cambric of her shift. Leannah moaned and arched her back, forcing her aching nipple against his palm.

"Yes, like that, Leannah. It feels good, doesn't it?" He rolled them again, pressing her back against the mattress so he could straddle her, capturing her thighs between his.

He had her arms, and raised them over her head, crossing the wrists just as he had the night before. "Now, you stay like that," he said. "Or I will have to be very stern with you." Before she could protest, he had her breasts in both his hands, and his calloused, clever fingers found her ruched nipples and began at once to pinch and play.

"Oh, yes." Her hips writhed, but he did not loosen his thighs at all. The burning confinement forced her legs to rub together, and that raised her desire as surely as if she'd been using her hand. Combined with his plumping and petting of her breasts, the feeling was entirely decadent. "Yes."

She couldn't stand to be still anymore. She must touch him. This heat, this need, would kill her if she did not. Mindful of his care of her hands, she chafed his arms with her wrists, reveling in the strong shape of them. He allowed it, and it was wonderful. Harry gathered up the wrinkled cloth of her shift, and drew it over her head. She was fairly certain she heard fabric rip, but she didn't care. She looped her wrists around his neck. He let her draw him down without protest, to kiss her and lay the whole of himself against her. This was what she wanted. His warm chest, his belly, hips, thighs, all pressed tight against her and it was wonderful. His hands caressed her back and sides, as hungry for her touch as she was for his. His member rubbed against her damp curls and the hot pleasure of it filled her, driving out breath and thought, and all other feeling.

He slid down her, kissing her shoulders and the swell of her breasts. He gathered both tightly and closely into his knowing hands. His tongue darted out to curl around her hot nipple, drawing another low moan from her throat. He tasted, he lapped, he sucked, and, gently, he nipped. The play was driving her into a divine madness. She could not touch him with her hands, but she could wrap her thighs around him and pull him against her. She could rub and writhe and urge him on. His body was hard and smooth against her softer flesh. She ran her heels down the back of his legs. She arched her hips, moving, adjusting until his shaft fitted into her slick folds. She wanted him inside her. She wanted to know how he would fill her, how he would feel when she tightened her core around him.

"Patience, Leannah." Harry nuzzled her wickedly. "You will have what you want. I swear it."

"Now, Harry." She arched her hips again, circling them against him. Oh, it felt good, but it was not enough.

His hand slid down her belly and lower. He cupped her curls, stroking and fondling her until she cried out and pressed into his hand.

"Yes," he hissed and his fingers slipped between her drenched folds. "You're very wet aren't you? You're ready for me."

"Yes," she cried. "Now!"

His hard fingertips ran up and down her folds again, stroking, exploring, enticing. He found her entrance and dipped inside. Pleasure suffused her and she felt herself opening wider for him. "Please, Harry."

"Well, since you ask so nicely . . ." His fingers withdrew, but before she had a moment to regret the absence, the blunt tip of his member pressed through her curls. Leannah arched her hips, opening, adjusting her own position so she could meet him. Even as she did, she knew a sliver of doubt. It had been over two years since she'd lain down with a man. Harry was much bigger than Elias had been, and much stronger. She wanted this with every part of her, but was she strong enough to take him in? Would he even *fit*?

But he was kissing her again, long, slow, languorous kisses. Thought retreated, and took uncertainty with it. Her body, it seemed, knew exactly how to accept him. Her inner folds, swollen with lust and want, loosened and opened. He took his weight on his elbows, and yet still managed to cup her breast in his hard hand. Fresh delight sang in her and she opened farther.

Slowly, determinedly, Harry's shaft sank into her heat. It felt too good. Her core tightened around him, as if her body had been starved, and now must take him all at once.

"Yes, Leannah," he gasped. "Oh, God, yes."

Power filled her in a rush as heady as all the other pleasures. Leannah wrapped her calves around his legs. She thrust her hips upward and that abrupt motion seated him entirely inside her. Harry gasped and Leannah grinned.

"Wicked. Wanton," he moaned.

"You have only yourself to blame . . ." She shimmied her hips under him and entirely forgot what she meant to say after that. It felt too good. He felt too good. She must have more. Her body tightened again, greedy, demanding, and so very ready for the pleasure he could bring.

Apparently aware she had reached a limit, Harry began to move. He pressed his hands on the mattress on either side of her head, holding himself on straightened arms. He gazed down on her, his eyes darkened with need, but strangely clear. He was here with her in this moment of pleasure and desire that was theirs alone.

Harry began to move. He thrust, slowly at first, making sure of her. She answered him, pressing her hips tight against his, using her legs to pull him close and hold him so he must fight her to move at all. She wanted him to feel her strength, as she felt his. Her own doubts had vanished. She had taken him in, and she knew her own power now. Harry must be made to realize she was his match, and more. He must know there was no need for restraint.

Not that he was showing much. His thrusts grew harder, deeper, driven by her urging, and his own need. His breathing was ragged and his skin glistened with sweat. He felt so good, so right inside her. Heat and pleasure filled her to the brim as he pressed and held her, sinking so deeply into her that his balls pressed against her folds and his weight crushed her back into the feather mattress.

It was too much. There was no more room for pleasure in

her body. She felt the first tentative, trembling waves of her climax.

"Yes, yes!" cried Harry. "Yes, come for me, Leannah!"

That heated command tipped her over the edge, and set her sliding down into those hot, honeyed waves. She cried out as the pleasure washed her beyond desire, beyond thought. Harry's thrusts grew frantic and her pleasure dragged him after her. She felt the throb of his climax echoing and brightening hers, heard his own shout of pleasure and release.

Slowly, the waves subsided. Harry's elbows buckled and he sank on top of her, gathering her to him, rolling them over once more, so he could cradle her body against his. Leannah sighed and snuggled close. Slowly, the warmth and relaxation took her, and Leannah drifted away into sleep.

Eighteen

There followed a long, timeless space of peace and darkness. Leannah drifted in and out of awareness. At one point, she felt herself being bundled into quilts and comforters. She swatted lazily at the hands that smoothed down her hair. She was so tired, and the pleasures Harry had so shamelessly bestowed had relaxed her so deliciously, that the only desire remaining in her was for sleep.

Slowly, however, several sensations dragged her reluctantly back into the waking world. The first was that her derriere and the backs of her thighs were cold. The second was that something important was missing from the bed, although she could not at the moment think what it might be.

The third was that she was unbelievably hungry, and she smelled bacon.

It was only then she realized what was missing. Harry was not beside her anymore.

Leannah scrambled to sit upright and push her hair back from her face. The room was awash with a gray twilight, but that was only because the drapes were still closed. The bright glow of watery daylight streamed around and under the closed curtains.

Clearly, she had slept through the night and well into morning. Leannah knuckled the sleep from her eyes. The chamber door was shut, but through the gap by the floor, she saw more light flicker. She kicked away the covers and got to her feet.

The fire in here had died. The chill air raised gooseflesh on every inch of her, reminding Leannah she had no wrapper, or nightdress, or anything else to wear.

There was a knock at the door.

"Leannah?" called Harry. "Are you awake?"

"Yes," she answered, looking around for something to cover herself with. Not that she was ashamed, not really. She was cold, and, if she was to admit it, an absurd sort of bashful uncertainty was creeping up her arms along with the gooseflesh. Now that he was no longer looking at her through desire's lens, what would Harry see when that door opened? She'd heard tales of ladies who engaged in passionate nights only to be profoundly disappointed with the man who they woke up beside. Some of these stories had been from the ladies themselves. She also knew the men could be disappointed just as easily, and just as frequently.

What did Harry feel about what had passed between them? Her own need had taken a near savage hold, driving out propriety or hesitation. She'd never felt anything like it. She was used to polite consideration from her partner, a swift completion of the act and a leave-taking that carried the feel of an apology. Not like this. Nothing like this.

"May I come in?" asked Harry.

"Yes." Leannah found herself crossing and uncrossing her arms, absurdly uncertain what to do with herself—just as Harry had been yesterday.

Harry opened the door. He wore a dressing gown of gray silk, and carried a bundle of claret satin slung over his arm. When he saw her there, he stopped dead. Leannah blushed, brightly and instantly. She turned to retreat to the bed.

"Don't," said Harry. "Please. There's no need."

"I'm cold." The words sounded exactly like what they were; a feeble excuse. Without their passion, she felt awkward—all knees and elbows and sagging breasts.

"I thought you might be. I brought this." He held up a wrapper of claret brocade with cream lace at the cuffs and hem. When she didn't shy away, Harry stepped forward. She turned, and let him help her into the gown. He closed it tenderly across her, bringing the sash up around her waist and tying it in a neat bow. The ease with which he folded his arms around her dimmed Leannah's worries. She could feel the entire hard length of his body at her back. A host of warm tremors rippled through her.

Harry gathered the entirely disheveled spill of her tresses, drew them out from under the wrapper, and spread the untidy mane across her shoulders.

"I love your hair," he murmured. "A thousand strands of silk."

"Hopelessly tangled silk." Leannah laughed. "It'll take a year with a brush to get it set to rights."

Harry settled his hands on her arms. "I could help." He planted a playful kiss on her ear. "In fact, I think I'd like to help."

"If you helped, I have a feeling it might take two years." He was nuzzling her cheek, and her neck. His hands caressed her arms possessively.

"So, it will take two years. I'll make sure you enjoy them."

She sighed, and relaxed backward. Harry cradled her, rocking them back and forth together in a motion that was provocative and yet sweetly soothing. His warmth embraced her as securely as his arms did. Lazy pleasure unfurled inside her. Unfortunately, her stomach chose that moment to emit a most undignified rumble.

Harry laughed. "Yes, I feel the same." He ran his palm across her belly. "Fortunately, precautions have been taken." He released her so that he could bow and gesture toward the sitting room. "If Mrs. Rayburn would care to follow me into breakfast?"

Leannah felt her cheeks blanch. Mrs. Rayburn. It was morning, and she was still Mrs. Rayburn. That was all very well and good. But it was also true that the world still waited right outside the doors, and those doors could not possibly remain closed for much longer.

"Did I say something wrong?"

"No." Leannah shook herself. "I'm sorry, and I'm famished. Please lead the way to breakfast."

Harry bestowed an uncomfortably thoughtful look on her, but said nothing more.

A round table laid for two had been set before the sitting room fireplace and a lavish breakfast now graced the sideboard. Covered dishes held poached eggs in hollandaise sauce, mutton chops, and cold ham, as well as the rashers of bacon that had smelled so enticing. There were fish croquettes with a boat of their own sauce, stewed greens, conserved fruits, cold rolls, and plum cake still warm from the oven. Of course there was a pot of tea, but there was also one of chocolate and another of coffee.

Leannah stared at the acre of food, and then turned to stare at Harry. He blushed.

"I don't know your tastes yet. I wanted to be sure there was something you'd like."

"I've married a profligate! I shall be quite spoiled before the week is out."

"Good." Satisfaction filled the word. In answer, Leannah felt an odd contraction that she couldn't quite put a name to. "Please, do help yourself."

Leannah made up her mind to enjoy a hearty meal. She truly was famished, and now that their wicked wedding night had passed, there was certain to be a very long day ahead. Also, the hopeful look in Harry's eyes warned her he would be made anxious if she did not fully partake of his breakfast.

She helped herself to croquettes and bacon, rolls, fruit, and tea. Harry pulled out her chair and saw her settled at her place before he loaded his own plate with chops, ham, eggs, and cake. He favored coffee over tea first thing in the morning and drank it hot and black. A habit, Leannah thought with something perilously close to wifely indulgence, he must have picked up in travels to barbaric foreign parts.

The food was excellent, and any lingering reluctance Leannah might have felt melted away as she tucked in. She did glance several times at Harry. A woman was expected to eat sparingly in public, to demonstrate her native delicacy and the care she took of her figure. But Harry did not appear at all taken aback at her appetite. In fact, he seemed quite pleased at her evident enjoyment of this morning feast he had arranged.

Which raised a question. "Whom do I have to thank for my dressing gown?" Leannah asked.

"Well," said Harry around a mouthful of ham. "I did say one of the reasons I chose the Colonnade was because they know me here. It was also because I know that some persons keep permanent rooms here. I had a word with Marshall, and it seems that at least one such gentleman is out of town at this time, so we might safely borrow a few necessaries for one night."

Leannah let all this unspool in her mind. "You bribed the maître d'hôtel to rifle some other gentleman's rooms, and what I am now wearing belongs to his mistress."

Harry looked pained. "I'll have you know, madam, I went through a lot of trouble not to put it like that."

"Well, one of you has excellent taste."

"Actually, I think Lewis made the selection." He sipped his coffee and eyed her thoughtfully. "Frankly, I would have rather you remained entirely naked, but I was concerned you might take a chill."

Leannah laughed, even as she felt herself blush. She could all too easily picture herself lounging quite nude on a chair or sofa for Harry's delectation. She'd enjoy it, and if she asked, she was sure he'd return the favor. She was equally sure she'd enjoy that at least as much. She'd barely had any chance to look at him last night before their passions carried them quite away.

"You are a wicked man, Mr. Rayburn."

"You provoke a man to wickedness, Mrs. Rayburn."

Leannah stopped. There it was again. Her thoughts would not settle. She was looking on this man with a burning desire. She was already dreaming of new and intensely erotic sport to enjoy with him. But every time he brought up her new name, it fell on her like a splash of icy water.

"Leannah," said Harry seriously. "Are you having second thoughts?"

"No," she answered quickly. "Not really. I just . . . I'm not sure what happens next."

"Neither am I."

Leannah frowned and pushed the remains of her bacon around her plate. This seemed a waste of good food, so she speared the last of her rasher with her fork and nibbled at it. She did all this without looking up. She could feel Harry watching her, and the tension growing between them was anything but warm. It was embarrassing. It was ridiculous. She had always prided herself on being able to act decisively no matter what the situation. Now, she couldn't even look at her lover.

This must end. She set her fork down and raised her eyes.

"Well, we are both going to have to go home," she said. "With Dorothea Plaice on the scent, the whole world will soon hear some version of what's happened. It would be wrong for our families to find out about our marriage via common gossip. I think you said you live with your parents?"

"Yes, and I agree with what you suggest. Do we go separately or together?"

"Would you be hurt if I said separately?"

"No. There's ground that needs to be prepared on both sides, I'm sure. Unless you think your uncle or your sister's already told your father?"

"No, I don't think they would do that."

Harry glanced at the carriage clock on the mantel. It had gone on half ten. "Father will be at his office already, but my mother and sister don't generally start making the social rounds until one o'clock. That means there's still time to break the news before they hear it in somebody's or the other's parlor. Shall we say we'll meet back here for supper at seven o'clock, perhaps? I've taken the room for a month, to give us time to plan and, well, adjust."

A month. I've married a man who can casually command a room in a first-class hotel for an entire month. It should have been exciting, or at least, comfortably reassuring. Instead, another cold wash of guilt threatened.

"I might have to stay," she told him. "This is going to be a severe shock to my father. If he has a nervous attack, I might not be able to leave at once. We have no regular nurse, you see."

"I understand. You can send me a note if that's the case. Direct it here. I don't expect to be delayed." He spoke to the bottom of his coffee cup. "Although, it's impossible to say. So, you'll leave me your direction, just in case?"

There was something unusually strained in the way he said this. Leannah didn't like it. "Of course."

His sigh held a little too much of relief in it to be entirely comforting. "Assuming all goes well, what then?"

"Then, I think I will need to talk with Meredith Langely. Do you know the Langleys?"

"I've heard of them, of Miss Langely, anyway. She's a sort of—social secretary to the ton at large—isn't she?"

"Something like that. She helps matrons and their daughters

organize successful seasons. In return, they invite her and her mother to stay for extended periods, or help with her expenses. It's an odd mode of existence, I'll grant you, but it allows them to manage. She's also a good friend of mine from boarding school." There was no need yet to explain that her stint at boarding school had been a whim of Father's. He thought that she might be able to make friends with more wealthy and powerful families there than she could being schooled by governesses in their country home.

It had lasted all of six months before she'd had to withdraw, and of the girls she'd met, only Meredith had become any sort of friend.

"The one thing we can be absolutely sure of is that there will be talk," she said. "Meredith will be able to help us manage it."

"Help us ride out the storm, you mean?" He nodded. "Yes. There's a great deal of sense in that. I hate having to give a fig about the haut ton and their fastidious attitudes, but I don't want things to be any more uncomfortable for you than necessary." He got up and helped himself to more ham, and coffee.

A scratching sounded at the door. Harry glanced at Leannah and set his plate down. He opened the door a fraction of an inch and then slid into the hallway. When he returned, he had a letter in his hand.

"There's a trunk waiting downstairs for you. It came with this." He handed her the paper. The direction was written in Genny's careless hand.

Leannah broke the seal at once, and with her heart in her mouth, she read:

My dearest sister,

I hope this finds you well and happy. You are not to worry a bit about us. All is just as it should be here. I've told Father and Jeremy that Mrs. Waterson suffered a sudden collapse, and that you went to stay with her until her niece could arrive. Uncle and Aunt have agreed not to contradict me.

I promise you that Father is none the worse for this news and Jeremy is only interested in whether he might be allowed to go out riding in Hyde Park today if the weather holds.

I thought you might be in need of a few things, so I took the liberty of packing your trunk and sending it along with this note.

Please convey my greetings to Mr. Rayburn. I know that we will see you both in due course.

Your loving sister,
Genny

"I trust all is well?" asked Harry with studied nonchalance as he carried his plate back to the table.

"Yes. Very. Genny just sent me some clothes. She says Father and Jeremy—my brother—are both well." Leannah took a deep breath and laid the letter facedown. "So, that's all to the good."

"I'm glad to hear it. You know, we should consider the matter of a house."

"A house?"

"Yes. We can't stay in a hotel forever. I was thinking we might look in the vicinity of Dobbsón Square."

It took a moment for Leannah's startled thoughts to catch up. "The Dobbson Square that is in the vicinity of Grosvenor Square?"

"Yes. Is that not posh enough? I'm not sure my finances run to St. James's."

Abruptly, Leannah began to laugh, and once she'd begun, she found she couldn't stop. Her letter fell to the floor, and her breath came short, but still the laughter would not cease. Harry joined in at first, but then seemed to realize something was wrong. Something was wrong. She needed to stop, but she couldn't stop. Tears ran down her cheeks and an entire tangle of emotion seethed painfully inside her.

Harry strode around the table. "It's all right, Leannah," he said as he wrapped her in his arms. "Truly. It's all right."

Leannah buried her face in the warm silk that covered his arm, and she sobbed. She couldn't help it. Too much was happening, and far too fast. She felt like a princess in a fairy tale. She'd made one wish, and now she had everything she could ever want. Except she couldn't keep it. It was not possible she could hold on to this kind, passionate man or this future of ease and plenty. Those times she had known plenty had always collapsed. So would this, except this collapse would be worse, because when it came, it would take Harry away.

Harry said nothing. He made no move to pull back from her. He just ran his hand across her shoulders in steady, soothing strokes and let her cry. Slowly, the storm eased, and Leannah was able to lift her head.

"I'm sorry." She sniffed and wiped at her eyes with the heel of her hand. "You must think me a complete hysteric."

"No." Harry retrieved her napkin, which had fallen to the floor alongside the letter from Genny. He passed it to her for use as a handkerchief. "I think that your life has been turned upside down. It would be very strange if you did not cry."

"But I did this to myself."

"Nonetheless."

"It's not regret."

"I know that, Leannah."

He leaned down and he kissed her. It was a soft gesture, filled with comfort and reassurance, at first. His hands closed around her wrists, so he could stand her up and more easily wrap his arms around her. Leannah's body softened instantly and she felt no reluctance at all when he pulled her close. The warm satin of her wrapper slipped sensuously against her as Harry cupped her face in his hands to hold her still while he continued the kiss.

She crossed her wrists around his shoulders and gave herself over to enjoyment. Time and worry melted away. When at last they broke apart, they were both breathless.

"We should see to your bandages," murmured Harry, as his fingers toyed with her hair.

"Later."

"It is not good to neglect such things."

"Later." How could he be even considering bandages, when they stood together like this, both practically naked? When she could clearly and wonderfully feel his growing arousal?

"But . . ."

What little patience Leannah still possessed ended at once. Before he could say another word, she claimed his mouth entirely with her own. She kissed him, heatedly, insistently. She leaned all her weight against him. Startled, Harry fell back against the table. She didn't stop. She thrust her tongue deep into his mouth, and she crushed her whole body against his. He had called up her need with his teasing and his kisses and he must now deal with the consequences. She would insist upon it. She rubbed her breasts against his chest and her hips against his. He was hard, deliciously hard. She wanted him to feel how her nipples had tightened with her need. She would not permit any mistake in his understanding of how very much she wanted him.

To this end, she drew her fingertips across his belly until she found the edges of his dressing gown. She pushed open the silk. All the while, she kissed him, held him in place with the press of her body. She felt him bending back, giving way. She slipped her hands underneath his robe. She let her fingertips graze down his hips and his hard thighs, and dragged them back up again to brush his erection.

The touch of him—velvet and steel and heat—filled her with fresh anticipation. She caressed his shaft fondly, but lightly, and only with the tips of her fingers. She would give him no excuse to continue his nonsense about her bandages. Harry groaned long and low, as his member swelled, hot and eager for her. She pressed forward, bending him farther back, so she could rub him against her belly, against her mound. Harry pressed his palms onto the table, striving to keep his balance.

Remembering her own earlier wish to see him nude, Leannah swiftly unknotted his sash. The gray silk fell open, revealing his broad chest and lean legs, and his member, jutting up proudly from the tangle of dark curls.

She surged close again. She couldn't help it. She had to hold him, dance her fingers along his exquisitely sensitive shaft. She gloried to see him let his head drop back as the pleasure her questing fingers brought robbed him of the strength to resist. She thought to kiss his member. She'd never done that particular thing, but knew it was done, and it seemed too delightfully wanton an impulse to resist.

She kissed his mouth first, and his stubbled chin. The rasp of it against her swollen lips only added to her excitement as she worked her way down past his jaw to his throat, and to his chest. She breathed in the scent of him, knowing it would arouse and entice her as surely as did the touch of his flesh. Her tongue found his flat, hard nipple and dabbed at it. It pebbled tight and hard and Harry hissed.

Leannah switched to his other nipple and set about pleasuring that as well. Only when she was sure it was as tight as she could make it, did she continue. With mouth and tongue she traced a line of wet heat down the center of his body, down to his navel, and lower.

"Leannah," Harry croaked.

"Hmm?" Her cheek brushed the blunt, impudent tip of his member. It felt extremely odd, but delightful in its own way. She curled her fingers around his shaft to hold him where she wanted him.

"This table's not going to stand it."

"Oh, dear." She lifted her eyes to meet his. "What would you suggest?"

Nineteen

❧

This woman was going to kill him. No one had ever been so quickly able to rouse him to desire or hold him at the pinnacle of his need. The butterfly brush of her questing hands against his member left him rock hard and burning. He gripped the table until his fingers hurt while she worked her wanton mouth against his throat, his chest, and—oh, God—his groin. His arms trembled, and the spindle-legged breakfast table trembled in answer.

Then she looked up at him with those incredible eyes and that wanton pout. All the while she kept hold of him, treating him to the most rousing and intimate of caresses. It was a wonder he didn't spill himself right then and there.

But she was waiting. She didn't move, didn't straighten. She just held him, torturing him with her lustful eyes as much as her warm fingers.

With a groan that might have been laughter or supreme frustration, Harry clamped his hand around her wrist and moved her hand away from him. Carefully. Keeping tight hold of her, he all but dragged her to the armchair. Positioning her in front of him, he lowered himself—again very carefully—onto the seat. He splayed his legs open so that she could see him, and what she had done to him. She looked—not shyly, but boldly, lingeringly. In fact, she feasted her eyes on him.

Harry would not have believed it possible for him to grow any harder, and yet he did.

"May I continue?" Leannah asked. He stared at her mouth as it shaped the words. With infinite grace, she knelt in front of him. "May I, Harry?"

He couldn't speak. Language had fled him. He could only stare at her luscious pink mouth. She was going to wrap those lips around him. She was going to kiss and suck him. She wanted it. She wanted him.

Harry managed a nod.

Leannah curled her fingers around him. Her thumb found the groove on the underside of his shaft and stroked it, tentatively, almost thoughtfully, at least at first. His blood pulsed and his groin tightened. The pain of it mixed with the breathtaking pleasure of her touch. She bent her head. Her gorgeous hair cascaded forward, obscuring her face. Her lips—warm, sweet, and infinitely desirable—pressed against his shaft.

He groaned again. He was sure she was smiling beneath the curtain of her hair. He meant to reach out to brush it back, but Leannah ran her tongue down his shaft and volition fled. His hand gripped the chair arm instead. Her rough, wet tongue glided back up his most sensitive flesh and Harry managed a strangled chuckling sort of noise. He could imagine nothing better than this, that was until her lips wrapped around the tip of him, and her tongue dabbed him there.

Harry moaned. He had been pleasured by more expert and experienced women, but nothing they gave him could match the intensity of Leannah's exploration of his body. The knowledge that she was discovering her own pleasure as much as his filled him with fresh fire. He was panting, he was groaning. She kissed him, she licked. Her throat made soft noises of enjoyment as she took him into her hands so she could hold him still, and take him more deeply into her hot mouth.

"Yes!" he cried. "Oh, God, yes, Leannah!"

She closed her lips. She swirled her tongue around him, and she moaned. She liked it, what she was doing, what she raised between them. The fire built higher inside him and his blood burned hotter. He had never been so hard, so strong, so frantic with the need for completion.

And he would be dead and damned if he didn't bring her with him.

With a mighty effort of will, Harry raised his hand and tangled his fingers in her hair.

"Leannah." He croaked as he pulled, not hard, just enough to urge her to lift her mouth from him. "Leannah, come here."

She understood at once, and she stood. Her mouth was wet and glistening from her work. A drop of moisture beaded at the corner, and her tongue darted out to lick it away. Oh, God, who was this woman? What was she doing to him? She was driving him insane, that's what she was doing. Well, if this was insanity, then let him be consigned to Bedlam because he never wanted to be sane again.

Leannah undid her sash and let the wrapper fall away into a heap. She stood before him trembling, but not with fear or cold. It was desire that shook her. He could see it in her face and her darkened emerald eyes. Her tangled hair cascaded down about her breasts so that the hard dusky buds of her nipples peeked out from between the elf locks. She was a goddess of desire, and he was nothing more than need given man's breath and form.

He grabbed her waist. She shrieked and laughed, but let herself be pulled forward and lifted. She understood what was required quickly, and straddled him so that her thighs pressed against his. Wonder and need lit her eyes as she leaned forward to kiss his mouth. She tasted of salt and musk and smelled of her own heady spice. Her naked breasts brushed his chest. He spread one hand across her buttocks, savoring their ripe curves. With the other, he sought the nest of curls between her thighs, and the sensitive, wet folds beneath. She moaned into his mouth as he parted her. She was hot and drenched, entirely ready for him. His shaft throbbed sharply, but he forced himself to wait. He let his fingers fondle her. Her soft sounds of pleasure and surprise washed over him like her scent and her heat. Her thighs tightened against his. She was rising up on her knees, seeking to press herself onto him, and as she did, he let his fingers slip up to the very top of her folds, to find and stroke the nubbin of flesh concealed there.

She cried out and he knew a fresh wave of delight, and triumph. She writhed against him, forcing his fingers to press her harder. Her red-gold hair rippled around her, offering him glimpses of her breasts and belly that were somehow more enticing than the full view could be. Leannah was radiant in her pleasure, lost to it entirely, knowing only that she needed, that she wanted.

"Oh, yes, Leannah. That's it. You like it."

"Yes!"

She was coming. Her thighs tightened hard and abruptly. Her hips rocked forward, pressing her nub tight against his fingers. He held her there, trapped between his hands. For a moment she was utterly still, her eyes closed, her body entirely alert to what was happening inside. Then she trembled, then she shuddered and her climax took her.

She rocked against him, crying out as he stroked her, prolonging her pleasure, ruthlessly, selfishly feeding his own greed and power on the sight of her, the feeling of her so helpless against his hands and body.

Her climax was ebbing and her strength at last beginning to flag. Leannah slumped forward and he embraced her and pulled her close.

"Oh, yes, my dear." Harry kissed her and brushed her hair back from her shoulders, which led him to brush his hand against her breast. Her nipple was pebble hard beneath his fingers. He tightened his arm around her. She shifted, slick and wet against him. The pain and need was robbing him of breath. He would not wait anymore. He could not.

Harry grasped Leannah's hips and raised her up. Her eyes flew open and her mouth made an O of surprise. For a moment he feared she might resist, and then he would have to die, because there was no way he could stand down from this. But a heartbeat later she grinned, and he felt her take her own weight on her knees, so he could reach a hand between them and position his iron-hard shaft at her entrance.

Leannah groaned and let her knees buckle. Harry shouted with desire and relief as he thrust up into her. Her heat tightened once around him, and he was lost—lost to reason, lost to restraint. Desire rendered him mindless. He thrust, hard, relentless. He grasped her, holding her tight and close. She struggled, she rocked, and then she found the rhythm. His rhythm, her rhythm. Now, she rode him. She rode him hard, and harder yet as pleasure drove them on.

Harry's climax took him without warning. He roared aloud as the waves of it rushed through him, lifting him high and crashing him back down hard to earth, to peace and relief.

To Leannah. His Leannah.

It was a long time before either of them moved. To Harry's surprise, he was the first to insist on it. He would have been vastly contented to spend the rest of the day with Leannah curled up in his lap. Unfortunately, she had been right when she said they needed to speak with their respective families before the gossip reached them.

Therefore, albeit with a great deal of reluctance, he got them both to their feet. It took a certain amount of highly enjoyable teasing and cajoling to convince her to reclaim her wrapper, retreat to her room, and ring for the maid. Lewis arrived promptly in answer to this summons with a pair of sturdy girls in tow. The trio had taken charge of Leannah's trunk and they disappeared into her room, presumably to take charge of Leannah herself. Harry chuckled and wished them luck.

Not that he didn't need similar assistance. Fortunately, Marshall was not slow in arriving with his own pair of subordinates to take charge of Harry. As a result he was washed, shaved, and dressed in short order. A green coat, clean shirt, plain blue waistcoat, and buff breeches had all been procured. By the time Harry knotted his cravat, he felt much more himself. He, in fact, felt entirely ready to brave the day and begin his new life as Leannah's husband. He even had time for another cup of coffee and an additional slice of cake. Fortunately, with Leannah in his life, he probably would not have to worry about growing stout anytime soon.

Harry leaned back in his chair and swirled the dregs of his coffee. He stared at the wall, but in his mind he saw her, his Leannah. In his vision, she was beautifully naked, and her red-gold hair curled around her lush breasts. The memory of her sang through him. He glanced at her chamber door. What would happen if he walked in there and dismissed the servants? Perhaps she wasn't even laced up yet. If that was the case, it would be the work of a moment to pull off her dress and corset and have her naked in front of him in reality. He could lay her

down on the bed and show her she was not the only one hungry
for exploration. He could suck her folds exactly as she had
sucked his shaft this morning, until a fresh climax overwhelmed her. Then, while she was still hot and pulsing, he'd
thrust into her, and drive her to distraction all over again.

Harry threw back his head and laughed. Great heavens, he
was a lost cause. No woman had ever gotten to him so quickly;
not even when he was a raw youth abroad in the world for the
first time. He'd taken full advantage of the privileges offered
a curious young Englishman with money in his pockets. Fortunately, he'd passed through all that without contracting a
serious disease, or fathering a bastard, which was something
on the far side of a miracle, all things considered. But that had
been simple lust, if lust was ever simple, and opportunity. What
he felt with Leannah was as far beyond all that as the sun beyond the clouds.

But just what was it he felt? Leannah delighted him phys-
ically and with her strength of mind and character. He enjoyed
sparring with her, teasing her, and laughing with her. She
turned him protective, mischievous, and wolfish by turns.
Could this be the love at first sight the poets nattered on about?
Harry sipped his cooling coffee. He'd never believed in such
folderol. But if it wasn't love at first sight, he'd bloody well like
to know what was. Which left him with a cold and vital
question.

Did Leannah's feelings match his? Did they even come
close?

As if summoned by that silent question, Leannah emerged
from her room. She wore a cream gown trimmed with peach
ribbons that brought out the warmth of her complexion and her
hair. The demure fichu at her throat was pinned by a plain silver
brooch. Her hair was dressed simply, swept back from her face
but with a shimmering spill of curls left to trail down her neck
and back.

Despite how well the dress suited her, Harry's expert eye
could see that it had been made over at least twice, and the trim
at the sleeves and hem was slightly worn. The pin was quite
plain, and it was the only jewelry she wore, besides his ring.
She'd said her family was short of money, and here was the
proof of it.

She was looking at him, shyly, uncertainly. She was ashamed, Harry realized. He would not permit that. He smiled as he got to his feet and crossed to her so he could take her hands and kiss them both. He noted with approval that they'd been freshly and lightly bandaged. He'd make certain Lewis remained in attendance on Leannah as long as they stayed here. Given the state of her dress, he had a feeling she didn't have a lady's maid of her own. That was on the list of things he could and would change.

"You are beautiful," he told her. "Are you ready for this?"

She squared her shoulders and tilted her chin up to meet his gaze. "As ready as I can be. You?"

"The same," he smiled, and kissed her. He'd meant it to be light, and brief, but when her lips trembled and parted beneath his own, he could not help but prolong the gesture. Anyway, what was the point of a kiss if he did not put his arms about her and hold her close? Just for a moment, of course; just long enough to relish the sensation of her magnificent curves pressed against him. She yielded to his attentions at once, leaning her whole body against his. She sighed into their kiss and he felt his member twitch.

"Oh, no," he said, when he finally had to breathe again. "We can't. Not yet."

"I know." Despite this, she kept rubbing her lips lightly along his freshly shaved jaw, all the while pressing those luscious breasts against his chest. His groin tightened abruptly. "I do know."

With an inward curse, Harry stepped backward. He took her face in both hands, and tipped her eyes up to his. "Tonight." He said firmly. "We are agreed. We will meet back here at seven o'clock for supper. After which, I will spend the rest of the evening showing you exactly how much I have missed you."

Leannah took a deep breath and nodded. "Yes. Of course. This is just the beginning."

But there was a tremor beneath her words, and something too close to fear flickered behind her gold and emerald eyes. Harry kissed her once more.

"We will be back together soon," he told her. "I promise you, Leannah."

When they parted again, he saw her touch her brooch, and

tug at her sleeve before she turned to pick up the reticule she'd laid on the table. A thought occurred to him.

"At the risk of turning this awkward . . ." he said as he reached into his coat.

"I think you mean more awkward."

"I believe I do. But, I wanted to make sure you had some money." He drew out his wallet, and his purse.

"Thank you."

He laid a stack of notes and coins on the table. Leannah stared at them and swallowed. Her brow furrowed, turning her expression almost angry as she swept the money into her reticule and drew the string shut.

He wanted to ask her what was wrong and where that anger came from, but something in him held back. He told himself it was that they had no time. It was already late. He was going to have trouble making his self-imposed deadline of getting home to break the news before one o'clock when the accepted time for paying calls began. There would be time to ask what so upset her later. There would be all the time in the world.

After that, they were caught up in the bustle of getting ready to leave. Bonnet, coat, and gloves had to be fetched for Leannah; hat, overcoat, and stick for him. Marshall had to be dispatched to see that the carriage was got ready and brought round. Once they descended the front stairs, there was a further short delay while Leannah meticulously quizzed the groom about the health of her horses, and the bona fides of the driver the hotel supplied. Fortunately, the groom had recognized the high-strung nature of the team, and had assigned an older man with a knowing eye and crisp manner to take charge.

Harry kissed Leannah's hand at the foot of the steps, and helped her into the barouche.

As she settled into her place he could not help but notice the contrast between her genteelly worn dress and the extravagance of the well-sprung carriage with its shining leather seats and team of matched grays. There was a story here, and while he had no notion what it might be, it left him uneasy, especially when it combined with the angry look on her face as she accepted the money. Still, he tipped her a jaunty wave as the driver touched up the horses and set them walking up the street.

He didn't move for a moment, although he couldn't have

said what he was waiting for. Then, he saw Leannah turn around, looking for him. She was too far away for him to see her expression, but he felt instinctively it was neither comfortable nor contented.

We will be back together soon. I promise you. His own words echoed in his mind, but now they took on a different tone; one that was anxious and far too uncertain.

Harry uttered a soft oath and wrenched himself around. This was not to be permitted. Leannah would return here, to him, just as soon as she was able. He'd close them both into their room and make her understand in the most direct way possible that the life she'd known did not matter. She was his wife now, and he would make all things right for her.

For them both.

With this single thought held firmly in his mind, Harry strode away down the street.

Twenty

Anthony Dickenson was not an impulsive man. His life's course had been set from the time he was breeched, and he followed it unerringly. From the care of his nurse and his tutors, he had gone to boarding school and then to university. There, he did well enough at his studies, but that was secondary. His father had been quite clear. The primary purpose of school was to meet the men and families with whom he would be associated with for the rest of his life.

After university, Dickenson was installed in the office next to his father's at the firm on Cornhill Street, four doors down from the Royal Exchange. There, he learned to navigate the world of shares and stocks, and how to buy and sell whatever would yield the best profit. His father sponsored him to join the correct clubs. His university acquaintances gained him invitations to dine at the correct tables. His older brothers taught him how to listen in those clubs and at those tables. Under their influence, Dickenson learned how to consistently put two and two together and make four when it came to business. Other men might approach the markets as they did the gaming tables, but Dickensons never did. They only played when they knew they could win. If necessary, they took steps to make certain of their victory.

So it was an unutterable shock to Anthony when the beautiful girl brought to his attention at the Mallon's New Year's affair turned out to be the daughter of Octavian Morehouse.

Old "Octopus" Morehouse was the most infamous gambling man ever to haunt the halls of the exchange. Anthony fully expected to forget Genevieve Morehouse as soon as he learned her name. Like his brothers, he was meant to marry to help raise the family's fortunes and position. Genevieve Morehouse could never be anything to him.

Except he couldn't forget her. He began to see her everywhere, and every time she appeared more lovely and desirable. He began to make excuses to speak with her. At first, when she returned her tart answers, he'd simply been appalled. This delicate creature who so attracted him could not possibly possess such an acid and impertinent tongue. It was not only unseemly, it went against the laws of nature. He, Anthony Dickenson, could never want such a creature, and yet he did want Genevieve Morehouse. She danced through his thoughts when he should have been concentrating on business. The vision of her smiled softly at him as he sat listening at the supper tables. His dreams at night quickly escalated from undignified to unendurable. He must have her.

However, Dickenson knew full well he could not claim her until he comprehended just how and why her character came to be so damaged. He could not make a wife of any girl who did not measure up to the Dickenson standards, however desirable she might be.

Fortunately, it didn't take him long to understand that the fault did not lie with Miss Morehouse's intrinsic nature. Rather, it originated with her sister.

Mrs. Wakefield was a cold, calculating woman. It did not take him much looking to see how she deliberately and maliciously poisoned Genevieve's mind and character in an attempt to make the lovely girl as unyielding, scheming, and proud as she was herself. Heaven only knew where that pride came from, considering the pathetic wreck she had for a father. But after a little conversation with those in the know, combined with a little impartial observation of the sort he applied to business matters, Anthony understood that Mrs. Wakefield was jealous of her unspoiled sister's youth and beauty. That jealousy led to the ongoing attempts to ruin her.

As soon as Anthony understood this, his course of action became clear. All he had to do was marry Genevieve Morehouse and get her away from her termagant of a sister. Once he had Genevieve all to himself, he could set about reshaping her character and behaviors. It would not be difficult. After all, he would only be guiding her back to what was right and natural. Within a matter of weeks, as long as three or four months, perhaps, Genevieve would be able to stand beside him as a proper wife.

When he'd heard that Terrance Valloy was planning on marrying Mrs. Wakefield, Anthony had felt quite fortunate. Valloy had a reputation as a sound businessman. He would not allow his wife to keep Genevieve unmarried simply as a sop to her own vanity, especially when there was an eminently eligible match on offer. All he had to do was wait.

And Anthony did wait. He waited for weeks. Those weeks stretched out into the months of an utterly interminable season. Still, he'd forced himself to be patient. The gossip he overheard indicated that Valloy had decided he'd given Mrs. Wakefield enough time to hide behind her mourning veil. Valloy told the men at his club it was time to close the affair. Anthony moved through his days confident that his period of suspense was nearly at an end.

Thus, it had come as a complete shock when Genevieve had written to tell him that her sister would in no way consent to the marriage. Worse, Genevieve told him Mrs. Wakefield declared she would not marry Mr. Valloy unless he agreed ahead of time not to sanction Miss Morehouse's marriage.

Disbelief had rooted him to the ground. Anger had nearly caused him to tear the letter in two before he'd finished reading it. Fortunately, his mind was too closely honed by business to permit him to discard any document before he'd thoroughly examined it. That was when he learned afresh that he had been right about his Genevieve. Her sister had not yet been able to eradicate her core of proper sense and feeling. She wrote that she wanted to marry him. She yearned to escape her sister's influence and put herself under the secure guidance that the right sort of husband could provide. Not that she'd put it that way, but he nonetheless knew it to be the truth. Had he not been so certain, he never would have agreed to the elopement.

Of course Mrs. Wakefield would attempt to interfere. He had attempted to plan for each contingency. He endorsed Miss Morehouse's notion of having her uncle (another member of the family who, despite all, maintained a sliver of good sense) meet them at the Three Swans. This not only made her attachment plain, but revealed a pleasing note of good sense. It also, not incidentally, saved him from having to manage an inconvenient, expensive, and tedious journey to Gretna. He did not like that she fabricated the tale of a bastard on the way. It did not suit his notion of his own character. However, if it overcame the old man's arguments, then it served its purpose and it was certainly no worse than any lie told upon the exchange in the name of business.

At first, everything had gone smoothly. Miss Morehouse had slipped away from her house and her escort. The old dame playing chaperone had assisted to the best of her strictly limited abilities. He would pension her off generously once the wedding was finalized. Then had come the weather and the delays on the road. Still, he'd thought nothing of it. All had seemed perfectly in hand.

Until they'd reached the inn and found that Mrs. Wakefield and her bullyboy had gotten there first.

Of course he'd retreated. He was a Dickenson. He could not stay and brawl in a public house, especially not with that unnatural bitch looking on and enjoying every minute of it. But his retreat was purely strategic. He'd circled back once daylight arrived. His idea had been to bribe one of the servants to get word to Genevieve of his presence. The idea of an unplanned flight to Gretna went against every fiber of his being, but if it got Miss Morehouse away from her sister, it would all be worth it.

That was how he had come to be in the yard and to hear the servants talking of the impromptu marriage taking place in the parlor. The application of a half-a-crown had secured the names of the couple. Mrs. Wakefield was not only favoring her bullyboy. She was marrying him.

This time Dickenson did retreat. He spent the entire cold, inconvenient drive back to town lost in thought, and by the time he arrived at his own door, he had his plan. It would be expensive. He would have to proceed with great care, but the knowledge that Mrs. Wakefield, now Mrs. Rayburn, still held lovely, innocent Genevieve drove him forward. She would not keep possession of his rightful bride, and she certainly would not be allowed to boast that she'd bested a Dickenson. He would destroy her for the very attempt. Fortunately, she herself provided all the means necessary for him to do just that. He did not even need to attack her directly.

What he did need to do was speak with Terrance Valloy.

Anthony arrived at the Exchange Club in Cornhill Street at lunchtime. A few inquiries had revealed that it was Valloy's regular habit to dine there in peace before returning to the riot of the Royal Exchange or Lloyd's trading rooms. A quiet word with one of the waiters allowed Dickenson to determine the man who sat alone at the table by the window, entirely concealed by his copy of the *Times* was the one he sought.

He made his way through the mostly empty room to the windows.

"Mr. Valloy? My name is Dickenson."

Valloy turned one corner of the paper down. He was a formidable man with a lined face and dark hair liberally streaked with iron gray. There was a great deal of iron in his cold eyes as well. Those eyes raked across Anthony, assessing each detail of his appearance.

It was only when this process was complete that Valloy closed the paper. "Ah yes," he said, gesturing for the waiter to bring another chair so Anthony could sit. "I've heard your name about the exchange." Valloy gestured to the wine carafe and coffeepot. Anthony declined both and settled into the chair. "What can I do for you?" asked Valloy.

"I've no wish to waste your time," said Anthony. "Therefore, I shall come straight to my point. You are, I believe, acquainted with the family of Octavian Morehouse?"

"What business might that be of yours?" Valloy spoke mildly. Clearly, he was not a man who shouted, or needed to.

"Forgive me. I would have hoped for a more proper way to broach such a private subject, but circumstances compel this direct approach."

"I do not understand you, sir." Again, the words were spoken with deceptive mildness. His black eyes though, were hard as flint.

"You intend, I believe, to marry Mrs. Wakefield."

"Once more, I ask what business is this of yours?"

"I am sorry to inform you that you will shortly find she has formed a mésalliance."

Valloy's hard eyes glittered. "You will explain yourself, Mr. Dickenson, or you will leave."

In as clear a fashion as he could manage, Dickenson laid out the situation. It was difficult, because each word reminded him afresh of the humiliation he'd suffered at the hands of Mrs. Wakefield and the callow brute she'd taken up with. Now that he'd had time to reflect, he realized he should not have been so surprised at this Rayburn's presence. What sort of man would she attach to her but a malleable, brawling brute who could be induced to obey her orders without thought? Yes, she'd probably already given him all sorts of favors in exchange for his assistance in blocking her sister's path to a woman's normal life.

When Anthony finished, Valloy stood. He faced the window with his hands folded behind his back, and remained in that attitude for a slow count of twenty.

When Valloy faced Dickenson again, his countenance was flushed scarlet, but otherwise his coutenance was under complete control. He lowered himself back down into his seat, and leaned across the table.

"You, sir, are either a liar or a blackmailer and you will get out at once."

Dickenson felt his own ears begin to burn, but he held his temper. "I regret that I am the bearer of such sordid news, but I am here in hopes of forming a partnership of mutual benefit."

"Again, I say, if you intend extortion of any sort . . ."

"I do not want to become angry with you on so short an acquaintance, Valloy, but I will if that word is spoken again. I am a man of business, and I am here with a business proposal. Will you hear me out?"

Valloy made no direct answer. First, he glanced about the room, making sure no one was near enough to overhear their conversation. Then, he flicked one finger toward Dickenson, indicating he should continue.

"The fact that there was a marriage ceremony is of little significance. Despite recent changes to the law, the actual statutes regarding marriage remain quite lax," said Dickenson. Like Valloy, he kept his words casual and calm. "A decent

lawyer and a decent payment to the proper parties will be able
to procure a quiet annulment. I can myself supply an affidavit
certifying that the circumstances were extremely irregular."

"Go on," said Valloy.

Dickenson took his time. This next part must be handled
delicately. Valloy was an intelligent man. It would not have
escaped his notice what sort of connection he would be acquir-
ing when he married Mrs. Wakefield. Still, if Dickenson
descended into unnecessary vulgarity, it could damage his case.

"While Mrs. Wakefield is not in every way a conventional
sort of woman, she does possess some very proper family
feeling."

Valloy's eyes flashed and Dickenson hurried on. "This may
also be seen in her sister, Miss Morehouse. I know that Mrs.
Wakefield does not wish to compound any lingering injuries
that may have resulted from mistakes made by certain other
members of the family. She especially does not want to be seen
to jeopardize her sister's reputation. Mrs. Wakefield's marriage
may be put down to an impulse of the moment, such as women
are subject to. After all, Miss Morehouse had engaged in what
might, under more usual circumstances, be considered an imprudent move."

"Might this imprudent move be your elopement with Miss
Morehouse?" murmured Valloy. "It is being rather talked about."

Anthony nodded his head, indicating the truth of this. Valloy waited for him to offer excuses, but he did not. Excuses
would only make him look weak.

"If Mrs. Wakefield could be shown that her marriage would
bring further disadvantage to her family, I believe she could
be convinced to give the thing up. There would of course still
be a scandal if she dropped the marriage so soon after it was
solemnized," Dickenson went on. "To keep it from erupting
uncontrollably, Mrs. Wakefield would have to marry yet again,
and quickly. This new marriage would have to be to a man with
the sensibility and resources to get her away from London, and
keep her away."

Valloy ran one finger thoughtfully across his upper lip and
lapsed into another of his long silences. For a moment, Dickenson feared he had gone too far. Planning to marry an ungov-
ernable widow was one thing. Actually marrying her while her

bed was still warm from the body of another man was quite another.

Valloy shuddered once, in anger or disgust, Dickenson could not be sure. Other than that, he remained completely composed. Dickenson saw Valloy was a man who had perfected the art of the facade. His cool demeanor was a mask he could don at a moment's notice, no matter what thoughts or emotions might be seething underneath. He could respect such a man. More, he could work with such a man.

"It is clear, Mr. Dickenson, you do not think much of Mrs. Wakefield. So, tell me, why should I simply not cry off? If what you say is true, she is now married to another man. If I pursue the subject, I will be involving myself in a most unseemly scandal. Should I still require a wife, there are others who may be had with less cost and trouble, and who have infinitely preferable connections."

"The Great Devon Road," replied Dickenson evenly.

"I beg your pardon?"

"The Great Devon Road, the one that is even now being planned in the bowels of the ministry. The route has not been finalized, as I am sure you are aware."

"Your point, Mr. Dickenson?"

"I am in a position to make sure that when the route is fixed, it will be fixed in a way that is advantageous to whomever holds the Wakefield lands." The lands that had been left in trust to Jeremy Morehouse, the lands that, according to Dickenson's informants, Valloy was willing to marry Mrs. Wakefield in order to control.

It would cost him thousands of pounds to make sure of the planning commission, and require that he turn over a few letters his family had been saving for just such an event, but if it secured Genevieve to him, the cost would be more than worth it.

Valloy's eyes flickered back and forth. He was thinking, and thinking quickly.

"Very well," he said at last. "On two conditions."

"Which are?"

"First, you will leave the matter of dissolving the marriage with me. I have made it my business to become fully informed regarding Octavian Morehouse's character. I believe I know how I may work on him to obtain a result that would be desirable for us both."

"And the second?"

Valloy's voice dropped to a bare whisper. "You will write out a letter guaranteeing the outcome you have just promised me regarding the Great Devon Road, and you will sign it."

Now it was Dickenson's turn to fall silent. This was dangerous in the extreme. If anything went wrong, he would be handing Valloy the means to ruin not just him, but his entire family.

But it was the only way for him to have Genevieve, to have her and hold her and keep her beauty away from all others for as long as they both lived.

Dickenson raised his hand to summon the waiter and give the order for quill, paper, and ink. When the man left, Valloy reached across the table and picked up the decanter.

"Will you change your mind about a glass, Dickenson? I can see we have a great deal to discuss."

Twenty-One

H arry's arrival at his parents' house in St. James Square was quiet, but only for as long as it took to hand his borrowed hat and overcoat to the footman.

"Harry!" cried Fiona. "At last! We were beginning to think you'd enlisted or some such thing."

Harry had just enough time to turn and stare, before his sister marched up to him and planted her hands on her hips. Harry felt his cheeks go pale, and he knew she saw it, but he had no chance to compose himself.

"Good morning to you as well, Fi," said Harry as coolly as he could manage. *She can't have heard yet.* "I'm glad to see you, too. You are looking well." Actually, she looked angry. Her face was roughly the same shade of rose as her walking dress. Harry's heart plummeted and he glanced at the case clock in the corner of the broad foyer. It hadn't even reached noon yet. He remembered his confident words to Leannah when he said his female relations did not go visiting until one o'clock. What if he'd been wrong?

Fiona ignored this bland greeting. "You must come in here at once. Mother's in a state! You have to contradict this viciousness immediately!"

Harry crossed the floor in a state that managed to combine the sensation of floating with the sensation that he could well sink through the marble floor at any moment. The footman, he noted, had very sensibly taken himself elsewhere.

The day had turned quite fine, and bright sunlight filled the morning room where their mother sat on a small beige velveteen sofa. As usual, Fiona exaggerated. His sister might be flushed with pique, but Mother appeared utterly calm. The only sign of agitation could be seen in the way she held her hands clasped tightly together in her lap.

Mrs. Nicholas Rayburn, née Louisa Amesworth, had been a beauty in her day. Time and a happy marriage had transformed her into a comfortable matron. Her thick fair hair was streaked with gray that she never troubled to dye. Gray hair, she said, was her badge of honor for having survived her youth, and her children. If she was plumper than fashionable, she was also more shrewd and more steady than the world tended to give her credit for. She had seen a great deal with her mild blue eyes, and those eyes looked straight through Harry now.

She knew. *They* knew.

The disembodied sensation that had carried Harry this far dissolved and he felt as if he were dropped, hard. Hard enough, in fact, to crush him down to a boy again, with Mother about to unwrap a handkerchief filled with fragments of the heirloom vase he had attempted to repair.

"Please sit down, Harold," said his mother.

Harry did. His first impulse was to choose the cane-backed chair, which happened to be the farthest away from her. But he rallied and instead chose the tapestry chair beside the sofa. Fi stationed herself behind mother like a guard of honor, her eyes blazing.

"There is a most unfortunate rumor abroad," Mother began.

"That odious Dorothea Plaice!" cried Fiona. "She positively barged into Lady Penelope's breakfast room . . ."

"I thought no one was at home before one!" Harry's words came out far closer to a yelp than they should have.

"It's the second Friday, silly," said Fi. "Lady Penelope always has a breakfast on second Fridays during the season and we were invited to—" Mother turned her face up to give her daughter a Significant Look. "But that's neither here nor there." Fi waved her own words away. "The point is that Dorothea Plaice waltzed right up to mother, and wished her joy on the marriage of her son! 'I can't believe you've kept it such a secret!' she says, right in front of Mrs. Candle and Lady Denmark and all the world!"

It must be a very large breakfast room. Harry decided against voicing this thought.

"Well, of course, Mother doesn't know what she's talking about and she says Miss Plaice must be mistaken. This is when Miss Plaice gets the slyest smile on her face"—Fi drew her own mouth up on a tight, simpering grin. Mother looked pained, but Harry couldn't tell if it was at the memory, or Fi's energetic recreation of the conversation—"and she says 'Oh! I'm sorry! Have I trod all over the surprise! I was only in such a hurry to congratulate you. Why I met Mrs. Wakefield . . . I should say the new Mrs. Rayburn, who is an acquaintance of mine—with *dear* Harry just last evening. They together confirmed everything, so naturally I assumed *some* sort of announcement had been made!' "

Leannah had warned him this would happen, and he hadn't believed her, not really. He'd have to arrange to kick himself later. Probably after he apologized and promised never to doubt her again.

"Now!" How Fi could imbue one word with so much menace was beyond him. "You must tell Mother that Miss Plaice got it all wrong. You have not married Leannah Morehouse Wakefield."

She crossed her arms, very obviously waiting for him to obey her instructions.

"Well, Harry," asked Mother, much more softly, "is it true?"

"It is not true!" declared Fiona, but Mother didn't look at her. Her gaze remained fixed on Harry. Fiona might be attempting to put on a brave show of denial, but Mother already had all the confirmation she needed. She'd seen it in his face the moment he'd entered the room. She was just waiting to see if he'd own up.

"I've sent for your father," Mother told him. "He should be here shortly."

"He's here now." The morning room door opened and Harry started reflexively to his feet.

Nicholas Rayburn was a large man with a ruddy complexion and a long, lined face. Like his wife, he had settled comfortably into his age and prosperity, as could be seen in his stout midriff and blossoming double chin. Despite this, the senior Mr. Rayburn still carried the hallmarks of an active life, for he was weathered, calloused, and tended to speak a little too loudly for any room he was in.

"Harry!" Father clasped Harry's hand in both of his. "Thank goodness! We've all been worried about you, you know."

"Yes, I do know, and I'm sorry."

"Something's happened, I take it? Louisa?" Father sank onto the sofa next to his wife.

"I am not quite clear as to just what's happened." She shook her head. "Harry was about to give us a fuller explanation of the circumstances." Mother continued to speak calmly, but it was clear that she held herself very tightly in check. "Harry, Fiona told us that Miss Featherington turned down your proposal, and that you left home understandably disheartened."

This was probably only distantly related to what his sister had actually said. Their mother, however, had ample experience with translating from the Fiona.

"Yes, that's all true. What happened afterward is a long story," Harry paused. "You may as well sit down Fi. You can glower at me just as effectively from the armchair."

Fi looked like she wanted to rebel, but a glance from Mother sent her flouncing to the cane-backed chair, just to prove that she was not following anyone's orders.

They all looked at him: the three people closest to him; the ones who trusted him to do as he should, to help support the family, to be a fitting son to his father and reliable heir to his business. He was not the one who created trouble, not here at home at any rate.

"I'm sorry you had to find out about this from Miss Plaice. I truly did mean for you to hear it from me first. It is, however, true—Mrs. Wakefield, Leannah, and I were, in fact, married yesterday morning by special license at the Three Swans."

Normally, Harry would have enjoyed seeing Fiona so completely dumbfounded. But any momentary satisfaction he might have gained was erased when his mother lifted her hand to cover his, and he saw how she trembled.

"Was this a long-standing acquaintance, Harry?" Mother breathed. "Why did you not tell us about her?"

"Did Miss Featherington find out?" boomed Father. "That's why she wouldn't have you? Knew there had to be a reason."

Harry shook his head. "No, and no. I met Leannah entirely by accident, after Miss Featherington turned down my proposal."

Guilt threatened as he met his family's anxious eyes, but Harry shoved it to one side. He would not feel guilty about Leannah. He had done the right thing by her and by himself. There was no other way for them to be together in the way they wished without sneaking about, or damaging her reputation past hope of repair. He would not present the news of her existence to his family with any taint of shame hanging about his words.

Instead, he took a deep breath, and he told them straight out. He gave a sketch of his disappointing encounter with Miss Featherington, and how he met Nathaniel at the club afterward, and how he decided to take a walk after that to clear his head. He told them about the "runaway" carriage, and how he'd tried to help; how Gossip had thrown her shoe and he realized he couldn't leave Mrs. Wakefield alone on the road. He told them about taking her to the Three Swans and about meeting Genevieve Morehouse and Anthony Dickenson there. He did not mention the very short and one-sided brawl. He did speak about the fear of scandal, and arrival of the Rev. Clarence Morehouse, and the plan—his plan—to deflect scandal from Leannah and her sister, and to allow he and Leannah to be together.

"I know it sounds mad," he said finally. "I don't know how to explain falling into a state of such deep feeling with someone within the space of a few hours. Before this I wouldn't have believed it possible. But it is what happened, to both of us."

Silence descended. It was not at all the sort of silence Harry was used to when seated comfortably with his family. This was hard and thick, and try as he might, he could sense no easy way to break it.

It was Fi, as usual, who found her voice first.

"Well, I suppose I should thank you, Harry. You've found an adventure that makes my exploits absolutely pale by comparison."

Harry ignored her and looked instead to his parents. Mother

knotted her hands even more tightly together. Father got to his feet. Where Mother had gone dead white, Father flushed red. He paced across the room, turning a tight circle in front of the hearth. He smoothed his sparse hair back across his permanently wind-burned scalp. He glanced at Harry, and smoothed his hair back again.

"Where is the woman now?" he barked.

"My wife," said Harry, "has gone to give her own family the news of our marriage."

Father faced the hearth and gripped the edge of the mantelpiece. Harry had seen his father heave fifty-pound sacks of spices and help sailors haul up great swaths of canvas without a second thought. For a moment, he wondered if the mantel could stand the strain.

"Have you given her any money?" Father asked.

The question came like a blow from nowhere, and left Harry just as stunned. "I beg your pardon?"

"I think the question is clear enough," said Father to the hearth. "Have you given her any money?"

"Not yet." The amount he'd given her for incidental expenses could not be considered real money. "But I will arrange a settlement shortly."

"Of course, of course." Father hung his head. "Because it's all above board—sudden, inexplicable, and romantic—but perfectly honest."

"I'm not sure what you're driving at, sir." Harry's gaze travelled uneasily from Father, standing at the hearth, to Mother, sitting grave and silent on the sofa.

Fi, naturally, took it upon herself to be direct. "Oh, come off it, Harry! You've been hoodwinked!"

"No. I know it looks odd, but . . ."

Fiona was in no mood to let him finish. "A damsel in distress, a sob story of her sister's elopement, and their uncle the clergyman just happening to show up at the inn? Harry! You've been played for a complete flat!"

"Fiona," said Mother sternly, "this is not helping."

"But it is the truth."

He was not hearing this. His family was not responding to news of his marriage by accusing him of having fallen for some elaborate trick. Not even Fi would do that. He'd expected shock, certainly. He'd expected questions, and lots of them. Perhaps there would even be tears, and some shouting. But to accuse Leannah of such an infamous scheme without even having met her . . .

Harry's hands shook. He couldn't even look at his sister. Not until he had control of himself. "Is this what you think?" he asked his father. "That I'm a dupe?"

Father lifted his hands away from the mantel, and turned. The look of disappointment in his eyes sent the blood rushing from Harry's heart.

"I think it's likely. Marriage traps are as old as, well, marriage itself."

No. Harry shook his head, hard, as if he needed to clear it. They didn't understand. He must make them understand. "How could it be a trap? We met entirely by accident."

"Yes, that is a point in favor, but these sharpers can be very clever. Some play a very long game, or it may just have been you were in the right place at the right time when they were setting out to catch their mark. You of all men should know how such gangs work."

Father was not comparing Leannah to some dockside smuggler or gambling hall sharp. Such an accusation was not to be permitted, not even from his father, not even under these admittedly extraordinary circumstances. Harry rose to his feet and faced him squarely.

"Here's what I know. I know that when it looked like Fi was all but throwing her life away, we all stood by her. I know that mother's family did not approve of her marriage to you, and that it was accomplished in haste, down by the Fleet, unless I'm much mistaken. Am I the only one of us to be judged because I act impulsively?"

"This isn't impulse!" cried Fiona. "This is you being robbed, Harry!"

"Then it is my money to lose!" he shouted. "Unlike what you . . ."

"Stop this at once." Mother's ice-cold command lashed across the room, completely silencing whatever Harry had meant to add. "Sit down, both of you."

Harry stared hard at Fiona. Neither one of them was going to directly defy Mother, any more than they had as children, but neither one was going to be the first to back down either.

"Sit," Mother repeated. Father drew himself up straight and folded his hands behind him, and simply waited. Between the pair of them, the senior Mr. and Mrs. Rayburn could wait until a very cold doomsday arrived or obedience was achieved. When he was a boy, it sometimes seemed to Harry they didn't particularly care which came first.

Somewhat to his surprise, it was Fiona who gave in. This time she did sit in the armchair, which was closest. She clasped her hands on her knees, and dropped her gaze. But in the instant before she did, Harry thought he saw the glimmer of tears in her eyes. He tried to tell himself this wasn't genuine feeling. It was just more of Fi's dramatics, but he couldn't quite believe it.

He dropped back down onto his chair.

"Tell us about her," said his mother softly.

"Mother . . ."

"Please, Harry."

He tried, but describing Leannah was even more difficult than making sense of the circumstances under which they met. Her looks were easy enough—but how to describe her demeanor, her wit, and her nerve? What words did he have that would make clear her genuine and anxious concern for her sister, or her steady good sense in the most difficult of circumstances? Could he speak of her physical courage? He wanted to tell them how the reins had cut her delicate hands and she'd barely flinched from the pain—but he was afraid that might just make her look hardened.

Nothing was made easier by all the things he could not say but that nonetheless filled his mind to the brim. He could not speak of Leannah's passion and her delight in his touch, much less the searing heat of her lovemaking. He could not explain how it was her voice that cut through the red haze of his anger as Dickenson lay on the floor in front of him. In that moment, all he could think was he hadn't punished the bastard nearly enough—until Leannah called his name. She reminded him that he was home and he was himself, not that wastrel on the docks who couldn't tell the dead from the living.

Where was Leannah now? Harry's gaze drifted toward the window and the square outside. What kind of reception was she getting from her own family? It must be cushioned by the fact that her sister and uncle already knew what happened.

They, however, would still have Dickenson to deal with, and her father, who was not well. Harry wished he were with her. It had been a bad idea to go separately, but how could he have known that? He'd never before felt alone when he faced his family.

It was thinking of Leannah that finally gave Harry his voice. He did not know if his words were the right ones, but they were all he had.

"I have no way to convince you that what has happened has happened honestly," he said. If his voice sounded hoarse, it was at least steady. "I am very aware of how fantastical it sounds. I can only tell you that it has happened, and that I intend to approach my marriage as openly and honestly as I can. If I have made a mistake, then I have, and I will deal with that as I must." For a brief instant, Harry's words, and his confidence wavered. He clenched his fist. He must finish. He must say the rest of it. "If you feel you cannot stand by me, then I will understand."

Now it was his parents who looked stunned. It was perhaps a paradox, but their shock lit fresh hope inside him.

His father came forward and gripped his shoulder. There was nothing tentative in the gesture, or the words that accompanied it. "Of course we will stand by you, Harry."

"You're our son," said Mother, her whole bearing filled with her familiar quiet dignity. "Nothing changes that."

His sister remained silent, which, Harry had to admit, made for quite the change.

"Fi?"

Fi snorted and looked away.

"Fiona, that is entirely unladylike," their mother informed her, but it had the air of a reflex rather than a genuine rebuke.

Fi, however, refused to be mollified.

"I'm sorry, but, but, Mother, this whole thing is impossible! You're only ready to believe it because it's Harry! If it were me, you'd already be talking to the lawyers about bringing suit for fraud!"

"Fiona!"

"It's true! Harry, you're my brother and I love you, but you've always been the one who got the benefit of the doubt. Good, solid, steady Harry." Her imitation of their father was nothing short of remarkable, especially considering she was a foot shorter than he and female besides. "But will you look at what he's done? He's gone from trying to marry Agnes Featherhead . . ."

"Featherington," said Harry, because he did not know what else to say.

Fi ignored the interruption. "We've all known for months the girl was entirely unsuitable, but no one said anything, because this is *Harry* and we can all count on him to do right in the end. Then, not a handful of hours after he's been jilted, he up and marries this Mrs. Wakefield person. Marries her! And here we are, once again ready to make any sort of excuse, because surely Harry's sound judgment must prove right! Well, brother of mine, you have excellent judgment when it comes to dry goods and spices, but none at all when it comes to women!"

"That's en—" began Mother.

"Yes, yes, I know, that's enough," Fiona said, and there was real bitterness behind the words. "It's always 'That's enough, Fiona' and 'You go on, Harry.' Apparently, marriage won't change that for either of us, no matter how it comes about."

Harry felt his mind reeling. He was used to all sorts of storms and scenes from Fiona, but this was different. He could count on the fingers of one hand the times he'd seen her truly, deeply angry. That her anger was reasonless and unjust only made it harder to bear. She seemed to be implying their parents had always been easier on him, when the truth was the exact reverse. It was Fi who had been indulged since birth.

It seemed, though, that he was not the only one who felt this had gone beyond one of Fiona's normal displays. Mother shot her a warm and quelling glance.

"When can we meet . . . Leannah?" Mother asked.

"Soon. We're staying at the Colonnade," he added.

"Very nice," said Fiona acidly.

Harry ignored her. "I'm sure she'll want to call as soon as may be, if you'll receive her."

"You'll consult with her and let us know, then?"

"Of course I will." It occurred to Harry he had just been dismissed. Oh, it was done politely, even gently, but that changed nothing. It was as if by his hasty marriage he'd become a distant acquaintance and this unexpected call had gone on just a little too long.

Something inside twisted. He didn't want to leave things like this, but he had no idea what to do to fix them. He got to his feet. He was shaking, but he couldn't stop himself. He turned toward the door, to find his father blocked his way.

"Harry, I think you and I should have a private talk."

Twenty-Two

"Father, is it true, what Fiona said? About how you regarded Agnes?"

They stood out on the flagstone terrace. The gardens were chill, and remained more gray and brown than green. But out here they were far less likely to be overheard than any in room inside the house.

"It is." Father rested his fingertips on the terrace railing and looked at the sky as if he was deciding if the good weather would hold, or if he needed to batten down the hatches. "We—your mother and I—did not think you and Miss Featherington were well suited. However, we were confident you'd see it was a poor match before you reached the point of making an offer."

Harry found he needed several deep breaths before he could continue. He knew his father well, better than many sons ever did. When it became clear that Harry wasn't really cut out for university, he had taken Harry to sea on a trading voyage. They'd travelled down the coast and around the Horn. They'd visited Constantinople, Cathay, and Bombay. From his father, Harry learned how to deal with importers, with manufacturers, with men of all stations in settings that ranged from drawing rooms, to government offices, to the docks of a dozen different countries. He'd learned more of the fair and the foul of what it meant to be a man in those years than he ever could have at university, and that wasn't all. By the time he came back and settled into his job managing the warehouses, Harry had learned to respect his father, and to be proud of him. He wanted to be worthy of his good opinion and his trust. He had come home today aware that his hasty marriage might have jeopardized the regard he prized most in the world, but he still shrank from hearing it said out loud.

"Do you believe I married Leannah simply because Agnes turned me down?"

Father's gaze did not leave the sky. It looked as if he meant to track to progress of each gray cloud.

"I believe that might have had something to do with it. Disappointment in love works hard on a man and clouds his judgment." It occurred to Harry his father wasn't seeing the sky, not anymore. He was looking into the long past. "It wasn't your mother I took to that Fleet marriage house, you know. It was quite another girl. I was sick with fury at the time, because I thought she'd betrayed me."

"I didn't know."

"Well, it's not something I'm proud of." Father paused. "Harry, I've never asked you what happened that night in Calais . . ."

Harry stifled an oath. Why was it that every time he thought he'd found his footing in this endless wrangling, someone was determined to throw him back off balance? He had not come here to discuss Calais. This visit had nothing to do with that incident, that accident.

But even as he opened his mouth to say as much, Harry could clearly see the dead man's eyes staring up at him from the filthy cobbles. Man. Harry hung his head. The fellow had been little more than a boy, and a very drunk boy at that. He was clearly lovesick over a girl who'd preferred the party of wealthy Englishmen to the youth, despite his smart new grenadier's uniform. Harry hadn't even heard the girl's name clearly, or the boy's either. He just knew the boy had taken offence at their laughing with the girl. He'd decided to pick a fight, and Harry had decided to oblige, more because he'd wanted to show off for the girl, and his friends, than for any real offence.

And then that young, drunk grenadier had slipped and hit his head on one of those damned cat's-head stones that paved the streets by the quay. But Harry was so far gone in his own anger he couldn't see how bad it was. He'd kicked him, hard, in the guts.

The boy was already dead, and he'd kicked him. It was only after his friends had hauled him back that he really saw the blood, and those startled, still eyes. It was like the body couldn't believe its soul had fled.

But as terrible as that moment had been, it was not the worst of it.

The worst had come when he'd gone to the boy's house. His friends told him to stay away. They told him to get on the next ship across the Channel and forget any of it had ever happened. But, no, Harry Rayburn was going to take responsibility. He was going to apologize, and to offer to make what amends he could.

So he'd stood before the dead man's two sisters and his widowed mother. He'd told them what had happened. He'd asked forgiveness.

The mother had climbed to her feet. Trembling, she'd walked toward Harry and looked up at him with rheumy eyes.

"You," she said, her voice breaking from the strain of her emotion. "You tell me. Where's his money?"

The words had sent him reeling. The sisters had joined in shrilly. They wanted to know where the money was. They'd sent their brother into that casino to try to win the money they needed for their dresses, for the house, and to keep up their appearances. He'd been supposed to bring them back the results. Now they would have to make excuses to their creditors, and to the world at large for his stupid neglect of his duty. How could he, they wanted to know, become distracted by a girl when they needed him? While the sisters tried to work out what story they would tell to cover up the incident, the mother screamed at Harry, demanding to know why he hadn't thought to rifle her dead son's pockets.

He'd torn his own wallet from his coat, dropped it on the table, and walked away. He hadn't looked back, but he always pictured them falling on it like vultures.

Harry grit his teeth and, slow inch by slow inch, he shoved the vision of those squabbling women away from him. He could not fall into this trap. He would not let that moment and its shock and horror consume him. It was only one man, only a fight, and an accident. The family had been in shock, that was all. They surely mourned their loved one later. Harry must put that whole incident firmly in the past, where it belonged. He must keep his attention here, now, in the present.

"Calais has nothing to do with my marrying."

"Doesn't it?" Father looked down at him. Somehow it never felt fair that even though he was a grown man, his father remained the taller of them. "You've all but chained yourself to your desk since we got back. Every time I've suggested another trip out, you've put me off. It's as if you didn't want to leave England again, as if you were afraid of something."

Harry gripped the cold stone railing in both hands and stared out across the damp lawn. The snowdrops and crocuses were the only color decorating the dark beds, although a few daffodils were showing their green spikes. Over the far wall, Harry could see the brick turrets of St. James's Palace and the royal pennant snapping briskly in the April breeze.

"Your mother spoke for both of us back in there, Harry," said Father from behind his back. "You are my son, and I love you. Nothing will change that. When you're ready to tell me what really happened, I will hear you, no matter what."

Harry found himself unable to answer. Anger roiled in his guts. He couldn't go on like this. If he did, he'd start shouting. He hadn't come here to start more arguments. This was about mending any breaches that had been opened by his marriage before they could grow into a genuine divide. He must ensure that Leannah was received by his family with the courtesy and kindness she deserved. He couldn't do that if he, and everybody else, was still dwelling on Calais.

"There's nothing to tell," Harry said to the muddy garden. "It was an accident, and I was at fault."

"Even accidents have consequences, Harry, and they leave their own scars."

He must put a stop to this, for good and all. If his family was going to persist in seeing everything the wrong way around, then they'd have to learn to do it in silence, at least within his hearing. "I did not marry Leannah because Agnes turned me down," he said flatly. "I did not marry her because of an accident in Calais. I married her because I fell in love—suddenly, perhaps foolishly, but that is the beginning and the end of it."

Love. It surprised him how easily the word slipped out. Was Leannah telling her parent the same? He wanted to believe that. He needed to believe it. It was all he had to hang on to as he struggled to stay calm under his father's searching gaze.

"Since you say so, Harry, I've no choice but to believe you," Father said. "But you'll have to give us time."

"I know. I do know."

"I'm sure Mother's put a flea in Fiona's ear about all this." A smile flickered across Father's face as he looked toward the house, and Harry felt the tension in his shoulders ease. "You will need to make sure the new Mrs. Rayburn comes to visit soon. If she's all you say . . ."

"She is." Hope rose again, and it was almost as painful as the anger had been.

"Then I'm sure that visit will go a long way toward smoothing things over." But Father's attention did not return to Harry. It remained fixed on the house. The relief and hope that had been building in him faltered.

"You're going to say 'but.'" Harry tried to make of joke of it, but he knew as soon as the words were out that he'd failed.

"Is she with child, Harry?"

"Not that I'm aware of." Harry stopped, frozen in place by his own choice of words. "Sir, you are not suggesting . . ."

Father did not even attempt to look abashed. His face had hardened into its most determined lines. "I am, and I am saying it now because others will say it later."

"No," snapped Harry. "I won't allow it. Not even from you."

"It hadn't even crossed your mind?" asked Father, and for the first time in this entire nightmarish conversation, he sounded truly aghast.

"Of course not! You still think she's trying to put something over on me!"

Father made no answer. In the face of yet another bout of silence, Harry felt all the anger he'd struggled so hard to hold in check boil over.

"Fiona was right about one thing. Nothing has changed. Any member of our family can commit any style of outrage, but not Harry. It's Harry's job to help clean it all up, but heaven forbid he get his own hands dirty!"

"You know that's not true."

"Oh, yes, of course I do. How could I possibly be angry when you are all simply so concerned for my well-being? That wouldn't be reaction of a sound, steady man. It certainly wouldn't be good and upright to say it out loud! Well, perhaps I'm not the man you all believe me to be."

"Harry, you're upset and I understand that."

"Yes, I am upset and I have a right to be. You're doing that exact thing you've always warned me against. You're rushing to judgment!"

"You just need to give us time . . ."

"And how much time have you given me? How much have you given her?" He jabbed his finger toward the empty garden, as if Leannah was even now hurrying across the damp lawn. "You haven't even met her and you've all gone from accusing her of dangling after a soft mark to trying to cover up a bastard!"

A dark flush crept up his father's neck, coloring his sallow cheeks. Harry stood straight and still. He would not back down. He would not apologize. He would not be accused of being a fool, or have his word doubted, not even by his own family.

When his father spoke again, it was plain he chose his words with great care. "This has been . . . an extraordinary few days and I understand why you might be unsettled. But you are better than this. You understand that it's hard for all of us, and that I have to ask exactly these questions. The family reputation . . ."

"Reputation!" cried Harry. "When have any of us given a hang about reputation? What is it you've always said? 'We are what we are, and the world may take us or leave us alone as it chooses.'"

"Of course, and I mean it. But with your sister's marriage . . ."

Harry threw up his hands. "We're back to Fiona. I swear, if I'd known what joining the aristocracy was going to make of us, I never would have helped James find her."

"If I didn't know you better, I'd think you were deliberately misunderstanding."

"And if I didn't know you better, I might believe you were

becoming a social climber. Reputation! I'll bet that's what the conversation's about in there." Harry's eyes narrowed as he glanced toward the sitting room window. Someone had drawn the curtains, so the Rayburn women could argue unobserved. "The two of them are busy concocting some sort of story, working out how to excuse my marriage, or, better yet, to cover it up entirely . . ."

"That, Harold, is taking it too far!"

"Is it? You can say that and still wonder why I don't want to talk about Calais."

"Enough!"

"Yes, I quite agree." Harry met his father's gaze without flinching. "I've heard everything from you I'm going to and I've said all I came here to say. What you choose to do with it is your business. I'm going back home to my wife."

Harry turned on his heel and walked away, and he did not once let himself look back. If his father wanted him to hesitate, let alone turn around, he'd have to call him back, and he'd have to apologize.

But he did not, and that silence followed Harry all the way through the gardens, and out the back gate.

Oh, Leannah, he thought as he let the latch fall closed. *I hope it's gone better for you. It must have gone better.*

Because in that moment, he could not imagine how anything could have gone worse.

Twenty-Three

The groomsman from the Colonnade pulled Rumor and Gossip up gently in front of the rented house in Byswater Street. It was not, however, any member of Leannah's family who loitered near the area railing to greet them.

Leannah recognized the thin man by his crooked neck and squinting gaze. His name was Dawes, and he worked for the livery stable where they kept Gossip and Rumor, as well as Bonaparte.

"Well, well, she decided to return after all," Dawes remarked as he sauntered toward the carriage. "I hope you're not planning to put those two up at Mr. Hughes's?"

"Have a care, fellow." The driver held up the whip. "You'll use respect when addressing the lady."

"So I will, so I will, squire." Dawes tugged his forelock a little too showily. "That is if the lady uses some respect with me and Mr. Hughes, and agrees to pay the bill for the housing and feeding of this very fine team, not to mention one saddle horse that eats enough for ten, if I may be frank."

"It's all right," said Leannah to the driver. "This man is Mr. Dawes, and he's right. We owe his employer money." She took a deep breath and attempted to assume a brisk air. "If you will send your bill to the attention of Mrs. Rayburn at the Colonnade, it will be settled immediately."

Very deliberately, Dawes leaned over the gutter and spat. "Mrs. *Rayburn*? Can we wish you happy, then?"

"If you like. You will be paid in any case," she said this with what she hoped was a careless tone. The house door had opened, and Genny stood watching from the threshold. Even at this distance, Leannah could see the worry written across her face. She made herself continue speaking to the driver. "Dawes will show you to the stables. You may give Mr. Hughes this on account." She handed over one of Harry's guineas. "And for your trouble," she added a shilling. She felt Dawes watching her. His eyes trailed over her old dress. At least she had a bonnet now, and gloves, although they were strained at the seams because of her bandages. Despite these improvements, she knew exactly what he was thinking about where the money she held out must have come from, and she cringed inwardly.

"Very good, ma'am." The driver touched his hat brim to her as he accepted the coins and then moved to position the step so she could get down from the carriage. "When I've seen to the horses, I'll be back to find out if there's anything more you require."

"Thank you." She'd seen for herself the man was more than capable of handling her team as he drove the barouche through the streets. So, it was with only a small tremor of concern she turned away to mount the steps to the door Genny held open.

Genny drew her at once into the dim hallway. There, she threw her arms around Leannah's shoulders and held her tightly. Leannah returned her sister's embrace for a long moment, as if she needed to reassure herself that the welcome was genuine, and her sister still real.

"You look very well," said Genny when they were finally able to pull away from each other. She spoke the words a little more judiciously than Leannah would have liked, but at least she meant them. That would be enough for now.

"You're exaggerating," Leannah chose to respond as if she heard nothing but the compliment. "I look like I've been ridden hard and put away wet."

Which, considering the passionate night she'd enjoyed in Harry's arms was an entirely inappropriate metaphor to choose. Leannah felt her blush raise immediately, and she could do nothing at all about it.

Genny quirked an inquiring brow, which deepened Leannah's blush, but also eased her worries. If anything were truly wrong in the house, her sister's less-than-ladylike sense of humor would not be in evidence now.

Then, over Genny's shoulder, Leannah saw Mrs. Falwell peering anxiously through the kitchen door. "We'll speak later, Mrs. Falwell," she said, and the woman all but fled. She sighed. What they'd speak about, she did not know. She should be very angry with her. She should even consider dismissing her outright, but there were so many other things that needed to be sorted out first.

Footsteps thundered overhead.

"Lea!" Jeremy cried as he barreled down the stairs and up the narrow hall. "Is it true? Is it really?"

"Is what true?" asked Leannah as her younger brother skidded to a halt in front of her. Of them all, Jeremy had the reddest hair, and the most freckles. Although he had only just turned twelve, it would not be too much longer before Jeremy was able to look her, or at least Genny, right in the eye.

"Tommy Hargrave says his sister said that you got kidnapped last night by a highwayman and taken to Gretna Green and married at pistol point! I told him he was a liar because it's three hundred miles to Gretna and no highwayman would have more than one horse, and he said it must have been a whole gang plotting marrying you for your money and I said you hadn't got any and he said it was jewels and I said . . ."

"Oh, good heavens!" Leannah grabbed her brother's arm and hurried him back up to the third floor, with Genny at her heels. She pushed Jeremy into his room and slammed the door shut. "What made you think such a ridiculous story could possibly be true?"

"Where did you hear any of this?" demanded Genny at almost the same moment.

"I told you." Jeremy dropped onto his narrow, wood-framed bed, and bounced. "It was Tommy Hargrave. But were you abducted? Did you get the pistol away from him and escape? You had Gossip and Rumor, so you should have been able to outrun any highwayman's nag. I wish I could have seen the chase. I would have gone after you, but Bishop hid my saddle and . . ."

"Jeremy, hush!" Her head had begun to spin. Leannah pressed her fingers to her temples to try to slow it.

"And stop bouncing!" added Genny for good measure.

Jeremy, for a wonder, both hushed and stilled, giving Leannah a moment to draw in several deep, shuddering breaths. "You know perfectly well you are spouting nonsense. There was no highwayman and no pistol."

"But Tommy . . ."

"Jeremy, no one was abducted." She paused. "No one in this family, at any rate."

"Then where'd you get that ring?" Jeremy jabbed a finger at the diamond flashing on Leannah's hand. "Did he steal it? Did he force you to marry him?"

"No!" cried Leannah and Genny together.

"Then did he force Genny . . ."

"No one was forced into anything! It was my choice to marry!"

As Leannah's words rang through the room, Jeremy leaned back on his pillow, folded his arms behind his head and put on an entirely self-satisfied smile.

Genny's jaw dropped. "You little *brat*. You made up that story about Tommy Hargrave!"

Jeremy shrugged. "It was the only way I'd get you to tell me anything. You were so busy hushing me and saying nothing had happened." He grinned up at them. "But I knew if I poured out enough outrages, you'd tell the truth." He paused again. "By the way, Tommy Hargrave did say Genny eloped. I knocked him down."

Leannah groped for the stool by Jeremy's battered writing desk, and sat down heavily. "That was wrong of you."

"Was not. You're my sister, and he's got no business talking about you."

"All right, Jeremy, all right." She waved her hand. "Yes, I'm married. His name is Harry Rayburn, and I am now Mrs. Rayburn. At the moment, that's all there is to the story."

"Is not."

"If you're going to interrogate me, Jeremy, you will at least use proper grammar."

Her brother rolled his eyes. "It is not, Sister dear. I am quite certain there is much more to this tale than you have said so far. For example, did . . ."

Leannah did not wait for him to finish. "Does Father know?"

Jeremy pushed himself up onto his elbows, his face suddenly serious. As difficult as Father's long illness had been for Leannah and Genny, it had been worse for Jeremy. He was young now, but he was growing fast. He had a quick mind and an engaging air. He also had his father who sat trembling in his study, afraid to go out of doors and entirely unable to aid or advise a youth who must soon find his own way in the world of men.

"I don't think he does know," Jeremy said. "Aunt's been sitting with him the whole time, so I can't really tell." He paused and Leannah's breath caught in her throat at the set of his jaw and the clarity of his gaze. He looked like their father, back in the very beginning, before she understood how his determination to make them rich kept their lives turning around in a vicious circle.

"Will your getting married fix things?" asked Jeremy.

"Of course it will," said Genny stoutly. "Hasn't Lea always fixed things whenever we've been in trouble?"

That might be true, but trouble kept coming back. Jeremy understood this as well as any of them, and that understanding showed in the way his doubtful gaze did not waver in the least.

"I don't know," Leannah sighed. "But it might."

"You shouldn't have to keep getting married to fix things. It's . . . it's . . . unseemly. When I come into my own, you'll never have to again. I'll take care of us all."

Leannah touched her brother's shoulder. She thought to hug him, but he was on his dignity now and she didn't want to let him know she still saw him as a little boy. "I know you will, Jeremy. But right now, we must all hang together as best we can." She took Genny's hand, making a circle of the three of them. "That means taking care of each other, and making sure as much of this as possible stays in the family, all right?" Her siblings nodded solemnly, and Leannah felt a twinge beneath her ribs. "It also means no more knocking down the other boys." She shook Jeremy's shoulder and tried to speak lightly. "If anyone asks you what happened, you say your sister got married quietly, and there's nothing more to it than that. Getting into fights will just make people believe the worst."

The look on Jeremy's face all but broke her heart. She'd lost count of the number of times she'd delivered similar instructions: Stay quiet. Don't fan the flames of rumor. Keep up appearances. Hide the truth behind closed doors.

It was no wonder the boy was turning devious. She'd been teaching him to lie since he could talk.

"All right, I won't do it again," muttered Jeremy, but that mercenary gleam showed in his Morehouse green eyes. "But only if you tell me what's really going on."

"And now it's blackmail!" Genny threw up her hands.

"Well, what am I supposed to do? *You* won't tell me anything."

Leannah put up her hands to forestall what was in danger of becoming a real quarrel.

"Jeremy, Genny, stop. I will tell you everything I can, as soon as I can. That's a promise. Just now, however, I have to go speak with Father."

"Of course. We'll wait here." Genny said this directly to Jeremy.

Leannah left the room before she had to acknowledge the way Jeremy muttered, "Will not."

The stairs creaked underfoot as Leannah descended. With each step, dread rose around her. When she was with Harry, everything had seemed new. In his arms, she had found a dream of the future, and for once that future was clear and uncluttered.

But could she hold on to that dream? Here in the dingy rented house, where her troubles seemed to whisper to her from the very walls, Leannah was no longer sure. She'd dreamed of new beginnings, for her siblings and for herself before. But they'd started over so many times, and they had always ended up in the same place—scrambling, and hiding.

If that happened this time, it was Harry she'd drag down into trouble with them, just as she had dragged Elias.

No, she told herself sternly. *I was just a girl with Elias. I was blind and trying to believe. I will not let Harry be hurt, whatever happens.*

"Lea."

Leannah jumped. She'd been so lost in her thoughts she hadn't heard Genny following her down the stairs.

"I'm sorry," said her sister. "I know I told you I'd wait, but I didn't want to say this in front of Jeremy. Is everything . . . all right? With Mr. Rayburn? And, well, being married?"

"Yes," Leannah replied at once. "Better than I could have believed."

This did not seem to reassure Genny much. "You've set up at the Colonnade? That's quite expensive."

Leannah frowned. Her sister was not given to murmuring about such matters. "Genny, what's wrong?"

"It's just me fretting over nothing, I'm sure." The forced cheerfulness of this statement was painfully obvious. "But you should perhaps know I overheard Bishop and Mrs. Falwell talking about the bills. The grocer's not going to extend us any more credit."

"Oh. Well. I'll go talk with him." She thought about the money Harry'd given her. She hadn't counted it, but surely there was enough there to renew the grocer's good faith.

This should have made her feel better. She should have moved at once to reassure Genny, but Leannah remained silent. This was her first day away from her husband, and it seemed that all she was doing was using his money to pay her family's debts. She remembered the look Dawes had given her and that memory was like a smear of soot across her skin.

She was sure Genny saw that thought in her. Her sister looked ashamed. She was thinking she'd driven Leannah into disgrace.

Or is it just me? Have I conjured up a dream of love for Harry Rayburn to try to convince myself that that is not what's happened?

No. That is not what happened. I will not let it be.

Leannah glanced up to the top of the staircase, looking for Jeremy. But of course, if the boy were listening, he'd be too canny to stand where he could be seen.

She took her sister's elbow and moved them a little farther out of the stairwell. "What else, Genny?" Leannah asked softly.

"Mr. Valloy came by yesterday. He said he had an appointment to call on you."

Leannah blanched. Mr. Valloy had been calling to make his marriage proposal, the one she'd given him every reason to believe she was prepared to accept. Except that when he'd come to make the thing formal, she'd been driving down the road with her new husband. Leannah closed her eyes.

"He was angry," said Genny.

"He has a right to be," said Leannah. *Think of Harry,* she told herself. *Think of all that you've done and all you will do. Think about your private vows when you married him. You knew then this would not be easy. You cannot shrink from it now.* "I'll write to him as soon as I've spoken to Father." She glanced down at the diamond band on her smallest finger, which Jeremy had spotted right away. Father's mind and eyesight were nothing like so clear, and yet it would not do for this stone to make the announcement for her yet again.

Leannah twisted Harry's ring from her finger.

"You'd better take this." She handed it to her sister. "Father's sure to notice it."

Genny held the ring up in her two fingers. The scrupulous look she leveled against it owed more to the jeweler than to a romantic girl looking at a lovely wedding ring. It crossed Leannah's mind that her sister doubted whether the diamond was genuine. "But you are going to tell him, aren't you?" asked Genny.

The remark stung. "Of course I am, but I'd like to tell the story in its proper order and not have him jump to conclusions, like Jeremy did."

It was plain Genny had yet more on her mind, but there was no time for that now. Leannah already felt her nerve straining. She had to face her father and tell him. She could not delay things any longer, especially not after Genny's reminder that Father was not the only man with whom she must speak regarding her new status as a married woman.

Leannah turned her back on her sister, dragged her composure together, and walked into the study.

Twenty-Four

❧

I t felt like a thousand years since Leannah had left this room
in such a rush, and it felt like no time at all. Almost everything was as she left it. The ledger still lay firmly shut on the
desk guarded by the neat piles of bills and correspondence.
The fire had been allowed to burn low in the grate to save coal,
and the curtains were drawn close to save father's nerves.

Father himself sat on the sofa, asleep with his chin on his
breast and his old green dressing gown wrapped loosely around
him. The only other person in the room was little Aunt Clarence, who put down her embroidery the moment Leannah
entered to totter over to meet her.

"I'm so glad you're back, Leannah." She murmured the
words so as not to disturb Father. "Are you quite well, my dear?"

Aunt Clarence was a tiny bird of a woman, complete with
big brown eyes and a crooked, beaky nose. Her years as a
clergyman's wife had not been easy. She spent her days per-
forming the sort of charity work that had little to do with drawing room committees and much to do with going from house
to house through the slums and rookeries. Her labors had
left her joints stiff and swollen and her breath short. Despite
this, her energy showed in her kind, clear gaze and she
embraced her wayward niece readily.

"I am quite well, Aunt." Leannah pressed her cheek to the
older woman's. "I suppose Uncle's told you what's happened?"

"Of course he has. He's been very worried about you, as have I."

"I'm sorry to have made so much trouble. How has father been?"

"Quiet and calm," she answered and relief rushed through Leannah. "He thinks you've been with Mrs. Watersen."

"So Genny told me. You can go now, Aunt. I'll sit with him until he wakes up."

"Leannah, I know that whatever you've done, you've done with the best of intentions . . ."

Leannah's mind drifted back to the money, and the debts it would pay. She tried to see past it, to Harry and all they had already shared, but it was so hard here with all her oldest doubts and fears crowding around her. "I hope that's true, Aunt," she murmured. "You will forgive me, but I do need to be alone for a moment."

"Yes, of course," replied Aunt Clarence. "I'll just go check on Genny." She moved away, but Leannah stopped her.

"My reticule is on the table in the hall. Will you see if there's enough in there for Bishop to go pay the grocer and the collier?"

An unmistakable flicker of concern crossed Aunt Clarence's face but Leannah turned away, quickly, casually, as if no one could possibly consider anything wrong with the request, or the circumstances. Of course, that was not true. She just had to hope her aunt was willing to let her pretend.

It seemed that she was, because Aunt Clarence took her leave without further comment. Leannah closed the door behind her with a sigh. She crossed the room to the hearth and very carefully poked up the fire. With a feeling of grim determination, she laid half a dozen fresh coals on the blaze. Then she went to the window and carefully lifted the edge of the drape. It was as if she needed to reassure herself that there was still a world outside and that she had not fallen into some sort of isolated nightmare.

But the street was there. A light rain had begun outside, and it lent a shimmer to the paving stones. Harry was out there someplace, in St. James Square to be precise, talking with his own family. She hoped, for both their sakes, it was going more smoothly than her encounter with her own family had so far.

Father shifted uneasily on the sofa and Leannah let the curtain fall closed. She sat down on the faded horsehair chair by the hearth and folded her hands. Her finger felt bare without Harry's ring. She wished he was beside her to fill this chill room with his good spirits and his banter.

We'll be back together soon. She rubbed her bare hands together. *We will.*

She looked at Father. Sleep had relaxed his face, but did nothing to remove the sadness. That worn expression of regret was as familiar to Leannah as his glow of pride and elation. It had accompanied each turn of their fortunes.

She tried to think what she would say when he woke, but the words would not come. The last time she and her father had spoken of marriage, he'd been at the height of his confidence and his power. They'd been back in Devon then, but not in their own house. The story they'd put about the neighborhood was that they'd taken the cottage because the larger house was in drastic need of repairs. They said that they had decided they would buy some land to build new, but until the sight was chosen, they would stay in this snug little cottage.

Father's study in the cottage had been lovely and sunny. His books and papers filled it to the brim, and the stacks of newspapers and magazines covered every empty surface. She'd remembered her heart was beating fast with anticipation as he sat her down on the leather sofa. She'd been so sure he was going to tell her that their fortunes had turned, and that she was going to be able to have a season after all.

Instead, Father told her he had fixed her future with his friend and neighbor, Mr. Wakefield.

"Now, Leannah, my dear, I know Elias Wakefield's not a handsome beau, but you'll soon grow to appreciate him. What good is a wild young buck as a husband, eh? He'd have no steadiness, and certainly no standing. He'll chafe at the marriage harness and be forever wandering off to chase after what he can't have. Would I marry my daughter to such an untrustworthy creature? No. Would a man of that kind be anything like good enough for a Morehouse? Never. I'll have only the best for you, Lea, and that means a sound man, an absolutely trustworthy man. A man who, above all, can keep you as you deserve to be kept. It's you I'm thinking of, Lea."

She remembered how the words had washed over her. She remembered allowing herself to sink into the flood of them. It was always easier that way. When Father spoke, she must believe him. It didn't matter how often he'd been wrong before. It wasn't his fault things hadn't turned out as they hoped. Misfortune could come to anyone. The great thing was how a man recovered from it, and how he provided for his family. Here he was thinking of how best to provide for her, and she must believe that.

This time, she remembered saying to herself, *it will be different.*

This time it will be different, the words echoed through her mind. They were practically the Morehouse family motto. It should be carved over the door of their house. Houses.

She'd taught herself to believe it, though. Leannah stared at the fire, but she couldn't see it clearly for the tears welling up in her eyes. She'd not only taught belief to herself, she'd had done her best to teach it to Genny and Jeremy. To do otherwise would mean she doubted her father's word and ability, and that would have broken her heart in two, as it had her mother's.

Because she believed, she hadn't worried about the conversations Father and Elias held behind closed doors. She hadn't worried about the bank drafts Elias wrote, or the legal men and their papers. What was there to worry about? Thanks to Elias, she was finally able to spend the season in London, not just once, but every single year. As a married, and wealthy, woman, society was entirely open to her. She made friends. She entertained. She went to the opera and the theater. What were a few whispers in the background compared to all that?

As for the fact that Elias placed so much money into Father's hands, that was nothing to worry about. Elias had more than enough, and Father understood investing. He could turn the Wakefield fortune into something extraordinary. All he needed was time, and enough money. There was plenty this time. A few losses could be easily born. They'd be recouped on the next upturn in the market. This time would be different.

A tear trickled down Leannah's cheek, leaving a trail of cold behind. Father stirred on the sofa and his eyes fluttered. She wiped away the damp on her cheek.

"Leannah?" Father's head jerked up, and for a moment, the confusion she so dreaded came over him.

"I'm here, Father." Leannah moved herself quickly into his field of vision.

"Ah. Yes. Your aunt said you'd be back soon." He smoothed and straightened his dressing gown. "How is Mrs. Watersen?"

She studied him for a moment before she framed her answer. This time, the confusion appeared to have been momentary. His eyes were already clear. His wrinkled hand held steady as he reached to the side table and poured himself a glass of watered wine from the decanter. She waited until he'd taken a sip.

"I was not with Mrs. Watersen, Father."

Father blinked. "But your aunt and Genny . . ."

"They did not want to tell you where I really was because we were concerned about the shock."

"I see." Father took another sip of wine, and stared into the glass. His pallid lips twitched as he attempted a smile. "I suppose I cannot blame you for that. Are you going to tell me now?"

Yes. She took a deep breath. "I'm married father. To a man named Harry Rayburn. He's a merchant and his family owns two warehouses."

Father said nothing. He raised his glass again but now his hands were shaking, and shaking badly. Leannah reached forward to take the wine from him, but he managed to lift the glass to his lips and drink. It rattled as he set it down on the table.

"You were to marry Mr. Valloy."

"I had considered it. I changed my mind."

"You did not tell me that, either." Uncertainty lay beneath the statement and she knew he was trying to remember if they had spoken of it.

"No. It all happened very quickly."

She could not tell whether he believed this. His face had settled into different lines—harder, far more bitter lines. He took up the wineglass and drank again. Leannah's heart quailed, because she knew what was coming.

"This . . . Rayburn, I think you said his name was? He has money?"

"Yes," whispered Leannah.

"Enough?"

Is there ever enough? But she didn't say that. "I believe his income is quite substantial."

She didn't look at him. She did not want to see the calculations passing back and forth behind his eyes. First would come the pitiless, cold, and endless inventorying of all he owned or could reach. This would be quickly followed by the decisions regarding what of that could be most easily converted into money to feed into his investments.

She waited for him to ask how much she could bring him. She steeled herself for it. She could not be angry with him. Anger would accomplish nothing. But at the same time, she knew she could not fall back into the easy habit of letting Father's words carry her away. He would talk of all the good to come if he just had a little money, just one more chance. He'd talk and talk, and keep on talking, until he believed it, along with everybody else.

She must not listen, not this time. If she yielded in the slightest when Father began talking, the whole terrible cycle would begin again. She must think of Genny and Jeremy, and herself. She must think of Harry as well. She could not fail Harry as she had failed Elias.

Where are you, Harry? What is your father saying to you? Please don't let it be anything like this.

But Father didn't ask for numbers. He didn't speak at all. Slowly, in a series of sharp jerks, he lowered his face into the palm of his hand. His thin shoulders shuddered, and he began to cry.

"What have I done to you?"

Leannah slipped from her own chair and knelt in front of him. She grasped his hand tightly and pulled it away from his face.

"Father, please! I need you to try to concentrate."

"On what?" The hand she held tightened into a fist. "On the fact that I'm the one who taught you to sell yourself for *money*?"

"That's not what this is, father." *Not this time. This time it will be different.*

"Can you swear to that? Can you really?"

"Yes. I can, and I do." She said it, and she made herself mean it. But at the same time in the back of her mind, the terrible little slivers of doubt dug that much more deeply.

I must think of Harry. I must think of his arms about me, of the laughter and all we've shared already. That is why I have done this. For passion. For happiness, and for the hope of love to grow from all that. To protect Genny and Jeremy, and yes, Father as well. It isn't about the money. This time it is different. It is.

"Well, if it's done, then it's done," said Father. His voice was flat, defeated. The defeat touched a spark to her anger. She was trying to help in the only way she could. How could he make her efforts sound like another failure? Leannah squashed the emotion, and the question, down.

"What will happen now?" he asked.

"I'm not entirely certain. There has been very little time to plan."

Father got to his feet. He turned, and he walked to the windows, where the drapes were closed tight. He reached out one crooked hand and grasped the edge of the hideous puce velveteen. He stayed like that for three long, deep breaths.

Then came the question she'd been dreading. "Has he settled anything on you?"

"Not yet. I don't know that he intends to."

Here it comes. I will not listen. No matter what he says.

Father turned his face toward her. *I will not believe it this time. He is not well, and I know that. Perhaps he was never well.*

"Don't . . ." he stammered. "Don't tell me about it, Leannah. No matter how much I ask you to. Don't tell me. Don't let him . . ." He swallowed. "Don't let him give me any money. Don't let me convince him to give me any."

In a heartbeat, Leannah was on her feet and embracing her father. He felt so frail, but still she hugged him as close as she dared and held on. She held him for love and sorrow and for the understanding of how much strength it took for him to speak those words. Uncle might believe he'd changed, but Leannah knew better, and in this one moment, so did Father.

"I will make sure he's careful," she told him. "I know you're not well yet."

He pulled back and nodded, patting her hands. "I don't . . . I don't know what to do, Leannah. Should I give you my blessing?"

She managed a small smile. "You don't need to do anything."

"Well, you have my blessing in any case. It might prove good for . . . something." He struggled and in the end he smiled as well. "So, Mrs. Rayburn. Will you stay and take some tea? We should all do some little thing to celebrate, don't you think? Perhaps Mrs. Falwell can make some of those scones of hers."

Leannah thought about the grocer and their credit, but she made herself reply lightly. "That's a lovely idea, Father. I'll ring for her, and then tell Genny and Jeremy to come down."

She reached for the bell, but a scratching sounded at the door, and Mrs. Falwell peeped inside.

"I beg your pardon, sir, madam, but Mr. Valloy is here."

Twenty-Five

When the house had been built, its tiny back parlor had probably caught the afternoon sun. Since then, other houses had grown up close around it. Now, the room remained gloomy no matter what the time of day. Its single window showed the brick wall and lace curtains of the neighbor's home. This was part of the reason the rent had come so cheap.

Terrance stood in the middle of the threadbare room, his hands folded behind his back and his face sour. Terrance Valloy was not a handsome man, but he was a striking one. His wide mouth could be expressive, his black eyes quick and penetrating. His dark hair had gone gray at the temples, which lent him a distinguished air that suited his serious nature. He was not given to wild swings of emotion, or swings of any sort. This fixedness of outlook and approach was part of what had attracted Leannah to the idea of the marriage, if not to the man himself. Terrance would not permit himself to be swayed by a plausible appeal to his heart. He would always consult facts.

"Mr. Valloy." Leannah closed the door. It was not, strictly speaking, proper to do so, but she was not going to let the rest of the house hear any more of this particular conversation than was necessary. "I must apologize about yesterday. It was entirely . . ."

"I know."

Terrance spoke the words so calmly and so finally, they caught Leannah quite off guard. "I'm sorry?"

"I know where you were, and I know you have married another man. One Harry Rayburn, if I recall the name correctly."

I certainly didn't marry several Harry Rayburns. Leannah swallowed those words. "How did you find out?"

"Mr. Dickenson called on me at my club."

Of course he did. Mr. Dickenson would not see any reason to speak to Genny before matters were settled among those with the power to make the pertinent decisions.

Leannah rested her fingertips against the round table. She wanted to lean against it. Her knees were trembling, but now was not the time to make any sort of display. Terrance abhorred display.

"I intended to be the one to inform you of the change in my circumstances." When she was sure she could do so smoothly, she lowered herself into the cane-bottomed chair and gestured for Mr. Valloy to take the tapestried seat. He did not move. "I have treated you in an unforgivably cavalier fashion. You have every right to be angry."

"Yes." Mr. Valloy's face and voice remained entirely bland as he uttered the word. She might have assumed him entirely indifferent to the whole affair, had it not been for the look in his hooded eyes.

An inexpressible weariness came over Leannah. She tried to set it aside. She had known this interview must come. It was better that it came now. The sooner matters were finished between her and Mr. Valloy, the sooner they could both return to their separate lives.

"Beyond apology, I have nothing to offer you, Mr. Valloy," she said, striving for something like the detachment he displayed. "The thing is done. If you wish to speak to my husband, I can . . ."

Terrance waved this away impatiently. "Contrary to popular belief, Mrs. Wake . . . Mrs. Rayburn, I am not an entirely unsympathetic man. I was aware that the foundation of the marriage I proposed was not any sort of undying affection on your part."

What on earth was one to say to that? "No, I'm afraid not."

"You must also be aware that I have it in my power to make your life with your chosen spouse difficult indeed."

Terrance's tone did not change at all as he spoke these words. The matter-of-fact demeanor that masked the chill anger in his eyes set her skin crawling. *I was going to marry this man.* Her throat tightened. *I was going to say yes.*

"Why would you bother to make my life difficult?" she asked. "You cannot possibly wish to prolong the scandal."

"No. I wish to walk away and wash my hands of you entirely. Unfortunately, there are factors at work that prevent me from following this course of action, at least in the short term."

He did not sit down, even now. He had barely moved since she entered the room. There was nothing restless or impatient in his attitude. He would say what he had to say, and he would return to his point as often as he must until he achieved the result he wished.

I was going to say yes to him.

"What is it you want, Mr. Valloy?" She couldn't look at him. Her guilt at having behaved so improperly, combined with her growing awareness that by her impulse she had achieved a narrow escape, made it impossible to keep her countenance.

"The Wakefield property."

Leannah's head snapped up.

"Sign the property over to me," he said as coolly as if they discussed a book, or a used newspaper. "Once that is accomplished, I will leave you to pursue whatever future you can find with your Mr. Rayburn."

Mr. Valloy's expression had not changed. There was no sign of greed in him, no desire, no care or concern, not even any satisfaction at seeing her so disconcerted by his outrageous demand. There was nothing in him at all except that terribly controlled anger.

"I cannot do what you ask. The property is not mine to dispose of."

"It's in trust for your brother, yes, yes, but the executorship of a trust may be transferred. I have reviewed the list of the lawyers and bankers who complete the board. They are men who will be amenable to my management. It will only require your father's signature on the proper documents to transfer his place on the board to me. You hold sway in this house. You will convince your father, and later, your brother, to do what is required."

"That property is worth relatively little," said Leannah, fighting to keep the confusion from her thoughts and her voice. "The rents are barely enough to cover the taxes. The house is in ruins. Why would you wish to burden yourself with it?"

"That, surely, is my business. The fact is I do want it, and in return, I am willing to give you what you want, namely, your freedom." As he spoke that last word, an emotion finally leeched into Mr. Valloy's voice—contempt.

"If you think you can frighten me with scandal . . ."

"I will do far worse than add fuel to a scandal, Mrs. Rayburn. I will make sure that your father's past comes back to haunt him, and you, in the most direct manner possible."

And there it was—the first, last, and greatest fear Leannah harbored.

After each of Father's failures, there had always been a mad scramble, not only to salvage whatever money and possessions could be salvaged, but to paper over the losses enough to prevent legal action. She was not aware that her father had ever stepped so far over the line that what he did could be called criminal, but he had come close. Certainly close enough that a case could be opened, questions raised and investigations begun, especially by a man of influence. Any such inquiry would raise all the old gossip right out of its grave. It would ruin Genny's future and it would ravage what little strength Father had left, even if it did not end with prison. Leannah's hands shook, despite how tightly she kept them clasped. It would destroy the fragile new beginning she had made with Harry.

Right up until the moment Mr. Valloy said the words aloud, Leannah had been able to imagine he would not stoop so low. She wanted to believe there was some shred of decent feeling in him. Perhaps it was only wounded vanity, but it cut deep to be confronted by the fact that she had been so horribly mistaken in this man's character.

"Was the property the reason you wanted to marry me?"

Terrance shrugged. "I see no reason to deny it, especially considering the turn events have taken."

Leannah felt a kind of panic descend. Her throat tightened around her breath and her heart began to hammer against her ribs. The house, the reality of her family and her past, they were closing in, smothering her up. Harry not only wasn't here, it seemed to her in that moment he couldn't be possible here. Such a good, open person as Harry couldn't live in this place where people were only seen in terms of how much money they could bring in.

She had to get out, get away into the world outside. She had to find Harry, and to wrap him in her arms. She had to love him with her body until she could be certain he was real, and never doubt it again.

Leannah closed her eyes. She must concentrate on what was in front of her. As much as she might wish it, Harry was not here. This was Mr. Valloy in front of her. If she gave him control of the land, she not only gave him a property worth thousands of pounds, but she signed away what small security her brother had. Indeed, the only security any of them had if . . . no, she would not think of anything happening to Harry.

But what would Harry do when he heard all of this? That thought sent a fresh tremor through her. Mr. Valloy's eyes darkened.

He thinks I'm afraid of him. He thinks it's his threat. He has no idea of the truth.

"I know you will be an ornament to any gathering, and will keep a man's house with great economy," Terrance went on. Perhaps he meant to salve her wounded pride, or perhaps he just meant to be sure his case had been stated fully and exactly. "These are important points, as are your personal assets of grace, poise, and refinement. These, however, are attributes that may readily be found elsewhere. The land is unique."

Why? Why unique? The questions cut right through the tangle of thought and feeling. *You have money enough to buy whatever parcel of land you wish. Why do you want ours?*

"That land is my brother's." Her hands had stilled, as had the tremor in her voice. "It is the security for his future."

"Surely your new husband is wealthy enough to provide for your brother as well as yourself. Indeed I would be surprised to hear that you had not already secured such promises from him, probably in writing."

Anger burned. It engulfed her, raising her to her feet. The

man in front of her was no longer an injured suitor entitled to some measure of consideration. Mr. Valloy meant to use her—like her father had used her, like even sad, kind Elias had used her. No more. She was done with it.

"You can hardly present me with such charming compliments and expect me to meekly accede to your wishes."

"I expect, Mrs. Rayburn, that you will consult your own advantage, as you always have. No." Mr. Valloy lifted his hand. "Do not turn righteous with me, ma'am. You were not marrying me for love, but for money and security. I must assume this Rayburn was able to tempt you with more of one or the other."

Leannah wanted to scream at him. She wanted to shout the truth of Harry's love and laughter, his kindness, and his honesty. Yes, honesty, which was entirely lacking in this conversation, despite Mr. Valloy's protestations.

But she would not bring Harry into this. Mr. Valloy would only accuse her of rubbishy sentimentality.

But the rest is real as well. The good is real. The passion is real.

"I did not have to come here," Mr. Valloy told her. "I do, however, retain some respect for you. Your conduct, up until now, has been forthright. I admire that. Now, I have made my offer. It will not be repeated. Assign the Wakefield property to me and my management, or you and your family will suffer."

He would do exactly as he said. Hadn't she considered this steadfast determination one of his great merits? He was also a powerful man with a far-reaching web of connections in the city. He would use them to get what he wanted.

But why was he threatening to use them at all? If he believed her to be acting solely for her own advantage, why was he not offering to buy the land outright?

"And that is all you want from me?" Uncertainty and confusion turned her voice hoarse. "If I arrange for the land to be turned over to you, you will leave us alone?"

Mr. Valloy's eyes flickered about the room, as if he expected the rest of her family to magically appear. "Yes." He said.

You're lying. The realization formed crystal clear in her mind. She had seen enough evasion in her life to know precisely what it looked like. In this moment, Mr. Valloy had descended from not telling the complete truth into deliberate falsehood.

"Will you give me some time to consider?" asked Leannah.

"No. I have seen what happens when I give you time. You will accept, or you will decline. If you accept, you will put your intentions in writing."

Such writing would tighten his grip on her. He wanted to make sure she understood that. He believed her weak and friendless. In fact, she could feign that weakness now. She could cry or even grow faint. Such a show would throw him off his guard, and make him believe the worst of her and the best of himself. Even men who prided themselves on their hard, logical minds could be made careless by their sense of superiority. She had watched her mother when faced with such men—landlords and bailiffs and creditors. She knew what they thought of women who found themselves in straits. She could use that presumption to buy time.

Leannah looked again at Mr. Valloy's face, and at the wintery disgust in his dark eyes. Oh, yes, if she began to cry now, he would believe her to be simple, weak, overwhelmed. She thought of her father in the study, of all his practiced manipulation of others. She thought of how he used his charm, his distracting humor, and ability to spin endless excuses and complex tales to turn away the troubles he himself had created. She thought about how her mother had cried and pleaded and swooned to help salvage what she could when the failures finally came.

Her hand curled into a fist, and she missed the touch of Harry's ring, the one talisman she had of him. Harry did not prevaricate. He did not manipulate those around him. He acted from honest and passionate impulse. He risked scandal and outrage to take the cleaner course, even when he had no idea where it might lead.

But Harry Rayburn was a man. His father was prosperous, his sister married into the aristocracy. They did not depend on him. If impulse and honesty led him astray, he alone would pay the price.

She was not a child this time. In this moment here, alone in her heart and her mind, she must choose, for her family and for herself. The weight was impossible to bear. It would crush her. It was crushing her. She must wrench each word out from under it.

"If you . . . if you must have my answer now, sir, then you will." Her fist curled tighter. The absence of the ring struck deeper. Harry was not here. He could not rescue her from this moment.

"My answer is no."

Twenty-Six

Dearest Harry,

I regret that I have been delayed. I still hope to meet you at our rooms tonight and will come as soon as I can.

I am sorry,
Leannah

Harry folded the letter carefully. Leannah had a neat hand, clear yet graceful. It suited her. The letter was unscented and sealed with a plain wafer. He was aware he was concentrating on these tiny details in a futile attempt to hold back the disappointment flooding through him. She had, after all, warned him something might happen. Her father's health was fragile, she said, and there was no denying the news of her marriage would be unsettling, if not shocking. Look at how his family had received it.

No, don't. Harry grit his teeth.

After his disastrous visit home, he took his time making his way back to the hotel. He hadn't wanted to return to Leannah until at least some of the anger and bewilderment faded. Nothing that had happened between his family and himself was her fault. He didn't want her blaming herself for it.

So, he dismissed the hack and started walking. He continued to walk until he was able to convince himself that it would all work out. This marriage might not last forever, despite his best intentions, but it was too soon for troubles to begin. Surely, they could have another little space of time with each other, to explore and understand, and to dream. He stood by the river and wondered how things could possibly have gone worse. He passed the Houses of Parliament and wondered exactly when his nearest and dearest had become so pigheaded. He made his way across Hanover Square, wondering exactly when that same state of mind had overtaken him.

Despite all that, he had not only wanted Leannah to be waiting for him in their rooms, he'd needed her. He needed to wrap her in his arms and reassure himself that she was real. After listening to his parents and his sister level accusations of deceit and fraud, he needed to not just hold her, but to talk with her. He needed to hear her say again what she felt and what she meant to do. She had to tell him that although she might not yet love him, she wanted time to find that love.

Harry stopped in front of the hearth and ran both hands through his hair. He was pacing. This was no good. He needed to get out, find some fresh air and clear his head. Then again, maybe not. He'd already walked half the length of the city and it didn't seem to have done much good. Still, if the choice was between walking and staying in here and brooding, he knew which he preferred.

"Lewis," he called to the maid who was at her station in Leannah's rooms. "If Mrs. Rayburn comes back, tell her I've gone for a walk. I won't be long."

"Yes, sir."

Harry retrieved hat, coat, and stick. At least it wasn't raining anymore. Marshall was running out of dry coats for him to borrow. Perhaps he'd walk to Hyde Park, take a ramble across the meadows. Or perhaps he should head for Bond Street. The idea pleased him. He was, after all, a married man. He should find a present for his wife; something that would bring a light to her lovely green eyes and maybe make her throw her arms around his neck and shower him with kisses. But his competency didn't extend to choosing hats or handkerchiefs. A pet didn't seem appropriate. A piece of jewelry? Something to make up for the fact that she was married with a borrowed ring that did not suit the size of her hand or the form of her character.

With these pleasant thoughts accompanying him, Harry walked down toward the lobby. But when he reached the broad landing, he froze. Two men stood at the front desk talking to the clerk, and he knew them both. The man doing the talking was none other than Nathaniel Penrose and behind him loomed Philip Montcalm.

Harry could not imagine his friends had arrived to wish him joy. Much to his chagrin, he considered hurrying back up the stairs before he was seen. But Harry dismissed that notion as soon as it occurred. Whatever else he did, he would not play the coward's part.

Taking a firmer grip on his stick and his nerve, Harry walked down the stairs and straight across the Colonnade's busy lobby.

"I suppose I shouldn't be surprised," he said as he came up behind his friends.

Both men turned. Seen side by side, they were a study in contrasts. Philip was tall, lean, and fair. His dark gold hair and deep-set eyes generally earned him the description of "leonine," especially back in the day when he earned his reputation as one of the most notorious rakes in all London.

Nathaniel was the shorter of the two, and broader. With his black hair and blue eyes, he could pass for an Irishman or a Frenchman as easily as he could an aristocrat. He had, in fact, passed as each when his work for the navy demanded it. Right now, dressed neatly in a plain black coat, white shirt, and dark trousers, and standing beside the impeccable Montcalm, Nathaniel looked more like a private secretary than anything else.

"So," Harry planted his stick firmly in front of him. "Who told you two about my marriage? No, wait, let me guess . . ."

"Fiona." They all said together.

"You can't blame her for being concerned," said Philip. Harry had known Philip Montcalm for less than a year. Last season Montcalm had entered into his own unexpected marriage. His chosen wife happened to be one of Fiona's best friends and a lady Harry had known since childhood. Since then, he'd discovered the former "Lord of the Rakes" was a good man, a devoted husband, and a steady friend.

Harry was not, however, in any mood to be mollified by anybody regarding yet another instance of Fiona's presumption. "I can blame her for interfering."

"Perhaps, perhaps not," replied Nathaniel calmly. "Either way, I don't think this is something you want to discuss in the lobby."

Harry didn't like the look his friend was giving him. It was too quiet, too calm. It made him feel as if Nathaniel was waiting for him to give something away. His temper was still sore, but he reined back his impulsive retort. This encounter with his best friends had to come, just like his encounter with his family. Better to get it over with.

Still, he was not going to risk Leannah returning to find these two in their rooms making whatever arguments or accusations they might have.

"I've arranged for a private room at the coffeehouse next door," said Nathaniel.

"Of course you have," muttered Harry. "Bloody spy."

Nathaniel smiled, and bowed, entirely unperturbed. "Are you coming?"

Harry sighed. "Let's get this over with."

As they started together for the doors and the street, Harry couldn't help but notice how Philip walked directly behind him. "What's the matter, Montcalm?" he muttered. "Do you think I'm going to make a dash for it?"

"Could you blame me if I did?"

"Yes, sir, I could."

"That's your prerogative." Like Nathaniel, Philip would not be drawn out.

St. Alban's coffeehouse was a noisy, smoky place, occupied by men who hunched over their cups and their newspapers. They clearly knew Nathaniel here, because when the three men walked through the doors, the stout dame who kept the moneybox hailed him immediately. She conducted them personally up to a clean but Spartan sitting room, where the coffee and cups waited on the sideboard.

Philip passed the woman a coin, and shut the door behind them. Nathaniel poured himself some coffee and stirred in a sugar lump, tasted, and added another.

Harry set hat and stick aside, and dropped into the nearest chair.

"All right, we're here. Now." He held up his fingers so he could tick off the various points his friends no doubt intended to make. "I'm a fool. I'm being imposed upon. No good will come of it. Is there anything else?"

Nathaniel and Philip exchanged glances that held more than a hint of amusement.

"It's what I admire about you, Harry," said Philip, settling himself into another chair. "Straight at 'em and damn the maneuvers."

"I'm in no mood to be mocked, Philip," Harry growled. "Or managed," he added to Nathaniel, who stood at the sideboard stirring yet another sugar lump into his coffee. He must be up to five by now.

"No one's going to do either," said Philip. "But we're your friends, Harry."

"Yes, yes, and my family's already thoroughly covered the subject of what an idiot Harry is. They did so, may I add, without ever having met my wife."

He sat back and waited for his friends, like his family, to protest, but Nathaniel only shook his head.

"Your family may not have met the new Mrs. Rayburn, but I have."

"As have I," said Philip.

Harry started, but then realized he shouldn't have been so surprised. Despite how it sometimes appeared, London society was a fairly small world. Any one person might easily be no more than two or three introductions from any other.

"She didn't come up to town until after she was Mrs. Wakefield," Philip went on. "Beautiful young woman." If Harry didn't know how firmly Philip had renounced his rake's existence, he might have been jealous of the keen appreciation that filled his voice. "Impeccable manners. A little wistful, perhaps, but she was married right out of the schoolroom to a much older man."

Nathaniel nodded, sipped his coffee, and got up to add yet another sugar lump. "Her marriage to Wakefield was very much the usual thing. He hoped to get himself an heir, and he made an excellent settlement in return for her hand."

Harry felt his gaze flicker from Nathaniel to Philip. They were working their way up to something, but he could not yet fathom what it was. "I'm sorry to disappoint you, gentlemen, but Leannah has already told me this." Most of it, anyway.

"Did she tell you what happened to the money?" Although Nathaniel had gotten his brew sweet enough, he didn't sit down. He stood by the window, drinking, and looking out at the street, apparently idly, but Harry knew that was a ruse. Nathaniel was watching for something, or somebody.

"She told me the money's gone, and yes, she told me *before* we married," he added.

"Did she tell you how it was lost?" inquired Philip.

"From the way you say that, I gather you feel it's important."

This last seemed to strain even Nathaniel's patience. "Stop it, Harry. You're acting like we're the board of inquiry."

"What you're acting like is a pair of barristers with me on the witness stand," he shot back. "Listen to me, both of you. You have clearly come to present some horrible secret about my new wife, so you may as well just come out with it and save us all a lot of time."

Philip set his cup down. "Harry, Mrs. Rayburn's maiden name is Leannah Morehouse, and her father is Octavian Morehouse."

"And?"

Philip's brows shot up in genuine surprise. "You never heard of him?"

Nathaniel uttered a soft oath. "No, he hasn't. Of course, I should have realized. He was out of the country when it all happened." His face turned dark, and blatantly suspicious.

"And the family cleared out so quickly, the immediate scandal died away. Even if the aftershocks didn't," added Philip.

"And the biggest part of that scandal was what didn't happen . . ." Nathaniel spoke these words softly, but his anger rang in each one.

"Are you two here to talk to me or each other?" cut in Harry.

"Sorry, Harry." Nathaniel took a healthy swallow of coffee, and glanced out over the street one more time. Was he looking for Leannah? Or somebody else? "The facts are these. Octavian

Morehouse was—is—one of those men who play the markets. A speculator."

"Unfortunately," sighed Philip, "he had a tendency to play with other people's money."

"I'm sorry?" When had the room turned so cold? Harry glanced toward the coffee service, but he decided he'd be damned if he got up to take a cup. He didn't want either man to see him in the least disconcerted. He wasn't disconcerted. He was angry that his friends were proving as unreasonable as his family. It was enough to make a man wonder how he'd ever decided to trust any of them.

Philip leaned forward and rested his elbows on his knees. "Morehouse would talk wealthy individuals into giving him their money to invest in various shares. Always claimed to have insight into some infallible scheme or the other. There was nothing he wouldn't touch—housing developments, canals, bridges, all manner of corporations." Philip paused, to make sure he had Harry's complete attention. "He tried his patter on me, not once, but several times."

"So you're saying Leannah's father is a fraud?"

"Not a complete fraud, no," said Philip. "A number of his investments returned incredible sums."

"Which were then followed by incredible losses," said Nathaniel.

"Stocks are a risky game." Now he sounded hesitant, like he was making excuses. *Dammit all,* Harry cursed silently. He needed to get a handle on himself. But his mind kept returning to his empty rooms at the Colonnade, and to Leannah's note where she said she'd been delayed. That led him back to his own walk across London, the one he took to try to escape all the accusations that had been made already.

I will not hear this. I will not let them slander Leannah in front of me. And yet he did not interrupt. He told himself he needed to hear everything they had to say, so he could refute it in its entirety.

"Yes, stocks are very risky. Which was why most people were inclined to excuse the losses, and why he was accepted in society for as long as he was. He did make money for some men, at least for a while. He was also notoriously charming."

Nathaniel took up the thread. "The last straw came after his

daughter's marriage. As I said, Elias Wakefield made an incredibly generous settlement on his new bride. He also gave
Morehouse carte blanche to manage his affairs."

We have no money. My father is not well, Leannah's words
came echoing back. Harry felt the blood drain slowly from his
face.

"There was never any evidence of actual fraud, you understand," said Nathaniel. "But Morehouse did burn through thirty
thousand pounds in less than five years. Apparently, the first
Elias Wakefield knew of how far matters had gone was when
the beadles showed up to take some horses that Morehouse had
put up as collateral for a loan."

"What did Wakefield do?" Harry's voice had gone hoarse,
and his temper turned on himself. It might sound as if he was
shocked, as if he had begun to doubt Leannah.

Nathaniel drained his coffee cup. "He paid off the loan.
Loans, I should say. There were several by that point. To say
he acted with charity toward the family that ruined him is
putting it mildly." He looked into the dregs. Harry found himself wondering if Nathaniel had known Mr. Wakefield's family,
and if he had warned him as he was now attempting to warn
Harry.

Stop, he ordered himself. *Do not even begin to think on it.
There is nothing to this, nothing that involves Leannah at least.
She is not responsible for her father's failings.*

"He had to sell off much of what he still owned to pay the
notes. He was dying at the time, and he knew it. In his will, he
left his remaining land in trust to his wife's younger brother."

Harry's mouth had gone dry. He looked to the coffee again.
This time, he knew Nathaniel saw him do it. Damnit. They
were getting to him, despite everything. He was tired, worn
down from his walk and his argument with his father. Harry's
hand curled into a fist where it rested on the chair arm. "If
Wakefield made her brother his heir, he must have loved her."
He must have known she was not to blame for what
happened.

"Or he wanted to avoid the worst of the scandals," said
Philip. "Which would have included admitting he was duped
for the sake of . . ."

"Don't. You. Dare." Harry leveled his gaze at his friend. He was fully aware of sizing the other man up. He couldn't stop himself. He didn't want to stop himself. If Philip finished that sentence, he'd serve him as well as he'd served Dickenson. Nathaniel could have his share, too, if he wanted it.

Philip held up both hands. "All right, I won't. But *think*, will you? A woman brings a wealthy and well-known merchant's son to a country inn. She's beautiful. She's heartbroken and in dire straits. Maybe it's a coincidence. All well and good. But then her uncle, who just *happens* to be a clergyman just *happens* to arrive on the scene with a special license on which the names have not yet been entered? If someone told you this story what would you say it sounded like?"

"You're saying I've been duped."

Philip didn't even hesitate. "Yes, that's what I'm saying."

"What we're saying," put in Nathaniel. "Harry, you're the perfect target. You're afraid to leave home, but you're restless. You've got money to burn, and you spent the better part of a season chasing after one of the worst flirts in London but you didn't even notice how she was leading you on, because you were so desperate to try to settle down and put Calais behind you."

Harry climbed to his feet. He would not take this slander sitting down. No one had the right to talk as these two did, not to him, or any man. "Is your little conspiracy now expanding to include Miss Featherington?"

"No," replied Nathaniel calmly. "But Anthony Dickenson isn't out of the question."

That knocked Harry back on his heels. "Dickenson? The man Miss Morehouse eloped with? He's . . ."

"Bent as a corkscrew," said Nathaniel flatly. "The Dickenson family likes to make money, but hates risk. This drives them to use various means to ensure they can't lose. But nobody's been able to catch him at it. Not, may I add, for lack of trying." He turned his face away again, watching the street. Perhaps it was Dickenson he was watching for. "The kind of schemes his people run, though, take a considerable bit of money."

"It comes together this way," said Philip. "Octavian Morehouse is known for his inability to resist an investment he thinks will provide a huge profit. So, Dickenson tells him about some new scheme. Morehouse starts looking for money to invest." He paused for a moment, and then went on more softly. "He hasn't shied away from using his daughter to raise funds before, and he might not be terribly fastidious when it came to how she acquired his new son-in-law. No offence, Harry."

"No, of course not. Why in heaven's name would I be insulted by a single thing either of you have said?" Harry's fists clenched and unclenched and he didn't have the strength to control them. It was taking everything he had to remember that these men were his friends. "You've only called me a fool, and my wife . . ." He was shaking, he couldn't say it. He wouldn't say it.

"All I'm calling your wife at the moment is another victim," said Nathaniel. "I have no reason to believe she's done anything more than what she's been pressed to do by her father."

"At the moment," sneered Harry. "I suspect this particular belief could change."

"Yes."

Philip spread his hands. "Harry, Morehouse has ruined one son-in-law already. Wakefield was Morehouse's friend and his neighbor, and Morehouse not only hooked him, he baited the hook with his beautiful daughter. Why would he stick at playing the same game with a stranger? Especially with Dickenson egging him on."

Harry struggled to remember everything Leannah told him about herself and her father. There had to be something he could throw in Nathaniel's oh-so-concerned face. Some way to make them both see. Make them all see. They had already judged her. They seemed to think they had all the evidence. But they didn't know her. She was not a fool. She was not deceitful. They hadn't seen her with her sister. They hadn't held her. They knew some story about her previous marriage and were spinning it out into a grand conspiracy. Even when, as Nathaniel himself had pointed out, it was the sort of arrangement that happened every day.

He had to get out of here. Anger and doubt tore into him, and he had no idea which would win. He couldn't stay here and argue this out. He had to find Leannah before these two did. He wouldn't put it past Nathaniel to have had her followed. He had to warn her. He had to find some way to protect her from their accusations.

A thought struck him, and Harry found he was able to turn to face both Nathaniel and Philip.

"What happened to her settlement?"

"I'm sorry?" asked Nathaniel.

"This incredibly generous settlement you alluded to, where's that gone? That would have been legally hers, no matter what debts her father had run up."

The other men exchanged glances. "It's assumed that she gave it to her father to invest, along with everything else," said Nathaniel.

"So you don't know everything after all."

"No," Penrose admitted.

"I see. Thank you." Harry picked up his hat and stick. "Good-bye."

"Harry . . ." began Nathaniel.

"Good-bye, Penrose. Montcalm."

For the second time that day, Harry walked away from those closest to him. They didn't follow any more than his father had. Either they recognized the danger in him, or he'd been mistaken about how much they cared for him. After all, they now seemed perfectly willing to let him walk away into what they believed was a trap and a fraud.

What kind of friends are they, then? He stepped out into the street. *What kind of men have they become?*

But he couldn't stop himself from realizing that up there in that private room, they were wondering the same things about him.

For a brief terrible moment, Harry found himself on the quayside in Calais again, with the dead man staring up at him. His anger was bleeding away like the other man's life. He'd been afraid then, afraid as he had never been, and he didn't even know what was to come at the house with the mother and the sisters screaming and squabbling, all over money, always over money.

"Harry?" called a woman's voice. Her voice. Over the noises of the traffic and the turmoil of his mind, he heard her clearly.

"Leannah!" Harry whirled around. It was her. She was climbing down from the barouche, without even bothering to wait for the driver to put down the steps.

Harry ran toward her. He saw nothing else. There was nothing else. She'd come back, as she promised. Leannah was in his arms and he was kissing her, in front of all the world and she was warm and vibrant and real.

There was nothing else, and there never would be.

Twenty-Seven

Leannah didn't remember how they arrived back in their rooms. She was barely conscious of Lewis making her hasty retreat, or the door slamming behind her. There was only Harry, whom she wanted, and who wanted her.

The moment the servants removed themselves, Harry wrapped his arms around her. He pulled her to him and pressed his mouth fiercely over hers. For a moment, Leannah knew fear at the strength of his embrace and the raw emotion of his kiss, but fear quickly melted into desire.

"I need you," he murmured against her mouth. "I need you now."

"You have me," she answered him. "Anything you want, you will have."

He groaned and pressed his face against her shoulder. "Don't say so, Leannah. You have no idea what I want right now."

She took his face between her hands, lifting and turning him so she could look directly into his eyes. "Anything," she said again. "Anything at all."

They were clumsy, fumbling, frantic, clawing away at clothes and shoes, at anything that in any way separated them. All the while, Harry's eyes remained wide, distressed. What had happened to him? Something had. This desperation had not come from a few hours abstinence. But the distress changed and grew dark when she at last stood naked in front of him.

He ran his palm roughly over her cheek, down her throat to her breast. He grasped her there. When she gasped, he smiled and circled his thumb hard over her ruched nipple. The sensation burned through her to her core and she moaned.

His smile was dangerous as he lifted her breast, lowering his mouth so he could suck on her. She moaned again as his tongue lapped hungrily at her nipple, and she dug her fingers into his shoulders. Pleasure overcame her strength and it was a struggle to stay upright. Harry felt her faltering and cupped his free hand under her buttocks to hold her. He squeezed her there, too, hard, possessively.

When at last he raised his head, he was panting. The danger in his eyes had not subsided in the least.

"Lie down for me," he ordered. "Open yourself for me."

She was reeling with pleasure and need. The heat in his eyes was as maddening as any touch could be. His need was so complete, his member was straight and hard, so ready for her. She wanted to take him now, immediately. She needed to take him.

"Lie down!" he barked and the command thrilled her.

She moved to the bed and fell back on the soft quilts and bolsters. Harry circled to the foot of the bed, watching her. Lust burned in his eyes and in each tightly controlled movement. Leannah ran her hands up her thighs and around her hips. She pressed her hands to her folds, and spread her legs, doing as he ordered and opening herself to him.

"Please, Harry," she whispered. Her breasts were so heavy with want, she could barely breathe for the weight of them. The touch of her own hands was not pleasing, as it might have been if she were alone. With Harry watching, it only increased her desperation. "Please, I need you."

Harry moved forward. He was staring at her hands, at her folds. His hands slid across the sensitive inner skin of her legs and all the way up until his fingers curled around her thighs. He pushed her open yet farther. He leaned forward. She felt his breath hot against her hips, against her folds. She knew a moment of confusion. Then, his mouth pressed against her and his tongue thrust inside her and she forgot everything else.

It was beyond wickedness. It was pure wantonness and she wanted it never to end. She knotted her fingers in his hair. Maybe she cried his name. She couldn't tell. Her whole awareness was centered on his mouth against her. Harry lapped, and he sucked. He found her hot, greedy nubbin and he licked it mercilessly. She was frenzy. She was desire incarnate. When she cried out, caught between the bliss and agony of his attentions, he only licked harder.

And then he stopped. He pulled away and reared back over her. She cried out, confused, lost. There was nothing left of mind or intelligence. He'd burned them all away. There was nothing left but need.

"Oh, yes, that's good," he growled, as she struggled against his hands as he pressed her down against the bed. "But I want to see you when you come."

Without warning, he thrust his fingers into her.

"Yes!" Her body tightened around him, welcoming the invasion. It was good. It was better as he began to move, pumping into her, circling the heel of his palm hard against her mound. He held her ruthlessly in place with his free hand, even as he fucked her relentlessly with his fingers.

Leannah moaned. She struggled, writhing her hips, but that only drove him deeper. It felt so good. He had three fingers inside her now. He thrust hard and deep. He circled again, grinding his palm against her.

"You're going to come for me, Leannah. You're going to come so hard."

"Yes. Yes. Please."

"Because you're mine. Only mine."

"Yes, Harry. Only yours."

"You're going to come for me now!" He pressed down, rubbing her, fucking her with his words as much as with his hands. "Now!"

She shattered. Her hips slammed against his hands as her body wildly sought the source of its pleasure. He withdrew abruptly and she cried out. Still shuddering, almost feverish with the heat of the pleasure he'd given her, she felt his member press against her wet folds, and thrust inside.

"Oh, yes!"

How could she want yet more? She didn't know and she didn't care. It was nothing but the truth. She wanted him more than her next breath. He filled her and her shuddering body clamped down around him, holding him in place. But he was in no mood to be still. He thrust, driving himself into her not once, but again, and yet again. His hands were everywhere; on her breasts, on her buttocks and thighs, wrapping her tight around him.

"Harder!" she cried. "Harder!"

He obeyed, his frantic desire driving them both on. She laughed with it, she cried out with it. She wanted this madness, this final proof of how much he needed her. She needed it to be rough, blinding, unendurable. Nothing less would erase her agonizing doubt. She pressed her thighs against him and thrust her hips up, meeting him, matching him. He would not escape her. He would not outstrip her in this journey of passion. He was hers, only hers, as she was his.

He was groaning, panting. She felt the stillness amid the frantic motion, the pleasure that built and burned in the deepest part of her. He roared and he thrust, and his own climax overcame him. That maddened pulsing inside her was too much. She was coming again, riding his waves and her own.

The waves calmed, lowering them both down into their bodies again. Leannah pressed close to him, reveling in their mutual warmth and spent strength. He smiled at her, but what she saw in his eyes was not just love or gratitude for passion. There was relief, and the sight of it sent a breath of cold slipping through the easy warmth their lovemaking had left in her.

"What happened to you, Harry?" she asked.

He shook his head. "Not yet. I can't tell you yet." He took her hand and kissed her fingertips. "We're here, together, and that's all that matters."

But as she took him into her arms and cradled him against her, she knew just what had happened. Someone had told him—about her, and about her family. That was what had been behind the darkness in his claiming of her. He didn't want to believe what he had been told, but he could not escape it, either.

Leannah closed her eyes, but not before a tear slipped out from under her lids. She waited until Harry's breathing deepened and sleep took the last of the tension from his shoulders before she reached up to wipe it away.

Leannah did not sleep. She lay quite awake as darkness slid into the room and the fire faded away to gently glowing coals.

She listened to Harry's breathing, and held him in her arms, savoring his warmth and the exquisite contours of him.

All the while she knew this might very well be the last time she did so. He might have said that their being together was all that mattered, but the desperation with which he had taken her told its own story. He'd been hurt by what had happened to him when he returned to his family. He'd doubted her, doubted them.

Worse than this, though, was the fact that she could not be angry about that doubt. She could only stare into the night and remind herself she had known full well such uncertainty must come.

Her arm tightened around him, involuntarily. Harry stirred, and she tried to loosen her embrace. She tried to pull gently away so he would fall back asleep. But his eyes opened, and he smiled up at her.

Leannah felt her heart constrict painfully. *How will I ever learn to do without you?* She brushed his hair back from his brow.

"What is it, Leannah?" Harry murmured, running his hand across the curve of her shoulder. "What's troubling you?"

She considered lying. It was dark. As close as they were, he would not be able to read her face. But she couldn't do it. Maybe the time would come when she could lie to him, maybe soon, but it was not yet.

"You've been given questions, about me, about what I've done." It was the only way she could think to say it. "I want you to know I'll answer anything you ask."

"Perhaps answers aren't what I want from your mouth." Harry traced the line of her lips with his thumb. She was coming to love that gesture and that realization left an ache inside her. She wanted him. She wanted to roll him over and do whatever was necessary to make him hard, so she could take him inside her again.

She grasped his wrist and pulled his hand away from her face. Her palms stung as the salt of his skin leeched through her bandages, which had been loosened and disordered from their rough lovemaking. She ignored it.

"Ask me," she said. "I'm going to tell you anyway, but it will be easier if I know what's hurt you most."

She saw he wanted to deny that he had been hurt, or perhaps

even that he'd heard anything at all of her past. But slowly he turned and shifted in her grip until he could wrap his hand around hers. A look of soft disappointment filled his face. Leannah's throat tightened.

I will not cry. If it is over already, I will not cry. It's better this way. He should go before he can be hurt, by me or Father or Mr. Valloy. Anyone.

"Tell me about your first marriage." He spoke to their fingers, twined together against the crisp white sheets.

Leannah nodded. It was as good a place to start as any. All the same, she did not begin immediately. First, she reached up and touched his face. She smoothed her fingers across his brow and combed them through his entirely ridiculous and overgrown sideburns. She could not leave off touching him. She would not pull away. If this was the end already, she would let herself drink in every detail of him, so she would have at least that much to hold on to through all the dark nights to come.

"I was married to Elias Wakefield when I was nineteen."

"Married to?" Harry murmured. "That's an old-fashioned way of putting it."

"It's what happened. It was a bargain. Elias Wakefield was a friend of my father's and my father wanted his money to invest with. Elias . . ." She smoothed her palm across his shoulder. She had to say it. She had to tell him what she had been. "Elias wanted a young bride who might be able to give him an heir."

"I'm sorry."

She'd meant to keep looking at him, but she couldn't. She'd never said any of this out loud before. Until now, those who had needed to know had done so without her telling them.

"It was not so very bad. I always knew I'd be married however it would help my family. I was even cheerful, because I thought Mr. Wakefield was rich enough that this time Father's schemes could flourish."

"This time?"

Leannah nodded. "Our family fortunes rose and fell with the success of his market stratagems. When he found a solid investor and when the markets or the schemes cooperated, we were rich. When they didn't . . ." She bit her lip. "He was never caught by the tipstaves, but it was close a few times." Her fingers curled into a loose fist against his arm. "He always seemed to need just a little bit more than he had."

"Than his family had."

She shrugged. "I didn't let myself think about that. If I thought of anything, it was that I was helping make a future for Genevieve and Jeremy. They could do what they wanted. There'd be money for Jeremy to go to school, or take orders, or gain a commission. Genevieve could marry for love, or not marry at all.

"And Mr. Wakefield was a kind husband. He gave me plenty of money. He was glad to have me as his hostess. I tried very hard to keep his house in the style his station required. There was plenty of society. I even made friends with some other young wives." She smiled again, but she knew the expression was, at best, wistful. "We called ourselves the Schoolroom Club."

Harry swallowed. She touched his throat. He was stubbled. She would have to make sure he was more adequately barbered. If she had a right to make sure of anything regarding him after this. "I was even allowed to drive out in my own carriage. Elias was rather proud of my driving, and laughed at the matrons who were so scandalized. And the rest of it . . ."

"He wanted an heir," said Harry.

"Very much. He came to me almost every night. He . . . mostly couldn't complete the act. It wasn't bad." She whispered this. Shame crawled up her spine. But she couldn't tell what that shame was for. If she had laid down for her other husband without desire, it was no more than thousands of wives must do without complaint. "He didn't turn angry like some men. He just got sadder, and sadder. He even—" She bit her lip.

Harry waited. His hands spread against her back. He wasn't pulling away. He wasn't shuddering, or flinching in disgust. His gentle, steady touch gave her courage, if not hope. "He more or less gave me permission to have an affair. He said, 'I know, Leannah, I'm no dream of young woman's love. You know I wish for children. You should also know I will love, and care for any child that comes into this house.'"

She couldn't go on. She was doing this all wrong. Harry would now think the worst of poor Elias, even though he had done nothing worse than want children, and feel guilty over having bought a young girl to try to get them. After the will was revealed, and she'd had time to reflect, she'd realized that everything Elias had given her, and her father, had been to try to assuage that guilt.

"He tried to let you know that if you got pregnant by some other man, he'd claim the child," whispered Harry.

"I think he was hoping I'd do it. There were opportunities, but I just couldn't. I thought about it. I was so ashamed. I didn't know which way to turn. It was as if I was being disloyal by *not* having an affair." She lifted her eyes to his. *I watched them—the men in the ballrooms, the rakes and the Corinthians and the officers. I stared at them and hungered after them. I imagined them with me while Elias tried his best, but when it came to it, I couldn't bring any of them to my bed.*

How is it I can do this with you?

"You weren't in love," Harry said. Was he answering her words, or her thoughts?

"Perhaps. I don't know. Anyway, after five years Elias died. Before that, though, Father had lost all the money. In the end, the only thing left was one piece of land, and some of my widow's portion."

"He settled nothing on you when you married?"

"Oh, quite a lot actually."

"What happened to that?"

"I spent it, very shortly after I was widowed."

"It was spent?" said Harry. "Not lost?"

"Oh, no. I know exactly where it went."

She waited for him to ask where. But Harry's face went still. A whole set of emotions flitted behind his blue eyes and Leannah found she couldn't read any of them.

He will tell me good-bye, that it's best we separate now. He will tell me it's just for a little while, but he will say it all the same.

That, however, was not what he said. His hand squeezed hers, and he spoke slowly. "Leannah, are you with child now?"

So that was what his family and perhaps his friends had been saying. They said she had conceived a bastard more than a year after her husband had died, and now she had to cover it up. She must not be angry about it. It was only natural that they should suspect her.

"If I am with child, Harry, it happened yesterday."

For a moment, Harry looked shaken. She couldn't blame him for that, either. Until she said the words, she hadn't truly considered it. She might very well be with child. They'd taken no precautions against the possibility. Harry laid his palm across her belly, and met her gaze. Leannah let the warmth of his touch spread across her stomach, up her torso, into her breasts, and her heart. What if it was true? What if inside her even now a baby was growing with steely blue eyes and fair hair? Wonder and fear shot through her veins.

"I may be cut off," he said suddenly. "My father is afraid for me."

Leannah remained silent for a long moment. This was warning, and it was test. It was bitter that it should have to be said at all, but it had to, just like the question about the child had to be asked. It was also, she knew, only the beginning, just as her confrontation with Mr. Valloy yesterday was only the beginning.

She could end this now. She knew how to do it. She could pull away from him at this moment. She could be the one to suggest they separate, just for a little while. Just until tempers cooled and his family was able to see things in a better light. He would think she was leaving him because he could not give her enough money. It would create the first crack in his feelings for her, and, given time, his family and friends could break that crack wide open.

But if there was a baby . . . No. She would not use the specter of a child to bind him to her, not if he did not wish to stay.

And she would not lie. Not yet.

As much as she could while lying on her side, she straightened her shoulders and lifted her chin.

"I've been poor before, Harry. Probably poorer than you ever have. I know how to manage."

Harry smiled. It was slow as sunrise and just as bright. It lit his eyes, and an answering warmth inside her.

I love that smile, she thought. *I love this man.* And she knew it to be true.

Harry's hand slid beneath her jaw, lifting her face toward his. He kissed her. The desperation that made him rough was gone.

"I won't let them take you away from me, Leannah," he breathed. "Not so soon, and not without a fight."

Should she tell him? Should she say it? No, not yet. It was

too new. There was still so much that could go wrong. She would keep this much to herself, just for now, just in case. At the same time, she did not want to leave him doubting.

"We will fight them together, Harry," she murmured in answer. "I don't intend to lose you to anything less than the decision of your own heart."

He kissed her again with the exquisite ease and warmth that gave her so much delight. She melted at once against him and lay warm and soft and still as his hands glided across her—her arms, her breasts, her thighs, and buttocks. He was learning her body, giving every inch of her his absolute attention. It was as if he knew what her words had cost her and now sought to soothe away all her doubt and worry.

Slowly she began to respond. She looped her wrists around his neck so she would not distress either of them about her injured hands. She opened her thighs so he could slip inside her. When he did, he did not move again for a long time. He simply held her against him, letting them be together as close as two people could ever be. Leannah drifted on a steady river of warmth, and when her pleasure did crest again, it was a soft ripple of feeling, enveloping her as gently as the light in her husband's eyes.

Twenty-Eight

❦

"**Y**ou are going to insist on keeping them, aren't you?"
Leannah and Harry lay in the bed, cuddled close in
each other's arms. Leannah ran her bandaged palm along her
husband's jawline, studying the sensation of the crisp, curling
hairs of his sideburns against her sensitive skin.

"My whiskers?" Harry pushed himself up a little higher on
the bolsters. This attempt at putting on his dignity was rather
spoiled by the fact that his broad chest was swaddled in lace
coverlets and starched sheets. "I'll have you know they are
highly distinguished and the first stare of fashion."

Morning had not only arrived, it had almost passed. After
the passionate tempest of their reunion, they had both slept and
woken easily. The lovemaking that followed was tender, teasing, and prolonged. Leannah convinced Harry to lie back on
the bed and let her thoroughly explore his body with eyes and
fingers and tongue. Only when she could stand it no longer did
she straddle him, and together they settled him inside her so
they could move in the dance of intimacy that was quickly
becoming as necessary to her as breathing.

A breakfast had been ordered, but sat on the sideboard,
almost entirely neglected, because when Harry reached across
the table to hand her the marmalade, their fingertips had met.
This, naturally, led to a long, exceptionally heated look between
them, which in turn led to her rising from her chair to round
the table and kiss him. This wifely gesture caused him to pull

her down into his lap so he could kiss her back more conveniently, and slip his hands into her loosely tied wrapper to more thoroughly fondle her breasts and derriere. It was then, with Leannah straddling Harry's lap, they discovered that the chair was not quite big enough or sturdy enough for her to ride him as she chose, so there had been nothing to do but return to the bed.

"Well, it could be worse, I suppose." Leannah sighed and let her hand drift from Harry's whiskers to his throat. She couldn't get over the strength of him, the delight in each line and curve of his body. His form was spare, hard, entirely masculine, but there was a clean beauty to him that fascinated her. "You could be one of those men who goes through fifteen cravats in a morning trying to get the folds right."

"I do thank you for your enthusiastic support, Mrs. Rayburn."

"I am given to understand that there are many things a wife must suffer in silence." To emphasize this point, Leannah rolled over on her back and laid her hand across her eyes.

In this private darkness, she heard her husband chuckle. She felt his now-familiar touch as he ran his hand down her shoulder to the swell of her breast. "Silence is not your primary characteristic, or so I've observed." He took her hand away from her brow to kiss, and ran his thumb across her knuckles, and stopped. "Leannah, where's the ring?"

Leannah stared at her bare hand, horrified.

After her meeting with Mr. Valloy, she had been too angry and too frightened to even remember the ring. She'd sat in the study for a long time. She'd been so lost in thought, she hadn't even answered Genny's soft knock. She had heard the hinges creak as the door opened, but she did not turn around. She just stayed as she was, standing with her arms folded staring out the window at the neighbor's brick wall.

"Is everything all right, Leannah?" Genny asked.

"No, it is not all right." She did not turn around then, either. "When has it ever been all right?"

"What did he say to you?"

"Nothing I did not already know." She was being unreasonable. She should not be angry at her sister. It seemed she should never be angry at anyone. Except possibly Mr. Valloy. Oh, yes, she could be angry at Mr. Valloy. She just couldn't tell anyone why.

"Please, Genny, leave me be."

"I won't," said her sister stoutly. "You're too upset."

That had been the last straw. "I said leave me be! I have enough to contend with. I don't need you twittering about pretending to be a grown woman!"

Genny had made no reply. Leannah had hung her head and listened to the sound of the hinges creaking once more as the door closed behind her. She couldn't breathe. She couldn't think. The house and the weight of her family, her past, her whole life pressed down on her. She could do nothing but run. She'd grabbed up cloak and bonnet from the peg in the hall and hurried from the house without a word to anyone. She'd had only one thought. She must reach Harry. She hadn't once stopped to remember about the ring.

"I took it off before I went to talk with my father. I was hoping to cushion the blow. I must have . . . I left it with Genny."

I should tell him about Mr. Valloy, she ordered herself. *I can't keep this from him.*

But her tongue didn't move and she couldn't make it. There had been so many confessions to make in such a short time. Surely, this one could wait one more day, perhaps as much as a week. By then, if all went well, she would know what Mr. Valloy was really up to and she could lay it in front of Harry all at once.

None of this, however, stopped him from brushing his thumb across the bare place where his ring had been. But he smiled, and he lifted her hand and kissed it. "Did it work? Cushioning the blow, that is?"

"It's difficult to say," she admitted. "Father tried to take it easily."

"Would my calling at your house make things better or worse, do you think?"

But I don't want you to go there. I don't want you to become part of all that trouble. I want you separate and safe. Of course she could not say that. "I think it will help set his mind at ease. Genny's, too, of course, and you should meet Jeremy." She paused. "When should we call on your parents?"

Harry's expression turned grim, and the pain of it twisted under Leannah's ribs. "Once they've all stopped being . . . stubborn." Something of her feeling must have showed in her face, because Harry leaned across and kissed her brow. "Don't worry. They'll come around." But she heard something else under those words. She heard him wondering what would happen if they didn't.

Since she suspected Harry could no more answer that than she could, Leannah decided it was time to change the subject.

"If you're quite done distracting me, Mr. Rayburn, perhaps we could proceed to breakfast? I have business to conduct yet today." Mr. Valloy's call yesterday made that business more vital than ever, but Leannah found she was not ready to talk about that, either.

"Me, distracting you, Mrs. Rayburn?" Harry drew back and favored her with a look of complete shock. "It was you who distracted me, you wanton minx!"

"What on earth did I do?"

"Only kissed me, like this." He cupped her cheek with his palm as he brushed his lips across hers. "And this." His tongue ran along the edges of her mouth, tasting and teasing and opening her again.

"Oh," she whispered. "Like this."

By the time they finally dressed and sat down again at the table, the breakfast had gone stone cold. They ignored the hardened eggs and chops under their congealed sauces in favor of muffins, marmalade, and butter. Now that they were both decently attired, they could safely summon Marshall and Lewis for necessities like fresh coffee.

"You said you had business today. What sort?" asked Harry as he poured Leannah a fresh cup of coffee and passed the milk.

"I sent a note to Meredith Langely asking her to call. I think you said you know the Langelys?"

"I know of them. I think I've met Miss Langely once or twice."

"Meredith and I were at school together for a time. I mean

to consult her on how we can create a proper—call it a debut—for us, as a married couple." She tried not to see how he glanced at the place on her little finger where his ring used to be.

"Good. I shall be glad you have a friend with you." He picked up his last bit of muffin and set it down again. "I should tell you that I'm going to interview my solicitor, and my banker, about a settlement."

"Oh. Don't you think it would be better to wait?"

"No, actually, I don't." There was steel in his words, but it was not for her. "I want this part of the business behind us."

"Harry . . ." She hesitated. She did not want to ask this question. She certainly did not want to hear his answer, but she must. There were already enough secrets brimming in the air. "What happened when you went home?"

"My family is angry," he said simply, but he spoke more to his muffin than to her. "I also have a pair of, well, I'll call them friends for lack of any other polite term, who are attempting to convince me you were a charlatan who is intent on swindling me out of my money."

"They're the ones who told you about my father, aren't they?"

"Yes." He stretched out his hand until their fingertips met, but this time there was no passion in the touch, only reassurance. "I know you would have given me a full account, had you been given the chance."

Would I? Leannah ran her mind back over the past few days and all the hours she had spent with Harry, driving and dining and simply being together. It would have been the matter of a moment to lay out the bare facts of her father's identity and her family's most recent ruin. But she hadn't.

"I should have done it right away," she whispered. "I should have made you understand who you were really marrying."

Now Harry did lift his gaze to meet hers. "I was really marrying the woman who abducted me on the road to Gretna." He spoke the words calmly, steadily, but there was a warmth behind them. The same warmth glowed in his eyes. "The one who can handle a team like Athena in her chariot and who drives me right out of my mind each time I look at her."

"That woman is Octavian Morehouse's daughter."

"And there's nothing that can be done to change that. I won't deceive you, Leannah. This is going to be more difficult than I had anticipated. I . . . my whole family is very worried. They do believe you ultimately intend to make a dupe of me."

"Settling any of your money on me will do nothing to change that opinion."

"No." He took sip from his coffee cup, made a face, and reached for the pot. "But as I said, it will get this over with. People will be watching whenever the settlement happens. The sooner we show them there's nothing to see, the sooner their attention will move on to other, more entertaining subjects." He lifted the freshened cup and eyed her over the rim. "I see some doubt in those lovely eyes, Leannah."

She smiled, but she also shook her head. "We all say that society has a short memory, but that is not entirely true. They just store gossip away, ready to pull it out whenever it might be needed again."

"I will not conduct my marriage according to the whims and fears of those who have not met you, much less those who know nothing about us together."

The bitterness with which he spoke this hurt. *I should let him go,* thought Leannah. *I am already hurting him.*

And if she did? This was the one question she had a clear answer to. If she did, she was acknowledging that she was nothing except Octavian Morehouse's daughter. She was saying her life was forever bounded and compassed by her father's mistakes.

But it was more than that. It was giving up this man forever. It meant never being near him again, never laughing with him again, never sharing a cold muffin and colder coffee again. She hadn't danced with him yet. She didn't know whether he preferred his beef boiled or roasted, and did he care at all for the theater? Or did he prefer a concert? Did he read French novels? Had he seen the panorama in Vauxhall Gardens and what did he think of that? Would he object to having a cat in the house?

She wanted to know all these things, and so much more. She let her hand close over his.

With Harry, she had a chance to make something new, something for herself and for her family. It would not be easy. With all that stood against them, how could it be? But if she didn't try, she was accepting a life without him, and that meant a life without hope.

"Harry, listen to me. I will not deny the money will make things easier, or that it will be a blessing to my family. It's already helped. But also be aware that I have been poor. I know what everything costs and I will not lose this . . . whatever it might be between us, over a settlement, or a salary."

"We will fight them together?" He said, echoing the words she'd spoken the night before.

"Yes. Together."

Her words lit his eyes with the spark of mischief she was coming to cherish as much as the touch of his hand, the sound of his voice, and yes, his ridiculous sideburns. She had not said love. She would not say what might yet be withdrawn. They would finish this fight first. Then, when family and friends and all their fears had been finally satisfied, and it really was just the two of them here, she would say it. Only then.

Twenty-Nine

"Meredith!" Lea got to her feet at once as Lewis ushered her friend into the sitting room. "Thank you so much for coming!"

The first thing the world usually noticed about Meredith Langley was her spectacles. Unlike most girls of the haut ton, Meredith did not demur about wearing them, no matter how grand the occasion. She was known to tell anyone who asked, "I would rather see than be seen."

If such a person bothered to take a second look, they saw a tall, slender woman with dark, lustrous hair and penetrating gray eyes. Her dress was generally becoming, but never anything approaching the first stare of fashion. Like Leannah, Meredith's circumstances were what was politely referred to as "reduced."

"Of course I came." Meredith handed Lewis her bonnet and wool cloak and hurried forward so the two friends could embrace and kiss each other on the cheek. "You're looking well, Lea."

"You mean considering what's happened?" Leannah gestured her to one of the chairs by the fire. The rain had begun again, and despite the drapes and the good fire, the room held a distinct chill.

"I'd be lying if I said I have no idea what you mean, and you'd know it, so I won't bother." Meredith accepted the cup of tea Leannah poured out. In anticipation of Meredith's arrival,

Leannah had ordered fresh tea brought and the service laid out on a small table along with some more of the excellent muffins from the bakeshop. She had to admit, at least to herself, she could conceive a great liking for hotel life.

"I take it Mr. Rayburn is not here?" Meredith was not a bashful soul and helped herself at once to a muffin.

Leannah shook her head and sipped her own tea. "He's gone to see his banker, about a settlement."

Meredith nodded. "Probably better to have that out of the way. It will help tamp down some of the nastier gossip."

"Do you know, that's what Harry said?" Leannah hesitated. "I almost didn't write to you," she said softly. "I didn't think I'd really need the help. I'm so used to being able to manage anything. After all, I've spent years dealing with the consequences of everyone else's disasters. But now I'm in the middle of a disaster of my own making, and I barely know which way to turn."

She waited for Meredith to speak some words of consolation, but that was not Meredith's way. "Is that how you see your union with Harry Rayburn? As a disaster?"

"No. It's many things, but it's not that. At least, not yet."

"You just fear disaster might still come of it." She clearly saw the agreement in Leannah's expression and nodded. "I will admit, it is a difficult choice to explain."

"Or understand. Yes. I barely understand it myself."

Another woman might have used this statement as an opportunity to deliver a lecture on the importance of self-control. Meredith however, only settled back in her chair, and sipped her tea. "Tell me what happened, Lea, from the beginning."

Leannah did, and she left nothing out except the details of those moments when she was alone with Harry and both were able to give free rein to their desire. Not even Meredith required that much information.

The entire time, Meredith sat quietly and listened. She did not touch her tea or her muffin. Indeed, she did not even let her eyes flicker once from Leannah's.

"And that is, more or less, where we find ourselves," Leannah said finally. "The question now becomes, how is the matter to be handled before the wider world?"

"That," said Meredith, finally reaching forward to take a

bite of her muffin and a sip of tea, "depends entirely on what your intentions are."

"I don't understand you. I've said . . ."

Meredith waved her words away. "Yes, yes, you said you hope to minimize scandal; which, by the way, is not generally accomplished by a runaway marriage." She fixed her friend with her piercing gray gaze. "Lea, you have asked for my help. I am more than willing to give it, but I must know where you want that help to take you. Do you intend to let this marriage settle into a matter of convenience, or do you intend to make a genuine future with Mr. Rayburn? Have you fallen in love with him?"

Leannah looked down at her hands, which seemed to be involved in attempting to crush her teacup. She set the delicate china object down before they succeeded. "I don't know. He is . . . an amazing man in so many ways but, there's also something secret about him. Something he's hiding."

"I expect he could say the same about you."

"Yes, he could." She sighed. "I suppose what I really want is time."

"Time?"

"To find out what's true. Can I be in love with Harry Rayburn or is all this . . . some temporary aberration." *Can I be in love?* The words repeated themselves inside her. It was a strange way of expressing the sentiment, but she made no effort to correct the statement. As odd as it might be, it was also what she meant. She had thought of love, she had felt what she was sure must be love, but she had not spoken the words to Harry, because inside, there was still that question.

Can I be in love? With all that I've done and all that I am, is it even possible?

Meredith did not answer for a very long time. She finished her tea, and then poured herself a fresh cup. She'd added a slice of lemon, and sipped. Apparently satisfied with the flavor, she set the cup down on the saucer.

"If time is what you want, I believe I can be of assistance. The great thing is to be seen to act with certainty. You and I might be aware you don't know yet what sort of future you will have with Mr. Rayburn, but the world must think that you do. If, for instance, you wished to get ready for the probability that this marriage would dissolve, I would advise that you continue the theme of running away. Undertake a grand tour—Paris, Switzerland, Berlin, Florence, the usual destinations. Call it a honeymoon. Stay away as long as you wish."

"Is that your advice? Run?" How could Meredith of all people not realize that if she ran, she would be followed—by Mr. Valloy, by her family's past and her own. There was nowhere she could go to escape that, or to shelter Harry from it.

"Certainly not. You should run only if you wish to be seen as having an affair or something of the sort. If you really wish to try to establish your marriage and to buy time to discover what love there may be within it, then you must set up your house, and reenter society as soon as possible."

"But will anyone receive me?"

That made Meredith smile, as if Leannah had said something hopelessly naive. "The question is not will they receive you, but will you receive them? You must arrange to hold a private party, and let it be bruited about that you're inviting no one."

"It won't be much of a party, then."

"Lea, now you're being silly. You have not been away that long. You know full well that nothing sets society into a frenzy faster than the perception it's being excluded from something." When this did not clear up Leannah's uncertainty, Meredith shook her head, probably at the fact of Leannah's being such a slow-coach. "Generally, it goes something like this; I know that Mrs. Wells does not like Lady Teal. If I tell Mrs. Wells that Lady Teal has something she doesn't—an invitation to a particular party, for example—Mrs. Wells will huff and puff and grow irate and feign elaborate unconcern. This will last for approximately three days, after which, she'll start asking me how can she get an invitation to this party. Now, when Lady Teal hears that Mrs. Wells is angling after an invitation to said party . . ."

"A tidbit she will just happen to hear from you?"

Meredith nodded in acknowledgement. "When Lady Teal hears she has an invitation that Mrs. Wells wants, she will become extremely proud of it, and start telling her acquaintance that she's to be included in what promises to be a most amusing little gathering, *terribly* exclusive of course . . ."

"At which point her acquaintances will start looking about

for their own invitations," said Leannah. "They might even apply to her for assistance, which increases her consequence among them . . ."

"Just so." Meredith raised her bite of muffin in salute.

"And this is what you do?" breathed Leannah.

Meredith's answering shrug was small, and dismissive. "This is what I do, along with getting favorable notices about everybody's business in the society columns, of course."

"You must hate society by now. It's all so . . . trivial." *It takes so much energy, with all of us running about in circles trying to keep our places. What is it even* for?

"And yet here you are attempting to return," said Meredith as if she heard Leannah's thoughts.

"I know. I'm including myself in that assessment of triviality." Leannah shook her head. "I tell myself I'm doing it for Genny, and Jeremy, but the truth is, I'm the one who wants to come back. It's like . . . like wanting to come home when one has been too long away." She paused again. "This time, Meredith, what I do, I'm doing for myself."

"And it is for yourself that you married Harry Rayburn?"

She nodded. "Am I being hopelessly selfish?"

"Never," said Meredith firmly. "You acted impulsively, but I believe there was more wisdom in your choice than you have yet realized. As for society . . ." Meredith set her teacup down. "For better or for worse, it is the world we were raised in and the people we were raised among. One might wish to leave, but how? And where does one go? There are not many of us who can live in exile among strangers without breaking our own hearts. So, we are left to make the best of it." She smiled, but a trace of wistfulness remained in her bright eyes. "I'd much rather manage people's social standing than be a governess or a companion. And, I've occasionally done a little bit of good, in my way."

"I know that you have, and you are now."

"So, I've your permission to arrange this for you?"

"Meredith, you have my most earnest plea that you begin as soon as possible."

"Excellent." Meredith reached into her reticule and drew out a well-thumbed memorandum book. "We will have to aim for late in the season to give the brew of rumor and exclusion time to work. Everyone will be tired by then anyway, and nosing about for something new. What shall the gathering be? A musical evening? No. Those are commonplace."

"It's to be a small gathering, is that correct?" said Leannah. "Fifty or so guests? Perhaps we could arrange for a viewing of some sort. A piece of art by an up-and-coming painter? Or a reading by a poet or novelist?"

"Why, yes, Lea, I believe that will be just the thing. I can speak with Gideon Fitzsimmons. He knows that world inside and out, and will be able to recommend just the person, someone shocking and innovative, but not overly so. Balance is critical. Once we have secured our artistic individual, we will need some select guests whose names can be dropped." She tapped her pencil against her chin. "We can begin with Mr. and Mrs. Montcalm. They've barely been seen at all since they came back from their own honeymoon. Everyone will be dying for a glimpse and they are such good friends of the Rayburns . . ."

"Unfortunately, I don't know them."

"Fortunately, I do. At least, I know Mr. Montcalm." She paused and ran her finger across her notes. "Now, if you are going to entertain, you need a home to do it in. Has any thought been given as to where you will set up housekeeping?"

"Harry suggested we might look in Dobbson Square. I think that will be a good fit for us."

"I agree. It's fashionable, but not ostentatious. He might be able to afford Grosvenor, but it would be reaching high enough to offend the fastidious." She tapped her book several times with her fingertip. "Perhaps I can plant a few words in the 'Arrivals' column in the *Woman's Window* . . . unless of course Genevieve would rather write them another of her letters?"

"It is my hope that once this fuss is over Genny will be free to write letters to whomever she chooses."

Meredith was looking at her again, and the sensations raised by that direct and thoughtful gaze were not at all comfortable. But she said nothing. "Once the house is taken, there will be the furnishing . . . but as it's you, we've no need to worry about taste in decoration or wardrobe."

"But you will come help me shop?"

"I wouldn't miss it for the world. Tell me, have you met your in-laws yet?"

"No. They've quarreled with Harry over me."

This did not appear to surprise Meredith in the least. "If it's any comfort, the Rayburns are good people. I think you will fit in well with them once the initial shock has passed."

"I hope so." Leannah picked up her cup and looked at it, and set it down again. Meredith waited in silence for her to find her words. "There is something else."

Her friend raised an inquiring brow.

"Mr. Valloy came to me after he found out about the marriage. He threatened to, in his words, make things difficult if I did not persuade Father to sign over his seat on the board of trust for the Wakefield land."

For the first time in the whole long conversation Meredith appeared genuinely shocked.

"I knew Terrance Valloy to be a hard man, but I would not have expected this."

"Neither would I. There is something more going on here than wounded pride. Do you think you could find out what it is?"

Meredith took her time in answering. "I think . . . yes. At least, I will do what I can. There's a particular gentleman at the naval office to whom I could apply. He has . . . some rather wide-ranging connections."

"It also might be that Mr. Valloy is in communication with Mr. Dickenson about the matter."

"Two jilted men pulling in harness?" Meredith's brows knitted together as she turned this possibility over in her mind.

"Stranger things have happened."

"They have. Very well." Meredith's gray eyes glimmered behind her spectacles. "I am engaged."

"Thank you. I feel so much better knowing you are with me."

"Put it down to my irrepressible romantic nature." Meredith closed her book with an audible snap. "Now, finish your tea. You've given me quite the list, and we must get started at once."

Thirty

❧

"**T**hank you for agreeing to see me, Anthony . . . Mr. Dickenson."

It was the fashionable hour, and Rotten Row—the broad avenue running along the southern edge of Hyde Park—was filled to the brim with horses and carriages. This was the time of day when members of the haut ton who particularly wished to see and be seen ventured out to bask in whatever sunshine there might be, and in each other's company. None of that top-lofty crowd paid any attention to the neatly turned-out young woman who strolled along the edge of the Row, even though she walked in company of an impeccably dressed and clearly prosperous man who wore his quizzing glass on a gold chain about his neck.

But they should have paid attention. To Anthony Dickenson's eyes, Genevieve Morehouse surpassed every single woman who passed by in a shining carriage or on the back of a high-stepping horse. How could anyone not be captivated by her, with her auburn hair, her green eyes, or her sweet, slender figure? Everything about her spoke of freshness, of innocence and femininity. She was a perfect jewel. All she lacked was her setting. All she lacked was him.

"Of course I agreed to come," he said. "I've been most concerned about you." *And about what* she *is whispering in your ears.*

Of course, her writing to ask for a meeting here in the park was most improper and inappropriate. But her evident unease as they walked, along with the distance she kept between them, was proof that she understood this. He did sympathize with her discomfort. Her sister's actions had placed her in an impossible position, and driven her to the extreme.

Miss Morehouse lowered her eyes with becoming modesty, further evidence of her proper feeling.

"Oh, no, not at all. Well, a little." Dickenson hated her bonnet. It was plain and unbecoming, and kept him from seeing if a blush rose in her cheeks at these words.

It was maddening to have her so close. If they had been alone, he would not have been able to resist seizing her, kissing her, and more, much more. It was weakness. She was his weakness. He must not give in yet, but he could soon. Very soon.

"I know how hard this has been for you, Miss Morehouse. It is natural you should be confused, and angry at this delay in our marriage."

"I . . . no . . . well . . ." She hesitated yet again. "This isn't what I'd wanted to speak to you about, not entirely. I . . . I had a favor to ask, but perhaps, as things stand . . ."

"You may ask me anything. Indeed, I am the first to whom you should apply."

She made no direct answer to this, only fumbled in her reticule. She paused, and fumbled some more. "Oh, no! Where is it! Where is it!" She groped in the bottom of the beaded bag.

"What is the matter? Calm down. Speak clearly."

"I can't believe I've lost it! Leannah will *murder* me!"

"What have you lost?"

"The ring! The ring Mr. Rayburn gave . . . "

"Did Rayburn give you a ring?" he demanded, but he already knew the answer. Rayburn most certainly coveted Genevieve. No one could want the older sister once they'd seen the younger. He could not help but imagine the brawler casting his lustful eyes over her, and offering her every manner of insult. He would kill the man. He would watch him die slowly for daring to think that Miss Morehouse could be purchased as easily as her sister had been.

"No! Certainly not! But he did give it to Leannah, and . . ." Genevieve let the words trail off. "Oh, I never should have come," she muttered. "I've made so many mistakes. Anthony,

I'm sorry. I haven't been at all fair to you, but I can't carry on with this anymore. You should go now. I'll . . . I'll write to you."

"I will not leave, not until you tell me what this about."

In that moment, a look of such unforgivable stubbornness crossed her delicate face that Dickenson could almost believe it was the sister standing there. But it quickly subsided, and when Miss Morehouse spoke, it was in her own sweet, modest voice. "Mr. Rayburn had a wedding ring with him when he married Leannah. It was just so strange that a man whom one met by chance would have a ring with him. I wondered, I mean, is it genuine?"

Of course she wondered. Of course she could not understand. Anger burned in him. He would track Rayburn down, catch him alone. He would make sure the brute never dared come close to Genevieve again, and he would bring men enough to do the job properly.

This thought warmed him enough that it was easy to speak gently. "Of course it was strange. It speaks well to your common sense that you should not only see this at once, but that you should lay the matter before me."

"I'd put the ring in my bag. I meant to bring it to you . . . I thought you might be able to tell me whether it was real. But now it's gone, and I must get home and find it before Leannah asks any questions . . ." She shook her head. "Oh, I'm sorry. I'm making a mess of things again. And a scene." She glanced quickly about to make sure no one was taking notice. But there was no one even near them, except some black-headed clerk sitting on a bench with a book in his hand. "You'd be well within your rights to cut me dead."

If only I could. "None of this has been your fault." Dickenson turned toward her. Despite the chill of the spring day, perspiration prickled under his hat and collar. It was impossible that so small and delicate a creature should exert such a hold over him. Dickenson's yearning and impatience had only increased since he'd taken up with Valloy. His family had even begun to notice, and to remark on it.

Miss Morehouse bit her lower lip. Dickenson stared, fascinated. Even beneath the shadow of her bonnet, her mouth glistened. "I'm afraid it is my fault. All of it. If I hadn't suggested we elope . . ."

"Which you only did because your sister refused to permit us to marry." Anthony reminded her. She must learn to stop making excuses for that harridan. She had to conquer family feeling, and not only see Mrs. . . . Rayburn clearly, but to speak clearly of her defective character and the atrocities against decency that she had committed. When Genevieve was his, he would explain all this to her—patiently, of course—until she did understand. "I might wish you had consulted me more closely on the subject, but please believe that I do not judge you at all harshly because of it. You have never known a man's proper guidance. Once we are married, things will be very different. You will be able to depend on me absolutely to guide you upon the right path."

The strength of her surprise raised Miss Morehouse's eyes directly to his. Dickenson felt an uncomfortable tightening in his groin. "A man's proper guidance?" she murmured.

"Of course. Unlike your sister, you are a natural woman. You know that's what's been missing in your life, and your instincts have drawn you to the best and strongest man of your acquaintance."

Miss Morehouse said nothing for a very long time. A thousand emotions flickered through her bright eyes and he heard her breathing grow ragged. His groin tightened again to see the color that rose in her pale cheeks and the light that burned in her gaze. Now that the truth had been spoken, her love was filling her, her love and her need for him.

"You . . . you . . ." She paused and pressed her hand against her bosom. "You think my sister is somehow . . . unnatural?"

Anthony blinked. *Be patient,* he reminded himself. She is not used to speaking of such things. "She is, and in your heart you understand this. Otherwise you would not be so eager to separate yourself from her."

She drew herself up straight. Pride showed in every inch of her bearing. Anthony's heart swelled. Once she was properly educated, she would be truly magnificent.

But her next words shook him to his core. "Perhaps, as I am from the same tree that grew such an *unnatural* branch, you should reconsider. I would so hate to disappoint your notions of what a proper and submissive wife should be."

"But you cannot disappoint, don't you see?" He strove to

keep his voice calm. She was innocent still. He must not over-whelm her with an undue show of ardor. "Every word you speak demonstrates that you possess in full measure those proper feminine feelings your sister lacks. I promise, I have already set events in motion. Soon, I will be able to claim you for my own, and you will have nothing more to fear of your sister or her bullyboy."

"What on earth are you talking about?"

"You must forgive me for speaking openly of such things, but I would have you understand that I know it all." He seized her hand. He could not help himself. "I see how she dominates you and she poisons your life with her scheming ways. This business with the ring as well. He is trying to make a conquest of you. But it is all right. I know you are innocent in the matter. You will never hear a word about it from me once we are mar-ried, and . . ."

"How *dare* you say such things about Leannah and Harry!" Miss Morehouse twisted her hand, Anthony tightened his grip. He had meant to wait until their marriage to begin her educa-tion, but clearly he'd already left it too long.

"I will forgive you for raising your voice to me this once," he told her firmly. "I know you are very confused."

"Unhand me, sir!"

She struck him. Hard, and right across the face. Not with an open hand, but with a balled fist. Anthony saw stars. Then he saw red, a brilliant scarlet haze between himself and all the world. She'd struck him. His free hand lifted over his head. The poisonous little creature had dared . . .

A hand slapped about his wrist, pinning his harm in place. Not a woman's hand. A man's. Realization brought him back to himself. He couldn't see Miss Morehouse. He could only see the black-haired fellow who'd been sitting on the bench a moment before now. He stood directly in front of Dickenson and clamped his coarse hand around Dickenson's arm.

"Is there some problem?" the black-haired man asked. His voice was calm, but his blue eyes were ice-cold.

"No," began Dickenson.

"Yes," replied Miss Morehouse. Now he could see she stood just behind the stranger, pale as marble and just as cold. "This . . . this . . . man is importuning me!"

The stranger's eyes did not even flicker from Dickenson's. "Sir, I think you had better leave."

Anthony wrenched his arm out of the other man's grip. It was more difficult than he would have credited. "This girl is my fiancée," he announced. "You will cease to concern yourself in my business!"

"I am most certainly not your fiancée, nor will I ever be!" cried Miss Morehouse. "Of all the mistakes I've made, you are the worst of all! Good-bye, Mr. Dickenson! Sir,"—she turned to the stranger—"will you be so good as to escort me back to my carriage?"

Anthony could only stand and stare as the clerk bowed, and took Miss Morehouse's arm. She was leaving. She was walking away from him and she was not even looking back. Her voice rang in his ears. The shrill contempt, the unnatural harpy's fury. She'd struck him. She'd raised her hand to the one she should have been swearing to obey for the rest of her life.

He'd ruin her. He'd ruin them all. He'd spare no expense, stop at nothing. Then, when she was broken, when she was crawling, only then would he relent, and agree to take her back.

First things first, he would remove her sister. Never mind Valloy and his scheming with the father. The woman could not be allowed a single day's more influence over his Genevieve. Fortunately, his family's extensive business dealings taught him exactly what to do, and whom to hire. There was, in fact, a fellow right in her neighborhood who could be trusted to take the job. All he had to do was wait, and watch.

Thirty-One

❧

For Leannah, the next weeks passed in a blur. Her days were filled to the brim with errands of all description. She had everything to buy, not only for herself, but for the beautiful house Harry had taken in Dobbson Square. The new brick residence was entirely unfurnished, and Harry left it to Leannah to choose how it should be fitted out—including the drapes, wallpapers, and all the movables. There were servants to be interviewed and engaged, a pantry to be stocked, and accounts opened with grocers and provisioners. Workmen had to be supervised, and everything in the house, or about herself, seemed to require endless amounts of measuring and remeasuring.

Not one item was to be puce, or even lavender.

The flurry of it all left her breathless, but nowhere near as breathless as the moments that came with the end of each day. That was the time when Leannah returned to the suite at the Colonnade to find Harry waiting for her. However tiring her day might be, however difficult the arguments with the workmen had been, it all fell away when Harry opened his arms and drew her to him. She did enjoy plundering the shops and warehouses with Genny and Meredith. That enjoyment, however, was nothing compared to the feelings that came over her when she remembered that come evening, she would again lie down next to Harry, and when morning arrived, she would wake up in his arms. Admittedly, most nights, they did not wait until the morning to wake, or until darkness to lie down. Her hands had healed, and she was able to caress his delightful body in the most intimate fashion without the irksome layers of bandages, or even his joking reminders to be careful. Although, more than once he did raise her arms above her head and order her to keep still so that he could pleasure her.

It was not only in the new house that things were changing for the better. With Meredith's assistance, Leannah engaged a new doctor for her father. The doctor, in turn, brought in a staff of nurses. There would also be a new cook, new maids, and two new menservants as soon as persons of suitable experience in invalid households could be located. Genny was to have her own maid, and a brand-new subscription to the circulating library, which Leannah suspected would please her far more than having someone to look after her wardrobe. The stable bill was paid in its entirety, as were the grocer's and the dressmaker's. Harry sent his tailor around to the Byswater house to see about new clothes for Father.

"It's too much," Leannah tried to tell him, as she saw him writing yet another bank draft.

"No," he said flatly. "It's just as it should be."

Those words were as close to anger as she heard him come in all those giddy days while spring warmed and brightened the world around them. She did her best not to dwell on the moment, but she still couldn't help wondering. Harry's family and friends clearly harbored serious doubts about her, and their marriage. So serious, in fact, that Harry made no move to introduce her to any of them. They did not go out at all. She once ventured the suggestion that they might have a small supper party, but he'd shaken his head and declared he wanted to keep to himself for a while yet. Then, he'd demonstrated the advantages of their absolute privacy to her in such a magnificently daring fashion that she quite forgot to argue the point.

It didn't matter, Leannah told herself. They were just beginning. There was plenty of time yet. They had so much to learn about each other, and a whole new life to build. They could take this time. Call it, as Meredith suggested, a honeymoon. It might be the oddest honeymoon possible, and the capper on the oddest possible wedding, but it was hers, and Leannah was determined to enjoy it.

Besides, she really couldn't find fault with Harry keeping her away from his family when she hadn't yet taken him to meet Father. Not that this meant anything, either. Harry really didn't need to meet Father until after the household improvements were complete and everyone was used to the changes. After all, her family would be moving in with them once the Dobbson Square house was ready. There was no need to rush the introductions, was there? She had told him the truth about her family and past. She would tell him anything more he wanted to know, as soon as he asked. She would hide nothing. He had only to ask.

But he didn't ask.

Not that the days passed entirely in isolation. Encouraged by Meredith's readiness to resume their relationship, Leannah wrote to some of her friends from the time when she had first married Elias—other members of what they'd informally christened the Schoolroom Club, because they had all been very young matrons and mostly married to older men. They'd formed a bulwark for each other against the usual slights and jibes that society leveled against girls in their circumstances. To her relief, Leannah found that not only was she remembered by her old friends, but she was readily welcomed back. She could pay at least a few calls, and to receive them in the suite at the Colonnade. She also found herself starved for news—of Amilee's baby; of Margaret's sister, who had become engaged to a member of the diplomatic corps; of Lucille, who had gone to Philadelphia of all places; and of Geraldine, who was whiling away her widowhood writing a fashionable novel.

Meredith had been right. It did feel like coming home.

If Genny hadn't lost the ring, it might all have been perfect.

"I've don't know where it is," she'd said when Leannah had asked her for it. "I'm so sorry, Leannah. It is entirely my doing. I'll explain to Harry if you want." Her agitation was so extreme that Leannah felt a moment of genuine alarm.

"No, there's no need," she said hurriedly. "I shouldn't have taken it off in the first place."

But even as she said this, something nagged at her. Leannah did not believe for a moment Genny could be so careless with something so important. Could Jeremy have taken it as one of his pranks? Or had Genny perhaps entrusted it to Mrs. Falwell, only to have it go astray afterward. Was she perhaps trying to protect one or both of them from the blame?

The very next day, Leannah stopped by the house to see how the new staff was settling in. She'd meant to raise the subject again, but Genny had shut herself up in her room with, the new maid said, a sick headache. She did descend eventually, but she was pale and distracted.

At another time, Leannah would have dug down to the bottom of it, but there were so many other arrangements and claims on her attention. Besides, by her next visit, Genny's spirits rallied, so Leannah was able to believe it had all been as it appeared, a sick headache. The ring would be found. All other things would follow in their own time.

At least, this was what Leannah was able to believe until she received the letter from Geraldine inviting her and Harry to the opera.

"I'd love to go, Harry, but I really cannot risk meeting your parents or your sister for the first time in the round room," she said, as she showed Harry the letter.

They had finished their supper and were now sitting together in front of the fire. Harry was reading the shipping news as he usually did, and making notes in the margin in pencil. Leannah was going over the lists in her new memorandum book, crossing off what had been completed and making additional notes next to those things that were not yet attended to. Geraldine's invitation was only one item among many.

Harry glanced at the letter she handed him and put it aside. "It might be better if you did meet Fi in a public place," he said, picking up his newspaper again. "That way she can't start one of her ridiculous interrogations."

Leannah closed her book slowly and contemplated her husband. She'd known something was wrong. She'd tried her best to ignore it because she'd grown to love the peace and private enjoyments of their life. But now, as he turned over the tightly folded paper, she could neither miss nor dismiss his bitter expression. Her heart twisted. He was afraid of his family. He was afraid that some part of his regard for them would prove stronger than the emotions that were growing in this marriage.

Because like her, Harry really did care, or he would be made to care. Sooner or later, they both would.

"No, she wouldn't be able to interrogate me, as you put it, but she could cut me dead in front of the whole world, which will not do our plan to be accepted by society any good at all."

Meredith had been giving Leannah regular updates on the progress of the whispering campaign surrounding their planned end-of-season party. So far, all things seemed to be going in their favor, but people were beginning to wonder why they weren't seen together about the town. Meredith warned her that fresh whispers might soon begin—ones that said Leannah and Harry weren't actually married.

"Have I asked to be accepted?" Harry snapped. "By anybody? The world can like us, or leave us alone."

For a moment, Leannah's nerve failed her. She looked again at her left hand, where the diamond ring had glimmered for so brief a time.

Leannah looked down at her bare left hand. On the list of things that had not happened was one very important item. Harry had not offered to replace the ring. She had not mentioned it. She had held hard to the belief it would turn up again. Besides, she told herself, Harry was already laying out so much money on her and her family that it was unthinkable to ask for yet another gift. There was one other reason she kept mum on the subject that she kept hidden, even from herself.

She did not want to hear him refuse.

"We have to try, Harry," she said.

"Why?" he shot back. "Why should it matter what anyone else thinks?"

"Because soon or late, we have to walk out of doors together. How can what we have be considered at all real if it only exists in a single set of rooms?"

Please, she whispered inwardly. *It can't be over already. We haven't even lived in our own house yet. There's so much left to do.*

"We are the ones who decide what we have together, Leannah," said Harry and her heart ached to hear the affection and confidence that filled those words. "The world and its appearances and its reputations don't matter. Not to me."

Tears pricked at the back of Leannah's eyes. She wanted so much to keep the doors to their private world closed. She wanted to move from the hotel to the new house in the dead of night, lock its freshly painted doors, close its new burgundy drapes, and never open them again. She wanted there to be only Harry and his arms and his passion and his smiles. Her fingers knotted together. She wanted to be selfish just a little bit longer.

But that was impossible and she knew it, just as she knew what she had to do. She had to make the first move.

"Harry? Will you come home with me tomorrow?" she asked softly. "It's high time you met my father and my brother."

The request clearly surprised him, and it was a long, painful moment before he answered her. "I'm not asking you to do this, Leannah."

But you should have. Why didn't you? What are you hiding from, Harry? "No. You are not asking me, I am asking you. Will you come?"

"Of course, if you want it." He hesitated. "But not tomorrow. I've a meeting I cannot miss. The day after will do just as well, won't it?"

Their eyes met for a long moment, and Leannah felt her throat tighten. She could tell he wanted her to change her mind and leave the doors of their life closed. When she did not speak, he turned back to his shipping news and she opened her memorandum book, and if they talked, they talked of new purchases and planned purchases and the tradesmen and the weather.

That night, his lovemaking was fierce beyond measure and afterward Harry held her like he never meant to let her go. Leannah lay awake for a very long time, listening to him breathe, and hoping he would not open his eyes to see the tear that trickled down her cheek.

Thirty-Two

❧

"Well now, Harry Rayburn." The grizzled man in the checkered waistcoat held out his hand for Harry to shake. "I hear you've been having quite the time of it."

Harry shrugged and took the chair the other man kicked out toward him. The Turkish and Mediterranean coffeehouse was filled to bursting around them and Harry had not even bothered trying to fight his way to the counter to get himself a cup.

"I've got married, Mr. Brooks." Harry shouted to be heard over the din. "That'll bring changes in any man's life."

Thomas Brooks was a short, stout man. The seams of his blue coat strained across his arms, and his waistcoat's silver buttons were on the verge of giving way. Combined with his gray hair, this might give him the appearance of being somebody's kindly uncle, but that impression would only last until a man looked into his glittering little eyes.

This wasn't any relatively genteel establishment, like St. Alban's. The Turkey and Mediterranean was as much a trading post as it was a coffeehouse, and just now it was getting ready for an auction. Men were crammed at the tables, watching the sacks of spice and bolts of cloth being brought in. The salesmen ran about waving papers, affixing seals to sacks, boxes, and bags, dodging in between those interested buyers who were prodding and fingering the merchandise. They skirted yet more men who stood around pursuing lists and bills and timetables that plastered the walls. All of these worthies seemed to be arguing with each other at the top of their lungs.

"Marriage ain't the beginning nor the end of your adventures from what I hear." Mr. Brooks planted both elbows on the splintered tabletop. "I hear . . ."

"I'm not here to discuss my home life, Mr. Brooks," said Harry quickly. "I'm on the lookout for new employment, and I heard you were in need of a new buyer."

"That I am." Mr. Brooks rubbed his double chin thoughtfully. "Some trouble with your father is it?"

"It's just time I struck out on my own," replied Harry evenly. He'd spent most of the drive down here getting ready for this line of questioning. The haut ton didn't hold any kind of monopoly on gossip. Coffeehouses and alehouses could spread rumors with an efficiency that would put many a drawing room to shame. "But my capital won't yet stretch to setting up my own establishment."

"Well, that'll come, that'll come." As he spoke, Brooks narrowed his keen eyes at Harry. A massive river of goods flowed up the Thames to supply the needs and desires of London and its surrounding towns. All of it passed through the warehouses that filled the labyrinth of docks and quays. The men who ran those houses were a sharp crew. They could all of them smell a rat, or the inland revenue, a mile upwind in a freshening gale. They could smell trouble just as easily, and they were used to making quick judgments about the character of any man in front of them.

Mr. Brooks sighed and shook his head. "Well, I'd be sorry if I was helping keep up any kind of quarrel between you and your father, Harry." He paused, and Harry held his breath. "But there's no denying I could use a man of your savvy and experience on my side. So, here's my hand on it."

Brooks held out his meaty hand for Harry to clasp and shake. Harry hoped the noise around them covered the sound of the long, relieved breath that rushed out of him.

"You turn up at my place tomorrow morning bright and early, and we'll settle the details. Are you staying for the sale?" Brooks nodded toward the men who were clustered by the hearth, arguing over yet another set of papers.

"No, not today. I've got some shopping to do." Harry got to his feet and reclaimed his hat and stick.

"Ah yes. Heavy is the lot of married men." Mr. Brooks winked. "Good luck to you, Harry. But if you don't mind a word of advice . . ."

"Depends entirely what it is, Mr. Brooks."

Brooks chuckled, but when he spoke, he was perfectly serious. "Mend this thing with your father. Won't do you nor your new missus any good to start out on the wrong foot."

Harry made no answer. Any reply he could muster would be an angry one, and this man was his new employer. He just raised his hat, and shouldered his way through the milling crowd.

Mend this thing with your father. Harry stepped out into the street and took as deep a breath as he could stand of the thick, dockside air. It took two to mend a quarrel, just as it did to make one. Since his disastrous stop home, all he'd had from his father—from any of his family—was silence. The message in that silence seemed to Harry perfectly clear. Unless and until he could return in the character of the son they wanted, he would be left to go his own way, alone and unacknowledged.

Very well. If they didn't want to know him, he didn't want to know them. He and Leannah would manage perfectly well on their own. He had plenty of money to take care of what was necessary to get them started, and now he had employment. He could look forward to making a clean start for them both. He didn't need his family's prevarications or any attempt to explain away his life.

Harry glanced at his watch. He'd stroll up to the carriage house and hire a hack to take him over to Bond Street. He'd finally settled on a gift for Leannah and it was promised to be ready for today.

Harry felt a smile form, and he was able to shake off the last of Brooks's remarks. Let Brooks or the world make as many remarks as they chose. They didn't matter. Nothing mattered but that he and Leannah were together.

He told himself this several more times, with improvements

and elaborations. He let his thoughts linger particularly over the feeling of Leannah's body in his arms, especially when they were in bed together and she turned toward him, her face flushed with heat and desire.

These pleasant thoughts so occupied Harry, he didn't notice the carriage pulling up beside him.

"Hullo, Harry. Thought I might find you down here."

It was Penrose. Nathaniel leaned out of an enclosed and thoroughly anonymous carriage. He also looked like he hadn't been sleeping well lately. His chin was stubbled and his deep blue eyes had rings around them. A twinge of concern at his friend's appearance touched Harry, but he did his best to ignore it. After their last conversation, he was in no mood to look with sympathy on any of Penrose's troubles.

"On your own today?" Harry peered into the carriage. "Montcalm too fastidious to come down this way?"

Nathaniel declined to acknowledge this barb. Instead, he unlatched the carriage door. "Get in, Harry. We've got business."

"I've got no business with you."

"Yes, actually, you do," replied Nathaniel evenly and he pushed the door open a little farther. "Because it concerns Mrs. Rayburn."

Anger rose instantly in him and Harry took a tighter grip on his stick. "Penrose, I'm warning you—"

"You may warn me all you like," Nathaniel cut Harry off with weary impatience. "Get in, Rayburn. This is important."

Harry opened his mouth, intending to growl his dismissal at the other man. He had no need of any friend whose goal was to end his marriage, or any other part of his life. But the years of friendship proved too strong for that, especially when coupled with the serious expression on Nathaniel's face. This wasn't Nathaniel in search of a quarrel. Harry looked again at his unshaved chin and rumpled coat. Something really had happened.

Frowning, Harry climbed into the carriage and closed the door. Nathaniel rapped his knuckles on the roof to signal the driver to start.

"So, what is it?" Harry planted his stick in front of himself and folded his hands across the top.

Nathaniel contemplated him for a long moment, but what he was looking for Harry could not tell.

"How have you been, Harry?" he asked, as if he'd turned up during some pleasant little outing in the park rather than trolling the Cornhill district in search of him.

"Perfectly well, thank you."

"Your family's worried about you."

"Then they can ask after me themselves."

Nathaniel shook his head. "And Mrs. Rayburn? Is she well?"

Whatever momentary patience Harry might have mustered for his friend's small talk snapped abruptly. "What's this about, Nathaniel? You didn't come to take me on a buggy ride so you could pry into my personal business."

"No," Penrose admitted. "At least, not entirely. Your family is worried and they have asked me how you've been. But that's not my mission today." He glanced out the window, and was apparently satisfied with what he saw, because he turned his gaze back to Harry. "Has Mrs. Rayburn ever mentioned a man named Terrance Valloy?"

"Not in my hearing," answered Harry at once. "Why should she?"

"It was widely expected the pair of them would become engaged, up until the moment she married you, that is."

"What of it?" Harry shrugged, irritated. If this was Penrose's new attack against Leannah, it was pretty weak stuff. "It was widely expected I was to become engaged to Agnes Featherington, up until the moment she turned me down."

"'Widely' is perhaps coming a bit strong, but never mind that. Terrance Valloy, like old Octavian Morehouse, is a speculator. Unlike Morehouse, Valloy is actually good at it." Nathaniel paused again, and perused the passing street again. "What do you know about the markets, Harry?"

"If you've a lecture to give me, get on with it, Penrose. Unlike you, I've got business to attend to."

Penrose sighed and rubbed his eyes, which once more emphasized their dark rings. Harry bit his tongue and tried to rein in his temper. Despite all, Nathaniel was his friend. He was wrong about Leannah and her character, but whatever "mission" brought him here, it was not mere gossip or vague suspicion. It took much more than that to rattle a man like Penrose.

"All right. Here's the long and the short of it. The financial markets are mostly illusion. That illusion is that anybody with a bit of money can get stinking rich if he's a little smart and a little lucky. But the truth is the ones who make money are the ones who already have it; they're the ones who know each other and who pass information along to each other from inside the exchanges and the clubs. Everyone else is just scrambling after their crumbs. Some of those men are more or less honest. Some of them, though, rig the game. They make sure of their outcomes by bribing public officials or the members of corporate boards to get the results they want. Others just pay for secrets, and get together to make sure they can play those secrets to their best advantage." He lifted his head. "Has Mrs. Rayburn mentioned any recent contact between her family and Mr. Dickenson?"

"What's Dickenson to do with it? I thought you were talking about this Valloy."

"I have it on very good authority that Dickenson has been meeting with, and writing to, Terrance Valloy." Nathaniel paused again. "He also recently had a meeting with the young Miss Morehouse. That meeting ended in a quarrel, and Dickenson raised his hand to her."

Harry felt himself go quite still. It was a long moment before he could speak again. He should have taken care of Dickenson when he had the chance. A man who would even threaten to lay a hand on a girl was no man at all.

When he regained control of his voice, he asked, "What did they quarrel about?"

"My source didn't hear the whole of it, but it seems she was supposed to bring something to him, and that something had gone missing. Afterward, he got angry with her, and threatened her."

Leannah had said nothing of this, and Harry knew she was in Genny's company almost every day. Worry rose in him, dark and restless. He kicked it angrily away. He needed to concentrate on essentials, and not let Penrose's innuendo and suspicion distract him. "Was Leannah at this supposed meeting with Dickenson?"

"She was not seen."

Bloody spy. Can't talk straight even when it's important. I'll bet you're your own "source." "Then she probably didn't even know the thing happened." If her sister was the victim of such an outrage and Leannah knew of it, she would tell him. They already had ample proof, however, that Genevieve could keep her secrets. After all, it was her elopement that had started this whole business.

Her elopement with Anthony Dickenson.

"It is not a supposed meeting. It did happen," said Penrose. How could a man speak so softly and yet remain so impossible to ignore? "I've told you, Dickenson is bent, and Valloy has been known to wander from the straight and narrow himself, when he thinks it will be to his advantage." Nathaniel leaned forward. "Harry, please believe me. I am here because I am your friend. There is an investigation happening. It's not public yet, but it will be soon. The Dickenson clan have all been very busy of late, and money is changing hands. They're covering their tracks well, so no one quite knows what their aim is yet. But the one straight line anybody's got so far goes from Anthony Dickenson to Terrance Valloy, and now it's headed for the Morehouse family."

Damn you, Penrose. Harry ground his teeth together. *Damn me, too.*

Because he couldn't stop his mind from running over everything Leannah had told him about her sister. He thought about all the time she and Genny had spent together, and the number of visits she'd made to her former home. She'd only shared the most trivial of news about what had happened there—new servants, new clothes, and such. He hadn't thought much of it before. There was so much else to occupy his attention when he was with Leannah, first and foremost Leannah herself. But Nathaniel's words cast a fresh, cold light over those vagaries, and they did not look so trivial at all.

Then there was all that Leannah had not said—like why she hadn't yet reclaimed her wedding ring. He'd given her plenty of time. In fact, he'd carefully avoided bringing the subject up. He'd hated the ring anyway, and it was entirely wrong for her, but still, he'd been waiting for her to bring it back or at least say where it had gone. It was irrational and perhaps even mean spirited of him, but it hurt that Leannah had taken the thing off, and given it away, even though she had the best of reasons for doing so.

And it was Genevieve she'd given it to.

The worry in him rose higher. It closed over his head and dragged him down.

"This . . . thing that you say Miss Morehouse was supposed to bring Dickenson. Has your source any idea what it might have been?"

Nathaniel shook his head. "No. Apparently, it was small, something that would fit in a lady's reticule: a letter, perhaps, or some other paper. Perhaps it was a key to a safe or strongbox."

Or perhaps it was a ring.

Thirty-Three

❧

"Yes, if you'll put that here." The four carters maneuvered the marquetry sideboard to the empty space Leannah indicated, careful to avoid bumping the new chairs that had been positioned around the equally new dining table.

The piece was perhaps a little showy, but its inlaid pattern of starbursts in four different colors of wood was so beautiful that Leannah hadn't been able to resist when she saw it at the warehouse. It certainly did look very fine in its place alongside the gleaming oak table and chairs. Leannah looked about herself. The room only needed its last few details; the two lamps and the silver candlesticks were also promised for delivery today. She should be feeling proud, and satisfied, but all Leannah could muster was a weak smile.

What good is it? The treacherous question rose once again in her mind. *What good is any of it when it could all be ending tomorrow?*

A dozen times already that morning, she'd tried to think of ways to retract her offer to take Harry back to the house and introduce him to the rest of her family. Each time she had berated herself as a coward. This must come. It did not mean the end. What she'd said to Harry had been nothing less than the truth. They could not know if their marriage was real if it only existed inside their rooms, and they had to know. She had to know. The honeymoon had to end and the rest of life had to begin.

Leannah rubbed the knuckle on her smallest finger. For her, endings had never been happy ones. How did she find enough trust to believe that this one could be?

From Harry, she told herself. *From need and laughter and desire. From love.*

She rubbed her knuckle again.

"Mrs. Rayburn?" Stella, a brisk, plump, efficient girl crossed the threshold and curtsied. Stella and Cook, and several other of the new servants had come in today to help with the deliveries and arrangements. "There's a Mrs. Westbrook downstairs who wishes to know if you are at home." She handed Leannah a card.

Leannah stared at the card. Her mouth opened, and then closed as she read the flowing copperplate script. Mrs. Westbrook was Harry's sister, Fiona, and she was downstairs, waiting to be received. She pressed her hand against her stomach and struggled for calm. What was she doing here at all? How had she even found them? Had Harry written to her, or gone to see her? Was that the business that was keeping him from going to meet Father today?

No, Leannah shook her head to clear it. She must not descend into suspicion. Harry would never spring his sister on her like some party surprise. However Mrs. Westbrook came to be here, it was her own doing, and now that she was here, there was nothing Leannah could do but receive her.

"Yes, Stella, I am at home," said Leannah. She glanced about her. The sitting room and parlor still smelled of paint and what furniture had arrived for them was still covered with cloths. "You may show Mrs. Westbrook in here, and then please go see if Cook can furnish us with some tea, and perhaps something light to eat."

"Yes, ma'am." The girl curtsied again and bustled away. Leannah reached out and gripped the back of the nearest chair, striving to regain her countenance.

When Stella returned, she was accompanied by a tiny, golden-haired woman who carried an air of energy and self-assurance about her. She was immaculately dressed in spring green and antique lace, with a necklace of peridots around her throat and the merest suggestion of a green lace cap on her gold hair.

Leannah straightened. She let go of the chair and she curtsied.

"Good morning, Mrs. Westbrook. Won't you please sit down?"

"Good morning Mrs. . . . Rayburn," answered Harry's sister. "Thank you."

Mrs. Westbrook sat or, rather, she perched on the edge of the nearest chair, like she might be required to leap to her feet at any moment. Despite this, she did not look at all nervous. In fact, her gaze was positively steely and the way she met Leannah's eyes indicated she was ready to stay put as long as it took to achieve her ends.

Leannah had the most uncomfortable feeling she knew what those ends entailed. Her heart quailed, but not for long. Pride, and her own native stubbornness came quickly to the rescue, and Leannah was able to take her own chair smoothly.

She did not, however, have any idea whatsoever how to talk to this woman. There was absolutely no etiquette for such a situation. Fortunately, Mrs. Westbrook did not seem to be one to stand on ceremony.

"Shall you begin, or shall I?" she inquired.

Leannah felt her eyebrows lift. "Oh, by all means, please do go ahead, Mrs. Westbrook."

Mrs. Westbrook nodded once. "Very well. Harry is my older brother and I love him more than just about anyone in the world. But he is quite capable of being an idiot." She paused.

"Am I meant to agree or argue?" inquired Leannah.

That seemed to startle her. The corner of her mouth twitched. "As you see fit, I'm sure."

"Very well. I might perhaps observe that all of us can take on the appearance of being idiots from time to time, especially when our emotions are engaged."

Mrs. Westbrook's bright blue eyes narrowed minutely, and Leannah had the feeling she'd scored a palpable touch.

"You can imagine the news of his having married you came as something of a surprise."

"I do not need to imagine. It certainly shocked my family gravely, I cannot suppose it had any less of an effect on yours."

Leannah waited expectantly for Mrs. Westbrook to once more take up her side of this decidedly odd conversation. For her part, Mrs. Westbrook cocked her head. Leannah suspected many people underestimated the delicate looking woman, rather like they mistook Genny's fragile appearance for a fragile nature. Along with the energy Leannah sensed when Mrs. Westbrook first entered the room, she saw the light of a sharp intelligence behind the other woman's eyes, and a willingness to dive headfirst into the unconventional if required.

"Did Harry tell you we'd taken this house?" Leannah asked.

"No. He's pouting. I had to discover it on my own." Mrs. Westbrook reached into her reticule and pulled out a scrap of newspaper. It was the "Arrivals" column, from the *Woman's Window*, neatly clipped out, Leannah noted, and with a circle in grease pencil around one particular paragraph.

It has come to our attention that one Mr. R, recently returned to town with his new bride, and will be taking an unfurnished house in Dobbson Sq. As that neighborhood is closely connected to both the R—s and M—s, the rumors of a rift between branch and tree cannot be perhaps quite so serious as previously supposed . . .

Leannah stared at the clipping. This was Meredith's handiwork. She should have thought things through more carefully when her friend offered to plant an item in one of the most popular women's papers.

"After I saw this, all that was left was to talk to certain persons and get the exact address." Mrs. Westbrook reclaimed the article. "I might have lurked about with a dark lantern, but as a married woman, I felt it best to minimize the theatrics, and since my best friend happens to own the ground your house stands on, I had little difficulty discovering you. Now that I have, I must admit, I do not find you at all as I imagined you would be."

"Given what you probably imagined, I will take that as a compliment."

"Hmm." The other woman pursed her lips tightly together.

Silence fell once more. *Perhaps it is time to test the limits of my sister-in-law's unconventionality,* thought Leannah. *If nothing else, it will end this charade all the more quickly.*

With the feeling that she was about to plunge headfirst into her own deep waters, Leannah said, "Mrs. Westbrook, I know perfectly well what is said about me, and my family. I've heard it being said for years. I also know that my marriage to your brother will be the sensation of the London drawing rooms. I suppose I should have been more sensitive to that when I accepted his proposal, but to speak the absolute truth, when we met, society's acceptance was the last thing on my mind."

"Hmm." The corner of Mrs. Westbrook's mouth twitched again, and she took her time considering the direction of her next salvo. "You know he's quarreled with our parents?"

And with you. But Leannah kept this addition to herself. "Yes, I did know, and that also was no surprise, all things being taken into account. Before you are bothered with saying so, Mrs. Westbrook, he did tell me his father might cut him off."

"He already has, or perhaps I should say Harry has cut himself off. He hasn't been to work, or by the house, in weeks."

Of all the declarations Mrs. Westbrook could have made, this was the one that hit home. Leannah felt the blood drain from her cheeks. "I didn't know, about his work. He hadn't told me."

Mrs. Westbrook nodded slowly and several times for emphasis. "Mother is nearly frantic, well, as near to nearly frantic as I've ever seen her. She's generally not the frantic sort, not like some others I could name. But she insists that Harry will come home when he's ready. In the meantime she's driving the rest of us mad with her attempts to keep busy, so I decided to take it on myself to make sure he's ready to come home as soon as may be." *With you or without you.* Mrs. Westbrook did not speak those words, but they hung in the air nonetheless.

"In other words, you're here to ask me what my intentions are toward your brother?"

There was that twitch again in the corner of Mrs. Westbrook's mouth. Was that possibly the hint of a smile? Did this severe and unconventional woman also possess a sense of the absurd? Harry certainly did. It could very well run in the family.

"Yes. I came to ask your intentions. No one else was going to do it."

Now it was Leannah's turn to be surprised. This frank and unashamed admission was not what she expected. It flew in the face not only of drawing room etiquette, but the accepted rules of verbal combat as practiced among cultured ladies.

Very well. Let me see what you do with a response in kind.

"You want to hear my intentions, Mrs. Westbrook, but will you accept my answer? Or will you just brush me off with a brisk cry of 'stuff and nonsense' because my past has already condemned me? I am not inclined to waste my breath on a hopeless effort to convince you of the purity of my heart and motivations."

"I never say 'stuff and nonsense,'" replied Mrs. Westbrook primly. "To begin with, it makes no sense. It's also Rebecca Islington's favorite phrase, and she never makes any sense even on a good day." She paused and rallied herself around to the topic at hand. "Mrs. Rayburn, we would seem to be at an impasse because I am in no mood to waste my time on trying to convince you to release my brother when you have no intention of doing so."

"Your brother is free to go or stay as he will. I have no way of holding him if he wants to leave, and no desire to do so either." Leannah eyed the other woman. "I suspect you don't believe me."

"I don't know."

Stella chose that moment to enter with the tea tray. Both of them fell silent at once in order to avoid the cardinal sin of gossiping in front of the servants. Stella curtsied and took her leave. Mrs. Westbrook looked at the service, which was new, as was everything in the house. Her mouth trembled and her brows knitted. She'd been right, Leannah realized. Mrs. Westbrook was doing her best to keep from smiling. Leannah understood the impulse. Their situation truly was absurd. Here they were, arguing over the course of their lives, but any unpleasant conversation must be set aside for a hot drink and sweet biscuits. Why? Because that was what was supposed to happen, and everybody knew it.

"Tea?" inquired Leannah politely.

"Thank you," responded Mrs. Westbrook with equal politeness, and with another mighty and obvious attempt to suppress her smile.

"Milk? Sugar?"

"A little of each."

Leannah fixed the cup and handed it across. "Gossip?" she added, just to see what would happen.

Mrs. Westbrook did not disappoint. "Only if it's fresh."

"I'm afraid I haven't had time to lay in a supply yet. Perhaps you've brought something?"

Mrs. Westbrook considered. "Mrs. Spinnaker spent three hundred pounds on her daughter's new dress, and it's hideous."

"That's because she didn't let Emily help choose it," said Leannah as she added milk to her own tea and stirred.

"You know Emily Spinnaker?"

"A little. She's friends with my sister, Genevieve. They had a bit of a girl's salon together, where some friends gather at the library and read the *Woman's Window*"—she gestured toward Mrs. Westbrook's reticule—"and the latest novels and so forth."

"Wait. Wait." Mrs. Westbrook frowned in furious concentration. "There's a G.M. House who writes these wildly radical letters to the editors, about how women should be allowed their own property rights, even after marriage. Is there possibly any relation . . . ?"

Leannah sighed. "Genny got hold of a copy of Mary Wallstonecraft's *Vindication of the Rights of Woman*, and none of us has ever been the same. Unfortunately, she found out that espousing unpopular views is difficult work."

"And the appeal of saving the world only lasts for so long." Mrs. Westbrook rolled her eyes. "I do understand. Harry went through a dreadful philosophical phase when he was still at Oxford. He slouched about the house, grew his hair long, and quoted dead Romans at every turn."

"That doesn't seem at all like him."

"It wasn't, but you know how young men can be such terrible romantics. They get all sorts of idealistic notions that they decide they simply must live up to. Harry was no different."

Leannah shook her head in sympathy. "They are not the only ones who get notions. You may trust me on this. Once I confronted Genny with those letters, I had to sit through her political readings at breakfast every morning for a month. It's not that I didn't agree with much of it, but not over the coddled eggs."

At this, Mrs. Westbrook not only smiled but chuckled. "I take it, you read the *Woman's Window* as well?"

"Is there anyone who doesn't?"

"Rather too many people, to hear Aunt Judith tell it." She

paused when she saw Leannah's inquiring look. "Judith Montcalm, she's the publisher. She's not really my aunt, of course. She's the aunt of my best friend's husband."

Which sounded so like a translation exercise from a French grammar book, Leannah couldn't help but grin. "Well, don't tell Genny you know her. She'd like to meet the publisher above all things."

"Oh, but Aunt Judith would love to meet her as well. I've heard her say several times those G.M. House letters showed a genuine journalistic flare. You must let me make the introduction and . . ." She stopped. She blinked. "Good heavens, Mrs. Rayburn, have we just become friends?"

Now it was Leannah's turn to blink. "Why yes, Mrs. Westbrook, I do believe we have."

"How wonderful! And you must call me Fiona."

"Isn't it? And I am Leannah."

Fiona raised her teacup to Leannah. They clinked the rims of their cups and sipped in unison, and in unison burst into laughter.

"Oh, dear," said Leannah when she could speak again. "This is not at all how I imagined this interview would go, or how it would end."

"I confess, I was just about to say the same. Now." Fiona set her cup down and scooted her chair closer to Leannah's. "Tell me quickly, how is Harry really doing?"

"He's doing well, or at least, I thought he was." Leannah frowned down at the remains of her tea. "I'm suddenly not so sure. As I said, he didn't tell me he'd lost his job."

Fiona waved that away. "He didn't lose it, he left it. But Father will take him back as soon as he's got over this fit of pride. It's just the same as when we were growing up you know. Harry's gotten stuck on an idea. We must put our own heads together and make sure it is knocked loose as soon as possible." She paused. "Under normal circumstances, I'd do the job myself, but he's been so dug in . . ." She met Leannah's gaze and went on more softly. "He loves you, you know."

"I love him." *There. I've said it. I've said it and it's true. Why haven't I been able to say it to Harry?*

Fiona nodded. "I believe that. I might not have before, but I do now."

Leannah set her cup aside. She also rubbed the knuckle on her little finger. It was becoming a habit. She should stop it, soon.

"I think . . . I think that he will be coming back to you before much longer."

"Really? Has he said so?"

Leannah shook her head. "No. But I am taking him to meet my family." Her throat tightened and she glanced about the room with all its lovely things and all its promise of peace and comfort. "After that, he will either want to stay or leave."

Fiona reached out and touched her wrist. "Listen to me, Leannah. This is all very strange and very upsetting, but I know my own brother. Not all the notions he gets in his head are mistakes. I mean, yes, there was Oxford, and Agnes Featherhead, and . . . well that's all water under the bridge. At bottom, he is a good man and a steady man. If he really does love you, nothing in the world will take him from your side. And if he stays, it will be from love, not just pride or stubbornness or honor or . . ." She blushed. "I think I'd best stop talking now. I'm not making anything better, am I?"

"On the contrary, you're making everything wonderful," Leannah returned what she hoped was a cheery smile. "Would you like to see the house?"

"Very much, thank you."

They got up from the table, and Leannah led her sister-in-law through the rooms. They discussed drapes and furnishings and the absolute impossibility of finding good servants, and other such housewifely details. All the while Leannah felt her heart tremble with the effort it took to dwell on what was pleasant and inconsequential. She wanted to nurse this new friendship, which was as quick and unconventional as all the other things that had happened to her since she met her first Rayburn. Part of her could not wait to meet Harry's parents and see where all this cheerful directness came from. Part of her wondered if she ever would.

Because Harry got ideas stuck in his head, and Harry hadn't told her he'd left his job, or his family.

Thirty-Four

❧

"Leannah," said Harry. "Would you like to drive us this morning?"

They were getting ready to leave for her father's house. Leannah was in the act of tying the blue ribbon on her new bonnet into a love knot under her ear as she turned toward him. Her face did not look loving. She looked tired. Which, Harry supposed, was only to be expected. It had not been their best morning, or their best night either.

Since his disturbing conversation with Nathaniel, Harry had been attempting to come up with some excuse to avoid this visit. He'd spent hours walking up and down the streets, trying to tell himself nothing Penrose had said meant anything. The man might be a bloodhound in the halls of government and a damned spy for hire, but he didn't know everything. Penrose didn't know Leannah and how good and beautiful she was, how perfect.

But wasn't that exactly how Harry had described Agnes Featherington?

The effort he'd spent in trying to banish these cowardly and unworthy thoughts had left little energy for conversation with Leannah when he returned to their rooms, especially when his greatest news—that he had new employment—was not something he could share. After all, he'd never gotten around to telling Leannah he'd quit his father's employ in the first place. He hated the feeling he was keeping secrets from her almost as much as he hated the growing suspicion that she was keeping secrets of her own. He couldn't stop thinking about the ring, and Genevieve's meeting with Dickenson, and this other fellow, whom Leannah had never mentioned. Why hadn't she told him about Valloy? He'd told her about Agnes, hadn't he? And why hadn't she told him that that Valloy knew Dickenson?

What else was she hiding? Harry hated himself for wasting even a single second on the question, but it had become like a wasp buzzing about the room. Now that he knew it was there, he could not ignore it.

Damn Nathaniel Penrose anyway. Leannah was already nervous enough about taking him to meet her father, and here he was making the whole thing worse because he wasn't man enough to dismiss his friend's ludicrous insinuations.

"You wouldn't mind me driving?" Leannah asked gravely. She knew something was wrong. She'd known it since last night. For the first time since the Three Swans, they hadn't made love. He hadn't gone so far as to sleep in his own bed, but he'd held her in the dark and waited for his desire to rise, and it hadn't. He'd felt her warm curves. He'd felt her breath against his cheek, and the brush of her skin against his as she finally curled up beside him to sleep. The whole time, he'd been silent and sorry, and nothing else.

"I don't mind you driving in the least. In fact"—Harry reached into his coat pocket and pulled out a slim package wrapped in brown paper and white ribbon—"I got you these."

Leannah took the package, undid the ribbon and pushed aside the layers of tissue to reveal a pair of bright green gloves. He'd had them custom dyed that exact color to match her eyes. They were smooth, supple leather, with wide cuffs and palms of double thickness. The shopkeeper told him they were made for those unconventional ladies who liked to ride to the hounds.

"They're beautiful, Harry," Leannah murmured, but she didn't look at him. Harry felt his heart twist uncomfortably. She sounded far too unsure. This was his fault. His and Penrose's. He must find out what was going on. He must get this mess with Dickenson and this Valloy character cleared up. But how could he dig into it without wounding Leannah's feelings any further?

Leannah drew the gloves over her hands. They went on

smoothly and they fit perfectly. She held both hands up and there was longing in her eyes.

"Harry . . ." She turned her beautiful, hungry eyes toward him. Just a day or two ago, he would have teased her and demanded some token of thanks that would have left them both breathless. But that hunger he saw in her now was not for affection, or even for simple laughter. It was for something deeper, and she was afraid that something would never be found.

"Harry, everything will be all right, won't it?"

Harry swallowed. "Why wouldn't it be?"

She had an answer. He saw it. No matter how she tried to close herself off from him, he could still read the truth in her lovely face. But she just turned away to pick up her reticule. Harry bit back his worry and his words, and followed her out the door.

For a wonder, Gossip and Rumor behaved themselves the whole winding way through the streets. This miracle owed not a little to Leannah's expert handling of the mettlesome team. Harry sat beside her on the box, and watched her work the ribbons with renewed respect. He also watched how she relaxed, even smiled, as she drove. The air of worry was slipping away as she navigated the traffic, alternately encouraging and scolding her team. Harry felt himself relax as well. This was more the thing. Soon, they'd be joking and laughing again. Soon, everything would be as it should.

The street where Leannah's family lived was a narrow one. London's soot had dimmed the brickwork and stoops on the houses, but that had not happened without a fight. Harry saw several raw-boned women out with buckets and brushes trying to scrub away the worst of it. The people who stopped to look at the gleaming barouche were respectably dressed, but all about them was just a little worn, and just a little tired. The children clapped and laughed at the high-stepping team, as if it was a treat to see such animals. It was hardly poverty, but it was a place where people feared it was easier to fall in the world than to rise.

When Leannah brought the carriage to a halt in front of one of the tall, narrow houses. Harry jumped down to help her down from the box. She handed the reins to the groomsman who'd come with them from the Colonnade. Harry found himself looking about sharply. The children were not the only ones who watched the carriage. Disheveled men lurked about the board fences and in the shadows of the alleys, eyeing carriage and horses, and Leannah herself, like they were contemplating their market value.

No wonder she was reluctant to return here.

Leannah opened the door to her father's house. The hall was dim and there was no real foyer. Battered matting covered its scuffed boards. The housekeeper, an elderly dame in a stiff, dress of black crepe bustled up.

"Good morning, Mrs. Rayburn!" she cried. "We didn't expect to see you today!"

"Good morning, Mrs. Falwell," replied Leannah. "This is Mr. Rayburn. We're here to see Father, if he's awake?"

"Oh, yes, yes, he is indeed. I'll go at once and let him know you're here."

As Mrs. Falwell busied herself collecting their hats and coats, Harry became aware of being watched. He looked up, and saw a boy of about twelve years hanging over the railing on the top floor. This must be the brother, Jeremy. Harry tipped the boy a salute, and received a narrow-eyed glare in return. He felt his eyebrows rise. A moment later, Genevieve, moved into his field of view. She grabbed the boy by the shoulder and hustled him away, giving him a shake in the process. But she did not get either one of them away fast enough that Harry missed how Genevieve beckoned to her sister.

Leannah didn't miss it either. "Go in, Harry," she said. "I need to have a word with Genny."

"All right." He took her hand, now free of her new green gloves. He looked into her eyes, searching for something—some sign to tell him that Penrose's suspicions were unfounded, as they were, as they must be.

But all he saw was that she was tired, and that her smile, though cheerful, was more than a little wary.

Harry let go of her hand before she could feel that his own had gone quite cold and turned to follow the housekeeper.

"Mr. Morehouse prefers to spend his mornings in his study." Mrs. Falwell spoke those words with an air of both pride and apology. If Harry had judged the narrow house right, there were not many other places he could spend his mornings.

The room was small and while the furniture in it was good, it was all worn. Still, everything in it bore signs of recent and thorough cleaning. The drapes, which were a truly unfortunate color, had been drawn back to allow what little sunlight the neighborhood afforded to shine into the room, and the good fire in the hearth made the place snug.

"Mr. Rayburn." The room's sole occupant got stiffly to his feet. Octavian Morehouse had once been a tall man, but he was now stooped and frail. His skin hung loosely off him, as if he'd recently lost a great deal of weight. Despite this, his step was spry as he came forward to take Harry's hand. If his grip was weak, his gaze was steady and his eyes clear. His dark coat and trousers both looked new. Harry suspected that, like the housekeeper's crepe dress, they had been purchased within the last few weeks.

"I am delighted to be able to shake your hand, sir," Mr. Morehouse went on. "Will you sit? It's too early for wine, of course, but would you care for some coffee? I know it should be tea, but coffee is a habit I acquired as a younger man, and I haven't been able to give it up."

The door opened, and Leannah slipped in. Harry saw at a glance she was paler than when they walked in the house. Whatever Genevieve had told her, it was not good news. He caught her eye, but she shook her head minutely. Harry's disquiet increased, but he said nothing. He did, however, glance at her hand. The ring was still missing.

"I'd be glad of some coffee," he said to her father. "Thank you, sir."

"I'll pour." Leannah crossed immediately to the coffee service that had been set out on the desk, as the room had no table for the purpose. While she poured, Harry and Mr. Morehouse settled themselves on the sofa.

"Now." Mr. Morehouse smiled genially. "Let us not stand on ceremony. It's of no use to us here and now. Thank you, my dear." Mr. Morehouse smiled up at Leannah as she handed him his cup. "Leannah has told me what happened, and my brother and my younger girl have both confirmed it. We needn't pick over the details. You have married my daughter, and you did so honestly and willingly."

"Yes, sir."

Leannah handed Harry a cup of coffee, black and

unsweetened, as he preferred. He tried to give her a reassuring smile, but she turned away quickly, moving to fix her own cup.

"Will you tell me something of yourself?" asked Mr. Morehouse.

"Gladly." Harry drank the coffee, which was hot and good, and began to recount the details of his life; his youth, his schooling, his travels, and his position at the warehouses his father owned. He talked a bit of his father and mother, of his sister and her marriage to the future Baron Eddistone. In short, he offered up the sorts of remarks that he would have in more ordinary circumstances made upon offering for Leannah's hand.

All the while, Harry watched Leannah. She lingered over fixing her own coffee. She stepped out into the hall, presumably to speak with a servant, and returned a moment later. She sipped the cooling coffee without sitting down, and added a little more milk and a bit of sugar and sipped again. She refilled her father's cup, and then Harry's.

She said nothing, but her restlessness spoke for her. Something was profoundly wrong.

But what could it be? Her father gave every sign that he was enjoying the conversation. The questions he asked were easy, comfortable ones—about Oxford, about travelling, and business. If Leannah hadn't told him the old man had been ill, he would have believed Mr. Morehouse to be nearly as hale as his own father. He was thin, and there was a tremor in his hands that occasionally rattled his cup against its saucer, but his eyes were keen and his mind seemed perfectly sharp and attentive.

Leannah had brought him here to meet Mr. Morehouse, to charm him and be charmed, and yet every single action she had taken since they arrived said something was going badly wrong. It made Harry look again at her father and listen closely to his easy questions. He had met charming men with something to sell, and plenty of them. He did not forget for a moment this man had gone so far as to sell his young daughter for money. He did not forget one word of what Nathaniel had told him about the line stretching from crooked Dickenson to the speculator Valloy to Mr. Morehouse.

What was it he was failing to see? What was happening on the other side of that door, and what had Genevieve told her?

"Well now, Mr. Rayburn . . . hang it all, may I call you Harry?"

Harry started. He'd been concentrating so intently on Lean-nah, he'd entirely lost track of what Mr. Morehouse was saying. "Of course, sir."

"Excellent. Now, Harry. The circumstances are maybe not what I'd have hoped for, but I trust my Leannah. She's proved her good sense time and again and you are her choice. There's no stronger recommendation that could be made in your favor—no, not if the Prince of Wales himself came into the room and spoke your name. But I'm a man accustomed to making up my own mind, another habit not easily put aside. Oh, don't worry." He laughed. "Your speech, your bearing, the story of your life, all commend you to me, as do your actions on behalf of my family these past days. I am content with my daughter's choice, Mr. Rayburn—Harry. I am most content indeed."

"Thank you, sir. I shall endeavor to be worthy of your good opinion, and Leannah's."

Mr. Morehouse nodded. "I know that you will," he said firmly. "Therefore, we must look to the future. I have no doubt, that my daughter, and others, will have informed you that our family recently suffered a great reversal of fortune."

Harry glanced at Leannah. She had finally sat down, but her eyes were lowered toward the coffee cup she held in both hands.

"The fault was mine," Mr. Morehouse went on. "There's no good in denying it. But we were not left entirely with nothing. There is a piece of land that . . ."

There was a crash. Harry jerked his head around. Leannah was on her feet. Coffee ran down the front of her skirt and the cup lay in pieces at her feet. She had not just dropped it, she had dashed it to the floor.

"Leannah!" cried her father. "Good heavens, what's the matter with you? Let me ring for the girl . . ."

"Why was he here, Father?" she demanded.

"Who, Leannah?"

"Mr. Valloy, Father. Why was he here?"

Thirty-Five

❦

Leannah watched, entirely unmoved, as her father's face turned chalk white. "Who told you Mr. Valloy had been here?"

It was Genny. Genny had signaled from the top of the stairs that she needed to speak with Leannah, and her eyes had been so wide and her face so pale, Leannah knew that something important had happened. Nothing less could have induced her to send Harry in to meet her father on his own.

Genny had drawn her into their old bedroom, and gripped both her hands.

Lea, I think we're in trouble.

"Never mind who told me," Leannah said sharply. "Is it true?"

"Yes, of course it is." The air of confused innocence on his face was almost too much to stand. "Leannah, let me ring for the girl. Your skirt . . ."

She slashed her hand through the air to cut him off. "What did Mr. Valloy say to you?"

Father didn't answer her. Instead, he turned to Harry. "Perhaps you should excuse us, Harry?"

"Leannah?" breathed Harry.

Yes, let Harry leave the room. It would be better. She did not want for him to see her like this, or for him to hear her say what she must. She could not stand to watch his love and respect falling away, not just yet.

She nodded her agreement without looking at him. Harry got to his feet and crossed the room. He paused beside her. Just a day ago, he would have kissed her cheek. Now he only took her hand. His fingers felt cold against hers. She lifted her chin and stared straight ahead. She could not look at him. She would not. She had known what would happen if she brought him here, and now it had. She had opened the door and let in their ending.

Harry closed the study door behind him, and behind her.

"Now, no more evasions," Leannah said to Father. "Why did Mr. Valloy come here? What did he want with you?"

"Leannah, please, don't look at me so. I accepted nothing. I swear upon your mother's grave I did not."

"He offered you something? What was it? Money? A position? You must tell me!"

His whole frame trembled as he collapsed slowly onto the sofa. It was as if the weight of his years bore him down.

"Close the drapes," he murmured. "Please close them."

Impatient, furious, and afraid, Leannah wrenched the drapes back across the windows. The ancient velveteen tore in her grip, leaving the ends flapping loose and ragged from the rings. She ignored this fresh bit of ruin as she whirled around.

"Now, tell me!"

Father coughed. He coughed again, and when he spoke he spoke to the fire in the hearth.

"Mr. Valloy came, I think, three days ago. I was . . . surprised to see him." Father tried to lift his coffee cup again, but his hand shook too badly, and he set it down again. Leannah did not move. She must not let herself take pity on him, not now, not ever again. *I should have known this before I ever brought Harry here. This is all my fault. This is what comes of trying to hide from who I really am.*

"I had expected him to be angry," Father said. "I wasn't sure what to say to him, since I knew so little of what had happened between you and him, and you and Mr. Rayburn."

Again, my fault. I wanted to keep you separate from my new life. I didn't want to risk you becoming agitated, or tempted by what was happening. Leannah hung her head. "Go on."

"But he wasn't angry in the least. In fact, he was very gentlemanlike. He spoke of his continuing admiration for you, and said he blamed himself for your elopement. He'd been too slow about the business, was how he put it. I began to think that he'd simply come to break with me and show there were no hard feelings."

"Then what happened?"

"He said he was sure there was still a way the business could be brought to a positive conclusion." Father's eyes grew bright. "He reached into his wallet, and he laid a note on the table. A banker's draft. It was . . . large. He said it was a first install-ment. He said he still wanted you, and he said . . . he said . . . it would be on the terms I'd had with . . . oh, heaven help me, Leannah, on the terms of your marriage to Elias."

Leannah closed her eyes, but only briefly. She couldn't hide from this, or refuse to see.

"He wants the Wakefield estate," she murmured.

"He said it was about to prove very profitable and that I would have my share of those profits, but any such arrangement was contingent upon his marriage to you."

"But, why should my marrying him make any difference? You're still Jeremy's guardian. You still have a say in what happens to the property. Who I am married to makes no dif-ference." *He wants more than the land, he must. There's some larger plan.*

"He was unclear . . . no." He must have seen the look on her face. "I didn't ask for details. I just kept staring at the draft. Leannah, I could do so much with that money. I know just what should be done with it. And the land! If he's right about the road, just think about the profits . . ."

"The road? What road?"

"The Great Devon Road. It's set to pass right by the estate. Think of it! It means traffic and business of all sorts. There'd be new shops, and mills and steam looms, and more money to invest. We wouldn't have to fear a few losses, because there would be plenty. I saw the numbers, moving back and forth, adding up so beautifully. I knew what to do. I knew *exactly* what to do."

Horror gripped her and Leannah felt it tear her heart as easily as ancient velveteen.

"All the while he talked, the draft just lay there on the desk. I thought of you, and my other children. How you should have the best, only the best. As I thought this, it seemed like that note began to grow. It was going to drape over the whole room, like a wedding veil, or a shroud . . ."

"Stop it!" Leannah cried. "Stop it at once! Just tell me what you promised him!"

Father trembled. His voice, when he spoke again, was nothing but a whisper.

"I promised him nothing, Leannah. I picked up the draft and threw it on the fire."

Is it true? Harry stared at the closed door, his brain spinning. *What Nathaniel said? Can it be true after all?*

Harry could hear them arguing in the study, but couldn't make out the words. He wanted nothing more than to press his ear to the door like a spying parlor maid. He turned away before that ludicrous idea could take a firm hold.

No. I won't believe it. There's some reasonable, innocent explanation for why Valloy was here. But the thought had no strength.

Harry walked to the end of the narrow corridor. He should have been angry, but he wasn't. He felt drained, numb. He'd reached the end of the short, dim hallway, and turned to stare again at the closed door. He walked back toward it a half-dozen steps, and stopped, swaying on his feet.

He should go, he knew that much. But he couldn't think where he would go, or how he would get there. He couldn't think of anything except that Leannah had lied.

A shadow fell across him. Harry glanced up the stairs. The boy, Jeremy, was back, leaning over the railing and scowling. They stared at each other for a while. Distantly, Harry expected Miss Morehouse to appear once more to take charge of her brother. Judging from the way Jeremy glanced over his shoulder, he expected the same thing. But his sister did not return. Instead, the boy started down the stairs, stepping over one in particular as he descended. Harry suspected that one creaked in the fashion of an alarm.

Jeremy came to stand in front of him and drew himself up, head back, arms folded.

"You're him?"

"Yes," admitted Harry. "I'm Harry Rayburn."

"Jeremy Morehouse." Jeremy frowned up at him. He was taking Harry's measure. It was popular to assume children were empty vessels waiting to be filled with the thoughts of adults. The people who went around preaching this view had never met the sort of boys Harry had grown up around.

"Come on." Jeremy jerked his chin toward the back of the house. "I want to talk to you and we'll never get a chance if my sisters catch up with us."

The boy opened one of the right-hand doors and Harry followed, because he couldn't think what else to do. At least, if he was talking to her brother, he was not standing about stupidly waiting for Leannah, and whatever lie she'd tell him next.

Jeremy led Harry down the back stairs and through the kitchen; much to the consternation of the cook and her girl, and the carter who was sitting at the table enjoying a mug of tea. A small and sooty garden waited on the other side of the kitchen door, complete with the obligatory cucumber frames and small brick shed. Jeremy retreated behind the shed. Clearly, this was a place where the boy discovered he could not be seen from the house.

Once they were both crowded into the shed's weak shadow, Jeremy straightened himself up to look Harry as directly in the eye as he could manage. He was going to be tall when he finished growing. Unlike his sisters, the boy was a genuine "ginger," with bright red hair and a spray of freckles across his sharp face. It was his wary obstinacy that touched Harry, though. That hadn't come just from facing a stranger suddenly thrust onto his family. It came from never quite knowing who or what to trust.

"I know what Lea's mad about," Jeremy said. "All right. I admit it. I took it."

What was this now? Harry felt his brows knit together. Was the boy somehow involved in his family's schemes?

"I'm not sorry," Jeremy informed him stubbornly. "It's my duty to look out for my sisters."

"Naturally," murmured Harry, bemused in spite of himself. "I've only got one question. What did you take?"

That caught Jeremy flat. "You mean they didn't tell you about the ring?"

The world froze. Not one thing possessed the power of movement. Harry's heart did not beat, his lungs did not draw breath.

"No, Jeremy," he said, and he was stunned by how calm his voice sounded. "No one told me about the ring."

Jeremy clapped his hand over his mouth. Harry strongly suspected he was uttering a whole string of words with which a young gentleman was supposed to be entirely unacquainted.

"Next time, don't assume the other fellow knows the same as you." Harry went on. "Let him do the talking and find out what he's really keeping under his hat."

Jeremy grimaced. "I'm still not sorry," he muttered.

Harry glanced around the corner of the shed. He couldn't see any sign of movement in the house. Were Leannah and her father still talking in there? Was she looking for him? If she wasn't now, she would be soon. He dropped his gaze to the boy again. It was wrong to be standing here quizzing Leannah's little brother, but he didn't seem to be letting that stop him.

"Will you tell me why you took your sister's wedding ring?"

Jeremy shrugged. "I wanted to find out if it was genuine. The fellow at the pawn shop said it was."

"You took a ring worth hundreds of pounds to a pawn shop?"

Jeremy shrugged with the affected casualness that was particular to young boys who wanted to look tougher than they felt. "We had to be sure. If the thing was a fake, you might be just stringing Lea along. You might be planning to leave her flat after a week or a month of high living at a hotel we couldn't never afford."

The ground shifted under Harry's boots. Of course. His family wouldn't be the only ones with doubts. The Morehouses knew all about dishonest dealings, large and small. This boy who had seen so much disaster come from money—and the lack of it—would want to be sure his beloved sister hadn't just thrown herself headlong into a fresh scheme. It all made complete and heartbreaking sense.

But it doesn't answer why Dickenson expected Genny to give the ring to him.

Jeremy was looking at him in confusion. Clearly, he was waiting to be yelled at. Harry shook himself.

"It was still not a smart move for all that," he said. "The broker might have thought you'd stolen the ring." *Which you did.* "He could have summoned the police, or might just have knocked you on the head and kept the ring as payment for his trouble." *Your sister might have been beaten by a callous brute for failing to deliver on a promise.*

"Oh." Jeremy shoved his hands in his pockets. "Hadn't thought of that."

"Next time you're making off with other people's property, do."

"Are you going to tell them?" He jerked his chin toward the house.

"I expect at least one of them already knows. But no, I won't say anything, as long as you tell me where the ring is now."

The fact was, he already knew. He saw Jeremy's hand shifting inside his trouser pocket, like he was fingering something.

It seemed the boy realized he'd been caught, fair and square. He pulled the ring out of his pocket, and handed it over. "Was going to put it behind Genny's dressing table, like it had dropped there, but never got the chance."

There were holes in that story, but now was not the time to pick at them. Harry took the ring, and tucked it into his waistcoat pocket. "Did you get your answer? Is it genuine?"

Jeremy nodded. "Doesn't answer as to what you were doing running around with a lady's ring in the middle of the night."

"I'd been turned down by the girl I meant to marry, and I hadn't gotten around to selling it back to the jeweler, or throwing it in the river."

"Oh. Well. Her loss, ain't it?" Jeremy added in the spirit of manly camaraderie.

"Thank you."

"You're not what I was expecting."

"Neither are you."

Now it was Jeremy's turn to glance toward the house. "Better get back. They'll be shouting for us before long."

"One minute," said Harry. Harry felt the tiny bulge of the

ring pressing against his rib. It seemed to remind him he shouldn't ask this next question. It was entirely dishonorable. He should speak directly to his wife.

"Leannah said Mr. Valloy had come to the house recently. Do you know what he wanted?"

Jeremy's face screwed up tight, like he was trying to hold back anger, or tears. "He's starting trouble, and he's doing it on purpose. He's got no business hanging about here offering our father his dirty money."

"What's he giving your father money for?"

"For Leannah, so he can marry her."

Thirty-Six

I don't know anything. Harry told himself. *I don't know anything.*

"You got it wrong," he said to Jeremy. "You misheard something."

"Didn't. You can hear everything goes on downstairs if you put a glass up against the chimney in my room."

Of course you could, and of course the boy would know that. He'd be suspicious of any man talking to his father, just as he'd been suspicious about the ring. He had seen what came of men having private talks with Octavian Morehouse.

"Valloy was offering a settlement," Harry said, painfully aware he was grasping at straws. "He must not have known she had married again."

Jeremy snorted. "Oh, he knew all right. Didn't care. He was talking big about 'their' plans and how there was going to be so much money to go around once everything came through."

She'd been hiding this from him. Spinning stories. Pretending. Lying. Using her sister as a go-between for herself and Dickenson and Valloy.

No. Don't think like that. You don't know. You've only got a boy's version of events. He's sharp, but he's still only a boy. Just because she married for her father's advantage once, it doesn't mean she'd do so again.

Jeremy eyed him nervously. "Got to get back in. I'm supposed to be doing lessons."

This probably wasn't true, but the boy didn't give Harry a chance to question him. He just turned on his heel and pelted back the short distance to the kitchen door. Harry heard it slam, and he heard the cook's indignant shout that followed quickly after.

He stayed as he was, standing in the shadow of the garden shed where he could not be seen from the house, trying to understand, trying to think.

It can't be her fault. She was used before. Her father's the fraud, not Leannah.

The money's gone. My father's ill. A weakness of nerves.

Except that Octavian Morehouse hadn't looked ill. He'd looked calm, and in perfect possession of himself. And why wouldn't he? Everything was going according to plan. Leannah's family needed money. Leannah knew how money could be gotten and she helped set the plan in motion.

Which was why she couldn't bring him here before. He might discover why she'd really taken off her wedding ring and given it to her sister, who was intimate with Anthony Dickenson, who was bent as a corkscrew.

Harry's guts knotted tight. He doubled over, as if he'd just taken a blow straight to his solar plexus.

I don't know anything!

But that was the problem. He didn't know anything. He'd let himself be led by lust and pride. He thought Leannah had needed him in a way that Agnes never did. It had been a magnificent relief to be with her and to not have to be careful of her person or her body, or of his. He hadn't wanted to understand what was behind her acceptance of him, or any of her actions after that.

"Harry?" a voiced called from the house. "Harry?"

Leannah. Harry straightened, startled. He shrank back, coward that he was, even as he cursed himself for his weakness. But before she had to call again, he stepped out to where he could see her, and she could see him.

"There you are!" she cried. She ran to close the last few feet between them, like any girl would on catching a glimpse of her own true love. "Oh, Harry, I'm sorry about what happened in the study. I was afraid there'd been new trouble, but everything's going to be all right."

"Is it?" he murmured.

"Yes, it is." She threw her arms around his neck and kissed his cheek. Even now, understanding all he did, his body yearned for hers. He wanted to catch her up in his embrace and bury his face in her hair. He wanted to tell her it didn't matter that she'd lied. It didn't matter that she tried to betray him. Nothing at all mattered as long as she stayed with him.

He didn't move.

Leannah pressed her face against the side of his neck so he could feel each movement of her warm, vibrant mouth as she spoke. "I know, I'm talking like a madwoman, only I'm so happy." She paused, and lifted her face away from his collar. "What are you doing out here? Did Jeremy bring you?" She smiled, her eyes alive with sparkling good humor. "He probably wanted to give you a thorough going-over to prove he's the man of the family."

"Yes, that's it exactly. He also wanted to give me this." Harry reached between them so he could draw the ring from his pocket. He waited for the shock to overcome her, but it didn't. She just clapped her hand against her cheek in surprise.

"My ring! Oh, thank goodness." She seized it and slipped it back onto her little finger. "I'd been absolutely sick about it. Did Jeremy take it?"

"Yes," replied Harry dully. "He wanted to make sure it was genuine."

"Why that little . . ." She shook herself. "Well, never mind. We've got it back, and that's what's important."

"I wish it was."

Leannah frowned up at him. God, he was going to miss her eyes. Even now, with her brows knitted and her face filled with confusion, her eyes remained beautiful. He could see all those tiny flecks of gold that added such luster to her brilliant green irises. It occurred to him that Leannah's wedding ring should not be a diamond, or even a ruby, but an emerald.

But then, perhaps Mr. Valloy and Mr. Dickenson didn't care for emeralds.

"Harry?" Leannah gripped both his hands and shook them. "What's wrong? What did Jeremy say to you?"

"It's not what he said, or not *just* what he said. Leannah, I know." Harry drew in a shuddering breath. "I know you gave the ring—your wedding ring—to Genevieve so she could give it to Dickenson."

For a moment, Leannah only stared. Then, she yanked her hands away from him, as if she'd suddenly realized she'd touched something rotten.

"What was it for?" Harry asked as Leannah backed away, horror rising in her beautiful, shining eyes. "Was it a pledge against future income? Or a down payment for another piece of land along the Great Devon Road? Or was he just supposed to pawn it to raise more cash for the bribes to the ministers so that the route would go ahead as you all had planned?" He paused. "Is that what happened to your settlement, which was spent, not lost?"

She swallowed. He watched the movement of the muscles beneath her golden skin. He remembered how the satin flesh of her throat had felt beneath his fingertips, beneath his mouth. She wasn't speaking. She didn't offer any excuse or defense. Like her brother, she knew she'd been caught fair and square.

"Although, I don't see why you'd need any more cash. Surely, I was pouring out more than enough." He couldn't stop talking. He should. He should get away from here. Run away. Run home. Beg his parents' forgiveness for his foolishness and lock himself in his room like a child. Lock away possibility of any more mistakes, lock away the memories of need and love—yes, love. Love that would never come again. A broken heart could never hold love, and his heart was broken—truly, utterly completely.

"You all must have had great fun creating those false bills for me to pay so you could take the money and give it to God knows how many corrupt men . . ."

"Enough!"

The word lashed out like a blow. Harry's mouth shut. Leannah stood in front of him, her face as wild with fury and determination as it had been that first night when she'd run away with him.

"Enough," she repeated. "You will not speak to me that way, Mr. Rayburn."

It is over.

Leannah heard the bitter words pouring from Harry's

mouth, the mouth she had kissed and teased. The mouth that had tasted every portion of her body. He kept talking, spouting the worst calumnies, but all she could really understand was it was over. She had been afraid his love would fall away slowly. She should have been afraid it would explode like a cannon shell.

"You got an idea stuck in your head," she murmured. "Fiona said you would."

That stopped the flow of outrages, at least for a moment.

"You spoke with my sister?" Harry asked.

"I did." Leannah felt herself nod. She didn't seem quite in control of her own body. It was as if she'd stepped outside it somehow. Perhaps her soul no longer cared to inhabit the flesh that would not be quite so cherished by Harry Rayburn. "She came to our . . . to the Dobbson Square house to tell me, among other things, that her brother tended to become fixated on certain ideas . . ." Her voice faltered. "I should have paid more heed. After all, I know how many ideas about me could come up. But"—she waved her hand—"I was sure what we'd shared would prove stronger than any stray ideas. Another mistake."

"Yes, it was," said Harry and his bitterness sank like poison into her mind. "Especially . . ."

She could not stand to listen to any more. A moment ago, all had seemed right. Father had turned away Mr. Valloy's attack. The danger had passed. Father was well in his heart and his mind—finally, truly well. She'd come out here to tell Harry everything. The new beginning, the one she had hoped for all her life, was at last going to come true.

Except, it seemed it was not.

"Especially what?" Leannah lashed out. "Especially since you've decided I'm a liar and, what else? A schemer? A whore? All because I lost your ring?"

"Because your family is consorting with corrupters and speculators and . . ."

"And because we're the Morehouses," she spat. "Yes. Thank you. And because I didn't tell you about Mr. Valloy and that put the seal on it. I couldn't possibly have any reason not to speak of the man attempting to manipulate my family when I've always been judged so fairly and so decently by the world at large."

This last seemed to hit home. Harry raised a shaking hand toward her. But she let all the contempt, all the outrage she felt show in her face, and he let it fall.

"I would have loved you," he whispered. "I did love you."

Now he said it. Now, when it would hurt the most. "I came out here to tell you that my father refused Mr. Valloy's money, as I had refused his threats previously. I came to tell you I sent Genny out with a letter for Meredith Langely. She'd been in touch with a man from the naval office about Mr. Valloy, and Mr. Dickenson . . ."

Now it was Harry's turn to stare. "Meredith Langely? *She* was the authority Nathaniel spoke about?"

He was talking nonsense. It was just as well she wasn't listening to him anymore. "I see now I needn't have bothered. We have all of us been tried and convicted in the court of Harry Rayburn's mind, and I should have known." She let her head fall back, as if she thought to see the heavens themselves open to pronounce judgment. "It's never different. There's never any new beginning. Not for us. Not for me. Not even . . . not even love is enough to make one."

"No," breathed Harry. "That's not true. I will not let it be."

Her throat tightened. The world was shifting around her. She couldn't think straight. It was all closing in, closing down. It was the same thing as she'd felt before. The house, the walls, all the troubles of her life, all the long, cold past was closing in, trapping her for good and all.

She had to get out. Leannah whirled around.

"Leannah, stop." She heard Harry's boots smack against the muddy ground. "Wait. We must . . ." She felt his hand on her arm.

"Get away from me!" she screamed and slammed her elbow backward. The blow caught him in the ribs and he fell back. Probably not hurt, probably just startled, but it didn't matter. He'd let go and she could run. Run for the gate, burst through it, run for the street.

She'd lost him. She'd come back and she'd lost him. She'd opened the door to the tangle of her life, her family, and she'd lost him. He saw what she was and where she came from and he couldn't trust her, couldn't love her. Who could? It didn't matter that there was no blame this time. The blame from the past smeared itself across the present and it always would.

She had to get away, had to run. There was the carriage, and the team but not the groom. Where was the groom? Why was it Dawes standing there waiting for his orders. It didn't matter. She clambered up onto the box, and grabbed the ribbons from Dawes's hands. She slapped the reins, hard across the horses' backs. Gossip and Rumor leapt forward. She couldn't see straight. Her eyes were blurred. It didn't matter. All that mattered was getting away, from the house, from herself, from her life, from Harry Rayburn.

From the fact that she had loved him, and now he would never know it.

The horses didn't want to run, but she wouldn't let them hesitate. She shouted and smacked the reins again. The leather hurt her palms and she didn't care. She heard a voice, shouting in her ear.

"Leannah! No! I was wrong! Wrong! I love you! You have to stop!"

Harry. It was Harry. How was he here, so close? It didn't matter. She mustn't turn, she mustn't slow down. She could not stand to see his face again. She couldn't stand to hope, to love. Not again. Not ever again.

The traffic was thick, the road was narrow. She hauled on the reins. There was just enough room to take the corner, if she pulled just enough . . .

Leannah had one heartbeat to feel that something was wrong before the leather snapped. Gossip veered in the traces, the carriage swung wildly. Something caught her elbow. The wheel hit the corner of the house. The world spun. She was aware of Harry's arms, rock hard around her. She saw the horses rear, felt the fall begin, felt herself wrenched sideways. But Harry's arms weren't there anymore. She had no shelter. She saw the pavement, and felt the pain as it hit.

Then there was darkness, and it dragged at her. Leannah cried out. She didn't want to go. Harry had come back. Harry had put his arms around her, and told her . . . told her . . .

But the darkness was too strong, and it pulled her down.

Thirty-Seven

❧

H arry felt the reins give. He threw his arms tight around Leannah, dragging them both sideways. He saw Gossip rear. Then, the world spun and they flew, and he couldn't hold her anymore. Gray sky tumbled into gray stone, and stone tumbled into sky again. Something hard slammed against his back and for a moment he saw nothing but stars. After that, he couldn't see at all.

But he could hear voices. They screamed and shouted and he knew some of them. There was Genevieve, certainly, and that hoarse choking shout, that was old Octavian Morehouse. And . . . Nathaniel?

"Harry? Come on, Harry! Open your eyes. Look at me. Come on, Harry. You can do it."

My eyes are closed? Harry thought in confusion. Yes, it seemed that they were. After a brief struggle, he was able to pull them open.

First, he saw Nathaniel. His face seemed damnably calm for all the bustle and hubbub around him. There was something wrong with the angle, though. Slowly, Harry realized he was lying on his back on a heap of trash and dirt.

"Steady, old man," said Nathaniel. "You just lie still."

But Harry didn't want to lie still. Something important had gone missing, and he had to find it. With a groan, he rolled onto his side, blinking hard to try to clear his blurred vision. For a moment, he was able to see past Nathaniel to the street.

He saw the overturned carriage.

He saw Genevieve dragging her sobbing father away from the wreckage and toward the house.

He saw Leannah, stretched out on the cobblestones, blood smeared across her brow.

Movement was pain, but pain was not going to stop him. Neither was Nathaniel, who grabbed at his arm and his shoulder. Harry crossed the distance between him and Leannah in a heartbeat to kneel on the stones at her side.

"Leannah!" he cried. "Leannah, I'm here."

She wasn't moving. Why wasn't she moving? The blood trickled in a scarlet ribbon down her pale brow. She was cold. He lifted her. He had to get his arms around her. Get her warm.

"Harry, come away. You've already done everything you could."

That was Nathaniel. He felt the other man's hands on his shoulders. But Harry wasn't listening to him, because he heard something else, something much softer and far more urgent.

Harry?

It was Leannah. Leannah was calling him.

"I'm here." Harry pressed his mouth against her brow, not where the blood spilled. He didn't want to hurt her. He had hurt her too much already. "I'm here, Leannah. Forgive me, my wife, please forgive me. I was wrong. I was so wrong."

"She's gone, Harry." Nathaniel was kneeling on the stones beside him. He was trying to pull Leannah from him.

"No! She isn't. Leave her be! I can hear her!"

Harry! She was calling to him, as she had called to him across the inn when he'd been about to lose himself to his anger. As she called to him across her tiny, sooty garden, and in the darkness of their room, to let him know she wanted him. Because she had wanted him. She loved him. He knew that. He would tell her so, and this time he would make sure she never had cause to doubt him again.

"It's your imagination, Harry. Come on, come away."

"No!"

He wrenched himself free of Nathaniel's grip but then he cried out, because he'd jarred Leannah. He'd hurt her, again. She was so still, so white. There was too much blood. But she wasn't dead. She couldn't be calling to him if she were dead.

He leaned over her, so his mouth touched hers, so his breath must brush her skin. "I'm here. I'm right here, Leannah. I hear you. I love you, Leannah."

There was a moment. There was an eternity. It was filled with nothing but doubt, and the complete awareness of Leannah so utterly still and cold.

Then, he felt it—the tiniest flutter of movement, like a moth's wings. Her mouth was moving against his. She was making no sound. He could not possibly have heard her, but he did. She had called him back again to her.

He raised his head so he could see. Leannah's eyelids fluttered, and they opened, revealing her gold and emerald eyes. For a moment, she looked around in confusion.

Then she saw him. "Mr. Rayburn?" she breathed.

"Yes," he breathed. "Mrs. Rayburn. I understand. I was wrong. I was so wrong. But we're together, Leannah, and we'll fight this, too."

"Yes," she whispered and this time there was light shining in her eyes. "This, too. Together."

Thirty-Eight

⚜

"Harry," murmured Leannah. "They're expecting us downstairs."

She was prevented from adding to this by Harry's mouth covering hers. She knew she should resist, but she could not. Especially not when his tongue glided so sensuously against hers, and his hand slid up the sides of her tissue of silver wedding gown.

He moved his mouth to kiss her cheek, and her jaw.

"Harry . . ." She meant to admonish him, but his name came out as a sigh.

"Yes, yes, they're waiting. I don't care. They can wait ten minutes. After all, I've waited an entire year." His hands pressed against her back, urging her closer to him. She struggled, but only briefly, only until he smiled. The heat, the sheer wicked delight of that smile dissolved all possibility of resistance. Leannah melted against Harry, reveling in the way her body molded against his.

He was not exaggerating. It had been a year; a long, slow painful year. At first, time passed for Leannah in fits of confused dreaming broken by stretches of sick agony as her body fought the fevers and the infections, and tried its best to heal.

Sometime during that year, Terrance Valloy and Anthony Dickenson were brought up on charges of public corruption and conspiracy. Mr. Valloy turned king's evidence against Mr. Dickenson in the form of a letter detailing his intent to bribe certain officials. For this, Terrance was sentenced to twenty years penal servitude.

When Genny had delivered her letter to Meredith, Meredith had sent at once for Nathaniel Penrose, because she knew he'd want to hear Father's story. Father's story in and of itself did not turn out to be of any help in court, but it proved very useful to Mr. Penrose in convincing other witnesses to speak of things that could be. These statements taken together with the broken carriage harness, which Mr. Penrose had thought to preserve, led to Mr. Dickenson having attempted murder added to the list of his crimes.

Anthony Dickenson was hanged less than a week after the completion of his trial. The Dickenson family found itself drummed out of a whole range of clubs and fraternal organizations, after which they decided to leave the country en masse for parts unknown.

Father was still nervous, but he was also able to walk about the streets, if they were quiet. The doctors began to talk of a holiday to the country, or at the seaside to complete the cure. A new tutor was hired for Jeremy, who point-blank refused to return to school until he was confident his sister was fully recovered.

Fiona Westbrook was delivered of her first child, a fine healthy boy named James Harold Nicholas Edward.

Plans were drawn up for the renovation of Wakefield House. Mrs. Westbrook, Miss Langely, and the senior Mrs. Rayburn completed the furnishing and decorating of No. 14 Dobbson Square.

G.M. House started writing letters to the *Woman's Window* again.

Leannah knew all this because Harry told her. He spent the entire year at her side. He drove the nurses and the doctors to absolute distraction until she was strong enough to order him from the room so he could get some fresh air and she could get some peace. Those intervals averaged five minutes in length.

He fed her broth until she could hold the spoon for herself. She hated gruel. She despised barley water. The nurse despaired. Harry coaxed her and teased her until she drank them both.

When she was finally able to sit up again, they talked. They talked about their lives and childhood. They talked about Devon and all that had happened there. She told him how she'd used Elias's settlement to try to pay back some of the money her father had lost over the years.

They talked about her mother, worn away by misfortune. They talked about his mother, who had been a runaway bride back in her day.

They talked about sisters and houses and horses and the merits of roast beef over boiled, and if French novels were really more scandalous than English or if they just sounded that way because they were, well, French. They talked about whether they should keep renting the Dobbson Square house, or buy it outright. He had no objections to cats, but had a strong distrust of small dogs.

They talked about Calais. They talked of forgiveness.

When she got tired, he stretched out beside her, and pillowed her head on his arms. They lay close, not kissing, not doing anything but breathing each other's breath.

When she was strong enough to stand, it was Harry who raised her from the bed. When she was able to walk, it was Harry who supported her across the room, and eventually down the stairs, and out into the fresh air of the little park at the center of Dobbson Square.

When she could receive visitors, he introduced her to his parents and she introduced them to her family, and to Meredith when she came to visit, and to the members of the Schoolroom Club.

After that, they walked out every day the weather was clear, until the day came when they could walk themselves to Uncle Clarence's tiny church and stand before him yet again. This time when he said "Dearly beloved," he was beaming, because their families and friends filled the pews. This time, Genny stood with Meredith Langely as Leannah's bridesmaids, and Nathaniel Penrose and Philip Montcalm stood with Harry to make a truly arresting pair of groomsmen.

The papers were sure to remark on the fact that she had worn a plain woolen shawl wrapped around her shoulders. The rough garment didn't in the least go with her elegant gown of champagne silk and silver tissue, but she did not care.

The wedding breakfast had been truly splendid, and all their guests were now waiting downstairs to see them off. She was supposed to be getting out of her wedding dress and into her travelling costume. But when she'd come into the bedroom, it was only to find that Genny and Meredith had slipped away down the servants' stairs, leaving her to her husband's tender mercies.

Not that Harry's expression spoke much of tenderness, or mercy, either. His blue eyes smoldered dangerously as his hands firmly caressed her back, and glided around to graze her breasts. Leannah hissed in a long breath as desire unfurled itself inside her.

"Ten minutes?" Leannah breathed, even as she shimmied her body against Harry. Oh, how she'd missed the brush of his chest against her breasts and all the delicious anticipation it raised.

"Ten minutes," he whispered as he brushed back her lace veil to plant a heated kiss on the bare top of her shoulder. "Perhaps fifteen." His hands had travelled around to her derriere, and he began kneading her there in that way he knew she particularly enjoyed, the way that lifted her onto her toes and pressed her hips snuggly against his.

She had loved this shimmering gown from the moment she'd seen the pattern card, but it was beginning to annoy her now. There were too many layers of fabric between her and Harry. He was hard, she could feel it, but she could not touch him. Not in the way she wanted to, the way she knew he wanted.

She sighed. She also kissed the tiny bit of his throat that showed above the high collar of his gray morning coat. "You have never taken only fifteen minutes."

"The longer you protest, Mrs. Rayburn, the longer we will be about this business." He shifted his warm grip to her wrists. Her new wedding ring glowed on the third finger of her left hand—a square-cut emerald of a green so rich it was nearly blue. Slowly, he walked her backward until her shoulders pressed against the wall. His eyes blazed and she felt the molten heat of pure desire fill her. Harry opened his arms out wide, spreading hers like wings. He raised them over her head, crossing her wrists, holding both in place with one strong hand. "You will stay just like that and you will let me please us both a little, or I shall have to tie you down, and that may take us all day. Do I make myself clear?"

"Yes," she murmured as his hands took possession of her body and her pleasure. "Yes, my love."

After that, there was no need for any more words.

READ ON FOR A SPECIAL PREVIEW OF ANOTHER
SIZZLING-HOT ROMANCE FROM DARCIE WILDE

Lord of the Rakes

AVAILABLE NOW FROM BERKLEY SENSATION!

Lady Caroline sat in her private study, staring at the letter Mrs. Ferriday handed her. The only sounds in the cool blue-and-cream room were the ticking of the ornate case clock and the crackle of the fire. A lump of coal clattered against the grate as it fell. Caroline did not glance around. It was not the sound she feared, not the sound of her brother's return. She dared make no noise herself, no exclamation of hope or surprise. It was as if she thought the walls would not only hear, but would betray her. Country houses kept all manner of secrets, but some of them were not kept for very long.

She'd already been nursing this one for weeks. She read her letter once more, and once more after that.

"Really, this is absurd," Caroline murmured to herself. "It's not as if it's going to change."

Despite this entirely sensible remark, she read it again. The clock ticked and the fire crackled, and there was no other sound.

Slowly, Caroline laid the paper down and rose to her feet. Several locks of her unruly chestnut hair had escaped their pins to dangle about her ears. She pushed them back as she stared down at the surface of the desk. From this distance the closely written words were little more than scribbles of black ink, but she could still pick out the words "trust" and "dividends" and "account."

Moving without real purpose, Caroline drifted over to the

window and pushed back the plush drape. Outside, the garden had turned gold and gray from the cold, March rain. She could just see the last of the snow lurking under the burlap-shrouded forms of Mother's rosebushes.

Caroline rested her fingertips against the windowpane, feeling the cold of the glass slip under her skin. She had often stood and stared like this, sometimes in this room, sometimes in Mother's bedroom when Mama had fallen into a restless doze, or one of her long, terrible spells of silence.

But if the man who wrote to her was being accurate and honest in his presentation of the facts, her days of standing, staring, and wishing might finally be at an end. Caroline pressed her hand flat against the glass. She had spent years trying to accustom herself to living within the constraints her father and brother laid on her. But now . . . now . . .

The door creaked. "My lady?" said a soft voice.

Caroline jumped and whirled around. Her eyes darted at once to her desk, and her first thought was to run and hide her letter. Then she realized the voice belonged to Mrs. Ferriday, her personal attendant. Caroline sagged against the window, at least as far as her corsets would permit.

"Yes, Mrs. Ferriday, what is it?"

"Miss Rayburn, my lady. She's just arrived and—"

"And Caro, I've got such news!" Before Mrs. Ferriday could finish another word, Fiona Rayburn burst into Caroline's sitting room. "Look! Look!" Fiona waved her left hand in front of Caroline's eyes.

Between her letter and Fiona's abrupt appearance, Caroline was so dizzied, she could barely see anything at all. "Fi! I thought you were still in London."

"I was, but *look*!" Fi shoved her fingers directly under Caroline's nose. Caroline took a deep breath, grasped her friend's wrist to hold her still, and forced herself to focus on what was immediately in front of her.

What was in front of her was Fiona's dainty, perfectly kept, and entirely ungloved hand, the third finger of which was graced by a bright, gold ring. A square-cut diamond nearly the size of Caroline's thumbnail flashed with a delicate pink tint.

Caroline's gaze jerked up to meet her friend's. Fi nodded energetically.

"He proposed! James proposed!"

"Fi, that's wonderful!" Caroline embraced her friend and tried to set all other feeling aside, but the tears stinging her eyes were not just from happiness. The hope and fear that came with Mr. Upton's latest letter would not be so quickly dismissed, not even for Fiona's joy.

"You're the first person outside the family I've told." Fiona pulled back, but only so she could grasp Caroline's shoulders. "And you are going to be my maid of honor, you know. I couldn't possibly consider anyone else."

This determined declaration allowed Caroline to smile in earnest. Three seasons in London had not changed Fiona in the least.

"So, you're going to be married from Danbury House?" Caroline settled onto the velveteen sofa and motioned for Fi to sit beside her. "That will be beautiful . . ."

"Danbury House? Oh, no, Caro. A country wedding would never do. James is the future Baron Eddistone, after all. We're to have a town wedding. A big one. In June, of course, and—"

"A town wedding? In London?"

"Honestly, Caro. Your sense of humor does make you say the oddest things sometimes. Of course London."

Caroline did not make any immediate answer. She could not. The reminder of her current circumstances—all of them—was too much. Fi's eyes narrowed. It was a look that turned her dainty face surprisingly shrewd. Few beyond her intimate acquaintance ever suspected the sheer force of personality and cleverness that lay behind Fiona's sky-blue eyes. "Caro? Has something happened?"

Yes, it has. The words flashed through Caroline's mind, but she still couldn't make herself speak. Her ears still strained to hear the distant scrape of a heavy door, or the echo of riding boots against marble tile from the foyer below—the sounds that would signal Jarrett's return.

"I know Jarrett will refuse out of hand," Fi went on. "I'm sure he thinks I'll whisk you off to some masked ball and throw you to the Lord of the Rakes."

"Who?" asked Caroline, struggling out of the depths of her own angry reverie. "Lord of the what?"

For a moment Fiona looked at Caroline like she couldn't

comprehend what she said. Then she clearly remembered her friend was almost entirely ignorant of town gossip. "Oh. I'm sorry. It was a joke. There's a rogue about town currently, Philip Montcalm. The matrons have made a bit of a hobgoblin out of him. They call him Lord of the Rakes and use him to try to frighten girls making their debut into good behavior."

"Does it work?"

"Not that I have noticed. But, Caro, you are missing the point. The point is that you are to be my maid of honor, and I am here to make sure Jarrett lets you come to me." Fiona drew herself up to her full height, which was, in truth, not that difficult. The epitome of the English Rose, delicate, golden Fiona had never grown an inch past five feet tall. Caroline, on the other hand, had inherited something of her father's height to go with her mother's generous curves and chestnut hair. She could never sit next to Fi without feeling gawky. "I'm going to ask Jarrett directly to allow you to come to me," Fi told her. "If I fail, Mother and Father have already said they will come next and make the case on our behalf."

Although she was the daughter of a wealthy earl, Caroline had never once been to London. Instead, she'd grown up feasting on her mother's stories of its parties, shops, and theaters. Her favorite times as a child had been when Mama decided they would be "paying calls" for the day. Together, they traipsed through the house, pretending it was the London streets and that the empty, quiet rooms of Keenesford Hall were populated by the ladies of the haut ton that Mama had known before her marriage to Earl Keenesford. But Mama's long series of illnesses and Father's orders had kept them from ever actually visiting the town. Now that Jarrett had inherited the title, he decided those orders should remain strictly in place. Caroline might visit the country house parties of their various acquaintances, if Mrs. Rayburn or some other chaperone he approved of was there. She might accompany him to an archery meet, or a hunt ball for some slice of society. Otherwise, her world was Keenesford Hall and its grounds, and would remain so.

At least, that had always been their father's plan, and Jarrett had enforced it rigidly. She'd never actually caught him going through her papers, but it was not out of the question. He'd asked so many sharp questions at the breakfast table this morning, she was sure he knew she was hiding something. If he even suspected she knew about the money . . . what could he do? What might he try to keep her here?

But that question played itself over in her mind once more. What could he do? If Mr. Upton was right, Jarrett could do exactly nothing.

"Caro, you're looking positively feverish. What on earth's the matter?"

Caro looked into her friend's suspicious, worried eyes. How to even begin? She squeezed Fi's hands once before she stood and walked over to her desk. She pulled out two of her recent letters and stared at them. If they told the truth, if she could bring herself to really believe . . .

"Caro," whispered Fiona. "Please, I'm asking as your friend. Tell me what's wrong."

"Nothing," answered Caroline. "That's just it. For once, I think, everything's right."

Caroline handed Fi the first letter. She watched her friend read. She did not need to lean over her shoulder to know what Fi saw. She had memorized the words the week the letter arrived. Possibly the first day.

Dear Lady Caroline:

I hope you will excuse the liberty I take in writing this letter, and permit me to congratulate you upon this occasion of your birthday, and the achievement of your majority. Now that you are in full possession of the funds your mother so prudently left in trust to you . . .

Fiona lowered the letter. "A trust? Your mother left you a trust? Caro, you never said!"

"I didn't know," Caroline croaked. "They . . . Father and Jarrett. If they knew about it, they never told me." As an underage girl, she had not been present at the reading of her mother's will. Certainly no man of business would think to discuss such things with a girl when her father and brother were alive to hear about them for her. When Jarrett inherited the title, he had continued their father's custom of receiving all letters into his own hands at the dining table. He himself would then distribute the few meant for her or the stewards and servants. Caroline wondered now if any of those had been deliberately withheld.

Fiona pressed her hand to her mouth, but continued reading.

> *. . . I wish to take this opportunity to assure you that if you have any question or direction regarding the disbursement of your dividends, you have only to write to me at this address, and I will do my utmost to provide answers. In the absence of other instructions, there is an account in your name at the Bank of London, where said dividends will be deposited quarterly.*
>
> *I am very much looking forward to hearing from you. Again, my best congratulations upon this anniversary of your birth. You may believe me to be entirely at your service.*
>
> *Sincerely,*
> *Theodore Upton*
> *Davis, Upton, Fordyce & Crane*

"Dear Lord, Caro . . ." Fiona slowly lowered the letter so she could stare at Caroline. "Do you really have an inheritance?"

Mutely, Caroline passed the other letter she had selected from the pile, the one that had arrived less than an hour before Fi herself.

> *Dear Lady Caroline:*
>
> *I was very glad to receive your letter of the twentieth. I am sorry your mother was unable to communicate the details of the trust before her passing. But in her stead, I shall do my best.*
>
> *The basic facts are these. The money in the trust comes from a series of leases on land purchased by your maternal grandfather, Karl Herresmann. That*

*land has since been turned into several very profitable
and fashionable housing developments in the heart of
London. The rents accruing from these leases were set
aside in a trust for which your mother was named as
beneficiary. Five years ago, she drew up a simple will
and placed a copy with the members of the trust
board. In it, she names you as her sole heir and
beneficiary.*

*As to your main question, I have investigated the
matter quite thoroughly and find that this trust was
never in any way tied to her marriage settlement with
the late Earl Keenesford, or the Keenesford estate.
Therefore, your mother was legally entitled to leave
the income to whom she chose, just as you are legally
entitled to receive it.*

*I trust this clarifies the points you raised. Do not
hesitate to write again if you have any further
questions.*

Yrs. Sincerely,
Theodore Upton
Davis, Upton, Fordyce & Crane

Fiona finished the letter and raised her eyes slowly to
Caroline's.

"You're an heiress," she breathed. "You have the income
from land leases in London! They must be worth thousands!"

"Ten thousand a year," Caro answered, and watched Fi draw
back. "I asked. Oh, Fi. It's been so wonderful and so terrible,
I've barely known which way to turn. I'm still trying to believe
it . . ."

"Believe later. Now you have to act. What will you do?"

Caroline took the letter that Fiona held out. "I will not stay
here, that much is certain," she said as she folded the paper
into thirds. "My mother was made a prisoner, supposedly for
her own good, and I saw what it did to her."

"I know, Caro."

Caroline glanced toward the door. Had she heard a man's
footsteps from below? She wasn't sure. Fear struck a chord
inside her, but she stilled it. Now that she was her own woman,

she would have to get over being afraid. She would have to meet the world with poise and dignity, as Mama told her a real lady did.

"You see what this means, Fi? I can leave. I can leave anytime I like. I'm free." This was the first time she'd said these words out loud and they felt rich and delicious against her tongue.

"Yes, but . . ."

"But what?" Now that Caroline had broken this last silence, the fact of her freedom began to fully blossom within her. She had laid up a wealth of dreams and plans during the lonely years since Mama's death. But any possibility of escape, no matter how modest, had lacked a single ingredient—money. Now the money was hers—all she could ever need and more.

"Jarrett's still Earl Keenesford," Fiona said uncertainly. "No matter how great an heiress you are, he could make terrible trouble for you, if he chose."

"Then I'll go where he cannot reach." Now that the doors of Keenesford Hall were thrown open, every other point in the world seemed within equal reach. "The Continent. Vienna. Switzerland. Florence. Oh, Fi! I've always wanted to see Florence, and Paris, of course."

"But, not alone, Caro," said Fiona, plainly striving for a practical tone.

Caroline waved this away. "Mrs. Ferriday will come with me. She's already said she would." In fact, it was Mrs. Ferriday who had been taking Caroline's letters to Mr. Upton to be sent by hand from the carriage house in the next village. "She's a second cousin of Mama's. That will do for the proprieties."

"Not for long, Caro. You don't know how the London matrons love to tear a newcomer down."

"But I won't be staying in London," Caroline reminded her. "After your wedding, I'll be going to Paris, and past it." What had been a dim possibility a moment ago now appeared to be the ideal scheme. "I'll be free of Jarrett and any London matron who might want fresh gossip. No one will know who I am, and no one will care. I'll have money enough. I can do anything. Be anything." Tears were rising in her eyes. "Oh, Fi, Mama told me I'd have the freedom she never did. She just couldn't say how it would come to me. She had to keep it secret. And by the time I was old enough to understand, she was too ill."

Fiona looked wary, clearly not convinced, but her natural high spirits were rising to the surface. A smile spread across her face, and Caroline could not help but grin in return. "Caroline, this is going to be marvelous! Think on it. You and I together in town at last. I'll introduce you to absolutely everybody. You'll have parties and balls, and you'll be able to get *married* . . . !"

"No." Caroline spoke the single word with absolute decision.

"What?"

"I will never marry, Fiona. That much has not changed." Caroline had made up her mind to this years ago. Part of her decision had come from watching her mother's decline in a loveless marriage to a titled man. The rest had come from the round of country house parties she'd lived through. She'd spent too much time listening to matrons who talked of their children like a dealer talked of horses. If any cement was needed to fix her decision into place, it was created once Jarrett started inviting what few friends he had to the house to dinner. Those gentlemen were clearly being invited to inspect more than just the new guns her brother had purchased.

"But, with independent means, and a life in town . . ." Fiona was saying, but Caroline shook her head.

"If I married, I'd be entirely in my husband's power. I am determined, Fi, that I will not be controlled by anyone again, ever."

"But . . . you can't mean to live without love, Caro. Or, well, passion."

Caroline met her friend's concerned gaze without flinching. "Why should I have to do without passion?"

"I don't understand you."

"If I am never going to be married, then there's no need for me to remain a virgin." She might be an aging spinster in the world's eyes, but she was far from an innocent. She knew perfectly well why some men went sneaking down the corridors at night during their stays at certain houses, and she knew why the women who were not their wives opened doors. More than once she had looked on some of the youths and men who vied for the attentions of the girls with less watchful relations. She'd wondered, if she had been alone, and if it was her door they knocked on, would she open to them?

But, clearly, she had passed the limits of Fiona's daring. "Caro, are you mad?"

"No, I am speaking quite coolly. I am free. Absolutely and completely free. Why should I not enjoy all that freedom allows?" *Including the freedom to open the door, to say yes to whatever one I choose . . .*

"All right, Caro. You've had a great deal of excitement. I'm going to make some allowances." For a moment Fiona looked exactly like her mother at the height of her displeasure. Caroline decided now was not the time to mention the resemblance. "But when you've had time to think, you will understand what you're suggesting. There are *plenty* of words for that sort of woman. 'Adventuress' is the most polite."

Caroline knew Fiona was only trying to look out for her best interests, and now was most definitely not the time to argue this particular point. "I'm sorry, Fi. And I'm making a mess of your happiness, and I don't want that, not when I'm able to be your maid of honor after all! And I might need your help. I'll need to rent a house in London, and Mrs. Ferriday doesn't know the town. And this Mr. Upton . . . he can be my man of business, but I don't know him personally, so can't rely on his judgment for this. You could help us find a good place, couldn't you?"

"You know I'll do anything I can to help you. And so will Mother and Father, of course. And Harry . . ."

"Oh, no, Fi. You mustn't tell them. At least not yet."

"Why on earth not, Caro? When have they done anything but try to help?"

"I know, I do. But . . . they are such good people. They'll wish for me to try to reconcile with Jarrett. They might even, quite accidently, of course, delay things . . ."

Fi nodded solemnly. "I do understand, Caro. Very well, I'll tell no one if that's what you want."

"Just for now. If all goes well, I'll be in London in plenty of time for the ceremony, and once you leave on your wedding trip, I can take my own leave for the Continent and never have to worry about Jarrett, or anyone else ever again."

But still Fi seemed hesitant. "Just . . . just don't do anything reckless. Give yourself time to get used to your circumstances. Money and freedom and London can be a strong combination."

Having Fi turn so uncharacteristically cautious stung

Caroline harder than she would have believed possible. "Fi, I never expected to hear you agreeing with Jarrett."

"Say that again and I will have to be cross with you, Lady Caroline. I've been out for three seasons. I've seen more than one girl let London go to her head. You might be free, but you must be careful."

"Or I'll fall into the coils of this Lord of the Rakes you keep talking about?"

"I don't keep talking about him," replied Fi with a fine imitation of being piqued. "I mentioned him exactly once. But yes, Caroline, you might fall for him or someone like him and then—"

But Fiona was unable to finish her sentence. Heavy footsteps fell against the hall carpet and an even heavier hand knocked at the door. Caroline sprang to her feet again, and just in time she thrust her letter into Fiona's hands. A bare heartbeat later, the door opened, and Jarrett Delamarre, Earl Keenesford, walked in.

FROM BESTSELLING AUTHOR
SHERRY THOMAS

The Luckiest Lady in London

❦

Louisa Cantwell must marry rich to support her sisters. But does she dare fall in love with a man who has as many dark and devastating secrets as the Marquess of Wrenworth?

"**Thomas is known for a lush style...[and] transporting prose even as [she] delivers on heat and emotion and a well-earned happily ever after.**"
—*The New York Times Book Review*

"**A masterpiece...A beautifully written, exquisitely seductive, powerfully romantic gem of a romance.**"
—*Kirkus Reviews* (starred review)

sherrythomas.com
facebook.com/AuthorSherryThomas
facebook.com/LoveAlwaysBooks
penguin.com

M1462T0314

Properly improper—and daring to love...

FROM NEW YORK TIMES BESTSELLING AUTHOR
JENNIFER ASHLEY

The Seduction of Elliot McBride

Juliana St. John was raised to be very proper. After a long engagement, her wedding day dawns—only for Juliana to find herself jilted at the altar.

Fleeing the mocking crowd, she stumbles upon Elliot McBride, the tall, passionate Scot who was her first love. His teasing manner gives her an idea, and she asks Elliot to save her from an uncertain future by marrying her...

After escaping brutal imprisonment, Elliot has returned to Scotland a vastly wealthy yet tormented man. Now Juliana has her hands full restoring his half-ruined manor in the Scottish Highlands, trying to repair Elliot's broken heart—and maybe finding a second chance at love along the way.

"Ashley writes the kinds of heroes I crave."
—Elizabeth Hoyt, *New York Times* bestselling author

jennifersromances.com
facebook.com/LoveAlwaysBooks
penguin.com

M1317T0513